CARTOON NETWORK

ADVENTURE TIME COMICS

VOLUME 6

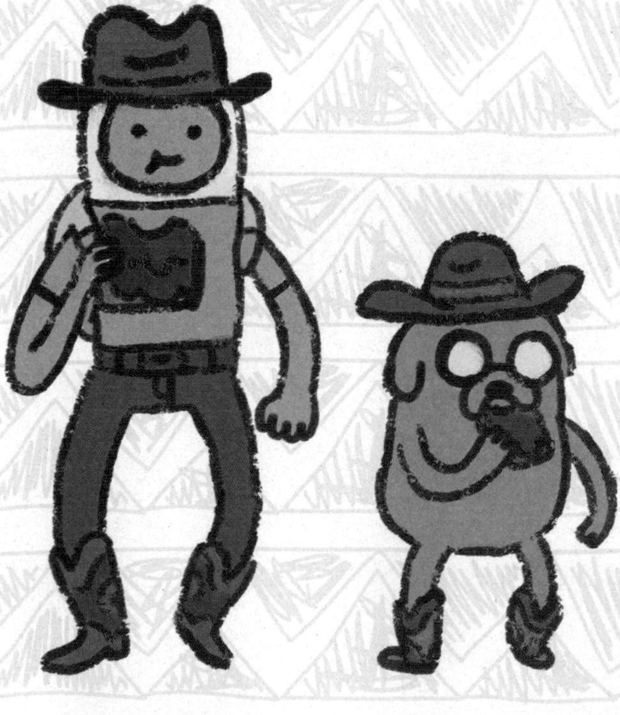

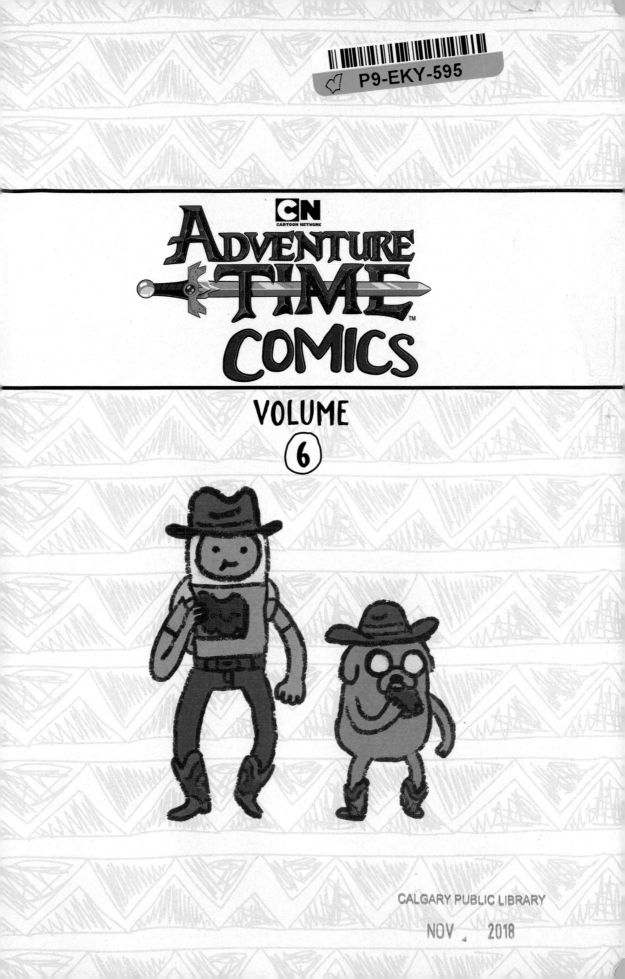

ROSS RICHIE CEO & Founder
JOY HUFFMAN CFO
MATT GAGNON Editor-in-Chief
FILIP SABLIK President, Publishing & Marketing
STEPHEN CHRISTY President, Development
LANCE KREITER Vice President, Licensing & Merchandising
PHIL BARBARO Vice President, Finance & Human Resources
ARUNE SINGH Vice President, Marketing
BRYCE CARLSON Vice President, Editorial & creative Strategy
SCOTT NEWMAN Manager, Production Design
KATE HENNING Manager, Operations
SIERRA HAHN Executive Editor
JEANINE SHAEFER Executive Editor
DAFNA PLEBAN Senior Editor
SHANNON WATTERS Senior Editor
ERIC HARBURN Senior Editor
WHITNEY LEOPARD Editor
CAMERON CHITTOCK Editor
CHRIS ROSA Editor
MATTHEW LEVINE Editor
SOPHIE PHILIPS-ROBERTS Assistant Editor
GAVIN GRONENTHAL Assistant Editor
MICHAEL MOCCIO Assistant Editor
AMANDA LaFRANCO Executive Assistant
JILLIAN CRAB Design Coordinator
MICHELLE ANKLEY Design Coordinator
KARA LEOPARD Production Designer
MARIE KRUPINA Production Designer
GRACE PARK Production Design Assistant
CHELSEA ROBERTS Production Design Assistant
ELIZABETH LOUGHRIDGE Accounting Coordinator
STEPHANIE HOCUTT Social Media Coordinator
JOSÉ MEZA Event Coordinator
HOLLY AITCHISON Operations Coordinator
MEGAN CHRISTOPHER Operations Assistant
RODRIGO HERNANDEZ Mailroom Assistant
MORGAN PERRY Direct Market Representative
CAT O'GRADY Marketing Assistant
BREANNA SARPY Executive Assistant

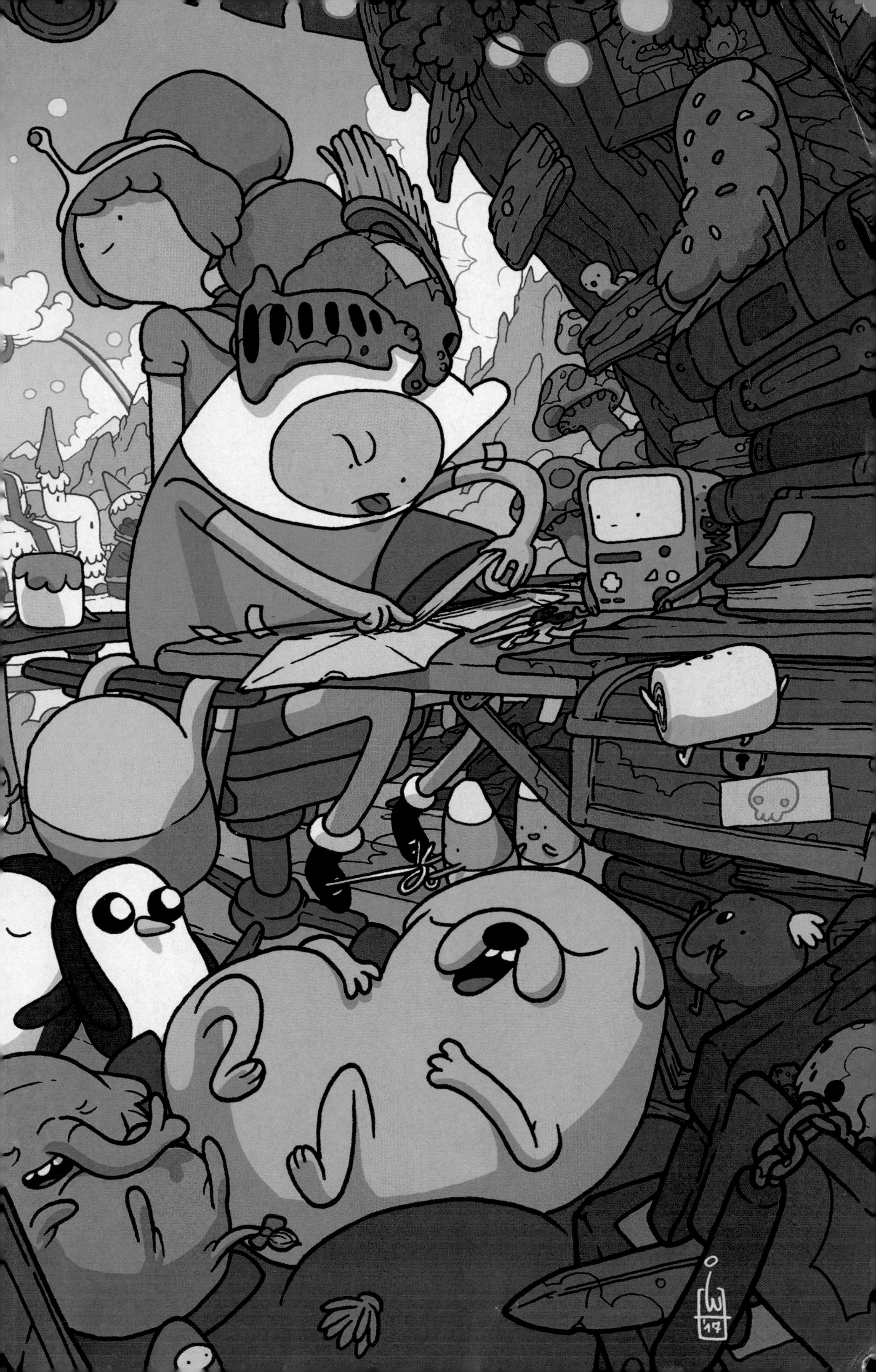

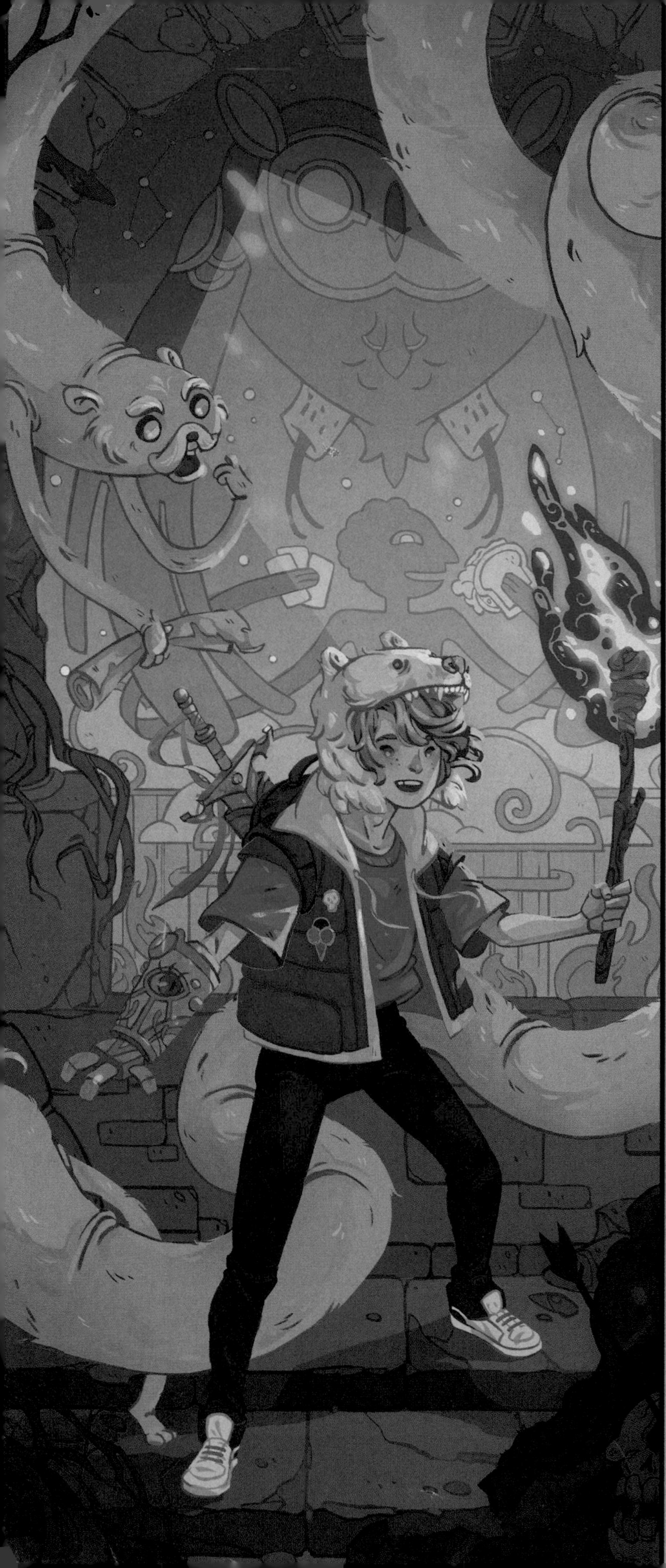

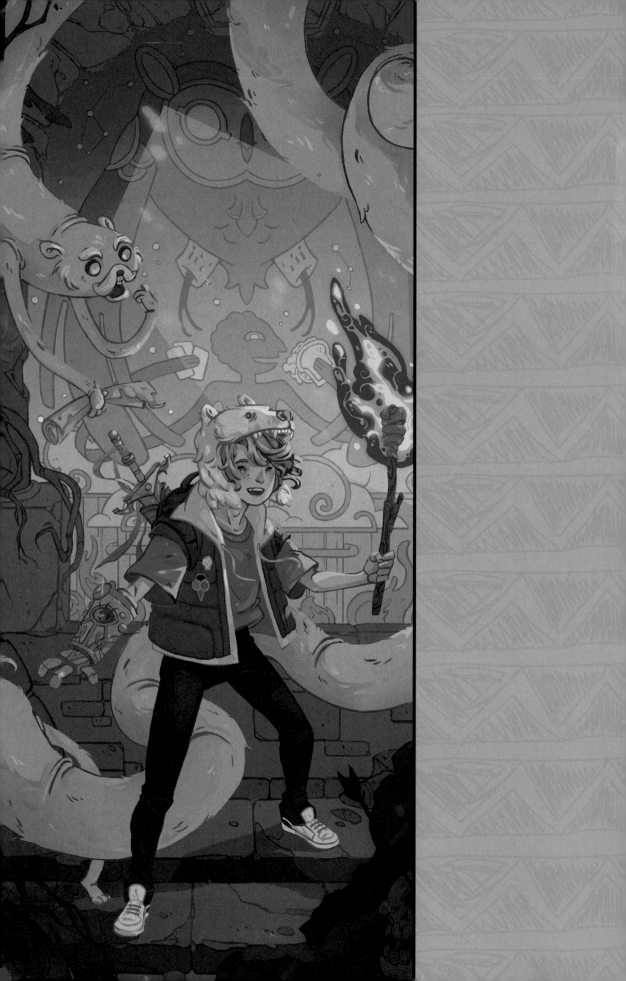

ADVENTURE TIME™
Created by **PENDLETON WARD**

"RICARDIO ARRYTHMIA"
Written & Illustrated by
AARON MCCONNELL

"MASTERS OF THE
POWERSKULL SWORD"
Written & Illustrated by
BENJAMIN MARRA
Colors by
ALEKSANDR GUSHKY

"GLADIATOR REALM"
Written & Illustrated by
JAMIE COE

"FAVORITE SHIRT"
Written & Illustrated by
REZA FARAZMAND

"SWORD OF THE SUN"
Written & Illustrated by
CARISSA POWELL

"BILLY THE HERO"
Written by
BRANDON ZUERN
Illustrated by
MATT FRANK
Colors by
GONÇALO LOPES
Letters by
MIKE FIORENTINO

"FOREVER (NOT) ALONE"
Written & Illustrated by
XIAO TONG KONG

"KEY TO THE BREAKFAST
KINGDOM"
Written & Illustrated by
JACK SJOGREN

"PICKLING WITH PRISMO"
Written & Illustrated by
JEAN WEI

"THE ARCADE"
Written & Illustrated by
MARI ARAKAKI

"MIGHTIER THAN THE FIST"
Written & Illustrated by
BEN PASSMORE

"BANDITOS"
Written by
TYLER JENKINS
Illustrated by
BOYA SUN
Letters by
WARREN MONTGOMERY

"CANDY FINN"
Written & Illustrated by
MORGAN BEEM

"BUS STOP"
Written & Illustrated by
SONNY LIEW

Cover by
RICHARD CHANG

Series Designer
GRACE PARK

Collection Designer
KARA LEOPARD

Assistant Editors
MICHAEL MOCCIO
KATALINA HOLLAND

Editor
WHITNEY LEOPARD

With Special Thanks to Marisa Marionakis, Janet No, Curtis Lelash, Conrad
Montgomery, Kelly Crews, Scott Malchus, Adam Muto and the wonderful
folks at Cartoon Network.

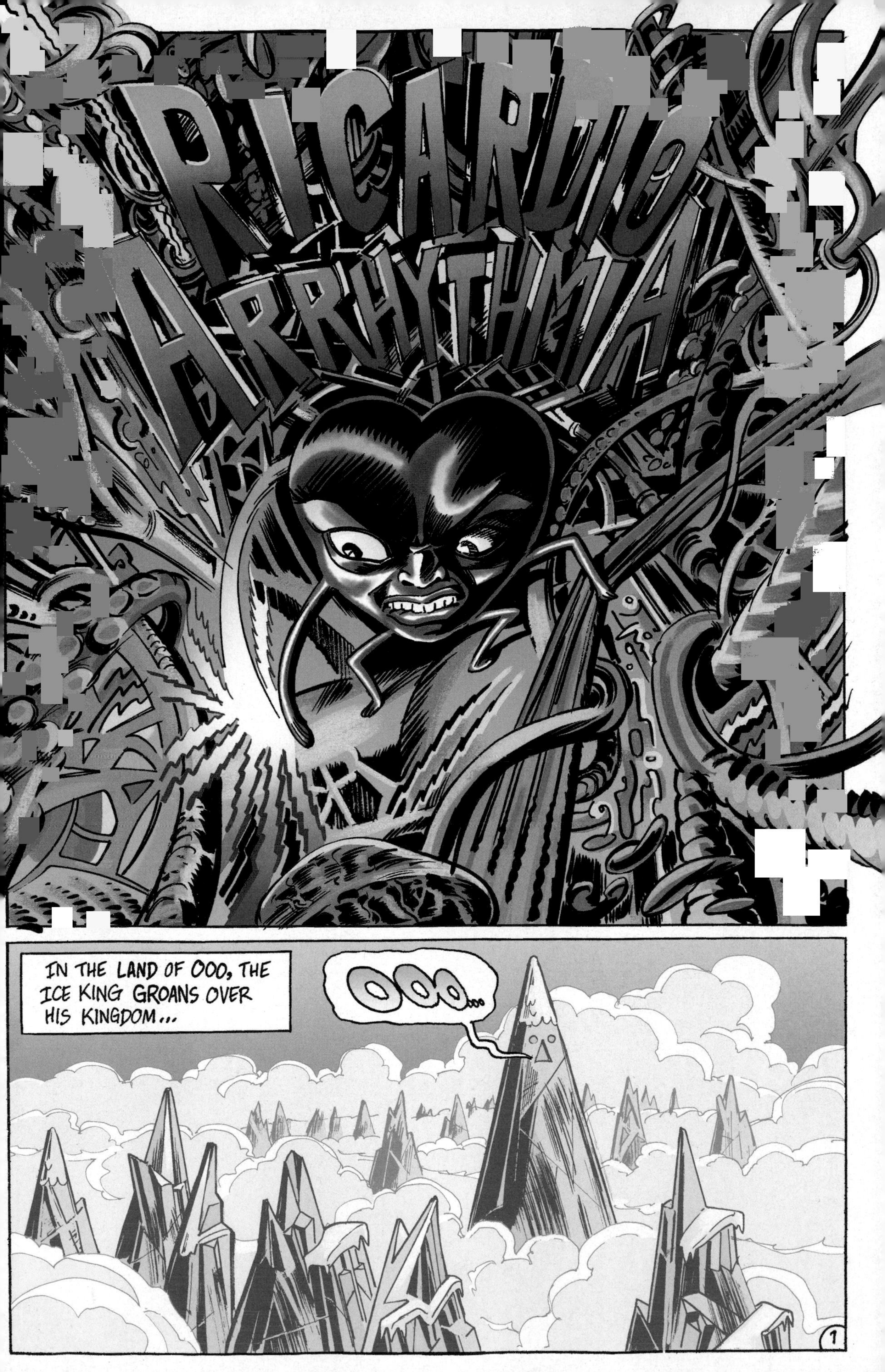
RICARDIO
ARRHYTHMIA
IN THE LAND OF OOO, THE ICE KING GROANS OVER HIS KINGDOM...
OOO...

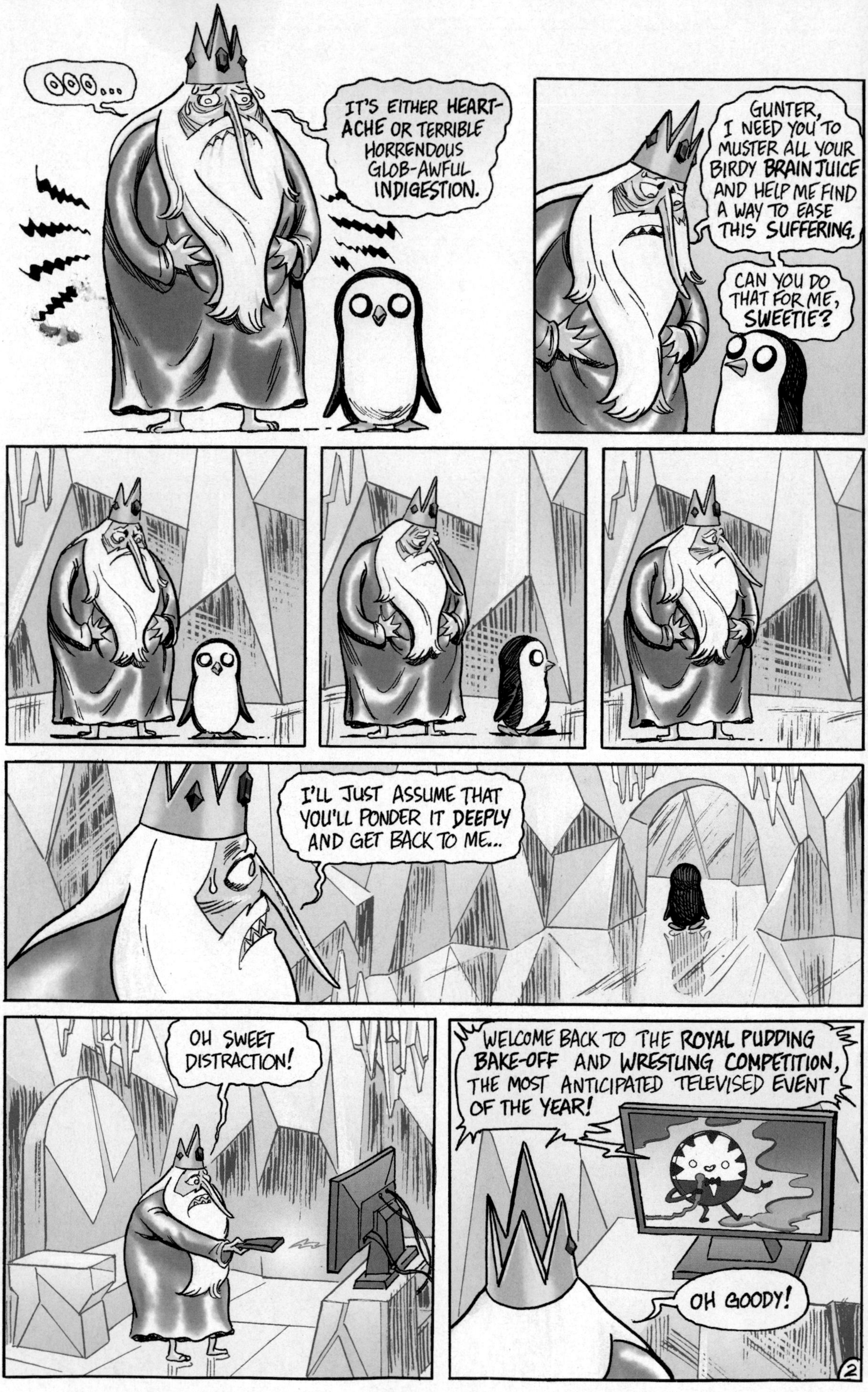
OOO...
IT'S EITHER HEART-ACHE OR TERRIBLE HORRENDOUS GLOB-AWFUL INDIGESTION.
GUNTER, I NEED YOU TO MUSTER ALL YOUR BIRDY BRAIN JUICE AND HELP ME FIND A WAY TO EASE THIS SUFFERING.
CAN YOU DO THAT FOR ME, SWEETIE?
I'LL JUST ASSUME THAT YOU'LL PONDER IT DEEPLY AND GET BACK TO ME...
OH SWEET DISTRACTION!
WELCOME BACK TO THE ROYAL PUDDING BAKE-OFF AND WRESTLING COMPETITION, THE MOST ANTICIPATED TELEVISED EVENT OF THE YEAR!
OH GOODY!

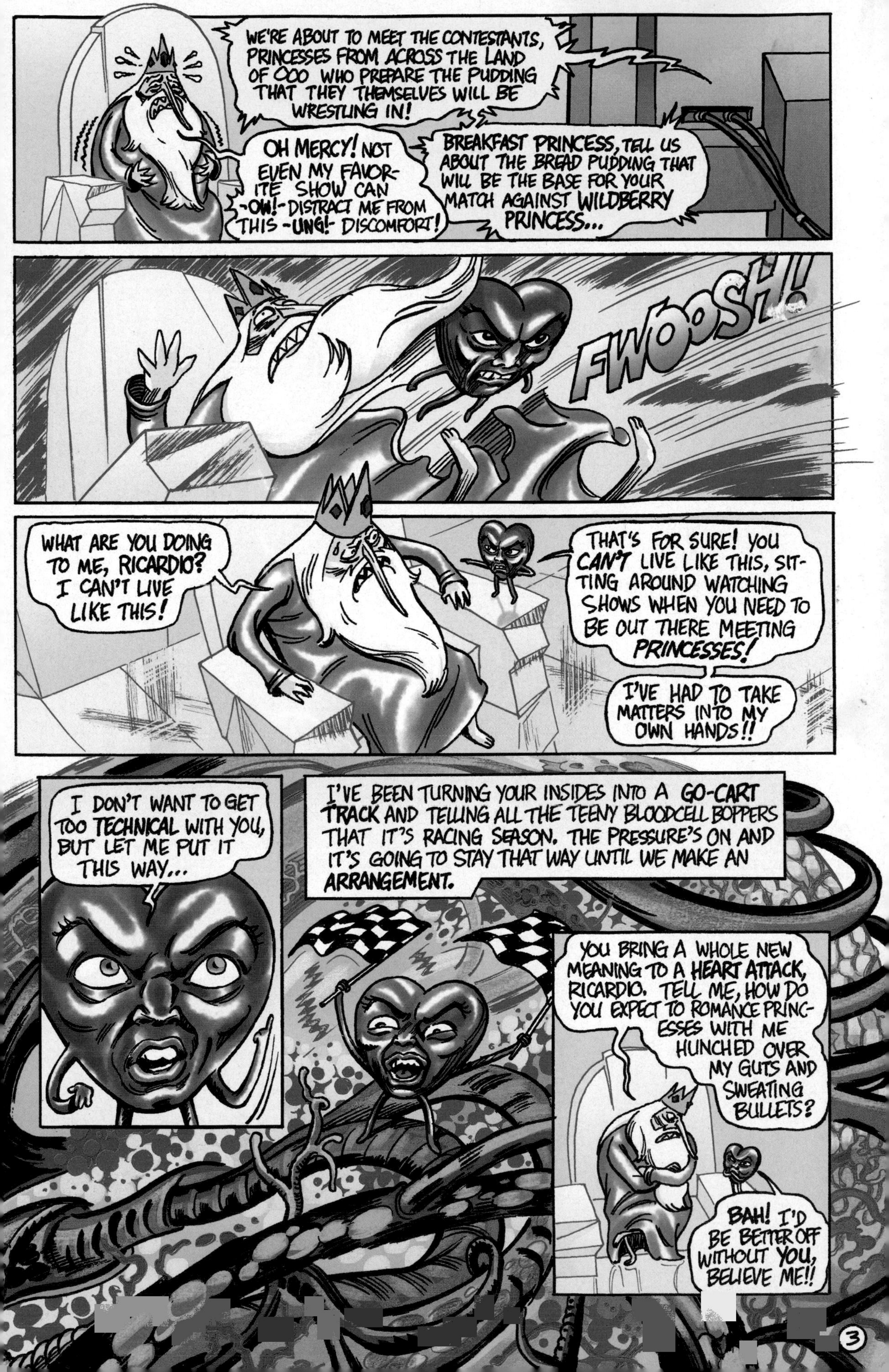
WE'RE ABOUT TO MEET THE CONTESTANTS, PRINCESSES FROM ACROSS THE LAND OF OOO WHO PREPARE THE PUDDING THAT THEY THEMSELVES WILL BE WRESTLING IN!
OH MERCY! NOT EVEN MY FAVORITE SHOW CAN -OW!- DISTRACT ME FROM THIS -UNG!- DISCOMFORT!
BREAKFAST PRINCESS, TELL US ABOUT THE BREAD PUDDING THAT WILL BE THE BASE FOR YOUR MATCH AGAINST WILDBERRY PRINCESS...
FWOOSH!
WHAT ARE YOU DOING TO ME, RICARDIO? I CAN'T LIVE LIKE THIS!
THAT'S FOR SURE! YOU CAN'T LIVE LIKE THIS, SITTING AROUND WATCHING SHOWS WHEN YOU NEED TO BE OUT THERE MEETING PRINCESSES!
I'VE HAD TO TAKE MATTERS INTO MY OWN HANDS!!
I DON'T WANT TO GET TOO TECHNICAL WITH YOU, BUT LET ME PUT IT THIS WAY...
I'VE BEEN TURNING YOUR INSIDES INTO A GO-CART TRACK AND TELLING ALL THE TEENY BLOODCELL BOPPERS THAT IT'S RACING SEASON. THE PRESSURE'S ON AND IT'S GOING TO STAY THAT WAY UNTIL WE MAKE AN ARRANGEMENT.
YOU BRING A WHOLE NEW MEANING TO A HEART ATTACK, RICARDIO. TELL ME, HOW DO YOU EXPECT TO ROMANCE PRINCESSES WITH ME HUNCHED OVER MY GUTS AND SWEATING BULLETS?
BAH! I'D BE BETTER OFF WITHOUT YOU, BELIEVE ME!!

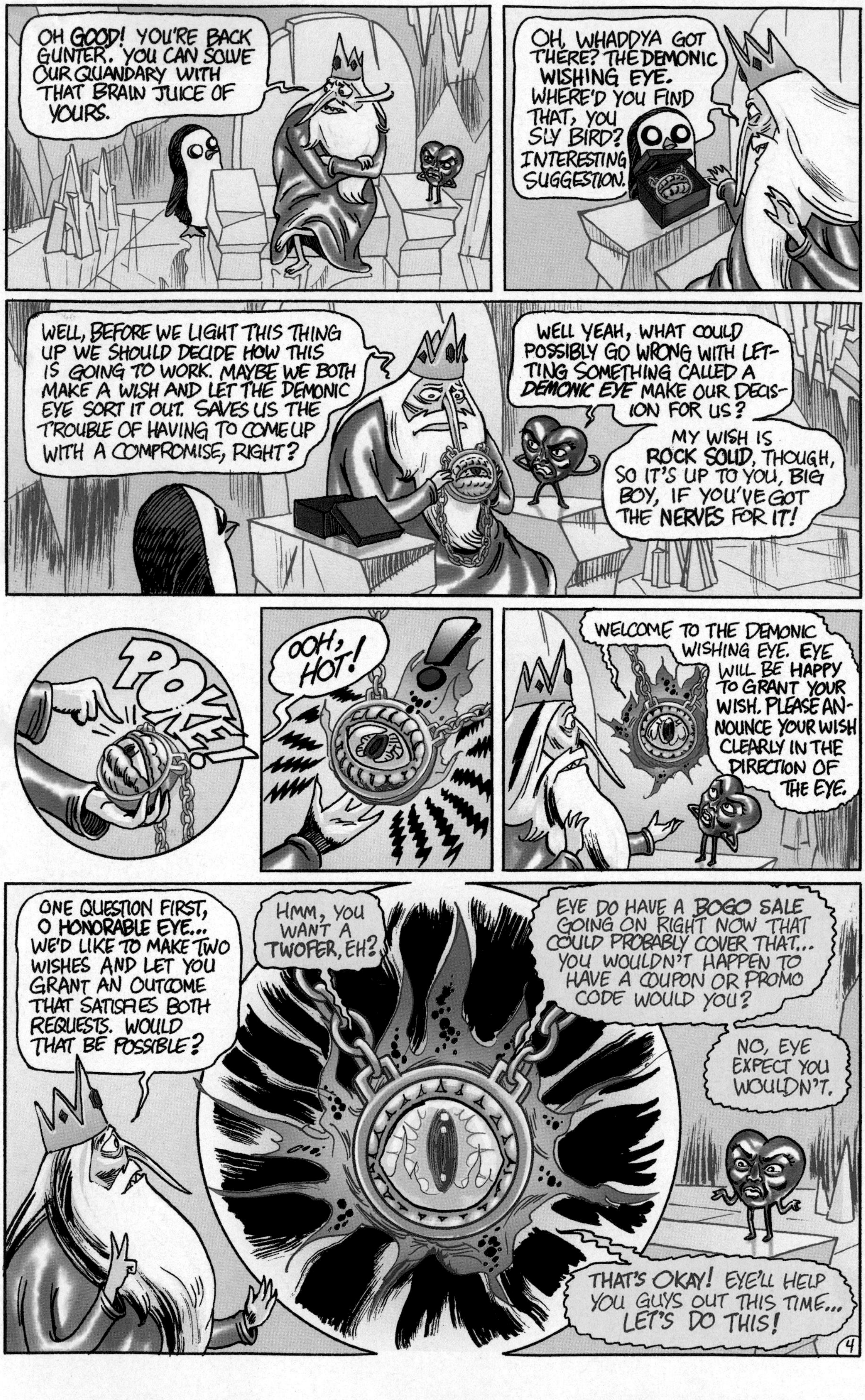
OH GOOD! YOU'RE BACK GUNTER. YOU CAN SOLVE OUR QUANDARY WITH THAT BRAIN JUICE OF YOURS.
OH, WHADDYA GOT THERE? THE DEMONIC WISHING EYE. WHERE'D YOU FIND THAT, YOU SLY BIRD? INTERESTING SUGGESTION.
WELL, BEFORE WE LIGHT THIS THING UP WE SHOULD DECIDE HOW THIS IS GOING TO WORK. MAYBE WE BOTH MAKE A WISH AND LET THE DEMONIC EYE SORT IT OUT. SAVES US THE TROUBLE OF HAVING TO COME UP WITH A COMPROMISE, RIGHT?
WELL YEAH, WHAT COULD POSSIBLY GO WRONG WITH LETTING SOMETHING CALLED A DEMONIC EYE MAKE OUR DECISION FOR US?
MY WISH IS ROCK SOLID, THOUGH, SO IT'S UP TO YOU, BIG BOY, IF YOU'VE GOT THE NERVES FOR IT!
POKE!
OOH, HOT!
WELCOME TO THE DEMONIC WISHING EYE. EYE WILL BE HAPPY TO GRANT YOUR WISH. PLEASE ANNOUNCE YOUR WISH CLEARLY IN THE DIRECTION OF THE EYE.
ONE QUESTION FIRST, O HONORABLE EYE... WE'D LIKE TO MAKE TWO WISHES AND LET YOU GRANT AN OUTCOME THAT SATISFIES BOTH REQUESTS. WOULD THAT BE POSSIBLE?
HMM, YOU WANT A TWOFER, EH?
EYE DO HAVE A BOGO SALE GOING ON RIGHT NOW THAT COULD PROBABLY COVER THAT... YOU WOULDN'T HAPPEN TO HAVE A COUPON OR PROMO CODE WOULD YOU?
NO, EYE EXPECT YOU WOULDN'T.
THAT'S OKAY! EYE'LL HELP YOU GUYS OUT THIS TIME... LET'S DO THIS!

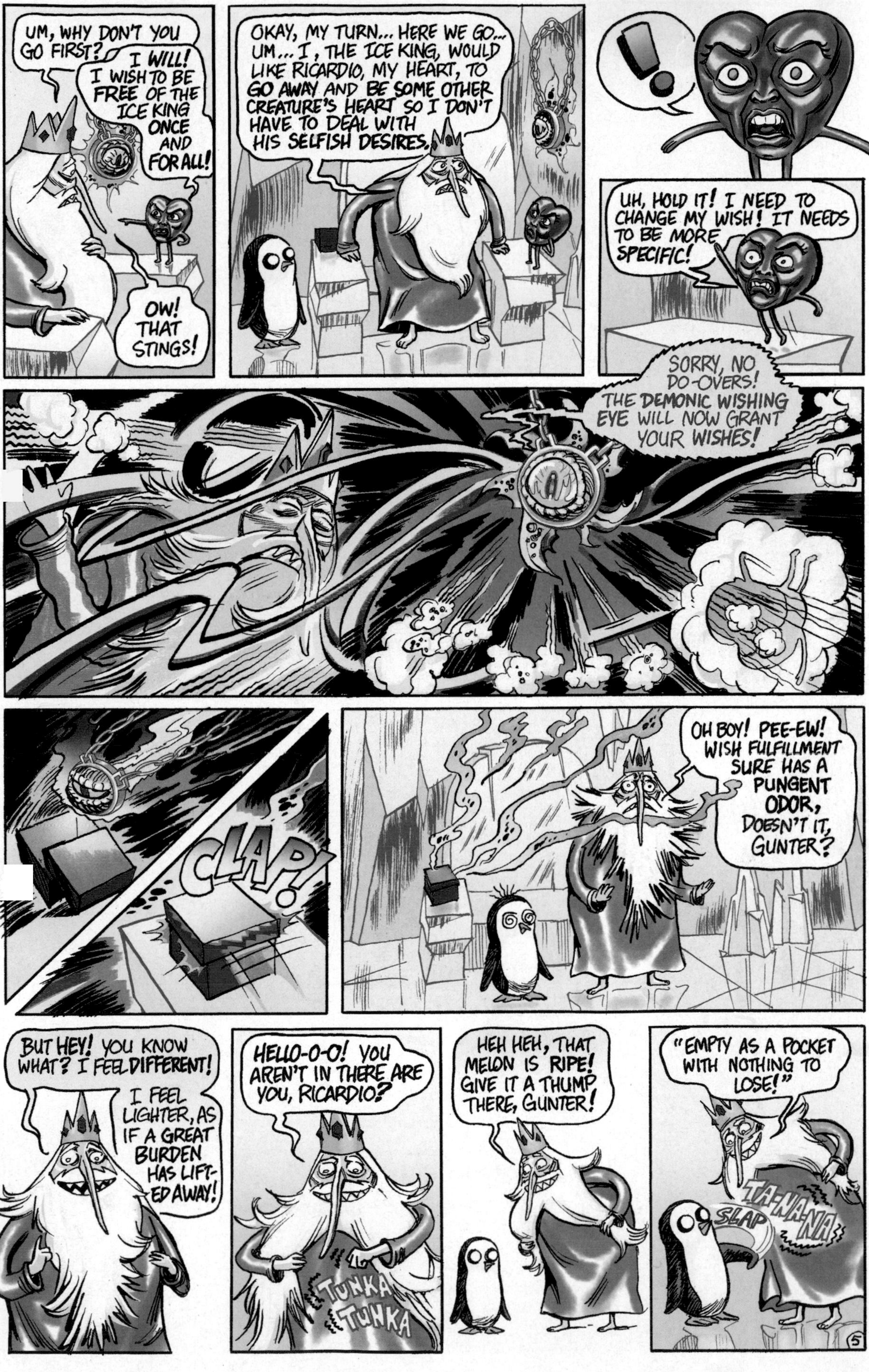
UM, WHY DON'T YOU GO FIRST?
I WILL! I WISH TO BE FREE OF THE ICE KING ONCE AND FOR ALL!
OW! THAT STINGS!
OKAY, MY TURN... HERE WE GO... UM... I, THE ICE KING, WOULD LIKE RICARDIO, MY HEART, TO GO AWAY AND BE SOME OTHER CREATURE'S HEART SO I DON'T HAVE TO DEAL WITH HIS SELFISH DESIRES.
!
UH, HOLD IT! I NEED TO CHANGE MY WISH! IT NEEDS TO BE MORE SPECIFIC!
SORRY, NO DO-OVERS! THE DEMONIC WISHING EYE WILL NOW GRANT YOUR WISHES!
CLAP!
OH BOY! PEE-EW! WISH FULFILLMENT SURE HAS A PUNGENT ODOR, DOESN'T IT, GUNTER?
BUT HEY! YOU KNOW WHAT? I FEEL DIFFERENT!
I FEEL LIGHTER, AS IF A GREAT BURDEN HAS LIFTED AWAY!
HELLO-O-O! YOU AREN'T IN THERE ARE YOU, RICARDIO?
TUNKA TUNKA
HEH HEH, THAT MELON IS RIPE! GIVE IT A THUMP THERE, GUNTER!
"EMPTY AS A POCKET WITH NOTHING TO LOSE!"
SLAP
TA-NA-NA

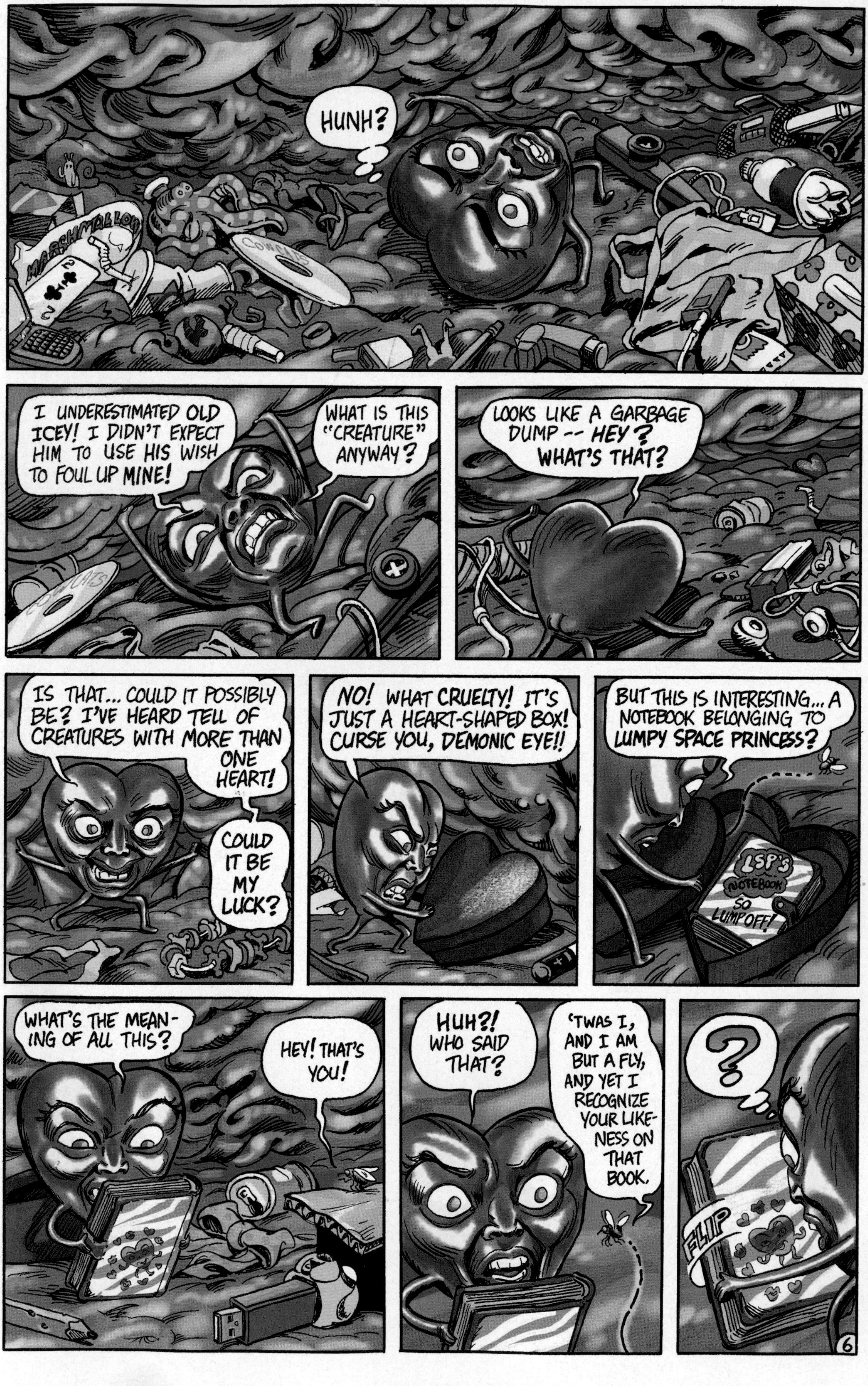
HUNH?
MARSHMALLOW
COWCATS
I UNDERESTIMATED OLD ICEY! I DIDN'T EXPECT HIM TO USE HIS WISH TO FOUL UP MINE!
WHAT IS THIS "CREATURE" ANYWAY?
LOOKS LIKE A GARBAGE DUMP -- HEY? WHAT'S THAT?
IS THAT... COULD IT POSSIBLY BE? I'VE HEARD TELL OF CREATURES WITH MORE THAN ONE HEART!
COULD IT BE MY LUCK?
NO! WHAT CRUELTY! IT'S JUST A HEART-SHAPED BOX! CURSE YOU, DEMONIC EYE!!
BUT THIS IS INTERESTING... A NOTEBOOK BELONGING TO LUMPY SPACE PRINCESS?
LSP'S NOTEBOOK
SO LUMP OFF!
WHAT'S THE MEAN-ING OF ALL THIS?
HEY! THAT'S YOU!
HUH?! WHO SAID THAT?
'TWAS I, AND I AM BUT A FLY, AND YET I RECOGNIZE YOUR LIKE-NESS ON THAT BOOK.
?
FLIP

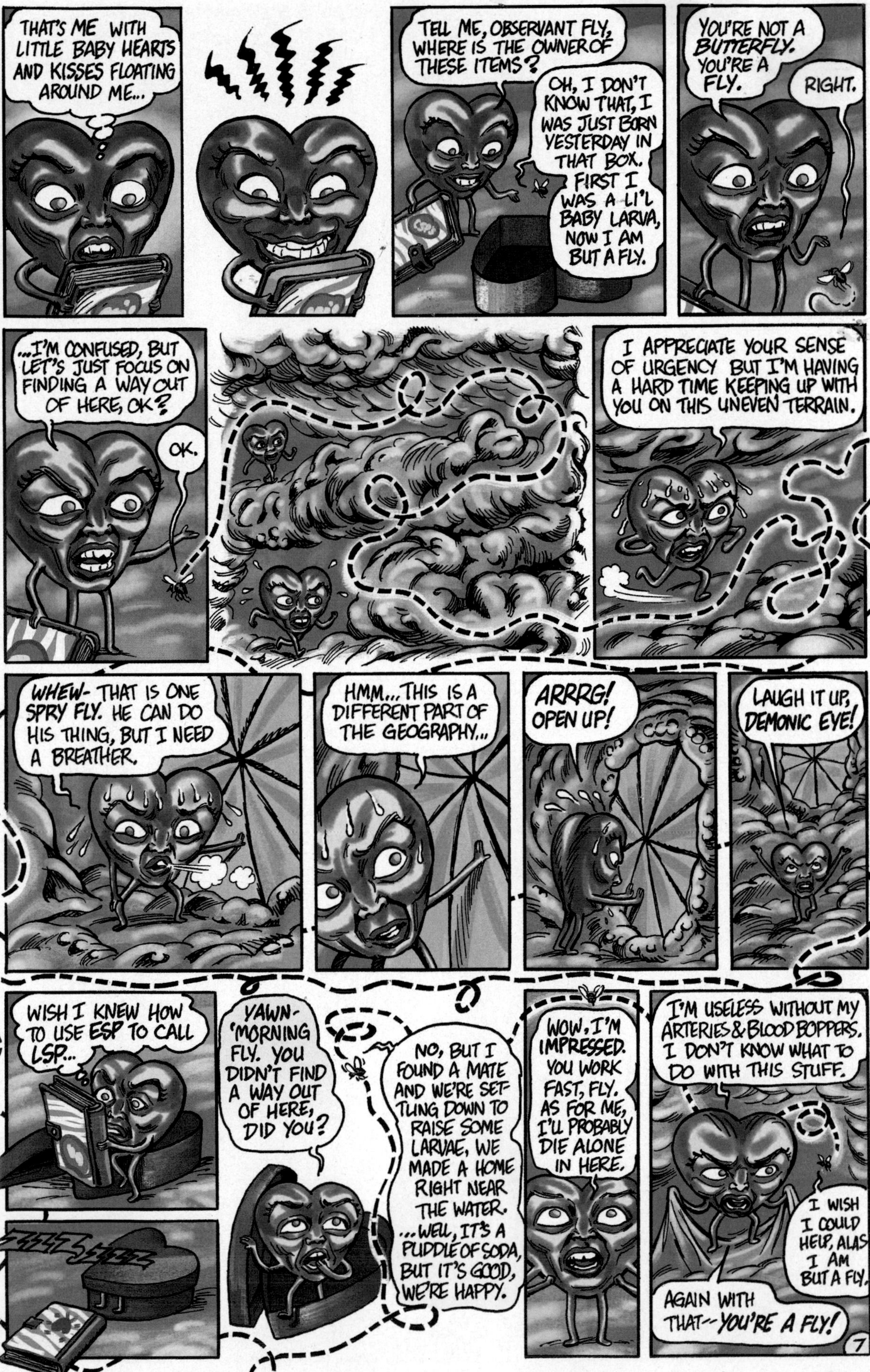

THAT'S ME WITH LITTLE BABY HEARTS AND KISSES FLOATING AROUND ME...
TELL ME, OBSERVANT FLY, WHERE IS THE OWNER OF THESE ITEMS?
OH, I DON'T KNOW THAT, I WAS JUST BORN YESTERDAY IN THAT BOX. FIRST I WAS A LI'L BABY LARVA, NOW I AM BUT A FLY.
YOU'RE NOT A BUTTERFLY. YOU'RE A FLY.
RIGHT.
...I'M CONFUSED, BUT LET'S JUST FOCUS ON FINDING A WAY OUT OF HERE, OK?
OK.
I APPRECIATE YOUR SENSE OF URGENCY BUT I'M HAVING A HARD TIME KEEPING UP WITH YOU ON THIS UNEVEN TERRAIN.
WHEW- THAT IS ONE SPRY FLY. HE CAN DO HIS THING, BUT I NEED A BREATHER.
HMM... THIS IS A DIFFERENT PART OF THE GEOGRAPHY...
ARRRG! OPEN UP!
LAUGH IT UP, DEMONIC EYE!
WISH I KNEW HOW TO USE ESP TO CALL LSP...
YAWN- 'MORNING FLY. YOU DIDN'T FIND A WAY OUT OF HERE, DID YOU?
NO, BUT I FOUND A MATE AND WE'RE SETTLING DOWN TO RAISE SOME LARVAE, WE MADE A HOME RIGHT NEAR THE WATER. ...WELL, IT'S A PUDDLE OF SODA, BUT IT'S GOOD, WE'RE HAPPY.
WOW, I'M IMPRESSED. YOU WORK FAST, FLY. AS FOR ME, I'LL PROBABLY DIE ALONE IN HERE.
I'M USELESS WITHOUT MY ARTERIES & BLOOD BOPPERS. I DON'T KNOW WHAT TO DO WITH THIS STUFF.
I WISH I COULD HELP, ALAS I AM BUT A FLY.
AGAIN WITH THAT-- YOU'RE A FLY!

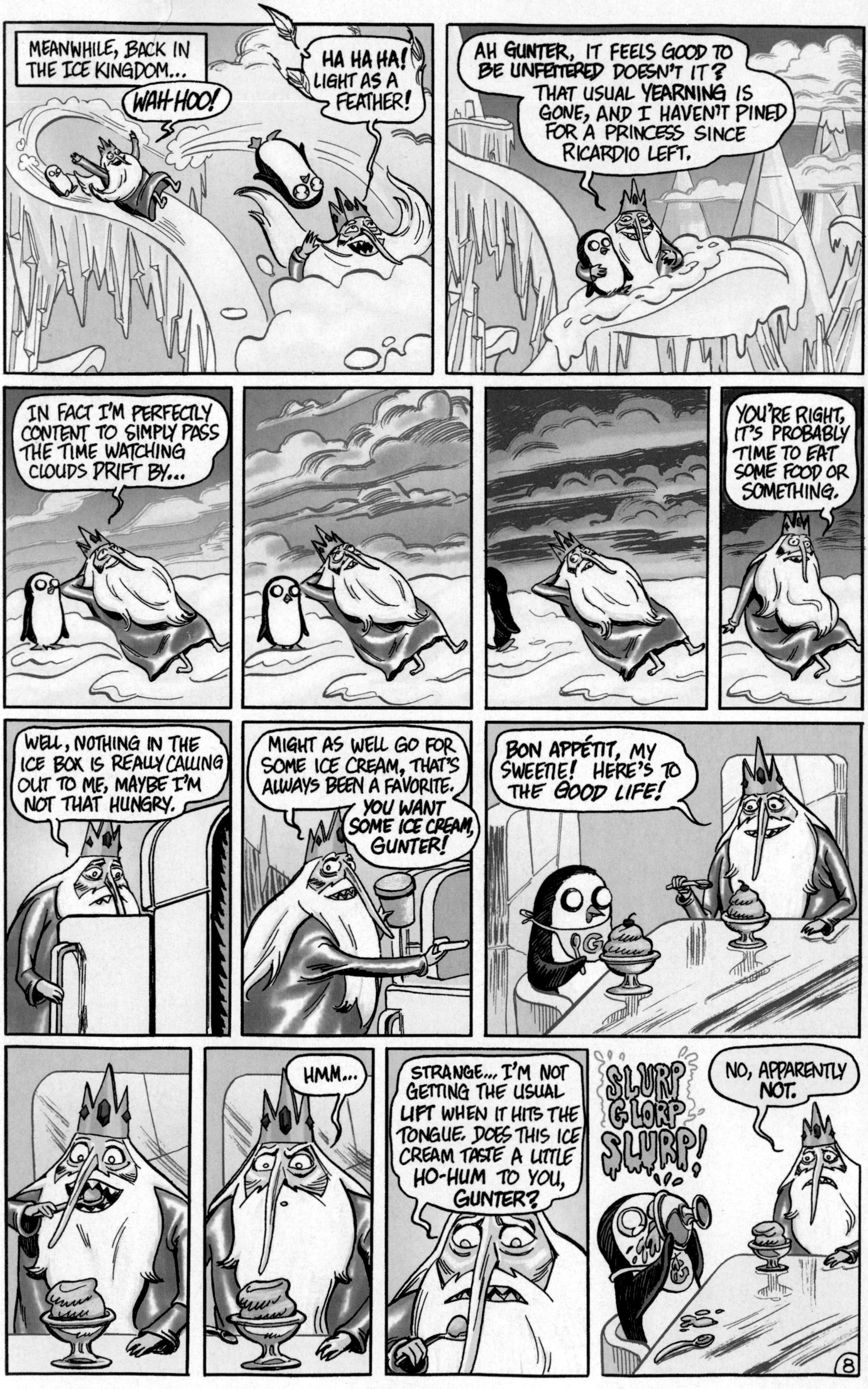
MEANWHILE, BACK IN THE ICE KINGDOM...
WAH-HOO!
HA HA HA! LIGHT AS A FEATHER!
AH GUNTER, IT FEELS GOOD TO BE UNFETTERED DOESN'T IT? THAT USUAL YEARNING IS GONE, AND I HAVEN'T PINED FOR A PRINCESS SINCE RICARDIO LEFT.
IN FACT I'M PERFECTLY CONTENT TO SIMPLY PASS THE TIME WATCHING CLOUDS DRIFT BY...
YOU'RE RIGHT, IT'S PROBABLY TIME TO EAT SOME FOOD OR SOMETHING.
WELL, NOTHING IN THE ICE BOX IS REALLY CALLING OUT TO ME, MAYBE I'M NOT THAT HUNGRY.
MIGHT AS WELL GO FOR SOME ICE CREAM, THAT'S ALWAYS BEEN A FAVORITE.
YOU WANT SOME ICE CREAM, GUNTER!
BON APPÉTIT, MY SWEETIE! HERE'S TO THE GOOD LIFE!
HMM...
STRANGE... I'M NOT GETTING THE USUAL LIFT WHEN IT HITS THE TONGUE. DOES THIS ICE CREAM TASTE A LITTLE HO-HUM TO YOU, GUNTER?
SLURP GLORP SLURP!
NO, APPARENTLY NOT.

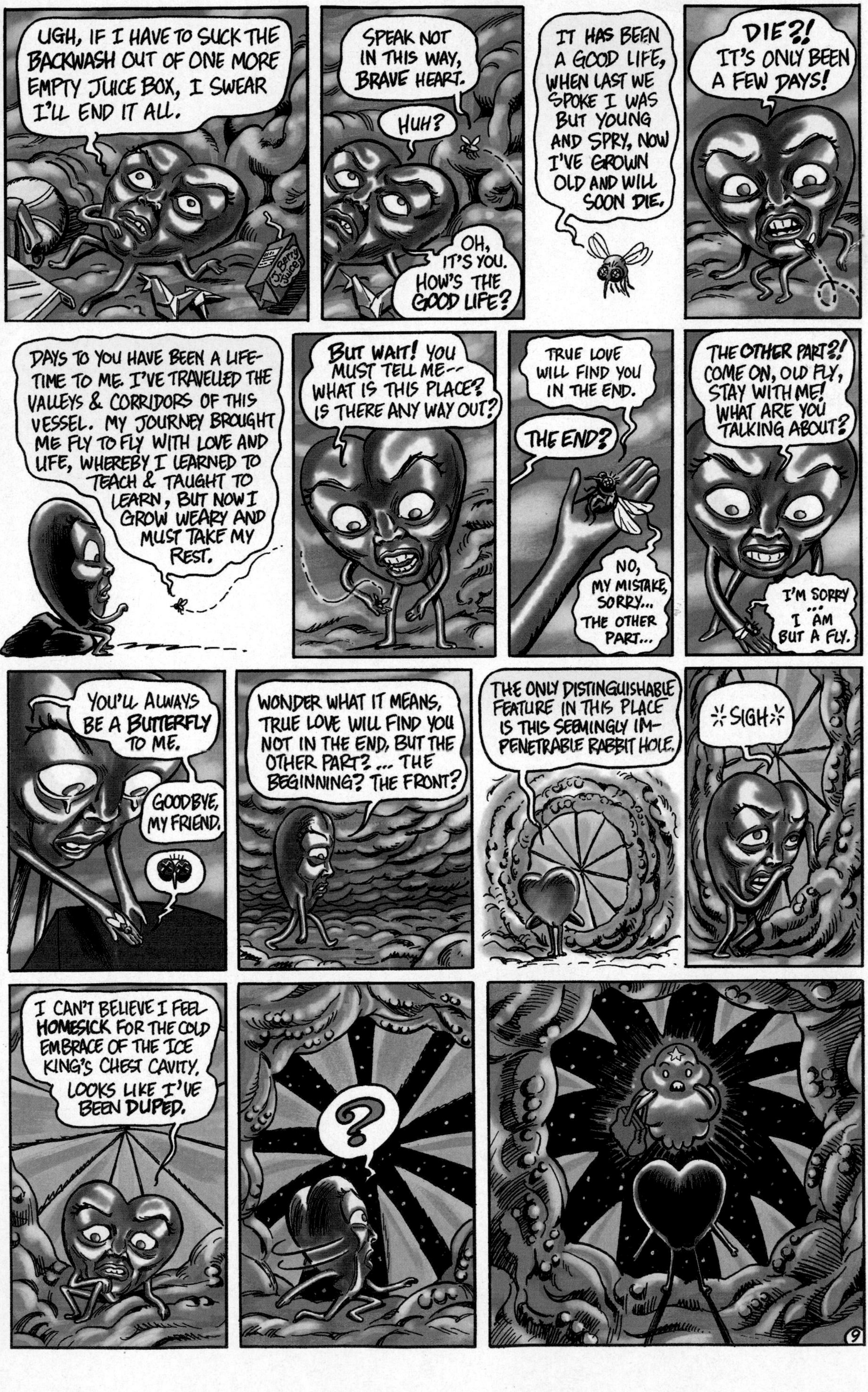
UGH, IF I HAVE TO SUCK THE BACKWASH OUT OF ONE MORE EMPTY JUICE BOX, I SWEAR I'LL END IT ALL.
J. Berry Juice
SPEAK NOT IN THIS WAY, BRAVE HEART.
HUH?
OH, IT'S YOU. HOW'S THE GOOD LIFE?
IT HAS BEEN A GOOD LIFE, WHEN LAST WE SPOKE I WAS BUT YOUNG AND SPRY, NOW I'VE GROWN OLD AND WILL SOON DIE.
DIE?! IT'S ONLY BEEN A FEW DAYS!
DAYS TO YOU HAVE BEEN A LIFETIME TO ME. I'VE TRAVELLED THE VALLEYS & CORRIDORS OF THIS VESSEL. MY JOURNEY BROUGHT ME FLY TO FLY WITH LOVE AND LIFE, WHEREBY I LEARNED TO TEACH & TAUGHT TO LEARN, BUT NOW I GROW WEARY AND MUST TAKE MY REST.
BUT WAIT! YOU MUST TELL ME-- WHAT IS THIS PLACE? IS THERE ANY WAY OUT?
TRUE LOVE WILL FIND YOU IN THE END.
THE END?
NO, MY MISTAKE, SORRY... THE OTHER PART...
THE OTHER PART?! COME ON, OLD FLY, STAY WITH ME! WHAT ARE YOU TALKING ABOUT?
I'M SORRY ... I AM BUT A FLY.
YOU'LL ALWAYS BE A BUTTERFLY TO ME.
GOODBYE, MY FRIEND.
WONDER WHAT IT MEANS, TRUE LOVE WILL FIND YOU NOT IN THE END, BUT THE OTHER PART? ... THE BEGINNING? THE FRONT?
THE ONLY DISTINGUISHABLE FEATURE IN THIS PLACE IS THIS SEEMINGLY IMPENETRABLE RABBIT HOLE.
SIGH
I CAN'T BELIEVE I FEEL HOMESICK FOR THE COLD EMBRACE OF THE ICE KING'S CHEST CAVITY. LOOKS LIKE I'VE BEEN DUPED.
?

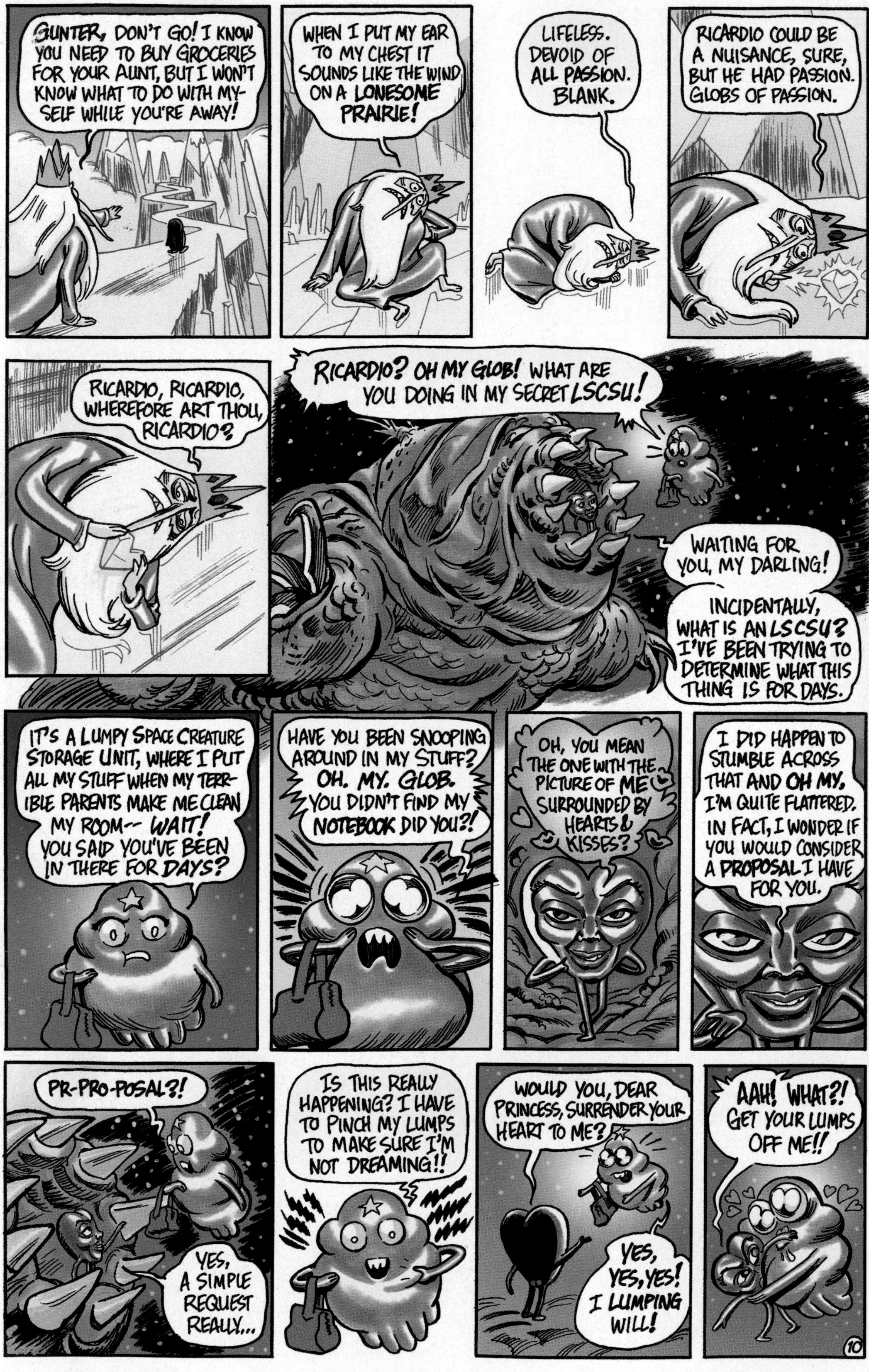
GUNTER, DON'T GO! I KNOW YOU NEED TO BUY GROCERIES FOR YOUR AUNT, BUT I WON'T KNOW WHAT TO DO WITH MYSELF WHILE YOU'RE AWAY!
WHEN I PUT MY EAR TO MY CHEST IT SOUNDS LIKE THE WIND ON A LONESOME PRAIRIE!
LIFELESS. DEVOID OF ALL PASSION. BLANK.
RICARDIO COULD BE A NUISANCE, SURE, BUT HE HAD PASSION. GLOBS OF PASSION.
RICARDIO, RICARDIO, WHEREFORE ART THOU, RICARDIO?
RICARDIO? OH MY GLOB! WHAT ARE YOU DOING IN MY SECRET LSCSU!
WAITING FOR YOU, MY DARLING!
INCIDENTALLY, WHAT IS AN LSCSU? I'VE BEEN TRYING TO DETERMINE WHAT THIS THING IS FOR DAYS.
IT'S A LUMPY SPACE CREATURE STORAGE UNIT, WHERE I PUT ALL MY STUFF WHEN MY TERRIBLE PARENTS MAKE ME CLEAN MY ROOM-- WAIT! YOU SAID YOU'VE BEEN IN THERE FOR DAYS?
HAVE YOU BEEN SNOOPING AROUND IN MY STUFF? OH. MY. GLOB. YOU DIDN'T FIND MY NOTEBOOK DID YOU?!
OH, YOU MEAN THE ONE WITH THE PICTURE OF ME SURROUNDED BY HEARTS & KISSES?
I DID HAPPEN TO STUMBLE ACROSS THAT AND OH MY. I'M QUITE FLATTERED. IN FACT, I WONDER IF YOU WOULD CONSIDER A PROPOSAL I HAVE FOR YOU.
PR-PRO-POSAL?!
YES, A SIMPLE REQUEST REALLY...
IS THIS REALLY HAPPENING? I HAVE TO PINCH MY LUMPS TO MAKE SURE I'M NOT DREAMING!!
WOULD YOU, DEAR PRINCESS, SURRENDER YOUR HEART TO ME?
YES, YES, YES! I LUMPING WILL!
AAH! WHAT?! GET YOUR LUMPS OFF ME!!

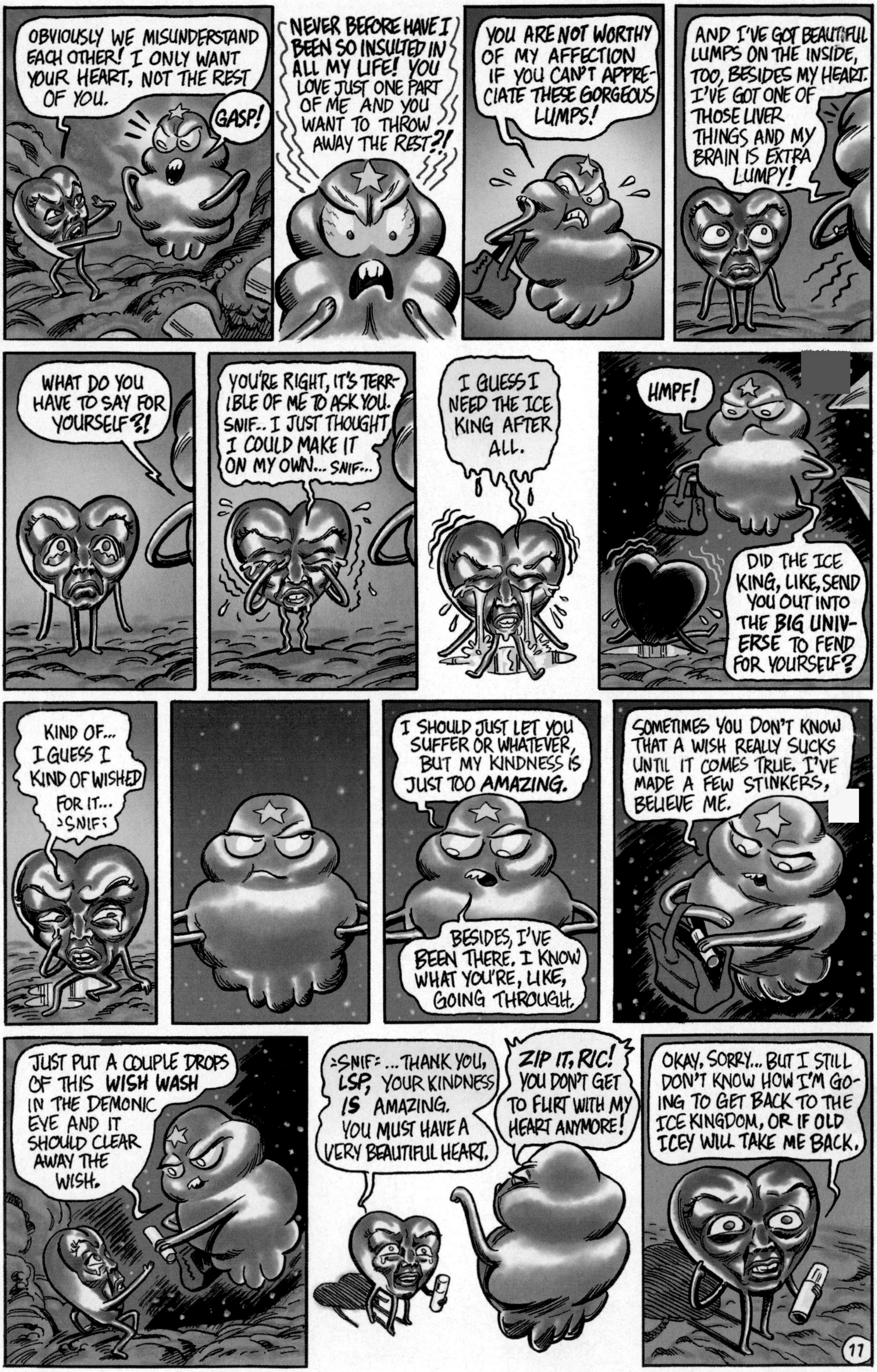
OBVIOUSLY WE MISUNDERSTAND EACH OTHER! I ONLY WANT YOUR HEART, NOT THE REST OF YOU.
GASP!
NEVER BEFORE HAVE I BEEN SO INSULTED IN ALL MY LIFE! YOU LOVE JUST ONE PART OF ME AND YOU WANT TO THROW AWAY THE REST?!
YOU ARE NOT WORTHY OF MY AFFECTION IF YOU CAN'T APPRE-CIATE THESE GORGEOUS LUMPS!
AND I'VE GOT BEAUTIFUL LUMPS ON THE INSIDE, TOO, BESIDES MY HEART. I'VE GOT ONE OF THOSE LIVER THINGS AND MY BRAIN IS EXTRA LUMPY!
WHAT DO YOU HAVE TO SAY FOR YOURSELF?!
YOU'RE RIGHT, IT'S TERR-IBLE OF ME TO ASK YOU. SNIF.. I JUST THOUGHT I COULD MAKE IT ON MY OWN... SNIF...
I GUESS I NEED THE ICE KING AFTER ALL.
HMPF!
DID THE ICE KING, LIKE, SEND YOU OUT INTO THE BIG UNIV-ERSE TO FEND FOR YOURSELF?
KIND OF... I GUESS I KIND OF WISHED FOR IT... SNIF
I SHOULD JUST LET YOU SUFFER OR WHATEVER, BUT MY KINDNESS IS JUST TOO AMAZING.
BESIDES, I'VE BEEN THERE. I KNOW WHAT YOU'RE, LIKE, GOING THROUGH.
SOMETIMES YOU DON'T KNOW THAT A WISH REALLY SUCKS UNTIL IT COMES TRUE. I'VE MADE A FEW STINKERS, BELIEVE ME.
JUST PUT A COUPLE DROPS OF THIS WISH WASH IN THE DEMONIC EYE AND IT SHOULD CLEAR AWAY THE WISH.
SNIF ...THANK YOU, LSP, YOUR KINDNESS IS AMAZING. YOU MUST HAVE A VERY BEAUTIFUL HEART.
ZIP IT, RIC! YOU DON'T GET TO FLIRT WITH MY HEART ANYMORE!
OKAY, SORRY... BUT I STILL DON'T KNOW HOW I'M GO-ING TO GET BACK TO THE ICE KINGDOM, OR IF OLD ICEY WILL TAKE ME BACK.

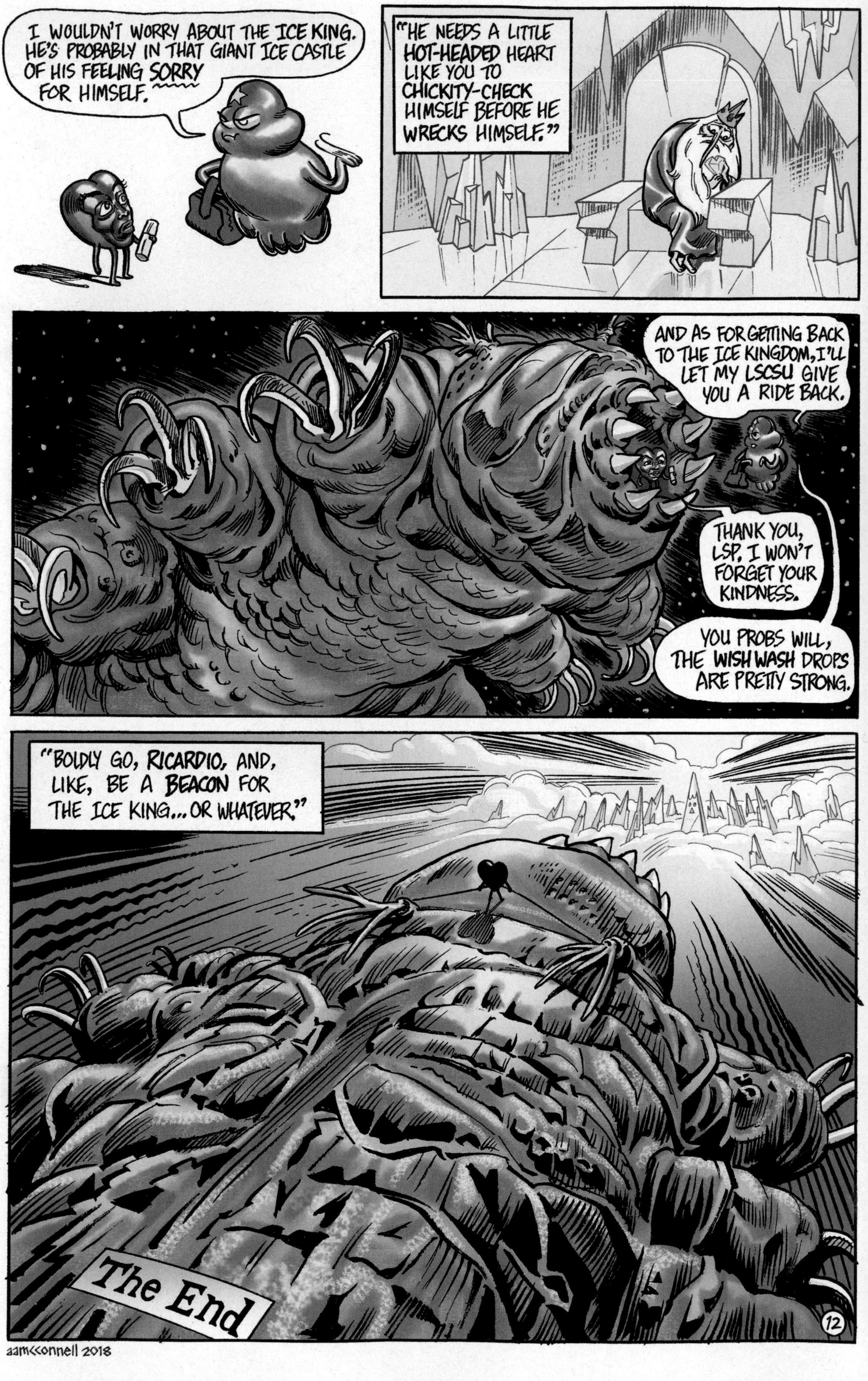
I WOULDN'T WORRY ABOUT THE ICE KING. HE'S PROBABLY IN THAT GIANT ICE CASTLE OF HIS FEELING SORRY FOR HIMSELF.
"HE NEEDS A LITTLE HOT-HEADED HEART LIKE YOU TO CHICKITY-CHECK HIMSELF BEFORE HE WRECKS HIMSELF."
AND AS FOR GETTING BACK TO THE ICE KINGDOM, I'LL LET MY LSCSU GIVE YOU A RIDE BACK.
THANK YOU, LSP, I WON'T FORGET YOUR KINDNESS.
YOU PROBS WILL, THE WISH WASH DROPS ARE PRETTY STRONG.
"BOLDLY GO, RICARDIO, AND, LIKE, BE A BEACON FOR THE ICE KING... OR WHATEVER."
The End
12
aamcconnell 2018

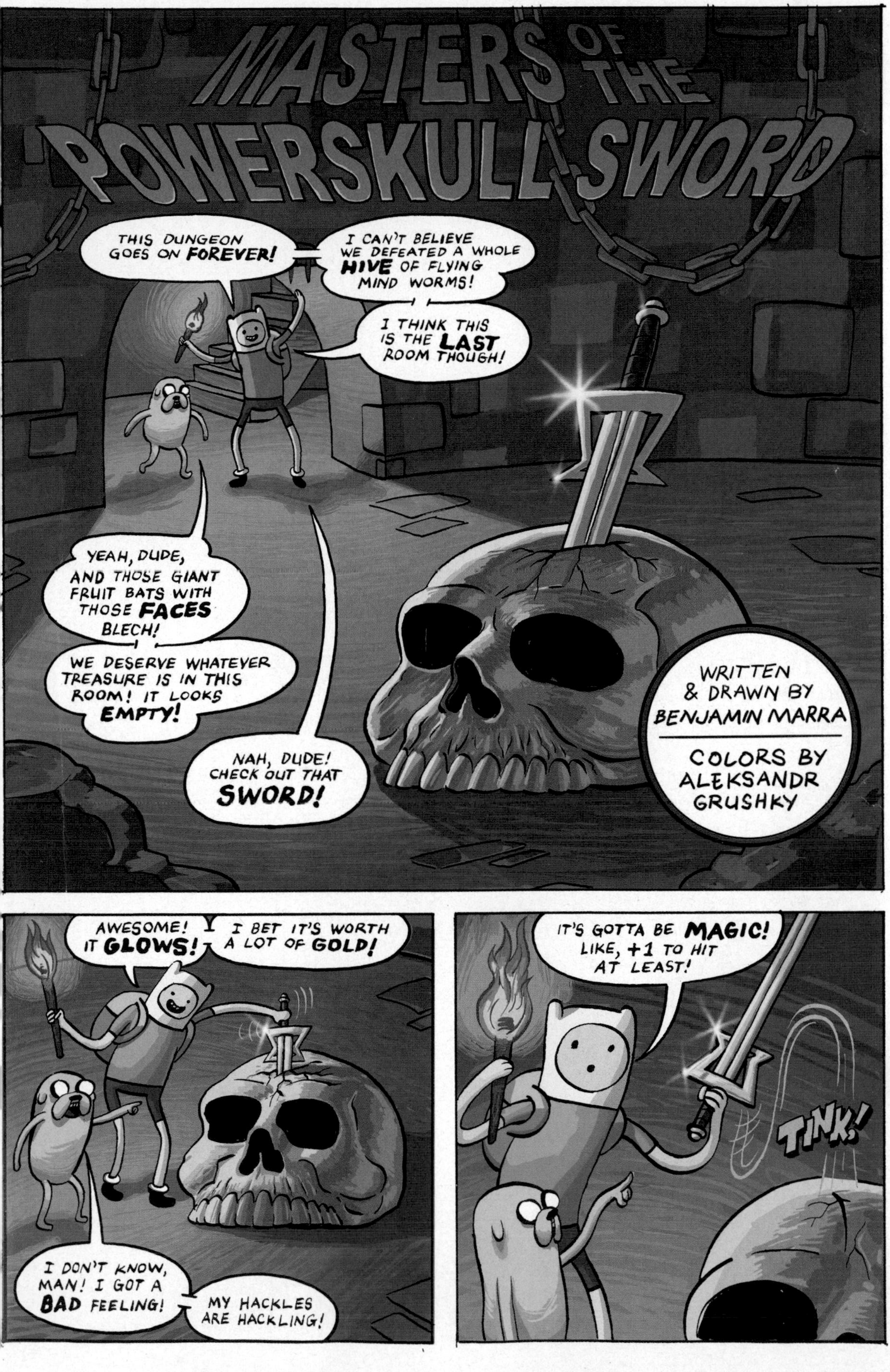
MASTERS OF THE POWERSKULL SWORD
THIS DUNGEON GOES ON FOREVER!
I CAN'T BELIEVE WE DEFEATED A WHOLE HIVE OF FLYING MIND WORMS!
I THINK THIS IS THE LAST ROOM THOUGH!
YEAH, DUDE, AND THOSE GIANT FRUIT BATS WITH THOSE FACES BLECH!
WE DESERVE WHATEVER TREASURE IS IN THIS ROOM! IT LOOKS EMPTY!
NAH, DUDE! CHECK OUT THAT SWORD!
WRITTEN & DRAWN BY BENJAMIN MARRA
COLORS BY ALEKSANDR GRUSHKY
AWESOME! IT GLOWS!
I BET IT'S WORTH A LOT OF GOLD!
I DON'T KNOW, MAN! I GOT A BAD FEELING!
MY HACKLES ARE HACKLING!
IT'S GOTTA BE MAGIC! LIKE, +1 TO HIT AT LEAST!
TINK!

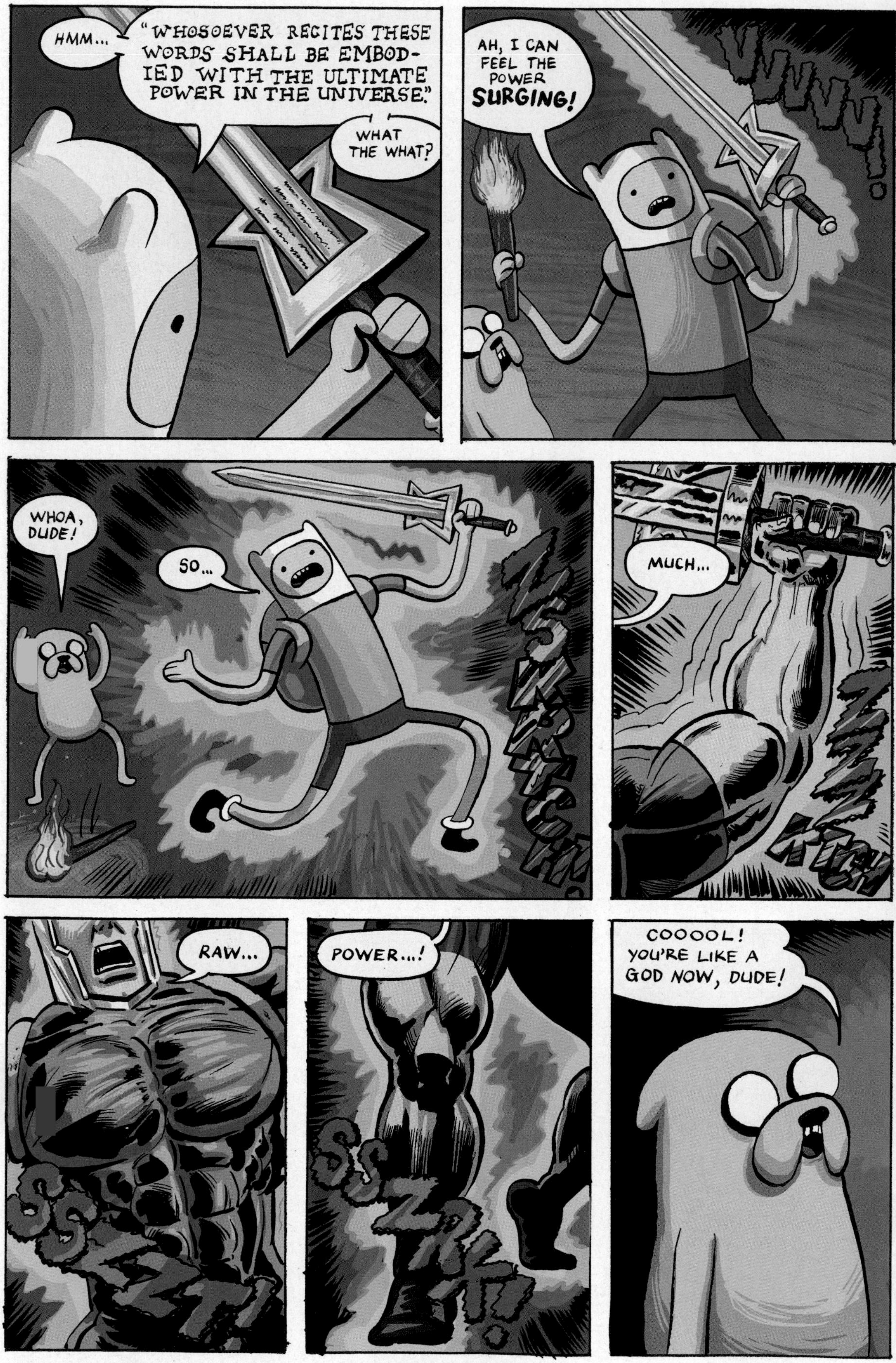
HMM...
"WHOSOEVER RECITES THESE WORDS SHALL BE EMBODIED WITH THE ULTIMATE POWER IN THE UNIVERSE."
WHAT THE WHAT?
AH, I CAN FEEL THE POWER SURGING!
WHOA, DUDE!
SO...
MUCH...
RAW...
POWER...!
COOOOL! YOU'RE LIKE A GOD NOW, DUDE!

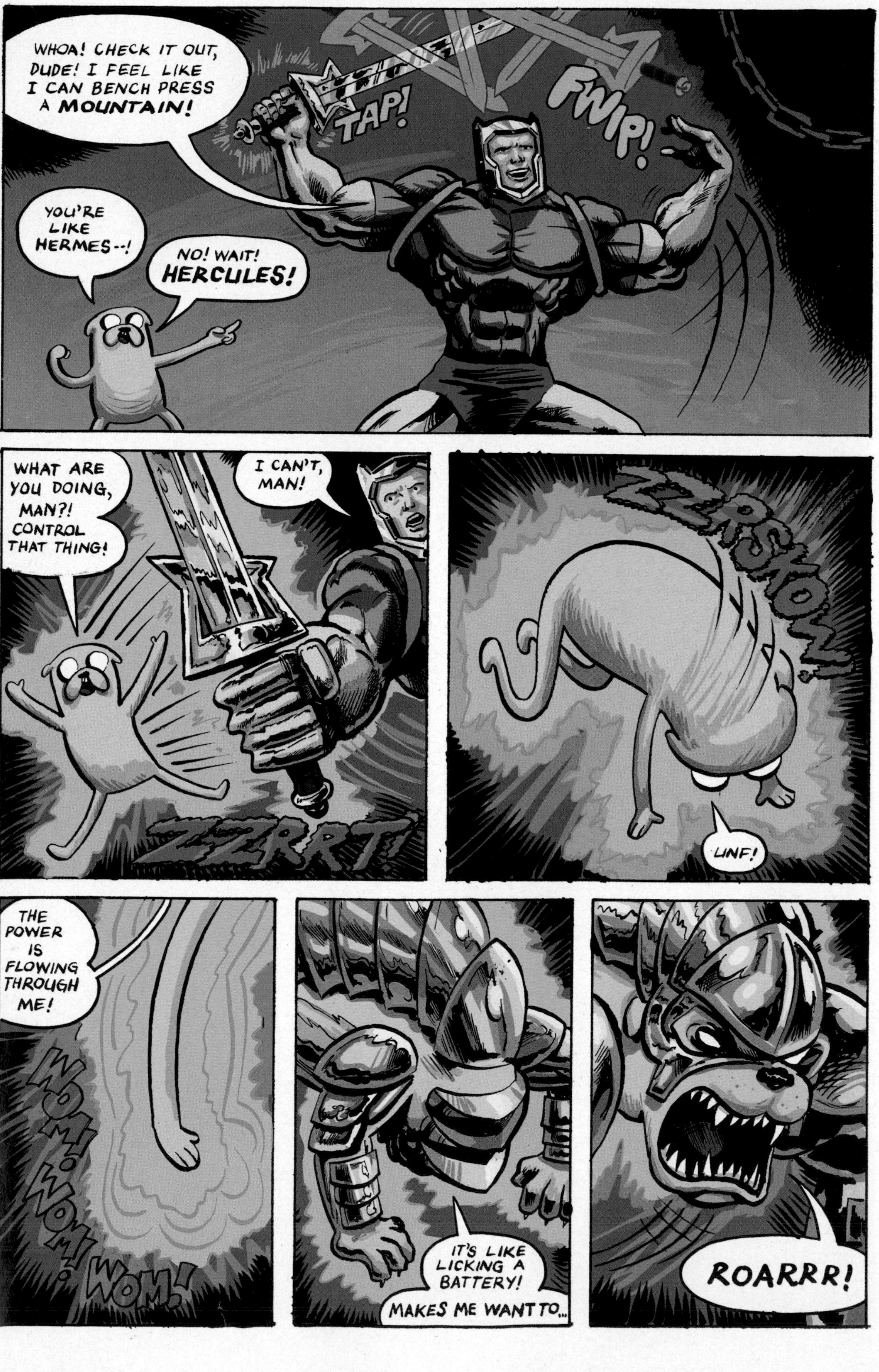
WHOA! CHECK IT OUT, DUDE! I FEEL LIKE I CAN BENCH PRESS A MOUNTAIN!
TAP!
FWIP!
YOU'RE LIKE HERMES--!
NO! WAIT! HERCULES!
WHAT ARE YOU DOING, MAN?! CONTROL THAT THING!
I CAN'T, MAN!
ZZRRT!
ZZRPSKOW!
UNF!
THE POWER IS FLOWING THROUGH ME!
WOM! WOM! WOM!
WOM!
IT'S LIKE LICKING A BATTERY!
MAKES ME WANT TO...
ROARRR!

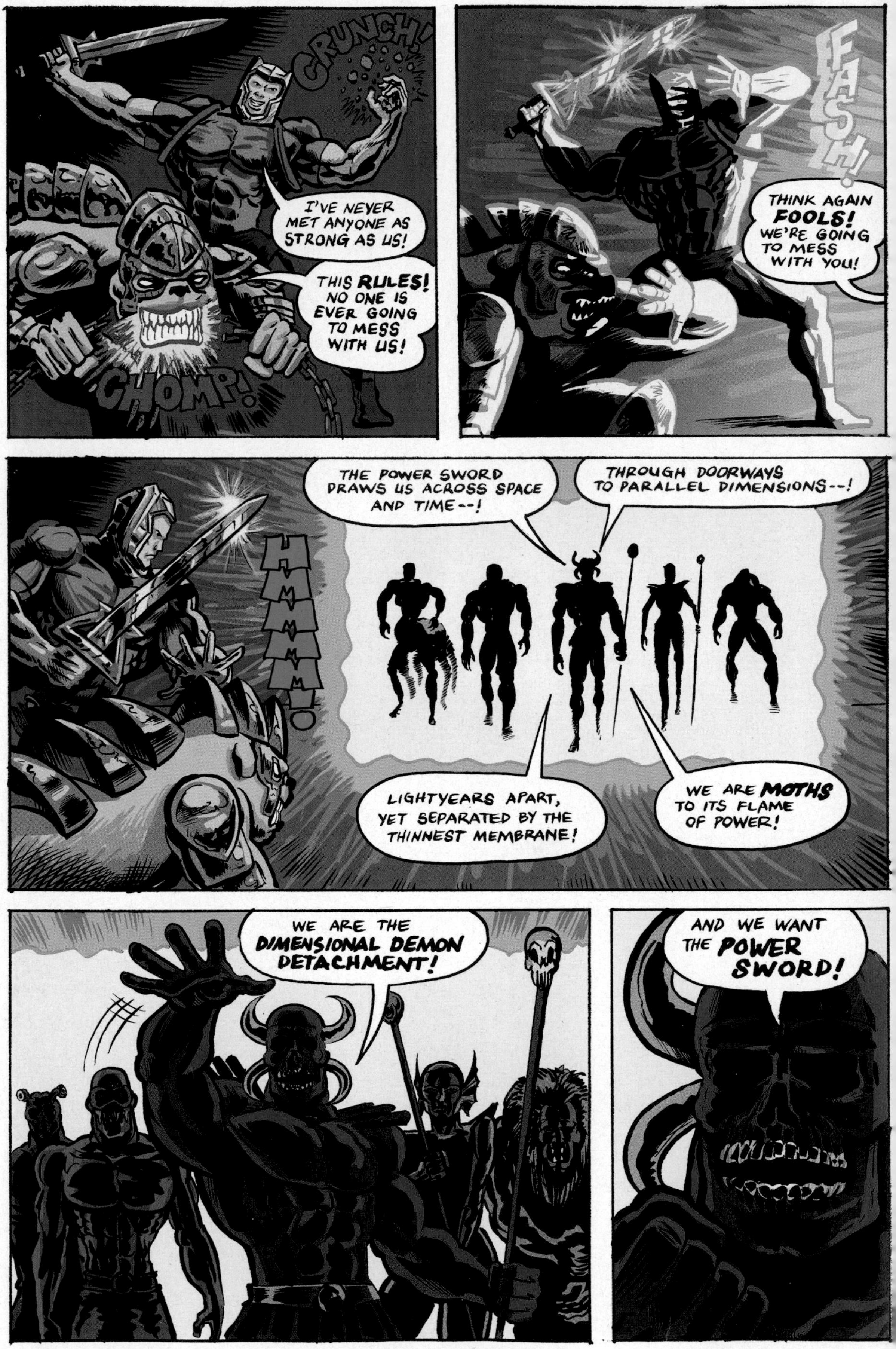

CRUNCH!
I'VE NEVER MET ANYONE AS STRONG AS US!
THIS RULES! NO ONE IS EVER GOING TO MESS WITH US!
CHOMP!
FASH!
THINK AGAIN FOOLS! WE'RE GOING TO MESS WITH YOU!
HMMMM!
THE POWER SWORD DRAWS US ACROSS SPACE AND TIME--!
THROUGH DOORWAYS TO PARALLEL DIMENSIONS--!
LIGHTYEARS APART, YET SEPARATED BY THE THINNEST MEMBRANE!
WE ARE MOTHS TO ITS FLAME OF POWER!
WE ARE THE DIMENSIONAL DEMON DETACHMENT!
AND WE WANT THE POWER SWORD!

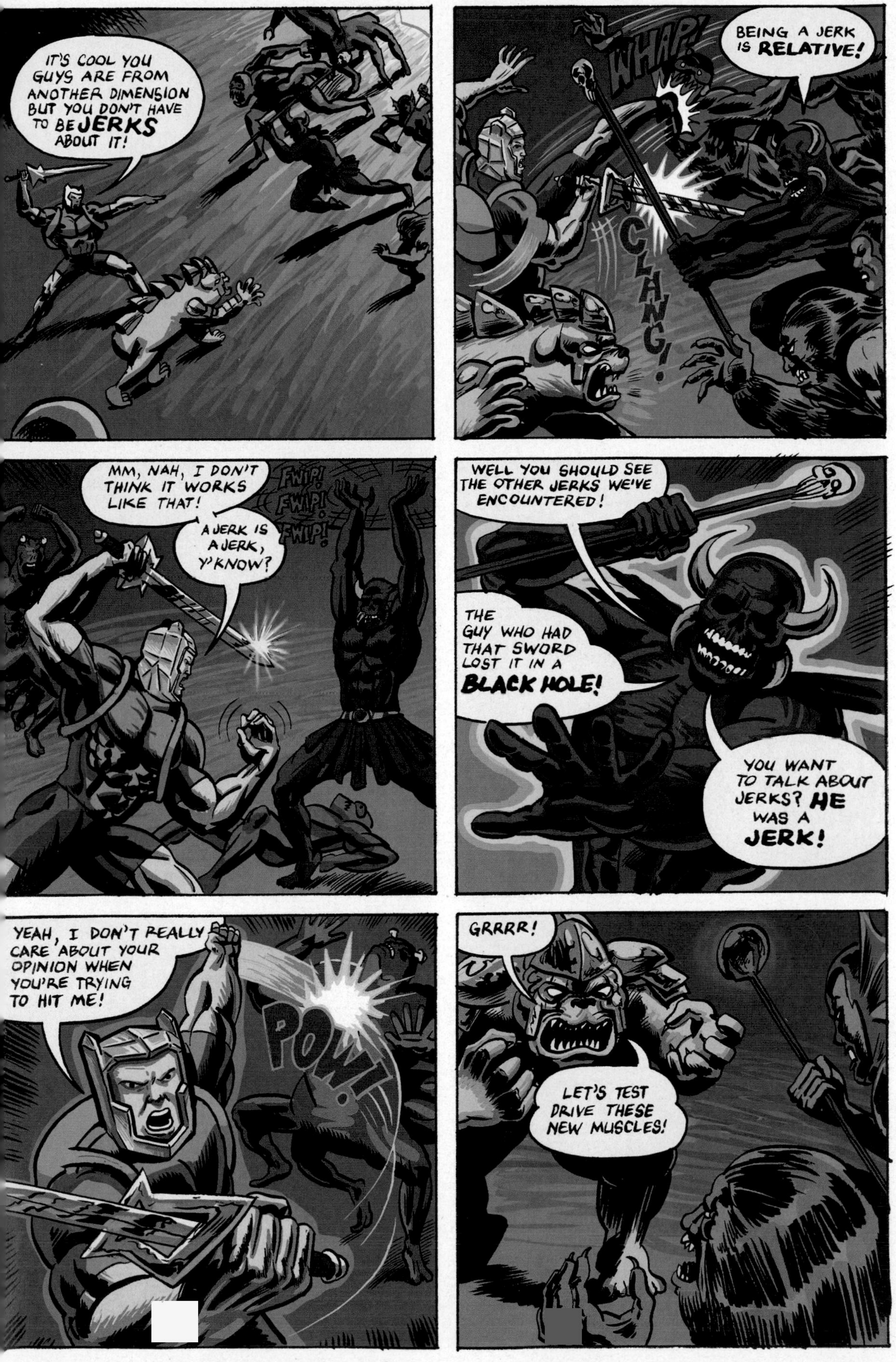
IT'S COOL YOU GUYS ARE FROM ANOTHER DIMENSION BUT YOU DON'T HAVE TO BE JERKS ABOUT IT!
WHAP!
BEING A JERK IS RELATIVE!
CLANG!
MM, NAH, I DON'T THINK IT WORKS LIKE THAT!
A JERK IS A JERK, Y'KNOW?
FWIP! FWIP! FWIP!
WELL YOU SHOULD SEE THE OTHER JERKS WE'VE ENCOUNTERED!
THE GUY WHO HAD THAT SWORD LOST IT IN A BLACK HOLE!
YOU WANT TO TALK ABOUT JERKS? HE WAS A JERK!
YEAH, I DON'T REALLY CARE ABOUT YOUR OPINION WHEN YOU'RE TRYING TO HIT ME!
POW!
GRRRR!
LET'S TEST DRIVE THESE NEW MUSCLES!

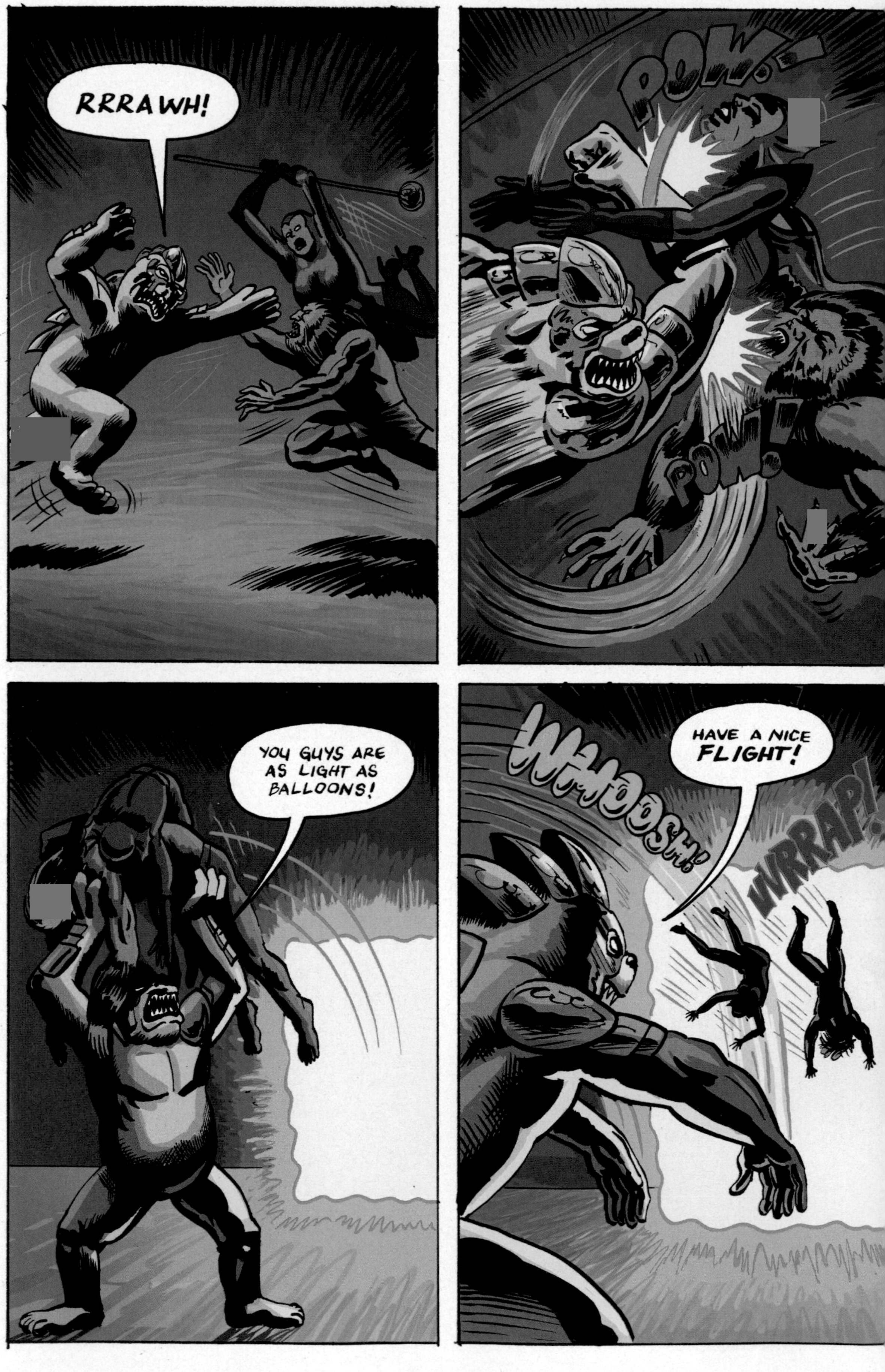
RRRAWH!
POW!
POW!
YOU GUYS ARE AS LIGHT AS BALLOONS!
WHOOSH!
HAVE A NICE FLIGHT!
VVRRAP!

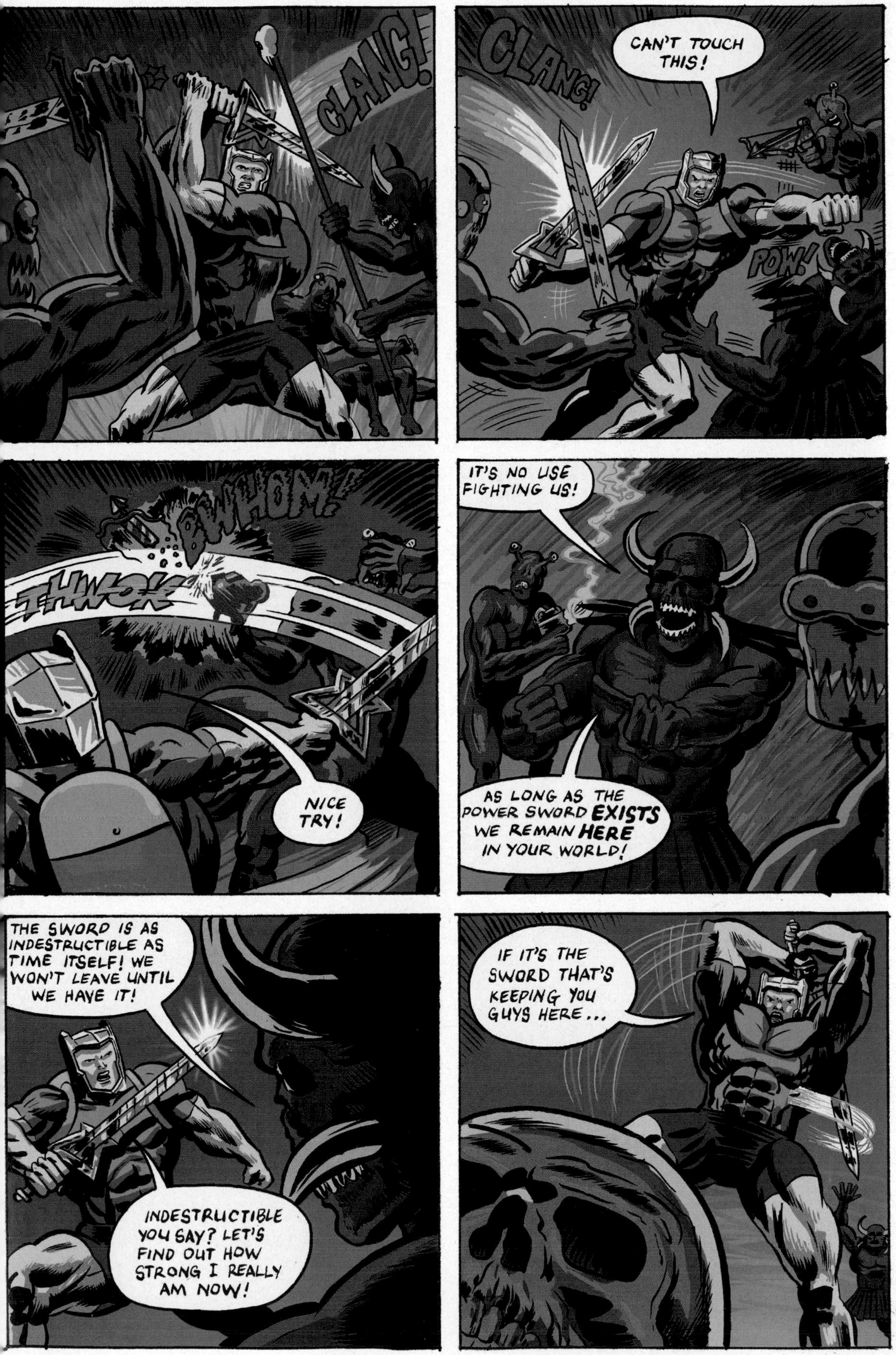
CLANG!
CLANG!
CAN'T TOUCH THIS!
POW!
BWHOM!
THWOK
NICE TRY!
IT'S NO USE FIGHTING US!
AS LONG AS THE POWER SWORD EXISTS WE REMAIN HERE IN YOUR WORLD!
THE SWORD IS AS INDESTRUCTIBLE AS TIME ITSELF! WE WON'T LEAVE UNTIL WE HAVE IT!
INDESTRUCTIBLE YOU SAY? LET'S FIND OUT HOW STRONG I REALLY AM NOW!
IF IT'S THE SWORD THAT'S KEEPING YOU GUYS HERE...

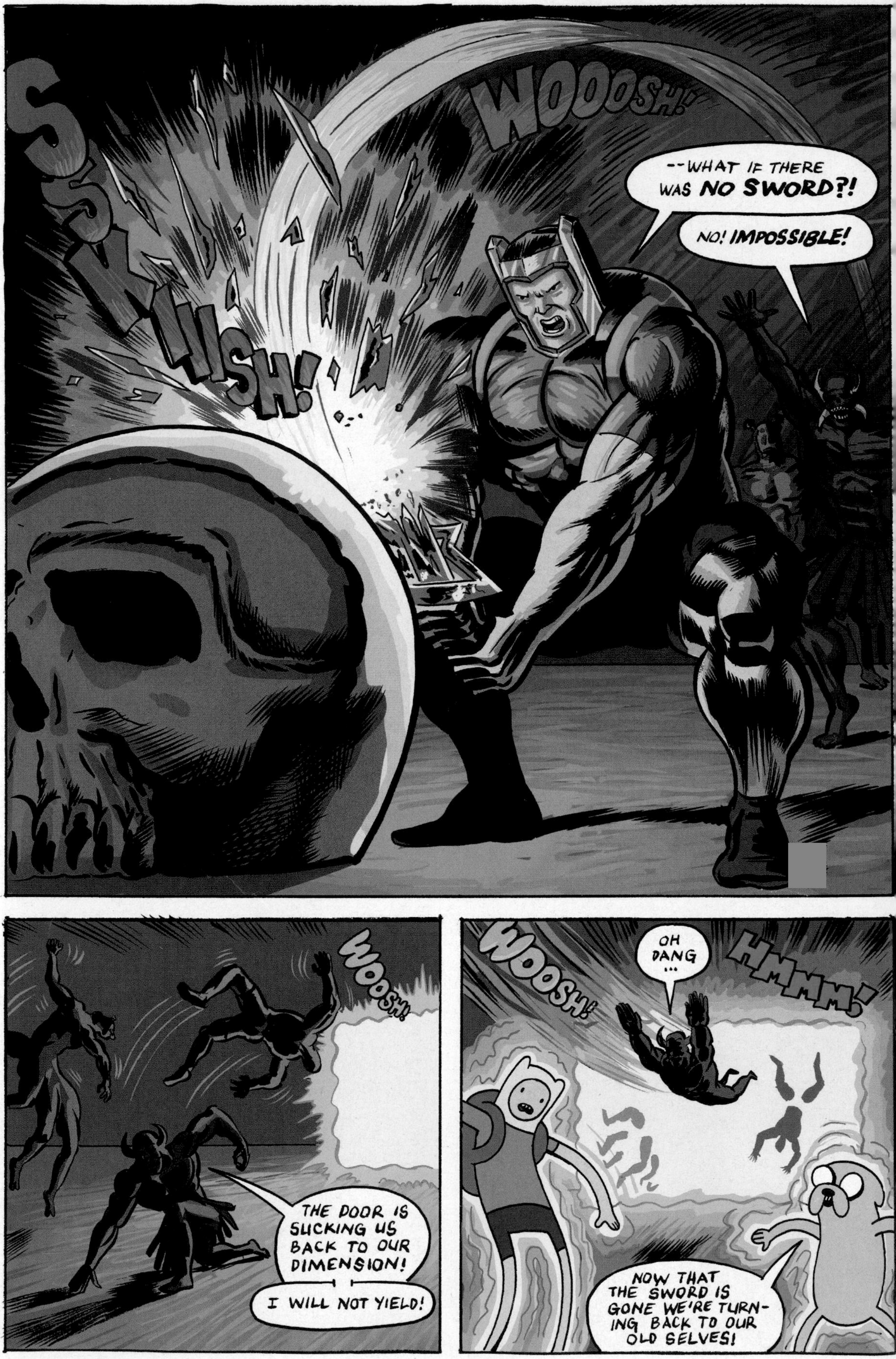
SKKIISH!
WOOOSH!
--WHAT IF THERE WAS NO SWORD?!
NO! IMPOSSIBLE!
WOOSH!
THE DOOR IS SUCKING US BACK TO OUR DIMENSION!
I WILL NOT YIELD!
WOOSH!
OH DANG ...
HMMMM!
NOW THAT THE SWORD IS GONE WE'RE TURNING BACK TO OUR OLD SELVES!

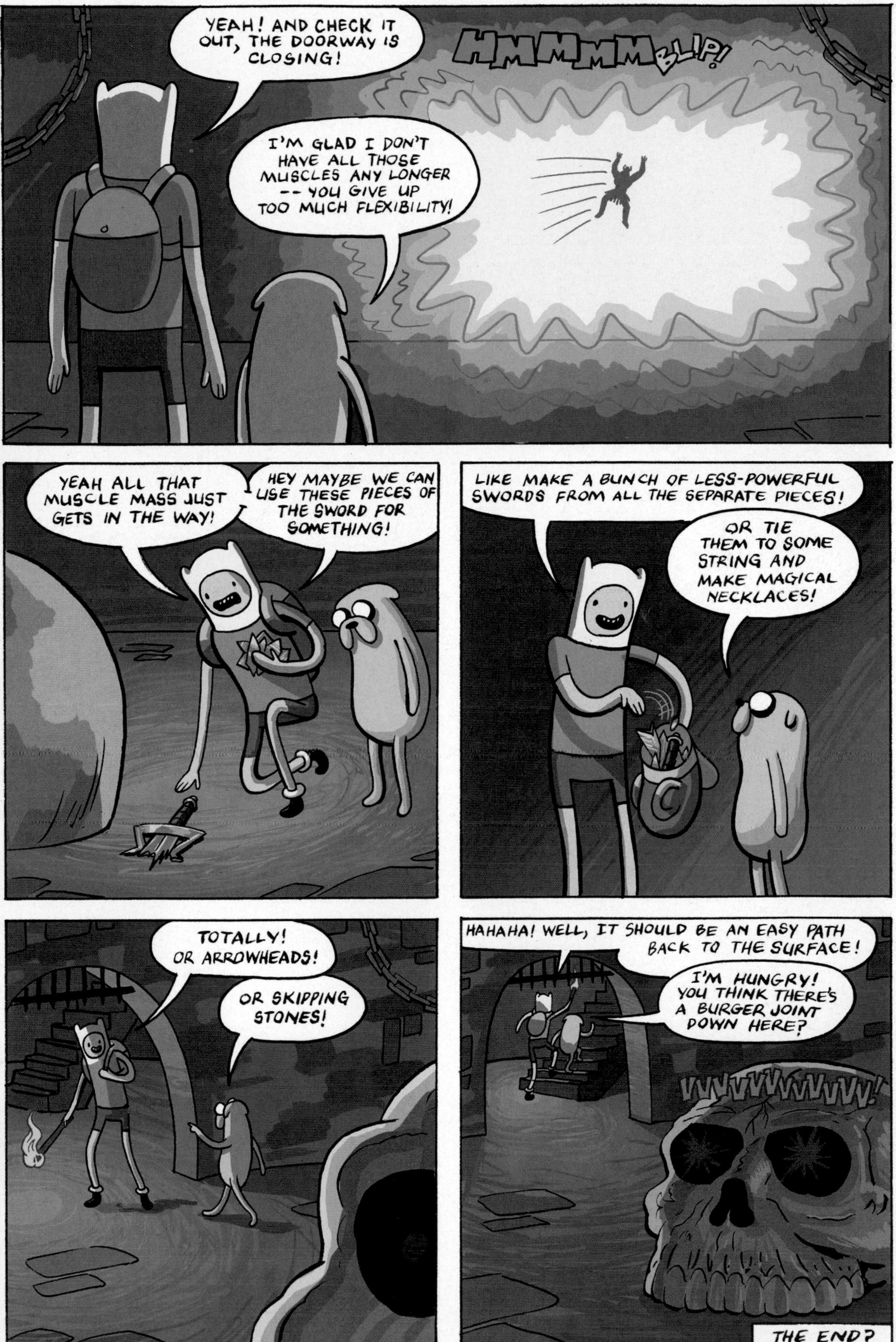
YEAH! AND CHECK IT OUT, THE DOORWAY IS CLOSING!
HMMMMMBLIP!
I'M GLAD I DON'T HAVE ALL THOSE MUSCLES ANY LONGER -- YOU GIVE UP TOO MUCH FLEXIBILITY!
YEAH ALL THAT MUSCLE MASS JUST GETS IN THE WAY!
HEY MAYBE WE CAN USE THESE PIECES OF THE SWORD FOR SOMETHING!
LIKE MAKE A BUNCH OF LESS-POWERFUL SWORDS FROM ALL THE SEPARATE PIECES!
OR TIE THEM TO SOME STRING AND MAKE MAGICAL NECKLACES!
TOTALLY! OR ARROWHEADS!
OR SKIPPING STONES!
HAHAHA! WELL, IT SHOULD BE AN EASY PATH BACK TO THE SURFACE!
I'M HUNGRY! YOU THINK THERE'S A BURGER JOINT DOWN HERE?
VVVVVVVVVVVVV!
THE END?

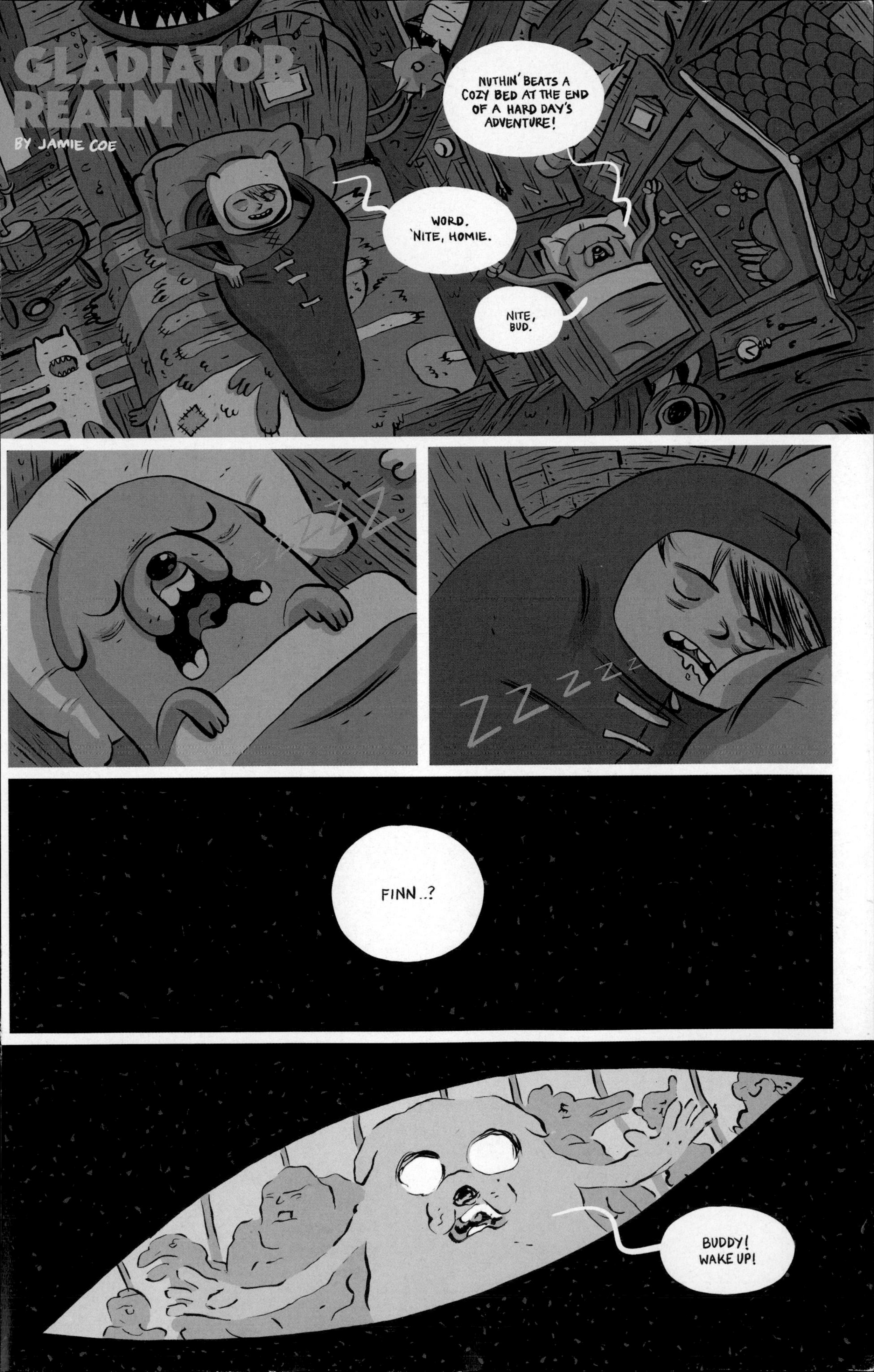
GLADIATOR REALM
BY JAMIE COE
NUTHIN' BEATS A COZY BED AT THE END OF A HARD DAY'S ADVENTURE!
WORD. 'NITE, HOMIE.
NITE, BUD.
ZZZZZ
ZZZZZ
FINN..?
BUDDY! WAKE UP!

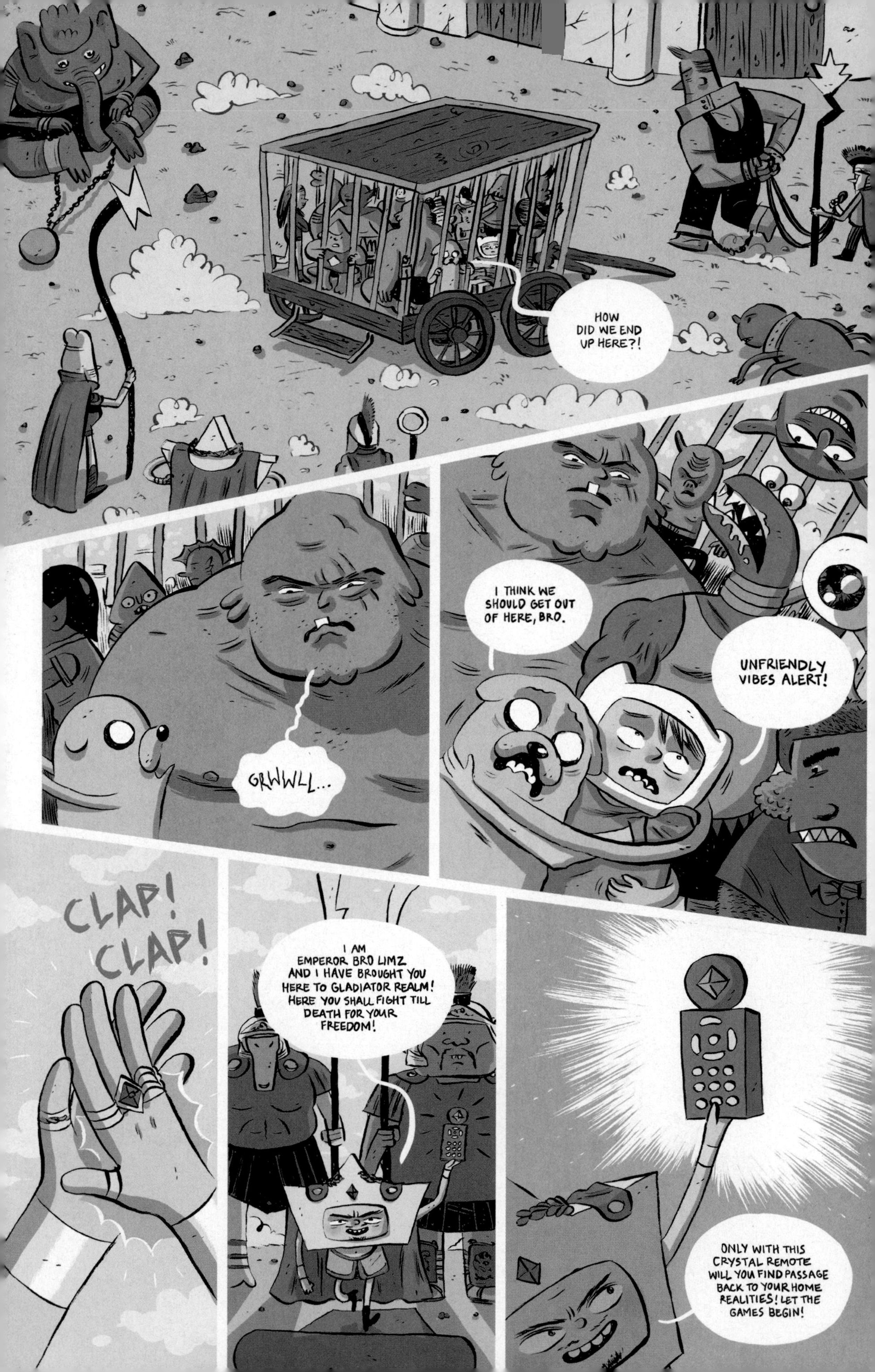
HOW DID WE END UP HERE?!
GRWWLL...
I THINK WE SHOULD GET OUT OF HERE, BRO.
UNFRIENDLY VIBES ALERT!
CLAP! CLAP!
I AM EMPEROR BRO LIMZ AND I HAVE BROUGHT YOU HERE TO GLADIATOR REALM! HERE YOU SHALL FIGHT TILL DEATH FOR YOUR FREEDOM!
ONLY WITH THIS CRYSTAL REMOTE WILL YOU FIND PASSAGE BACK TO YOUR HOME REALITIES! LET THE GAMES BEGIN!

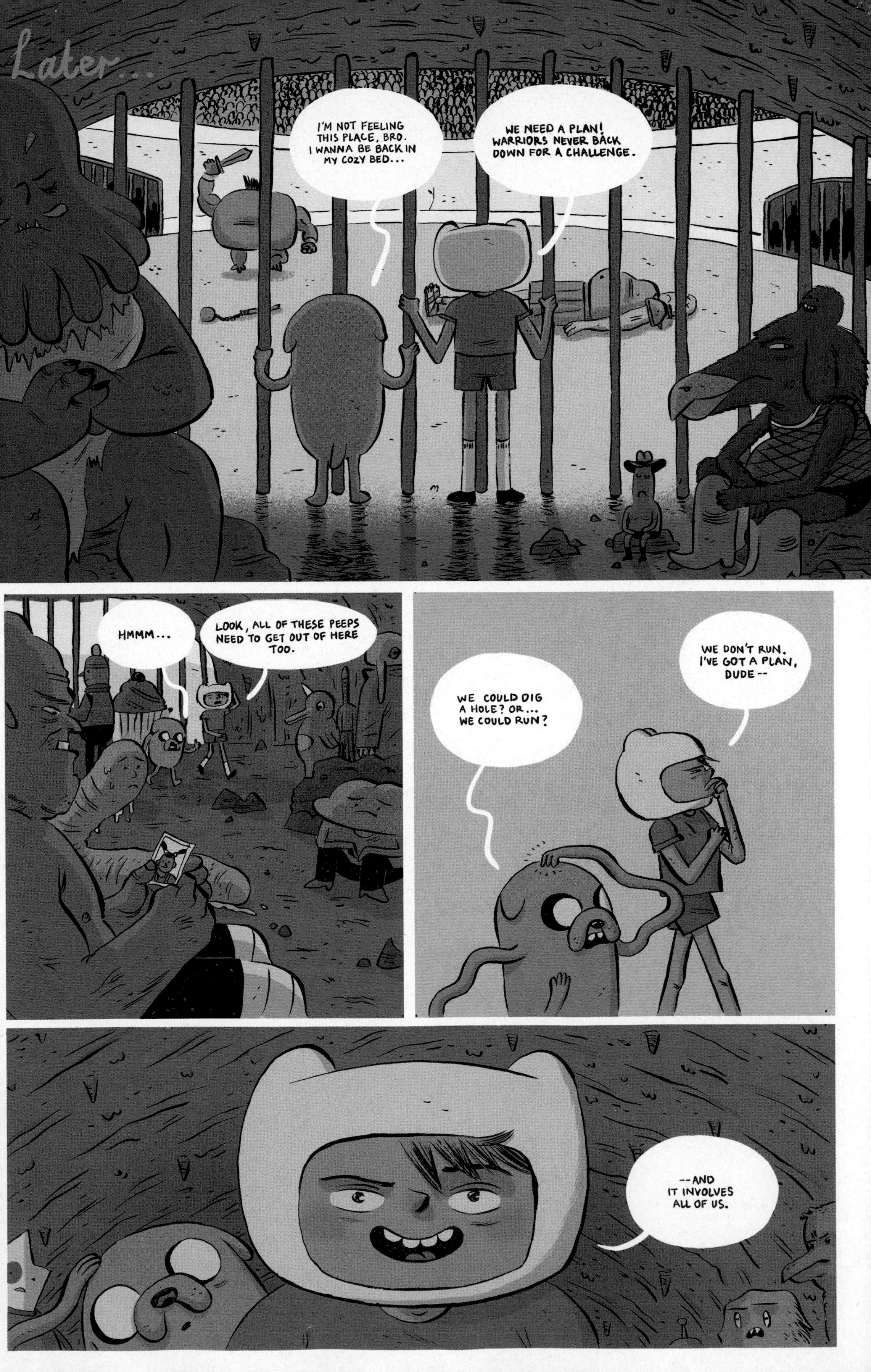
Later...
I'M NOT FEELING THIS PLACE, BRO. I WANNA BE BACK IN MY COZY BED...
WE NEED A PLAN! WARRIORS NEVER BACK DOWN FOR A CHALLENGE.
HMMM...
LOOK, ALL OF THESE PEEPS NEED TO GET OUT OF HERE TOO.
WE COULD DIG A HOLE? OR... WE COULD RUN?
WE DON'T RUN. I'VE GOT A PLAN, DUDE--
--AND IT INVOLVES ALL OF US.

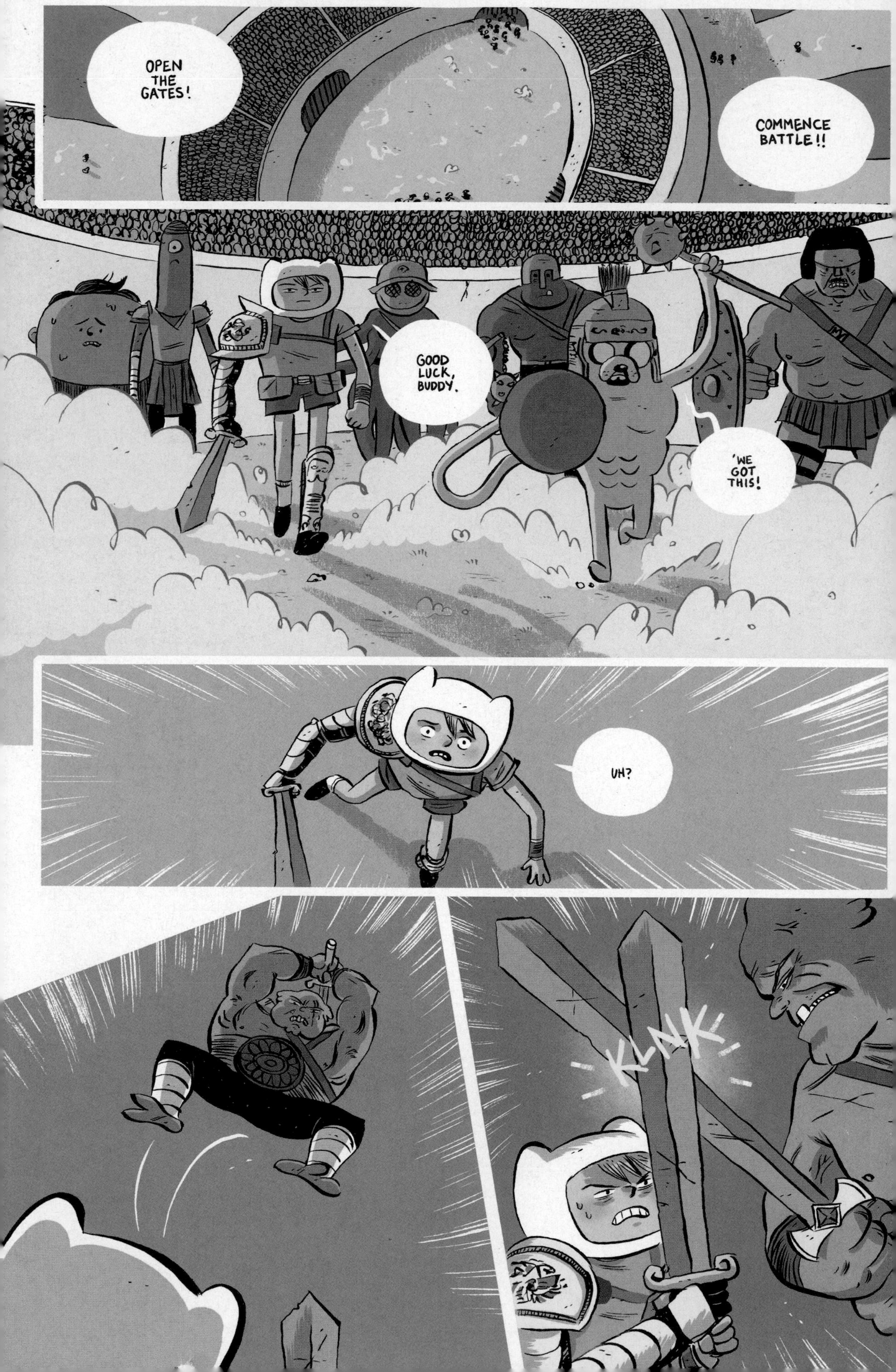
OPEN THE GATES!
COMMENCE BATTLE!!
GOOD LUCK, BUDDY.
'WE GOT THIS!
UH?
KLNK

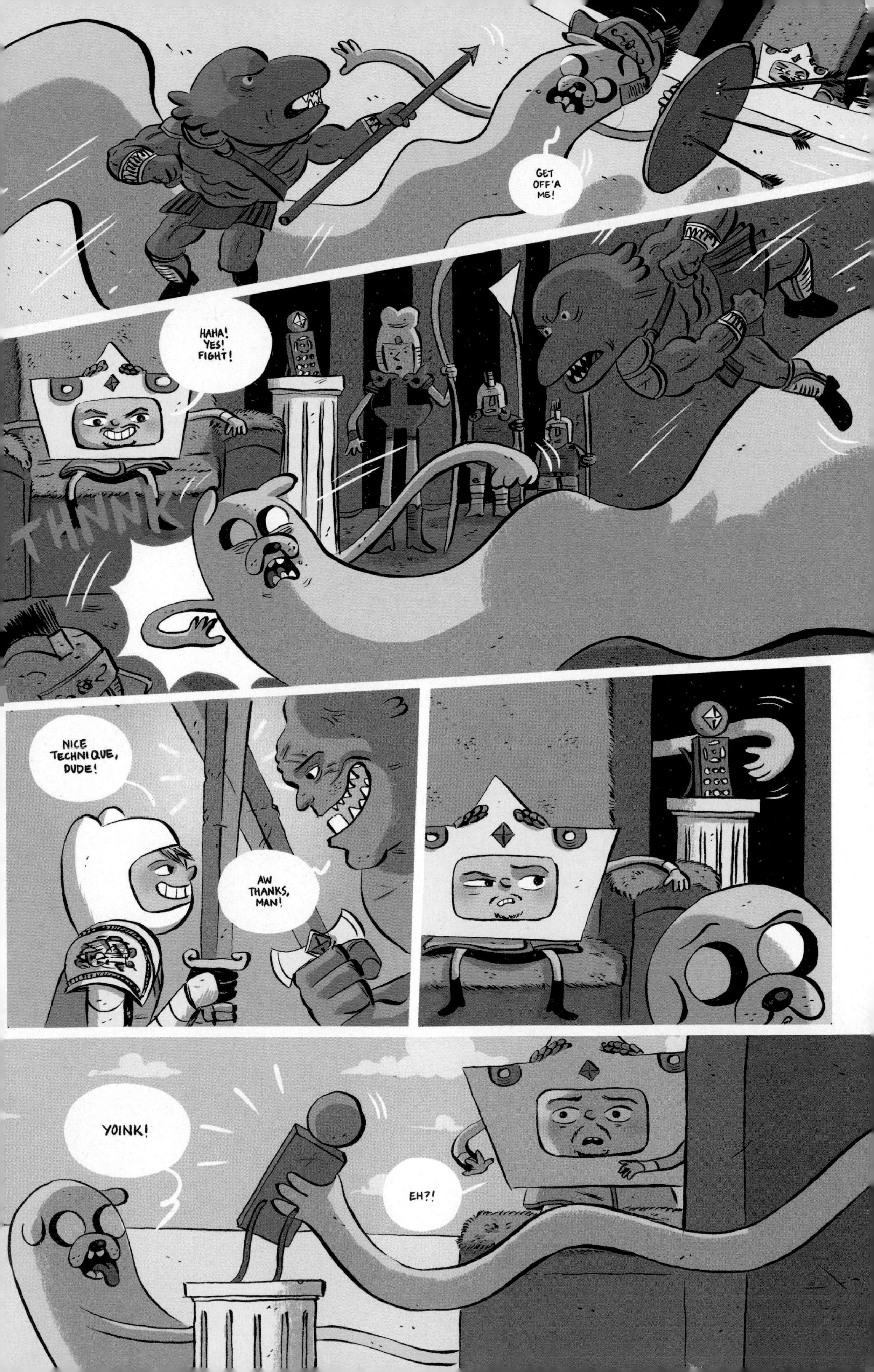
GET OFF'A ME!
HAHA! YES! FIGHT!
THNNK
NICE TECHNIQUE, DUDE!
AW THANKS, MAN!
YOINK!
EH?!

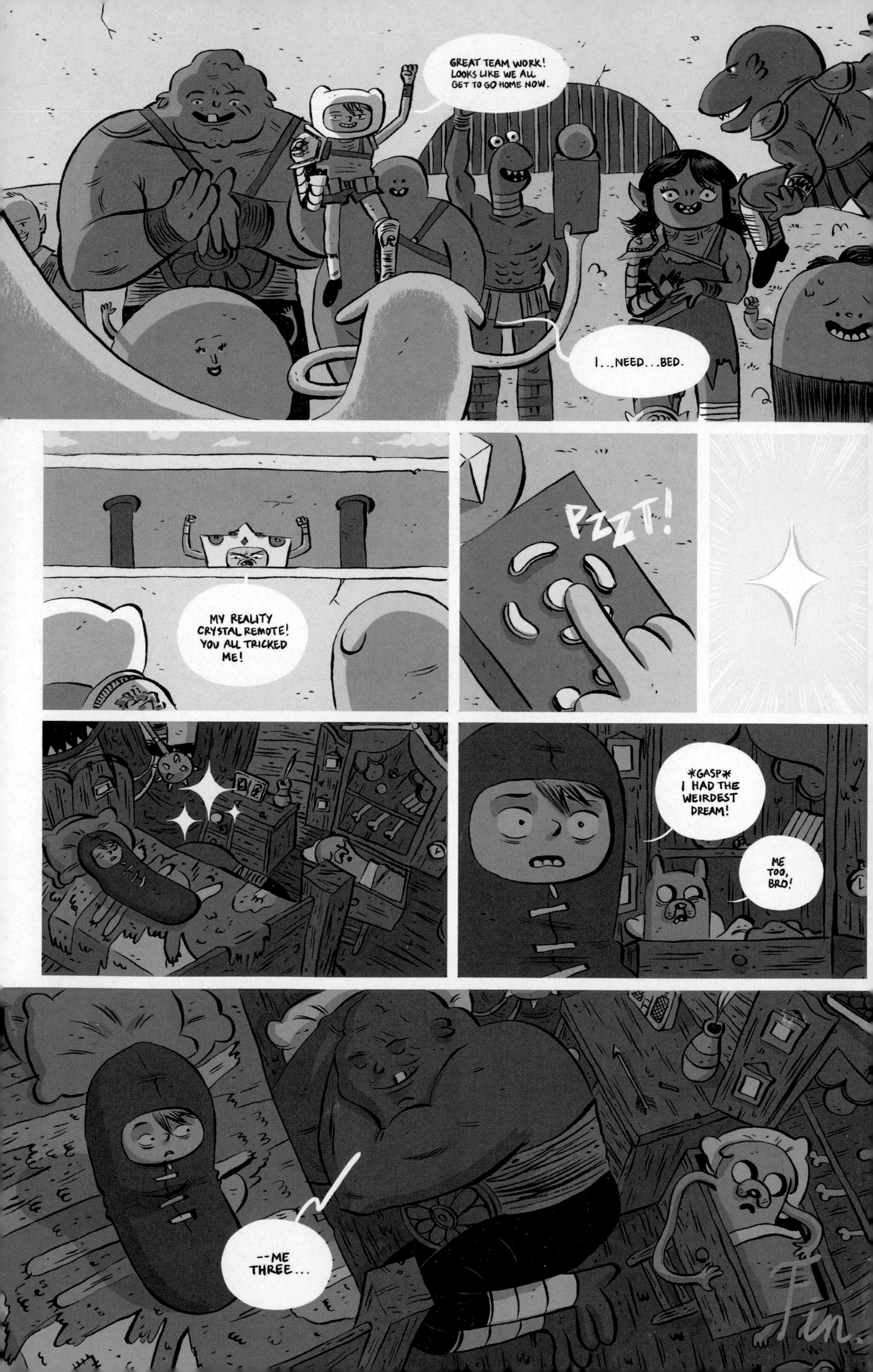
GREAT TEAM WORK! LOOKS LIKE WE ALL GET TO GO HOME NOW.
I...NEED...BED.
MY REALITY CRYSTAL REMOTE! YOU ALL TRICKED ME!
PZZT!
GASP I HAD THE WEIRDEST DREAM!
ME TOO, BRO!
--ME THREE...
Fin.

PEPPER POWER!

BY DANIELLE CHENETTE

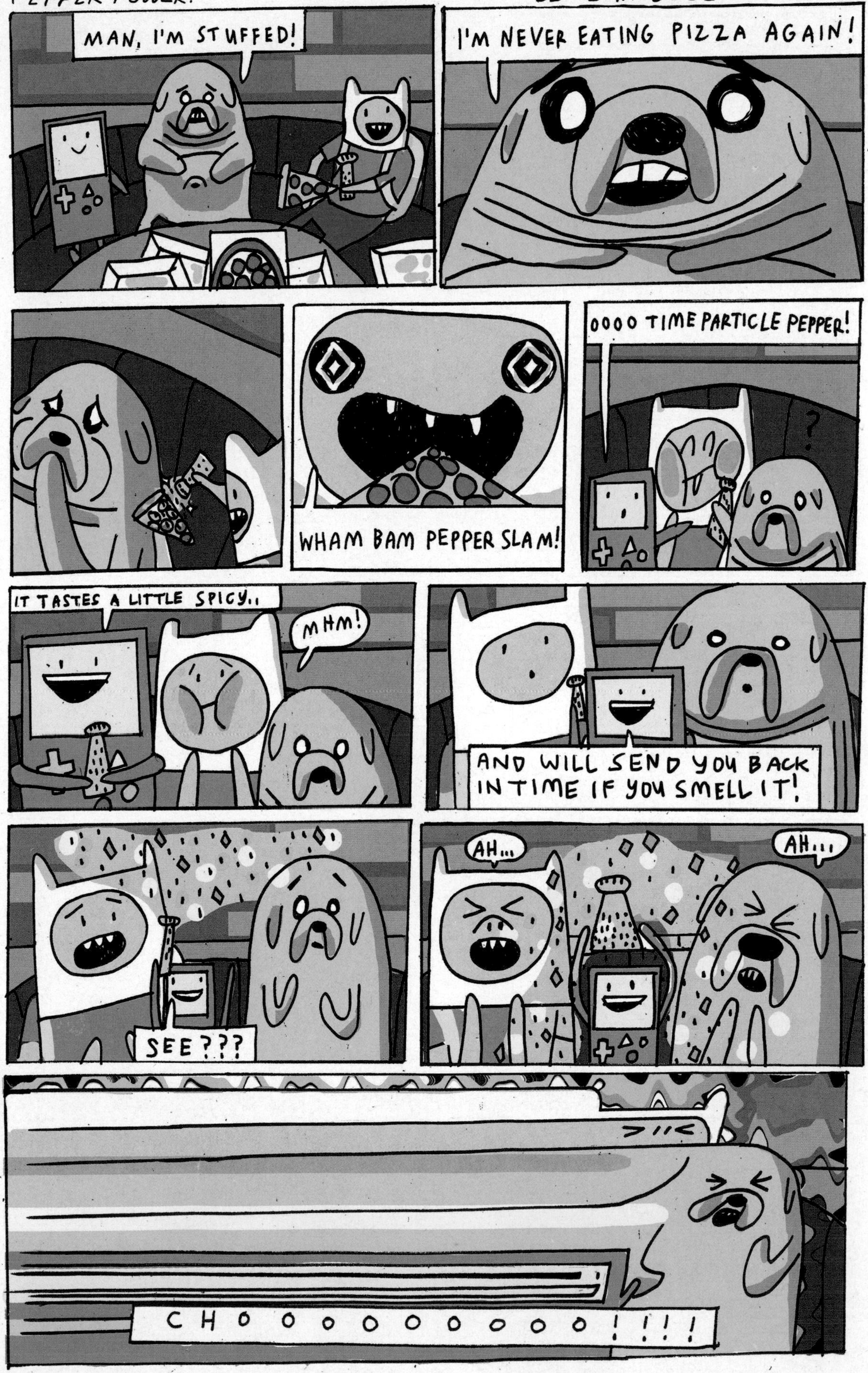
MAN, I'M STUFFED!
I'M NEVER EATING PIZZA AGAIN!
WHAM BAM PEPPER SLAM!
OOOO TIME PARTICLE PEPPER!
?
IT TASTES A LITTLE SPICY..
MHM!
AND WILL SEND YOU BACK IN TIME IF YOU SMELL IT!
SEE???
AH...
AH...
CHOOOOOOOOOO!!!!

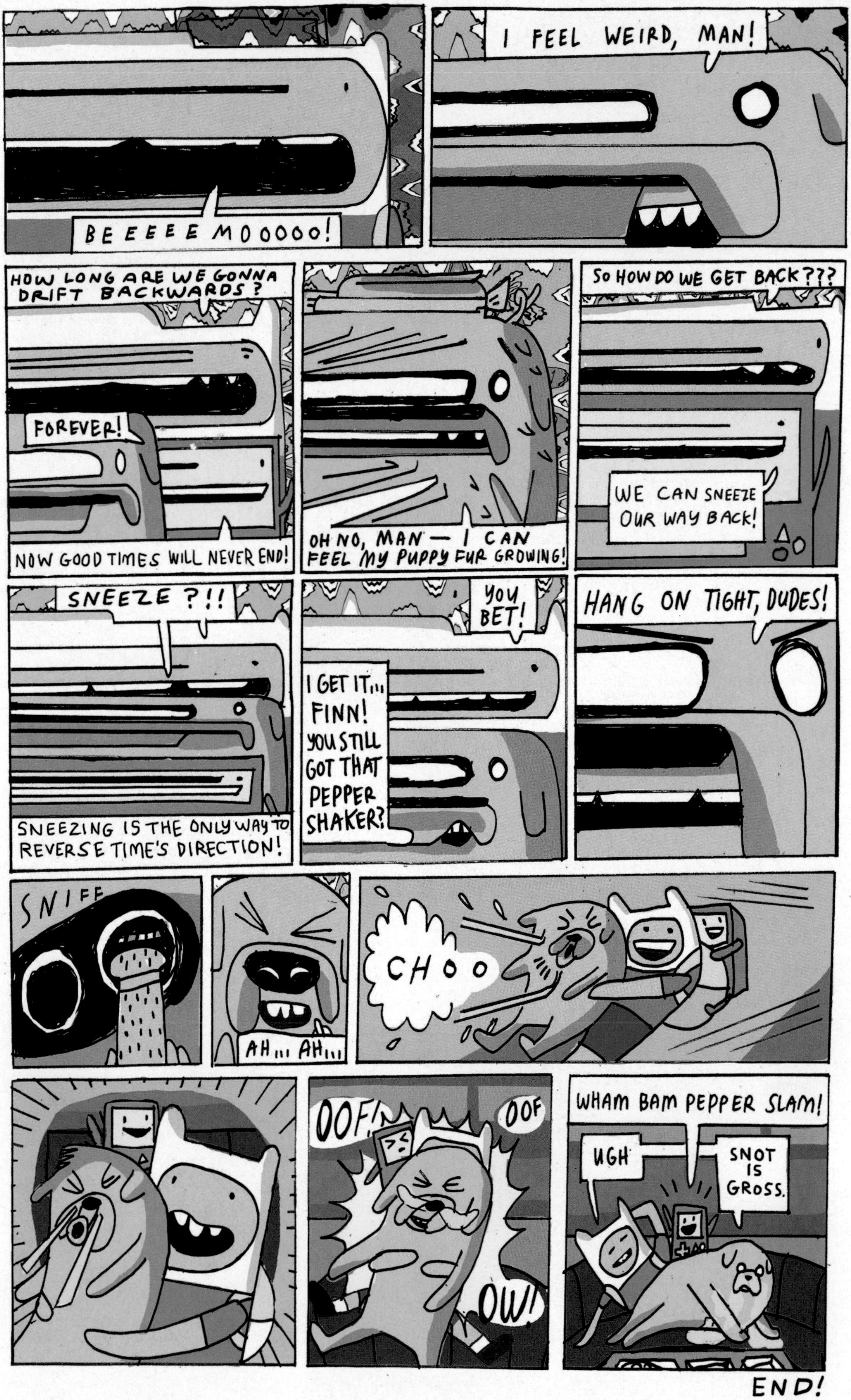
BEEEEE MOOOOO!
I FEEL WEIRD, MAN!
HOW LONG ARE WE GONNA DRIFT BACKWARDS?
FOREVER!
NOW GOOD TIMES WILL NEVER END!
OH NO, MAN — I CAN FEEL MY PUPPY FUR GROWING!
SO HOW DO WE GET BACK???
WE CAN SNEEZE OUR WAY BACK!
SNEEZE?!!
SNEEZING IS THE ONLY WAY TO REVERSE TIME'S DIRECTION!
YOU BET!
I GET IT... FINN! YOU STILL GOT THAT PEPPER SHAKER?
HANG ON TIGHT, DUDES!
SNIFF
AH... AH...
CHOO
OOF!
OOF
OW!
WHAM BAM PEPPER SLAM!
UGH
SNOT IS GROSS.

END!

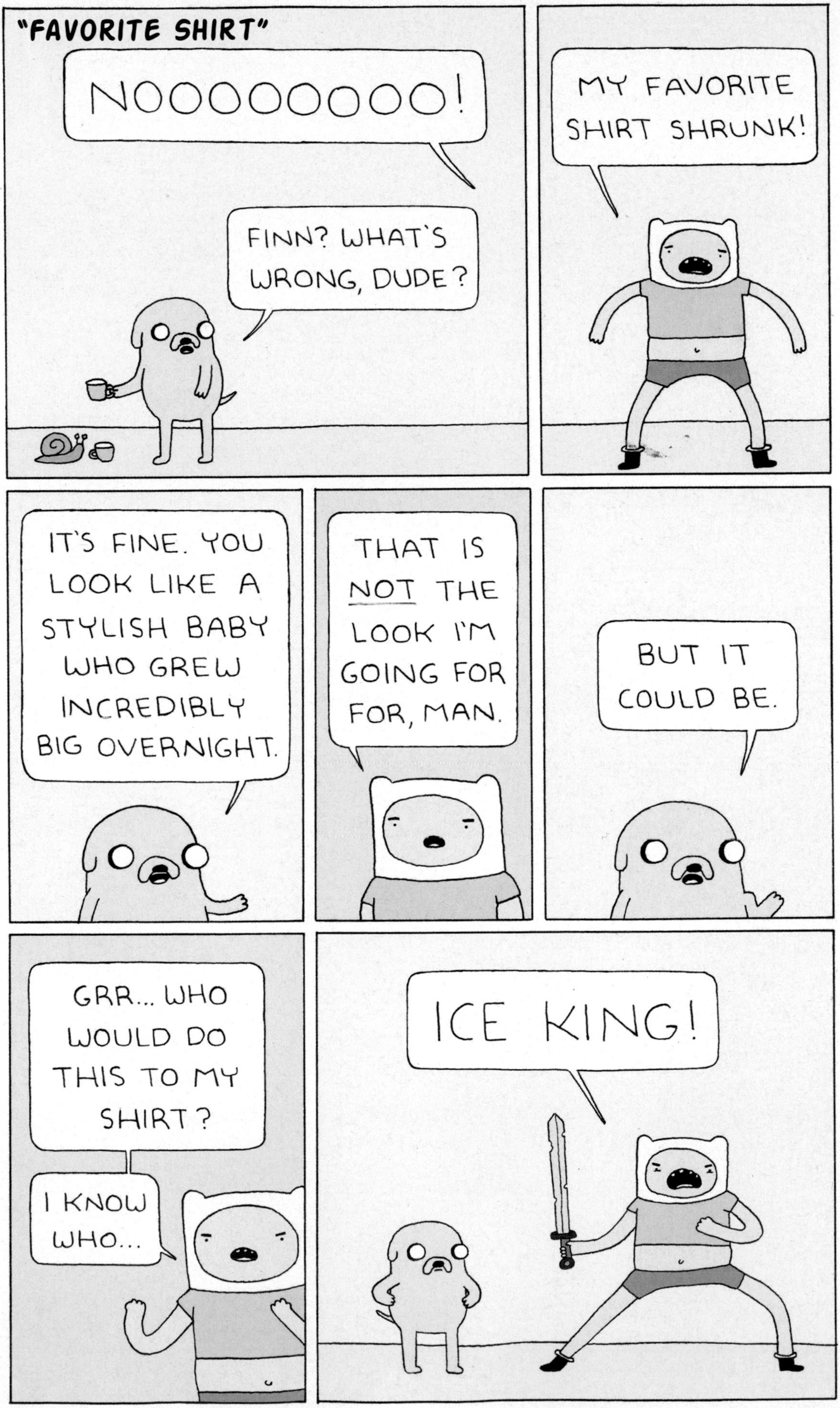
"FAVORITE SHIRT"
NOOOOOOOO!
FINN? WHAT'S WRONG, DUDE?
MY FAVORITE SHIRT SHRUNK!
IT'S FINE. YOU LOOK LIKE A STYLISH BABY WHO GREW INCREDIBLY BIG OVERNIGHT.
THAT IS NOT THE LOOK I'M GOING FOR FOR, MAN.
BUT IT COULD BE.
GRR... WHO WOULD DO THIS TO MY SHIRT?
I KNOW WHO...
ICE KING!

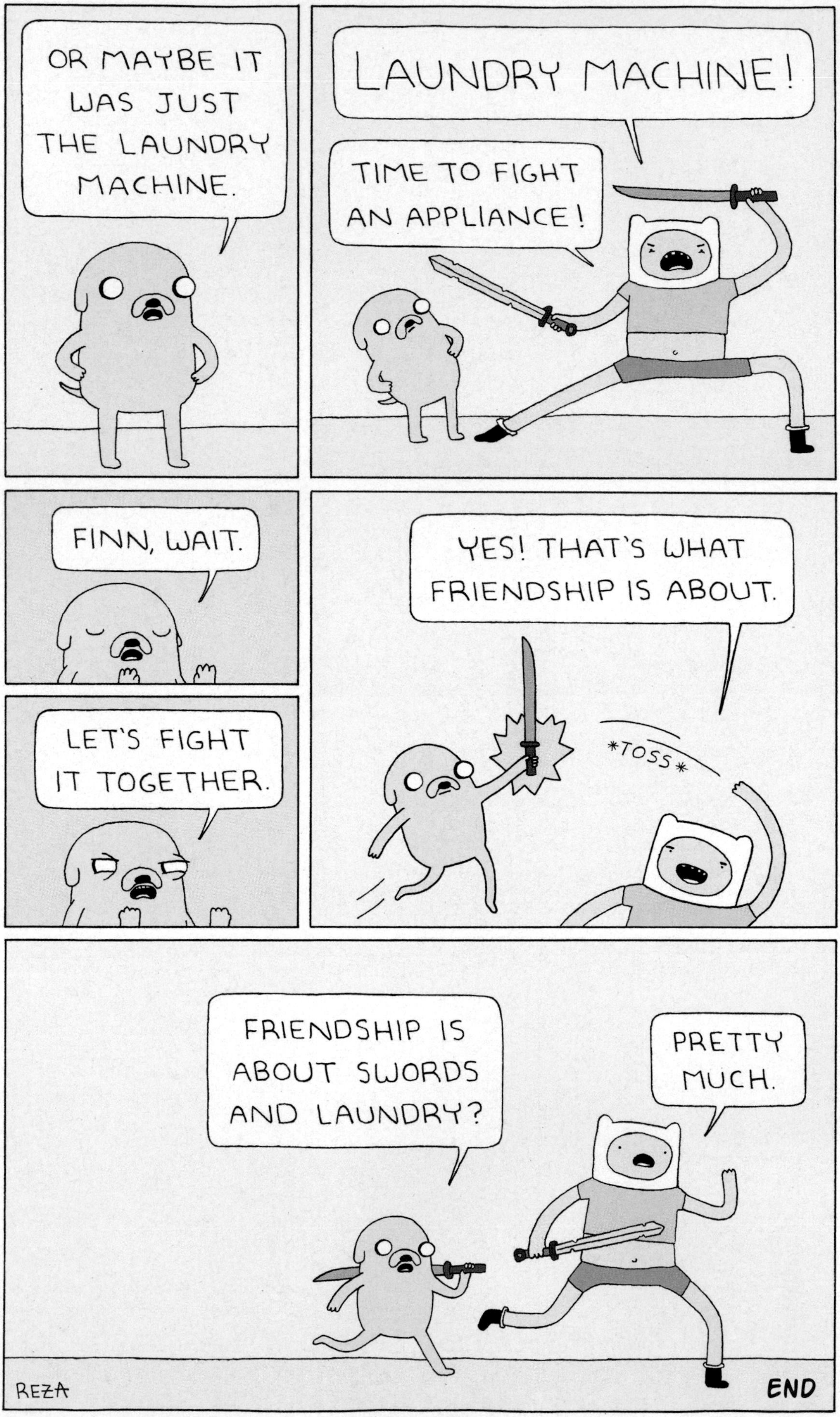
OR MAYBE IT WAS JUST THE LAUNDRY MACHINE.
LAUNDRY MACHINE!
TIME TO FIGHT AN APPLIANCE!
FINN, WAIT.
LET'S FIGHT IT TOGETHER.
YES! THAT'S WHAT FRIENDSHIP IS ABOUT.
TOSS
FRIENDSHIP IS ABOUT SWORDS AND LAUNDRY?
PRETTY MUCH.
REZA
END

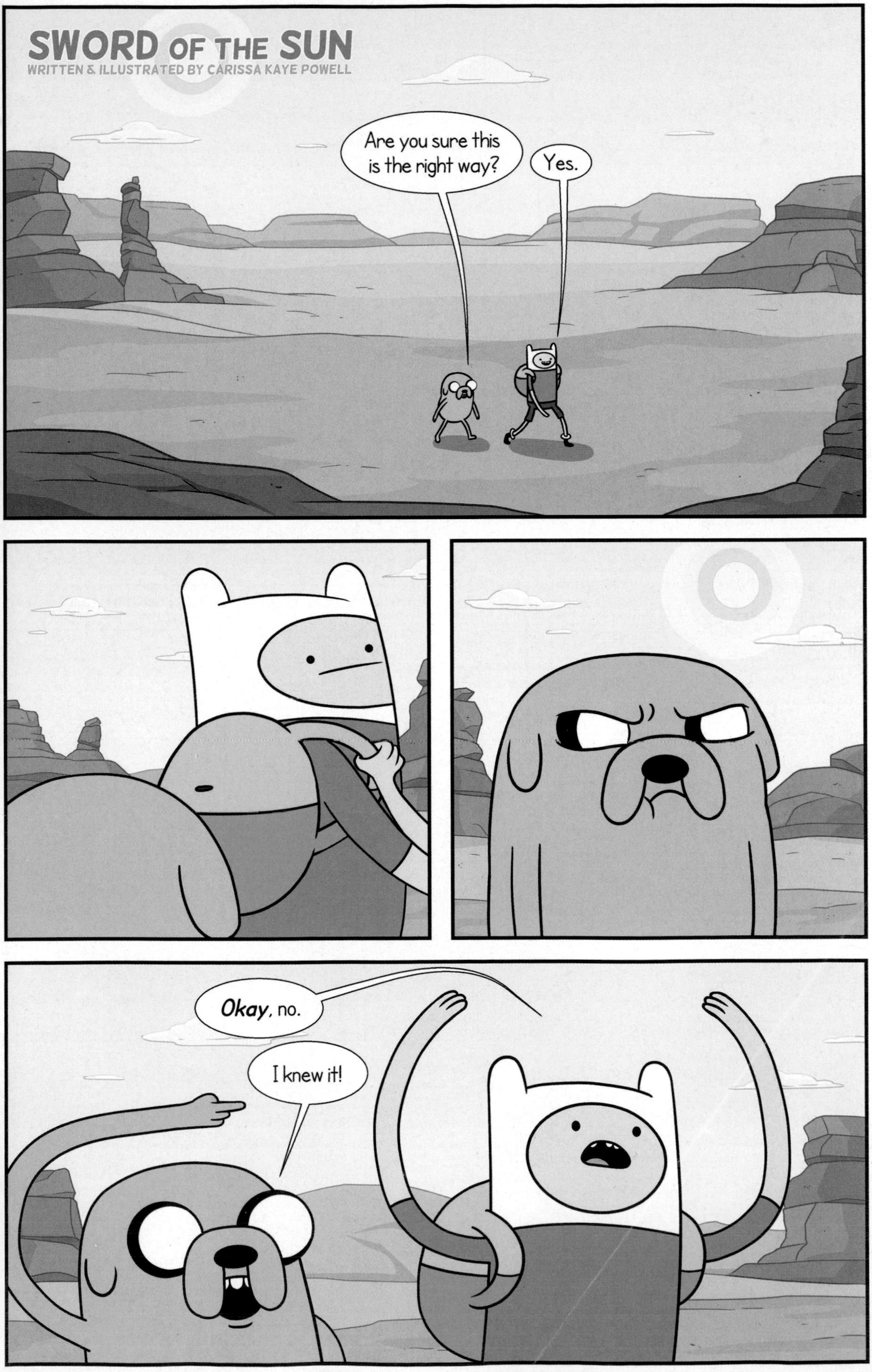
SWORD OF THE SUN
WRITTEN & ILLUSTRATED BY CARISSA KAYE POWELL
Are you sure this is the right way?
Yes.
Okay, no.
I knew it!

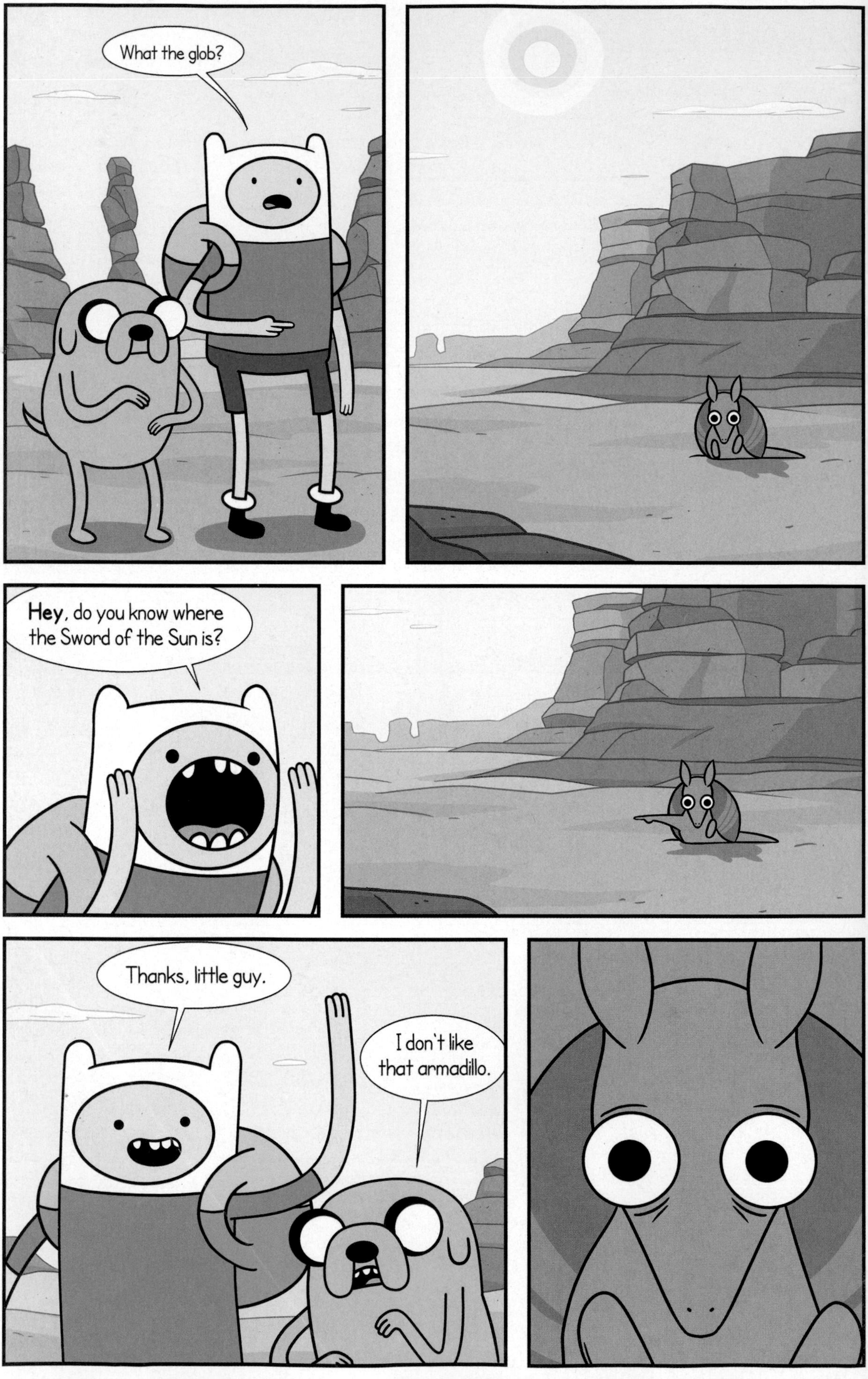
What the glob?
Hey, do you know where the Sword of the Sun is?
Thanks, little guy.
I don't like that armadillo.

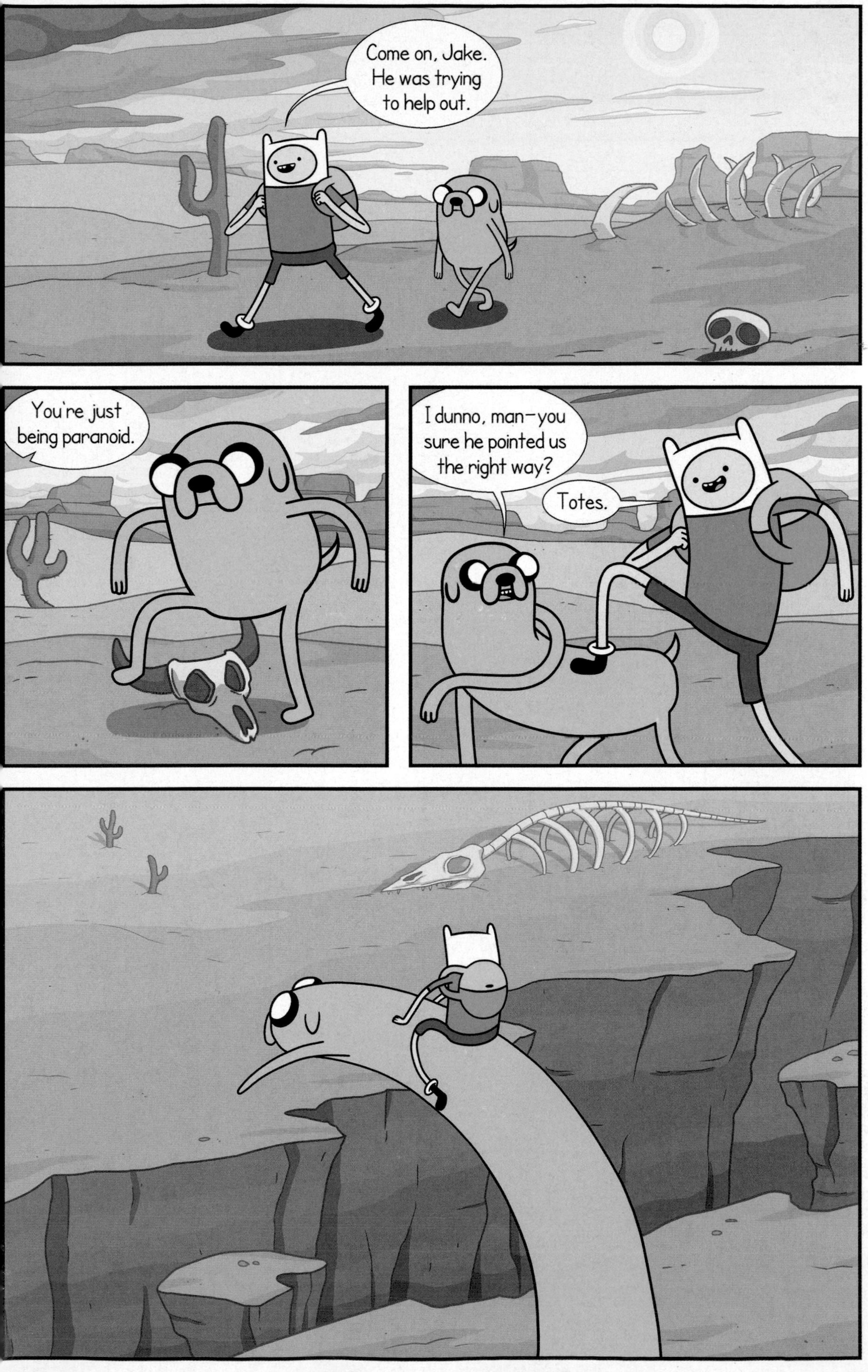
Come on, Jake. He was trying to help out.
You're just being paranoid.
I dunno, man—you sure he pointed us the right way?
Totes.

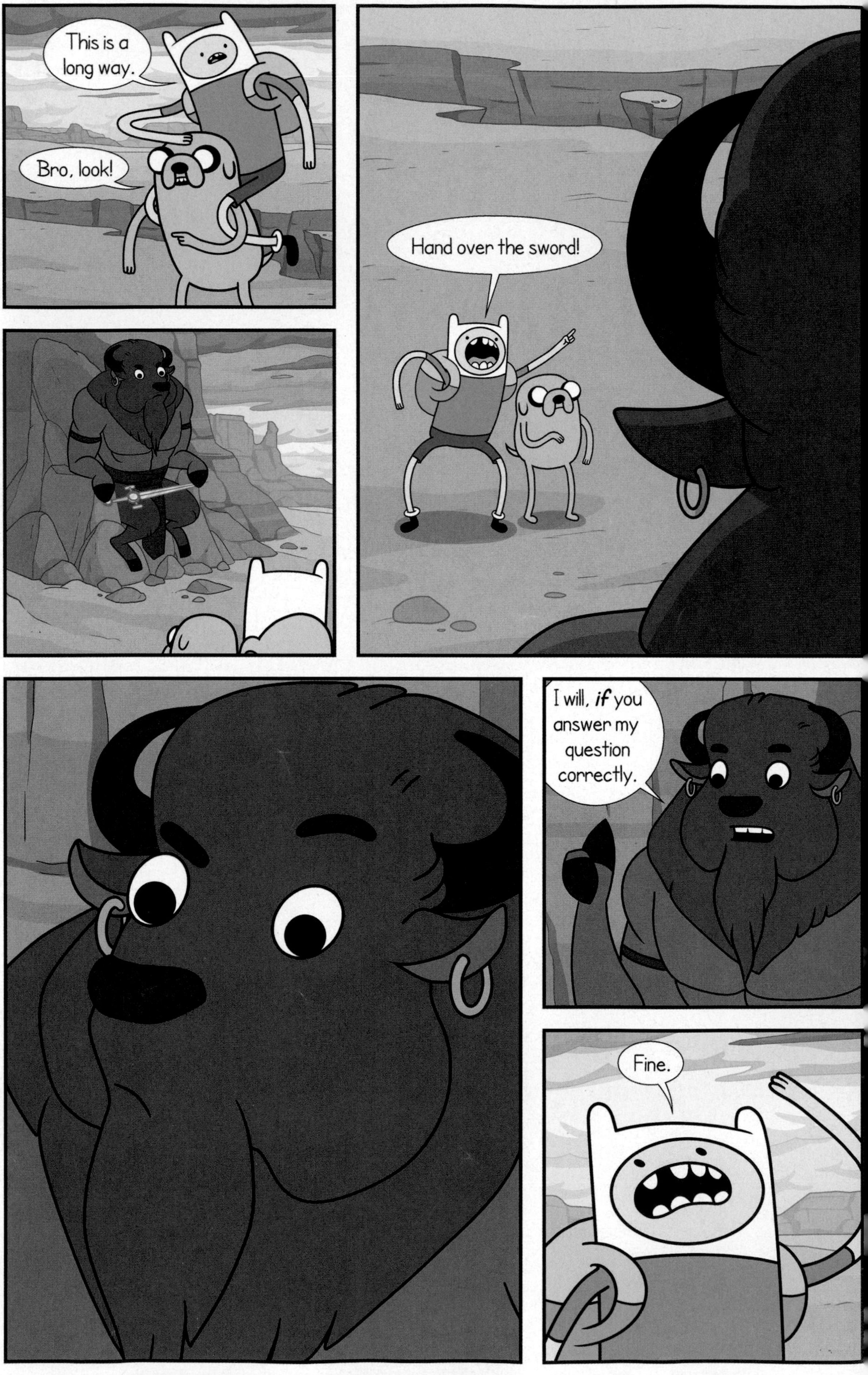
This is a long way.
Bro, look!
Hand over the sword!
I will, *if* you answer my question correctly.
Fine.

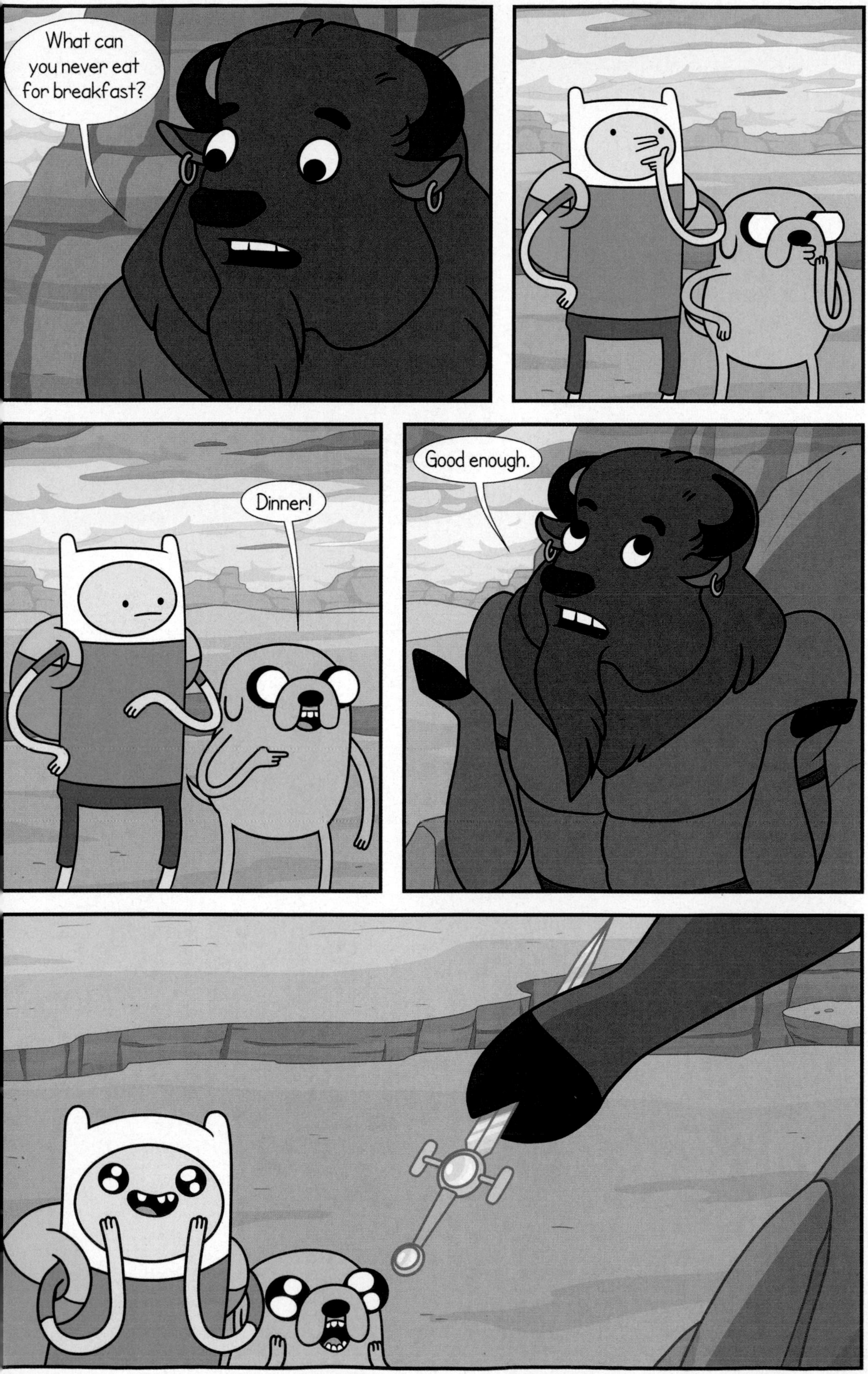
What can you never eat for breakfast?
Dinner!
Good enough.

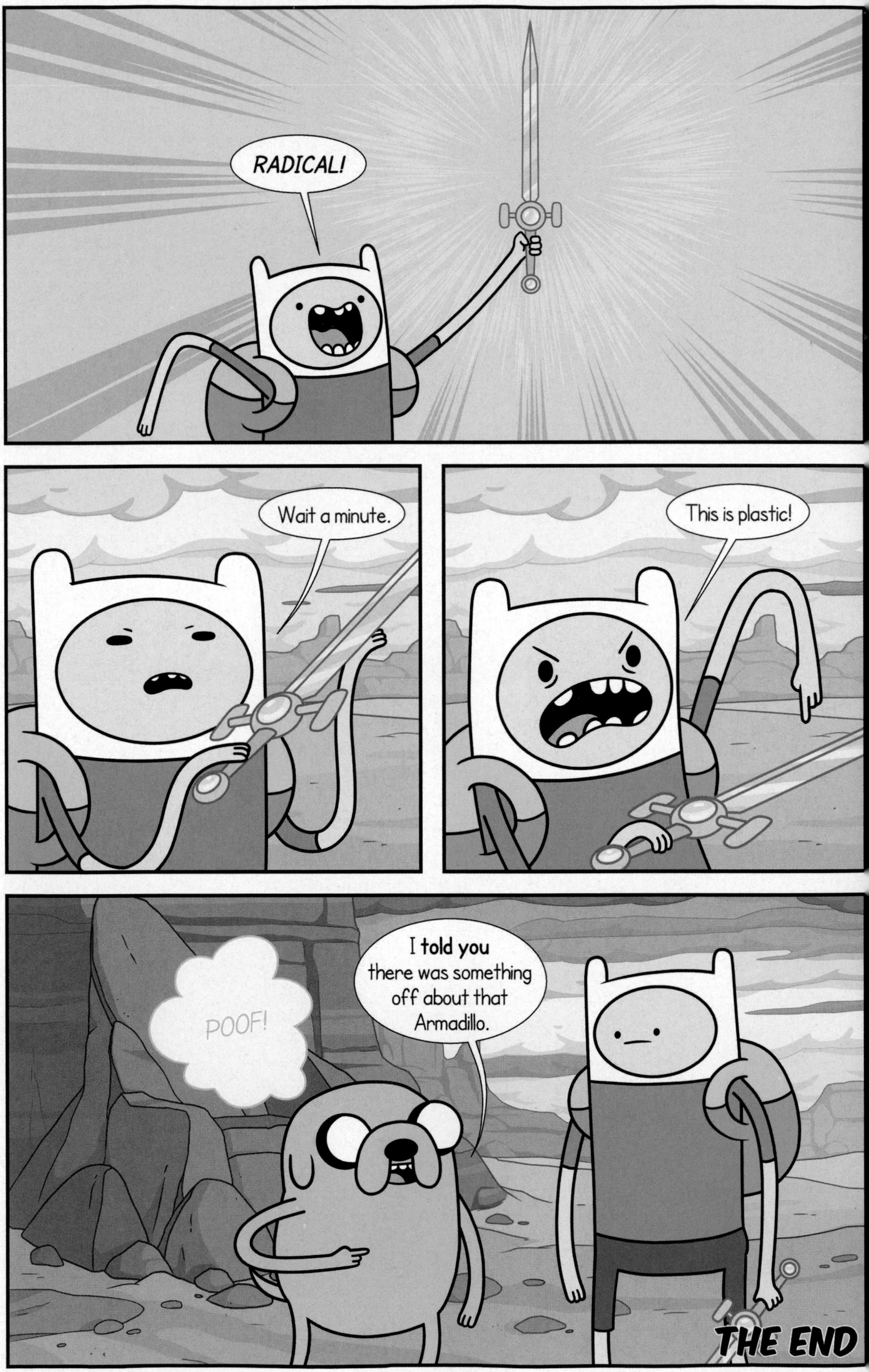
RADICAL!
Wait a minute.
This is plastic!
POOF!
I **told you** there was something off about that Armadillo.
THE END

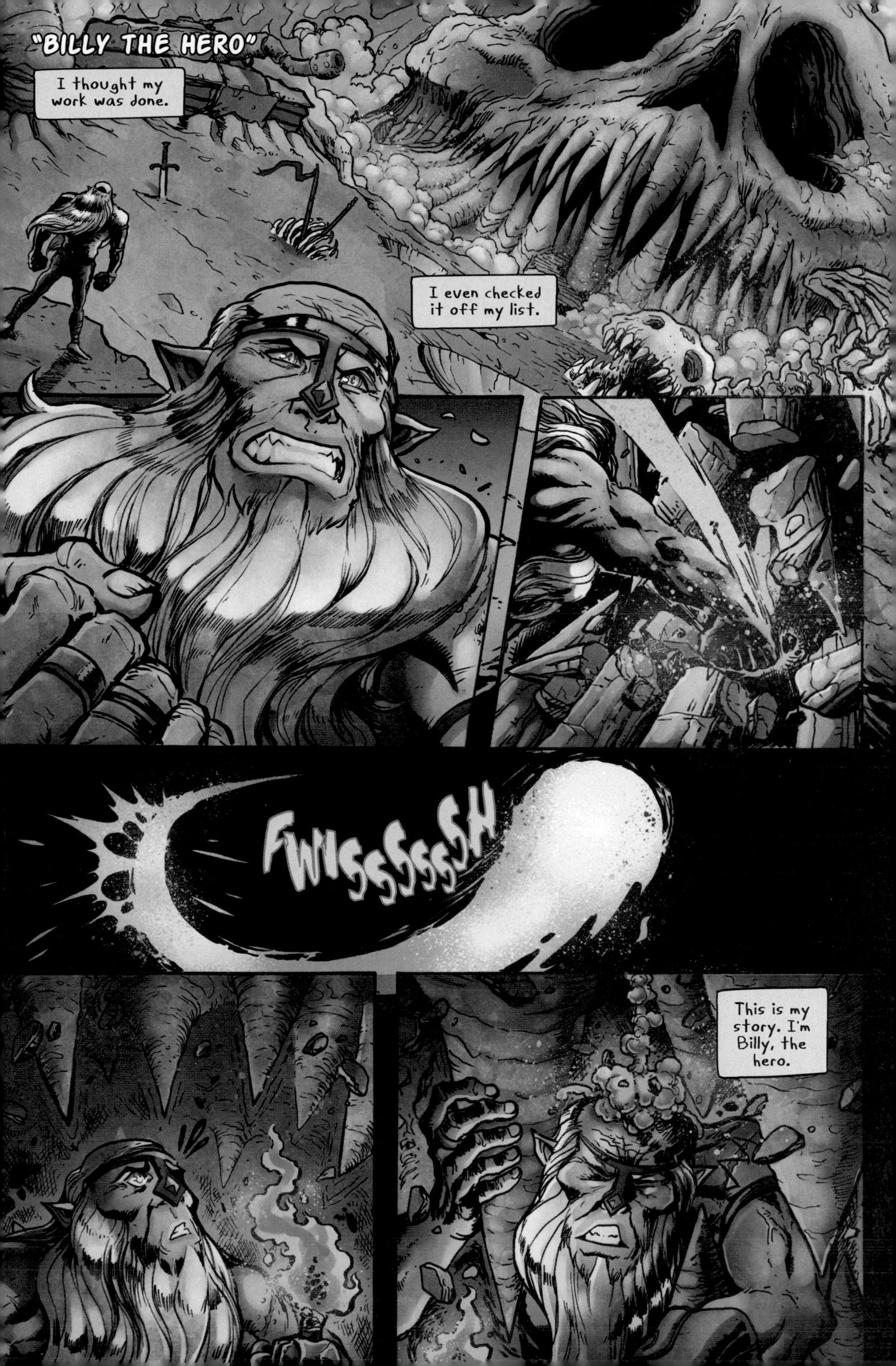
"BILLY THE HERO"
I thought my work was done.
I even checked it off my list.
FWISSSSSSH
This is my story. I'm Billy, the hero.

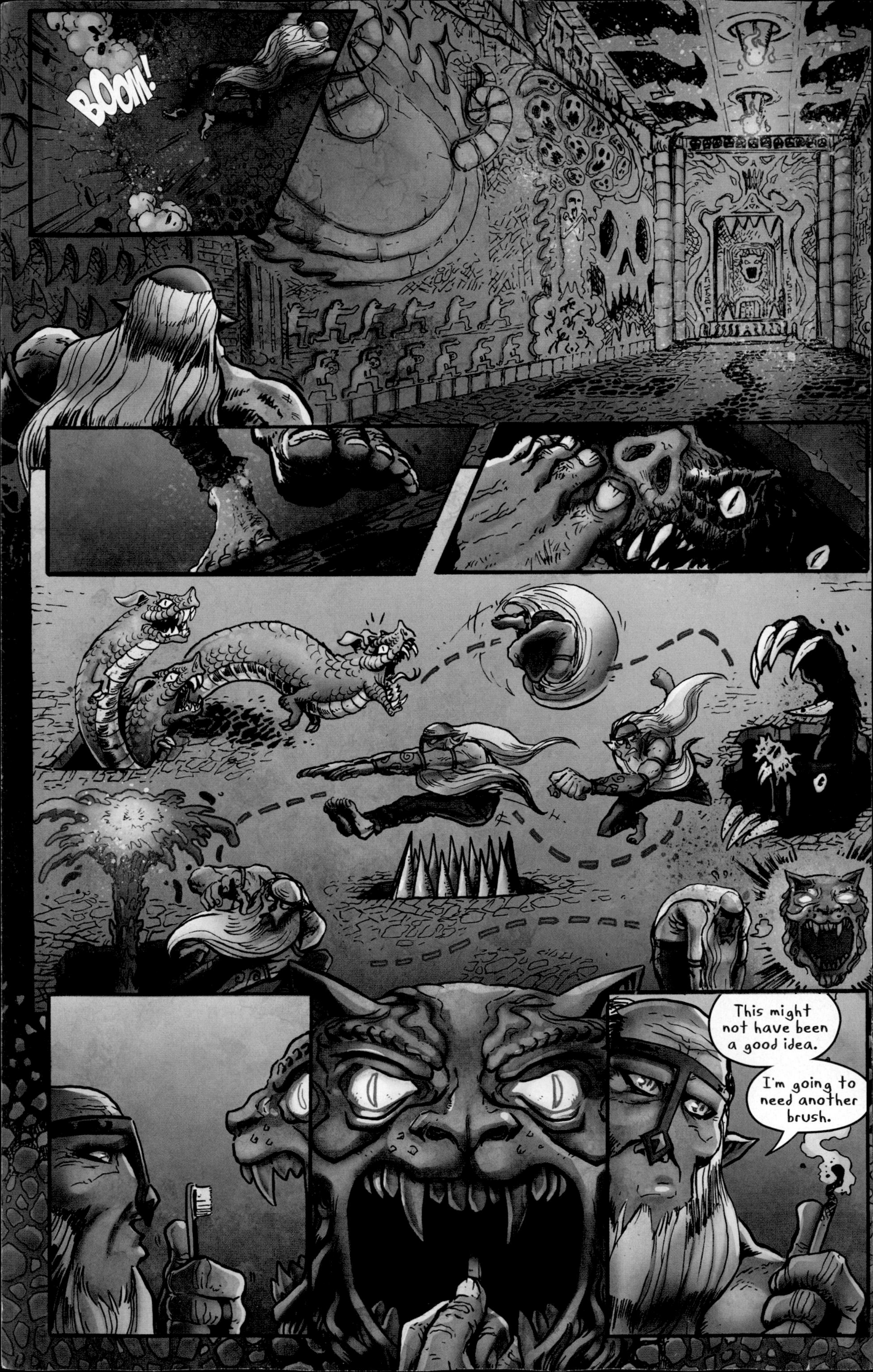
BOOM!
This might not have been a good idea.
I'm going to need another brush.

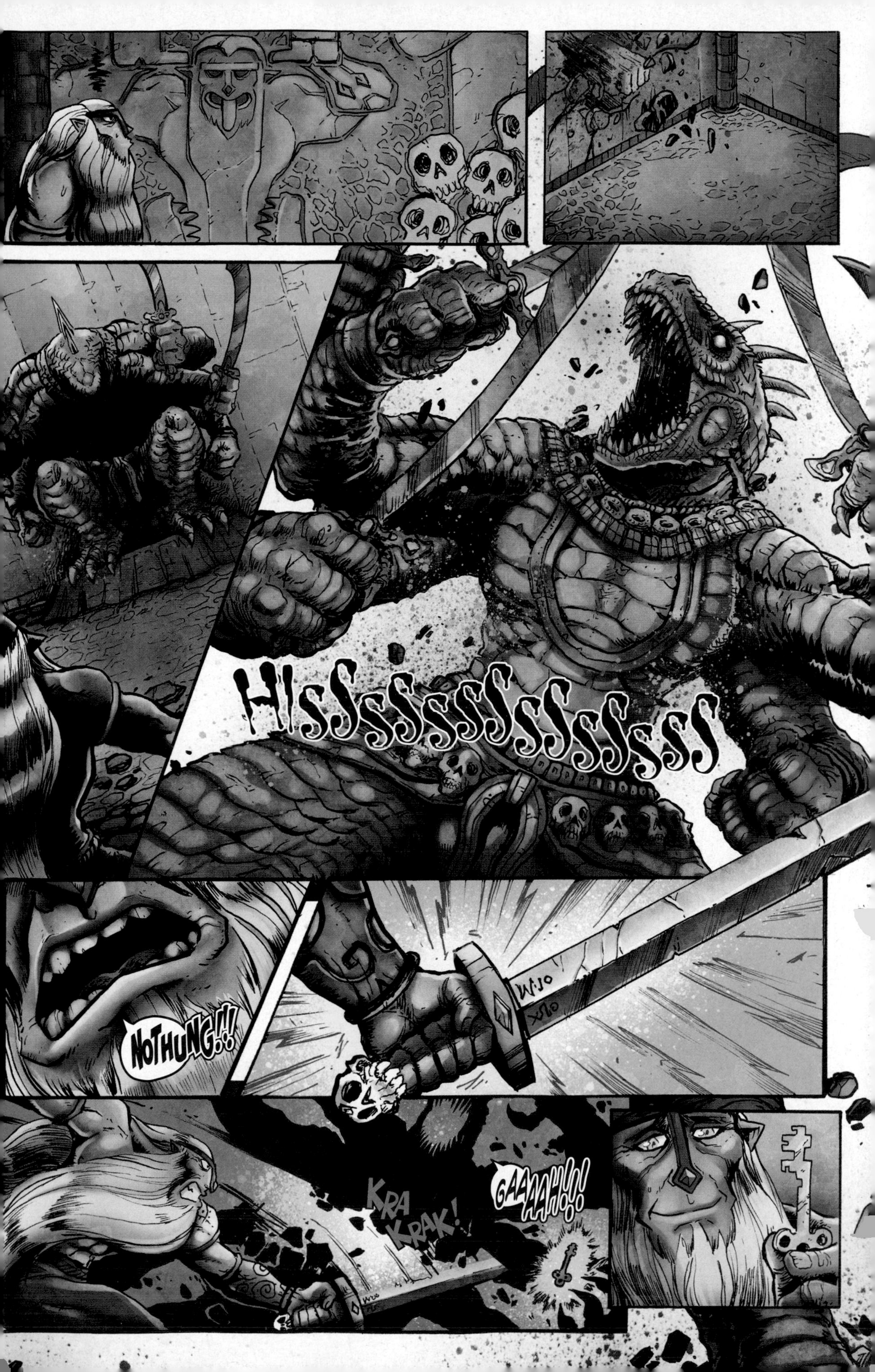
HISSSSSSSSSSSSSS
NOTHUNG!!!
KRAKRAK!
GAAAAH!!!

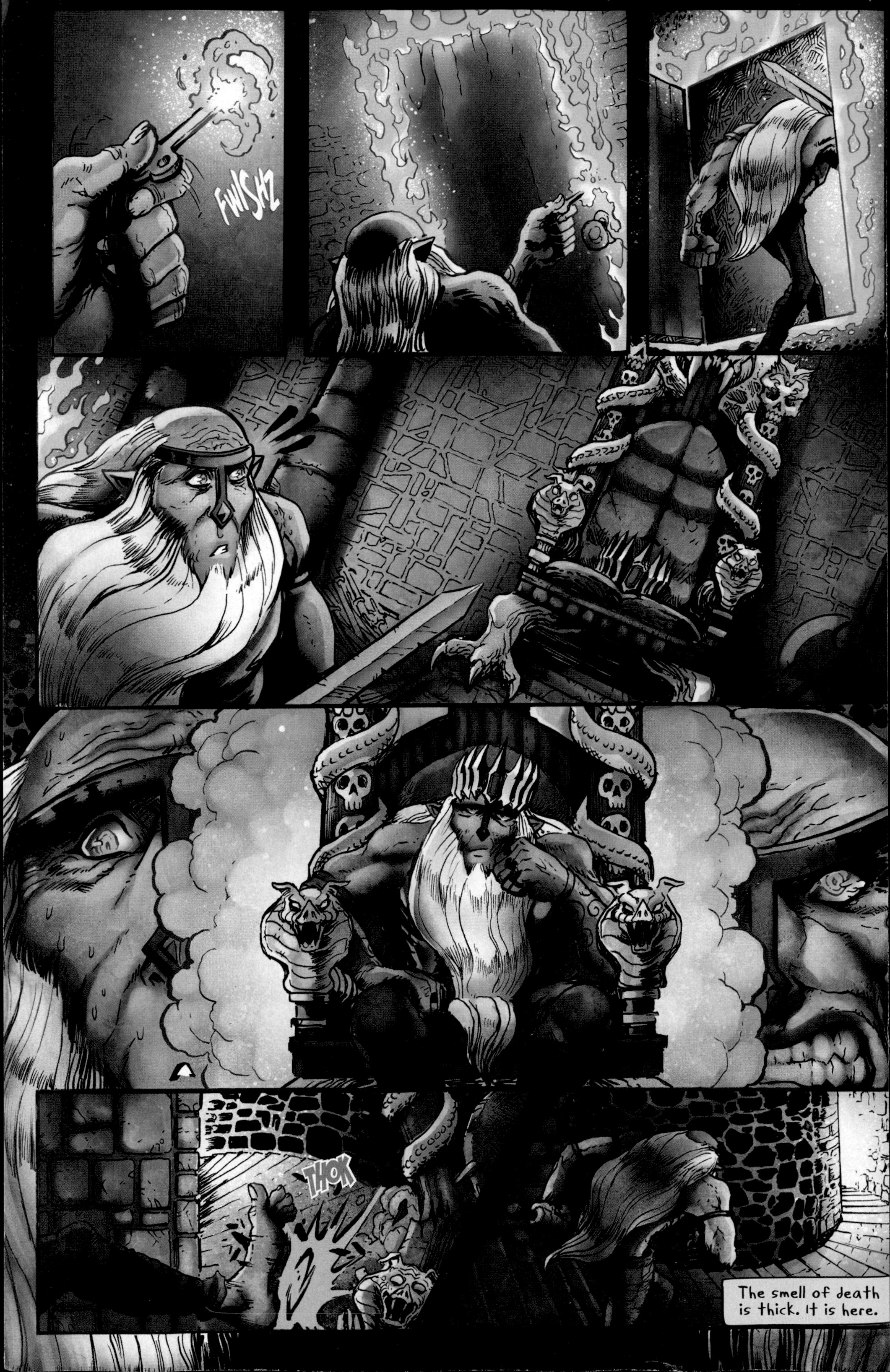
FWISHZ
THOK
The smell of death is thick. It is here.

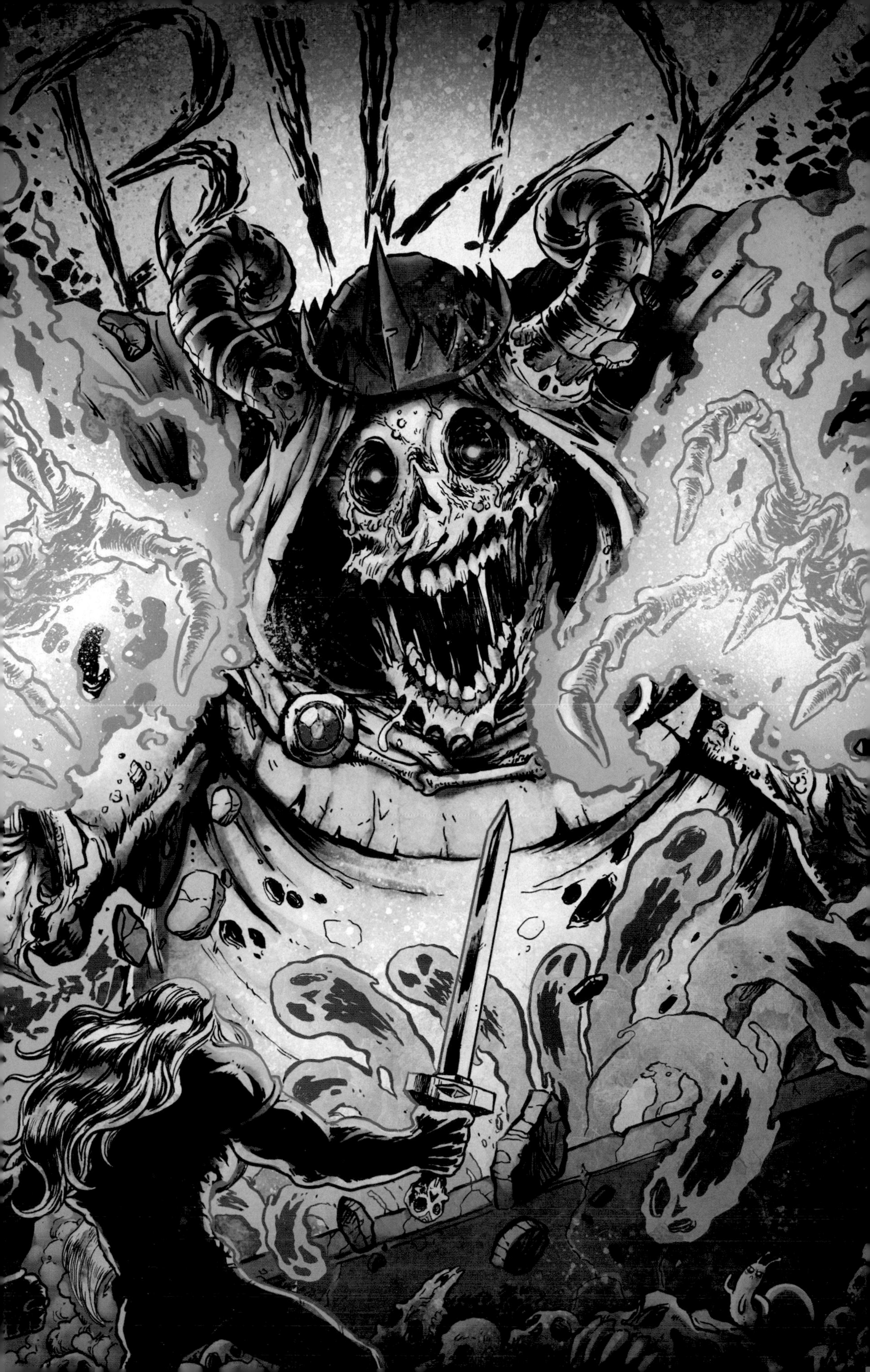

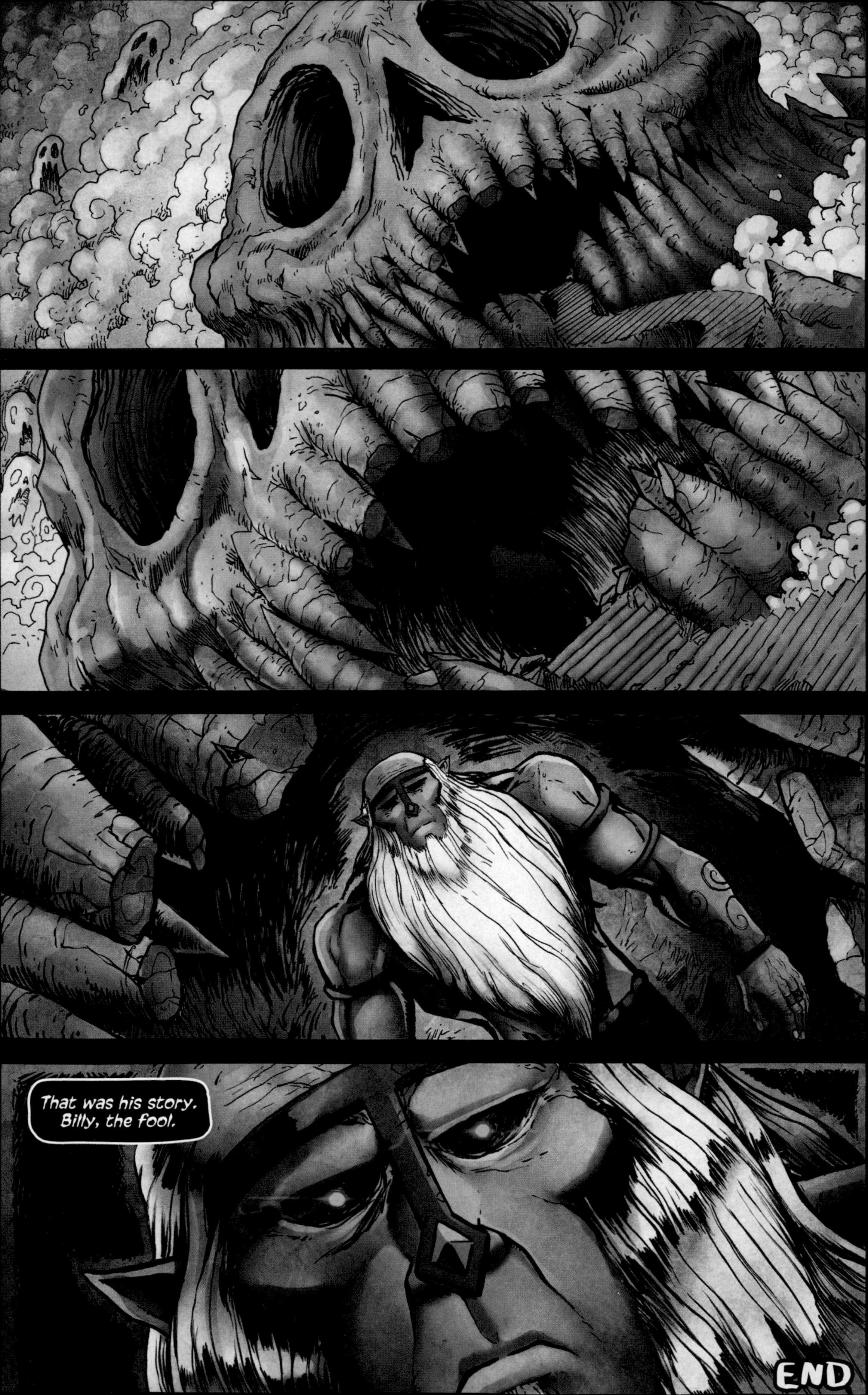
That was his story. Billy, the fool.
END

FOREVER (NOT) ALONE

By Xiao Tong Kong

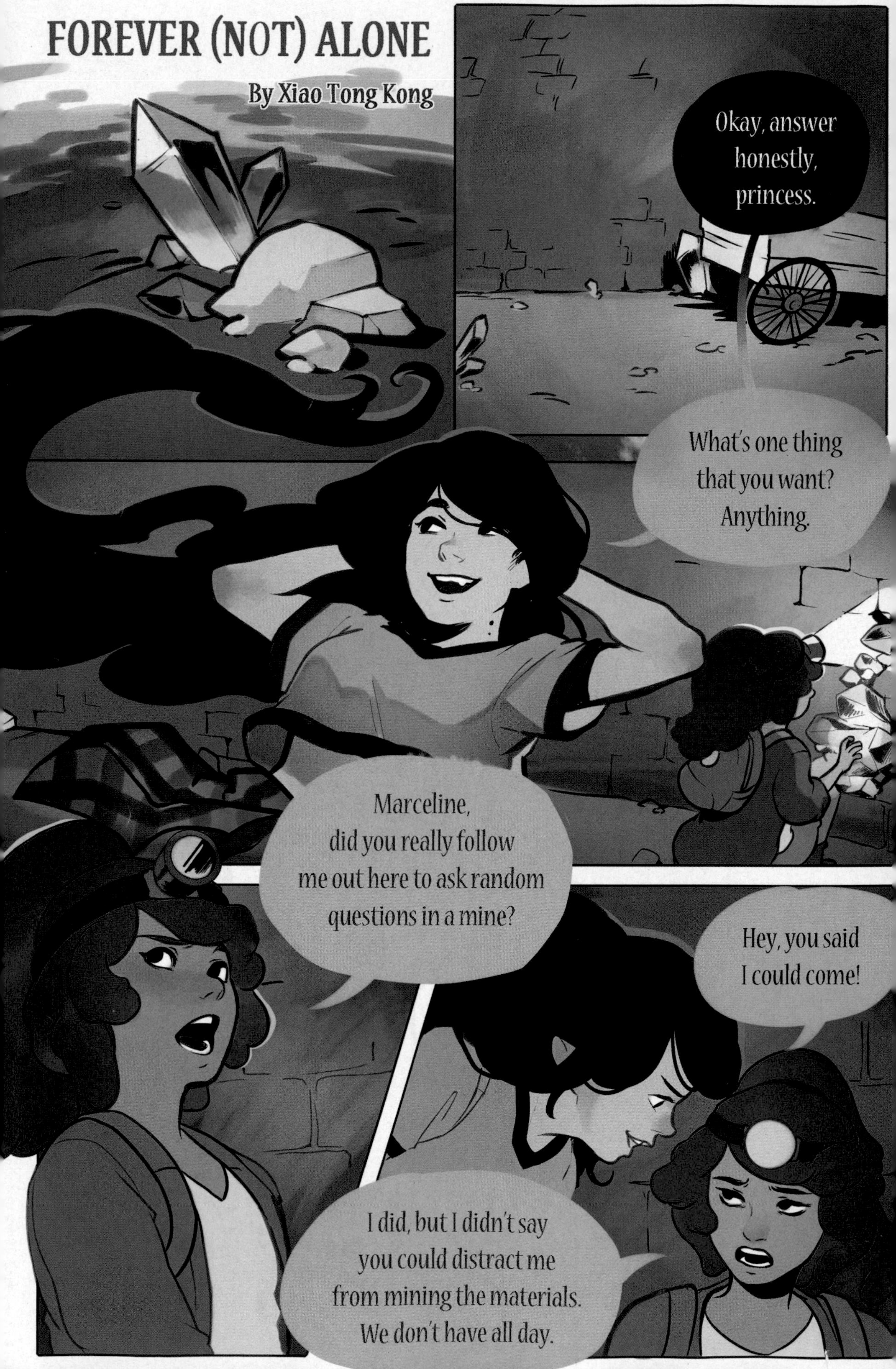

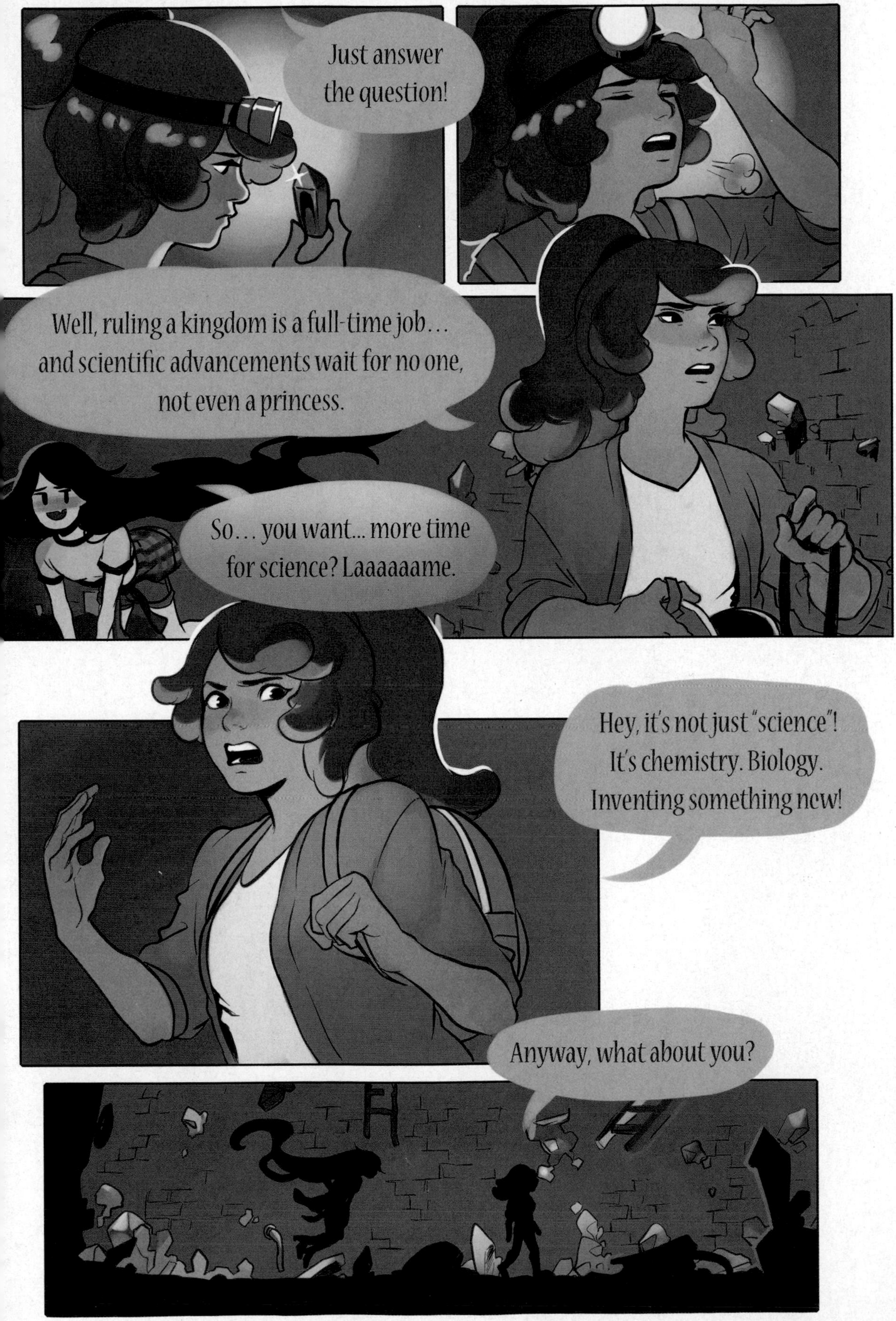
Just answer the question!
Well, ruling a kingdom is a full-time job... and scientific advancements wait for no one, not even a princess.
So... you want... more time for science? Laaaaaame.
Hey, it's not just "science"! It's chemistry. Biology. Inventing something new!
Anyway, what about you?

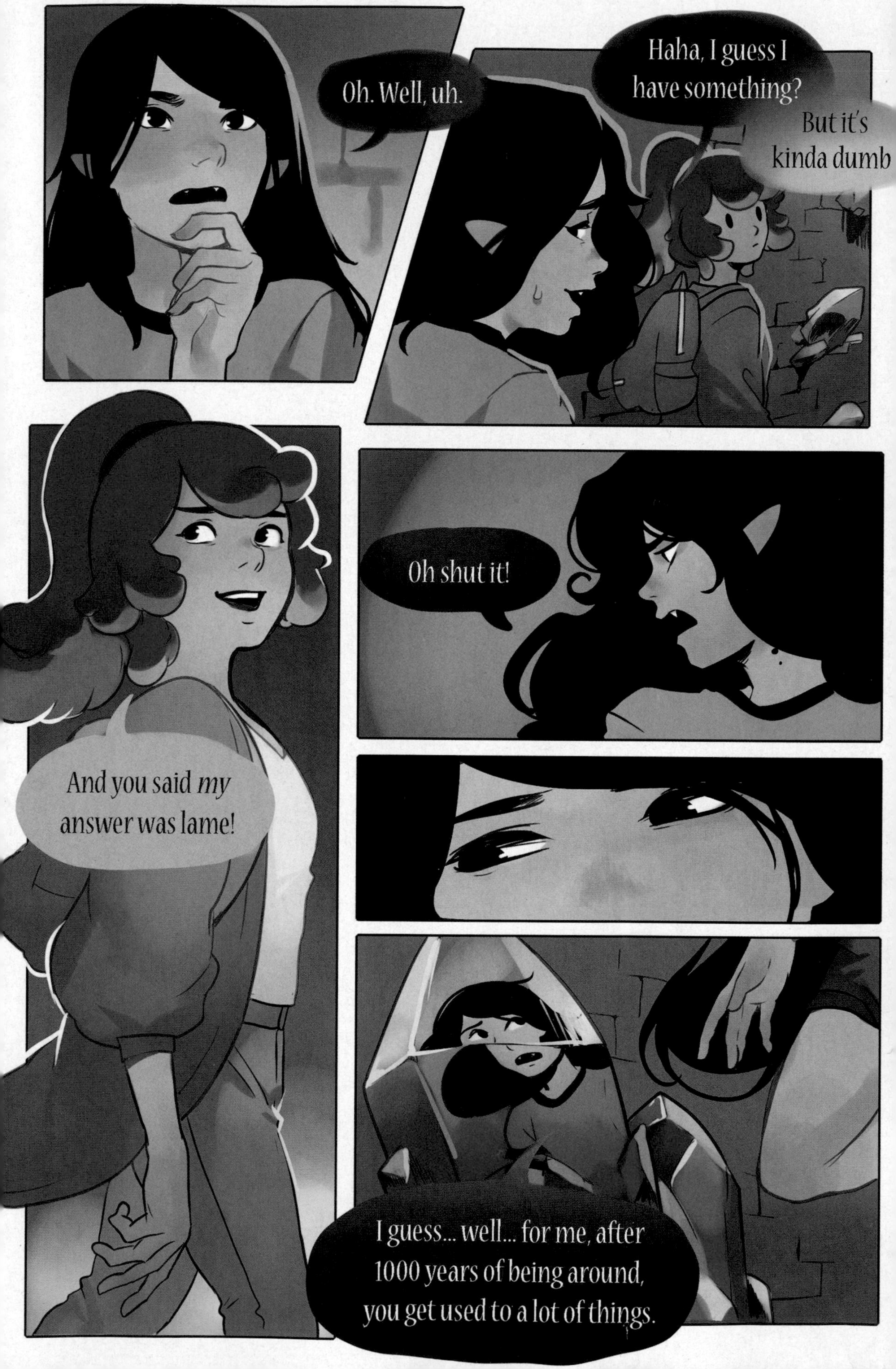
Oh. Well, uh.
Haha, I guess I have something?
But it's kinda dumb
And you said *my* answer was lame!
Oh shut it!
I guess... well... for me, after 1000 years of being around, you get used to a lot of things.

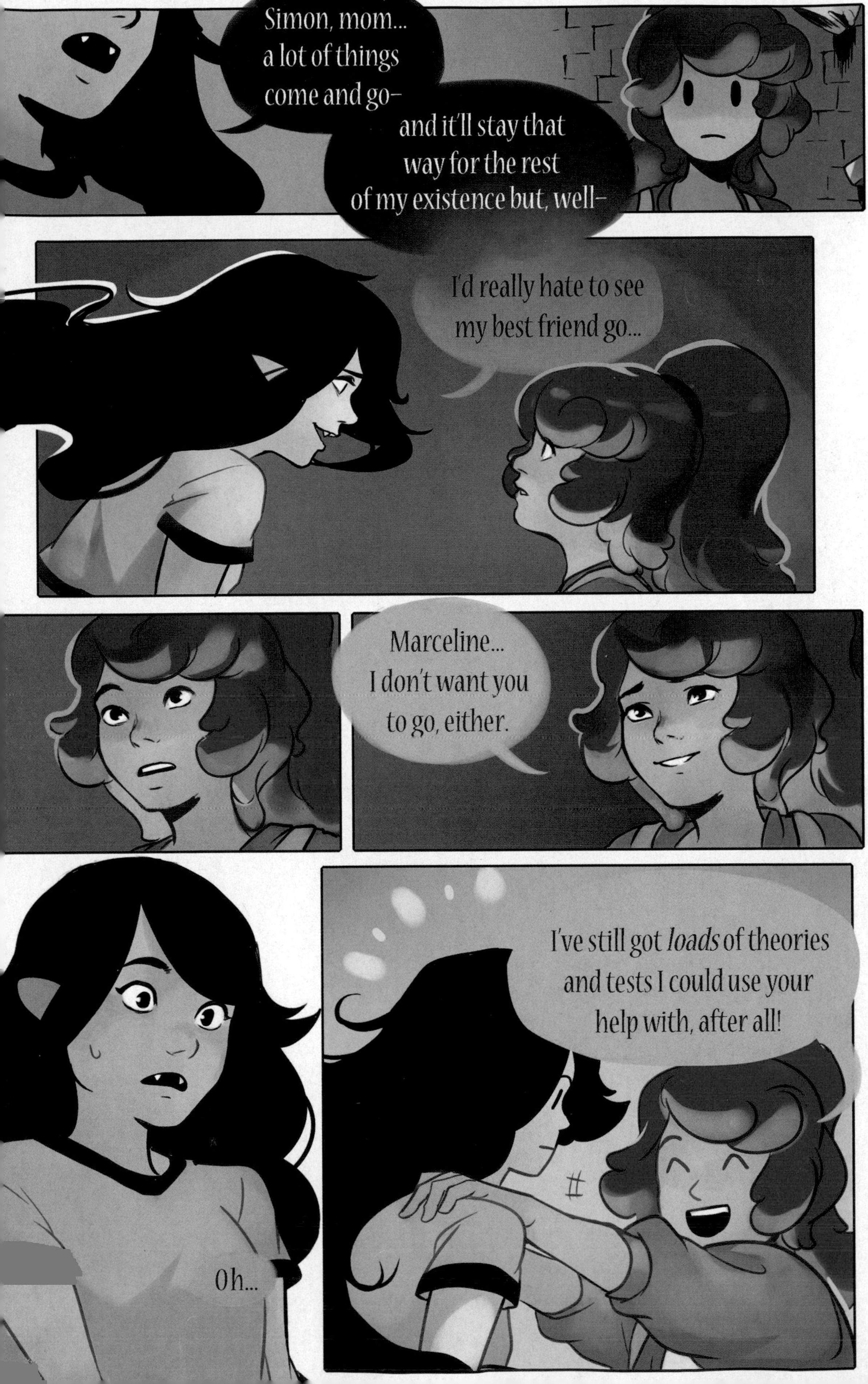
Simon, mom... a lot of things come and go–
and it'll stay that way for the rest of my existence but, well–
I'd really hate to see my best friend go...
Marceline... I don't want you to go, either.
Oh...
I've still got *loads* of theories and tests I could use your help with, after all!

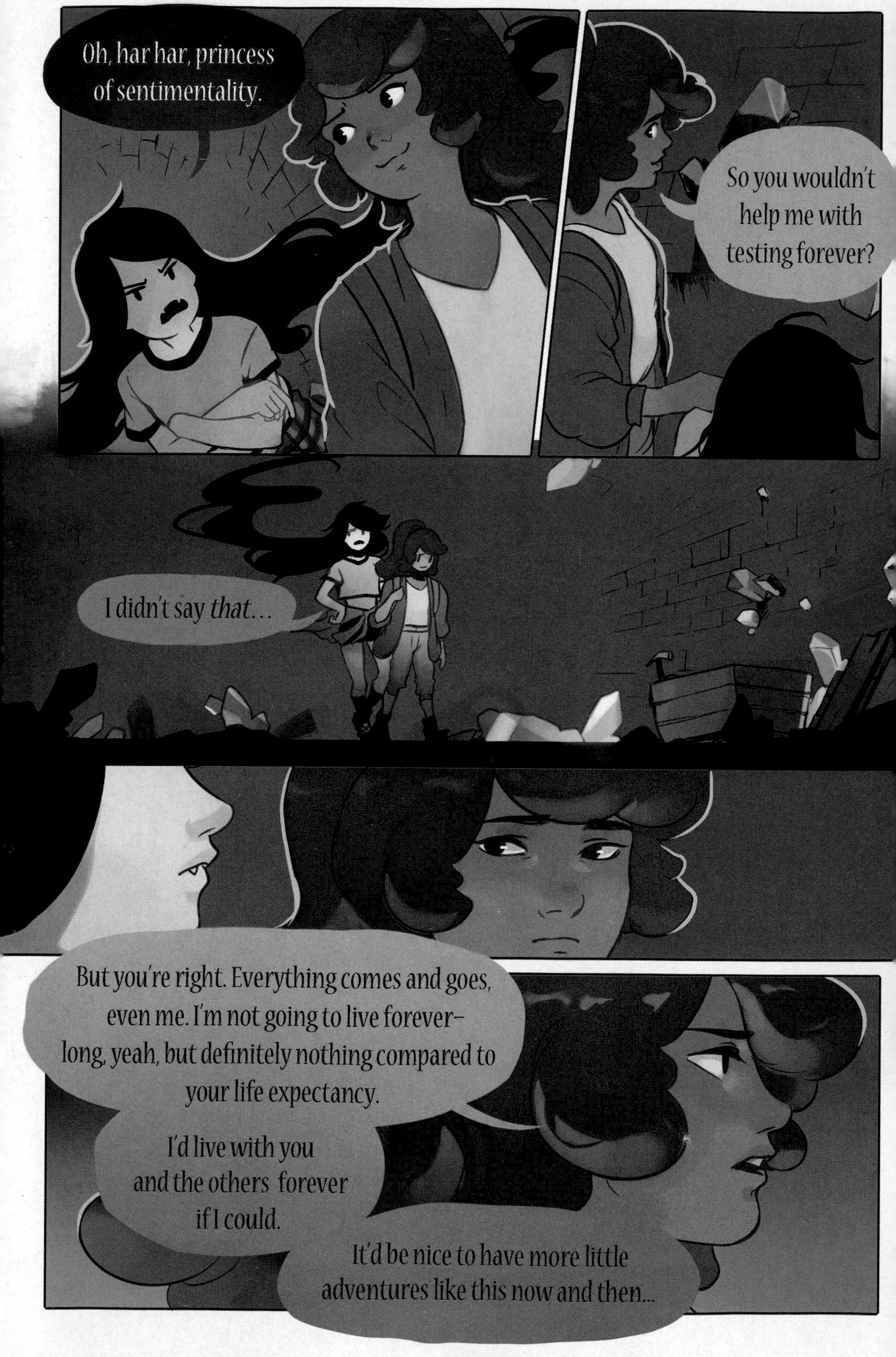
Oh, har har, princess of sentimentality.
So you wouldn't help me with testing forever?
I didn't say *that*...
But you're right. Everything comes and goes, even me. I'm not going to live forever–long, yeah, but definitely nothing compared to your life expectancy.
I'd live with you and the others forever if I could.
It'd be nice to have more little adventures like this now and then...

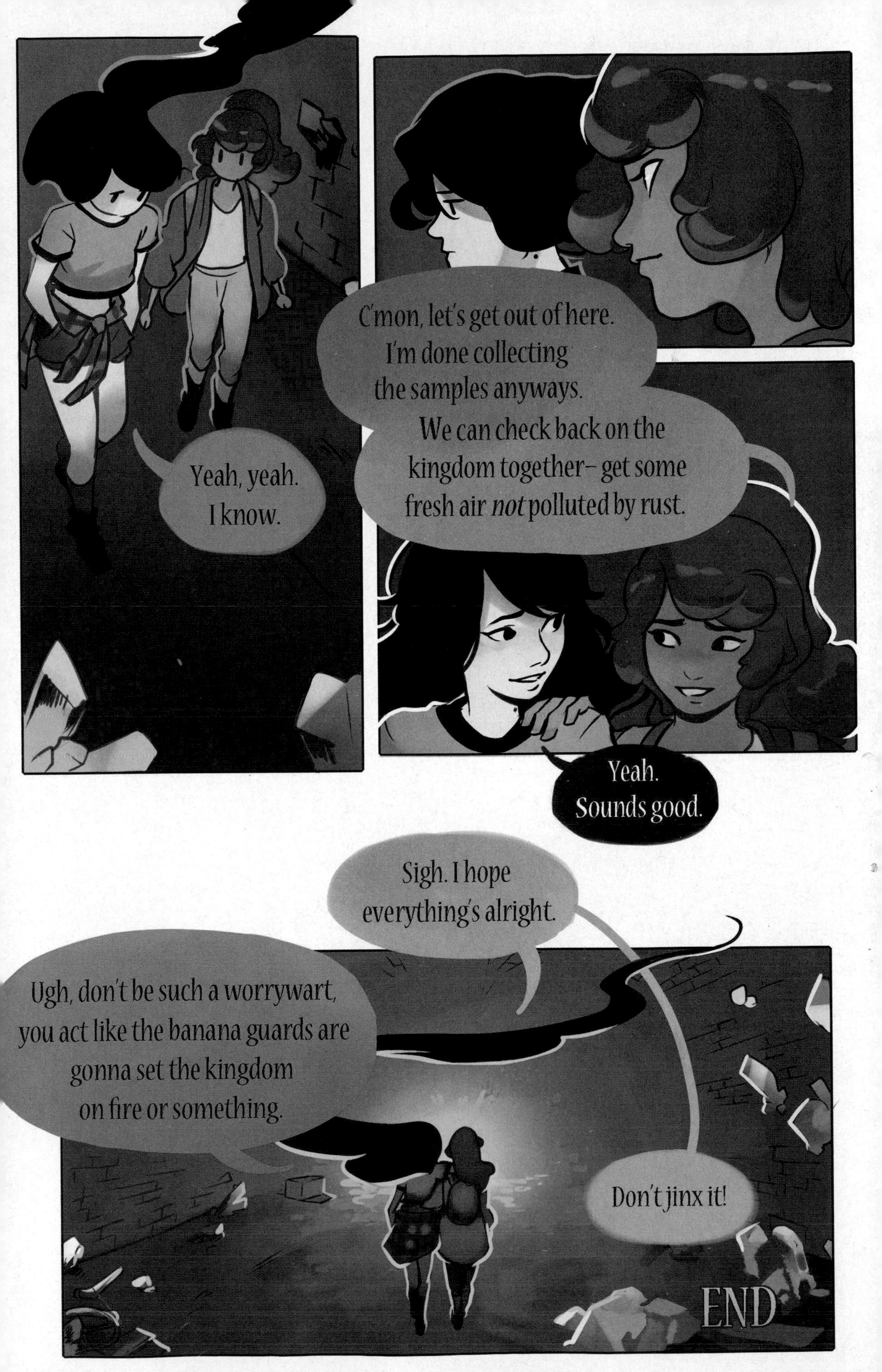

C'mon, let's get out of here. I'm done collecting the samples anyways.
Yeah, yeah. I know.
We can check back on the kingdom together– get some fresh air *not* polluted by rust.
Yeah. Sounds good.
Sigh. I hope everything's alright.
Ugh, don't be such a worrywart, you act like the banana guards are gonna set the kingdom on fire or something.
Don't jinx it!
END

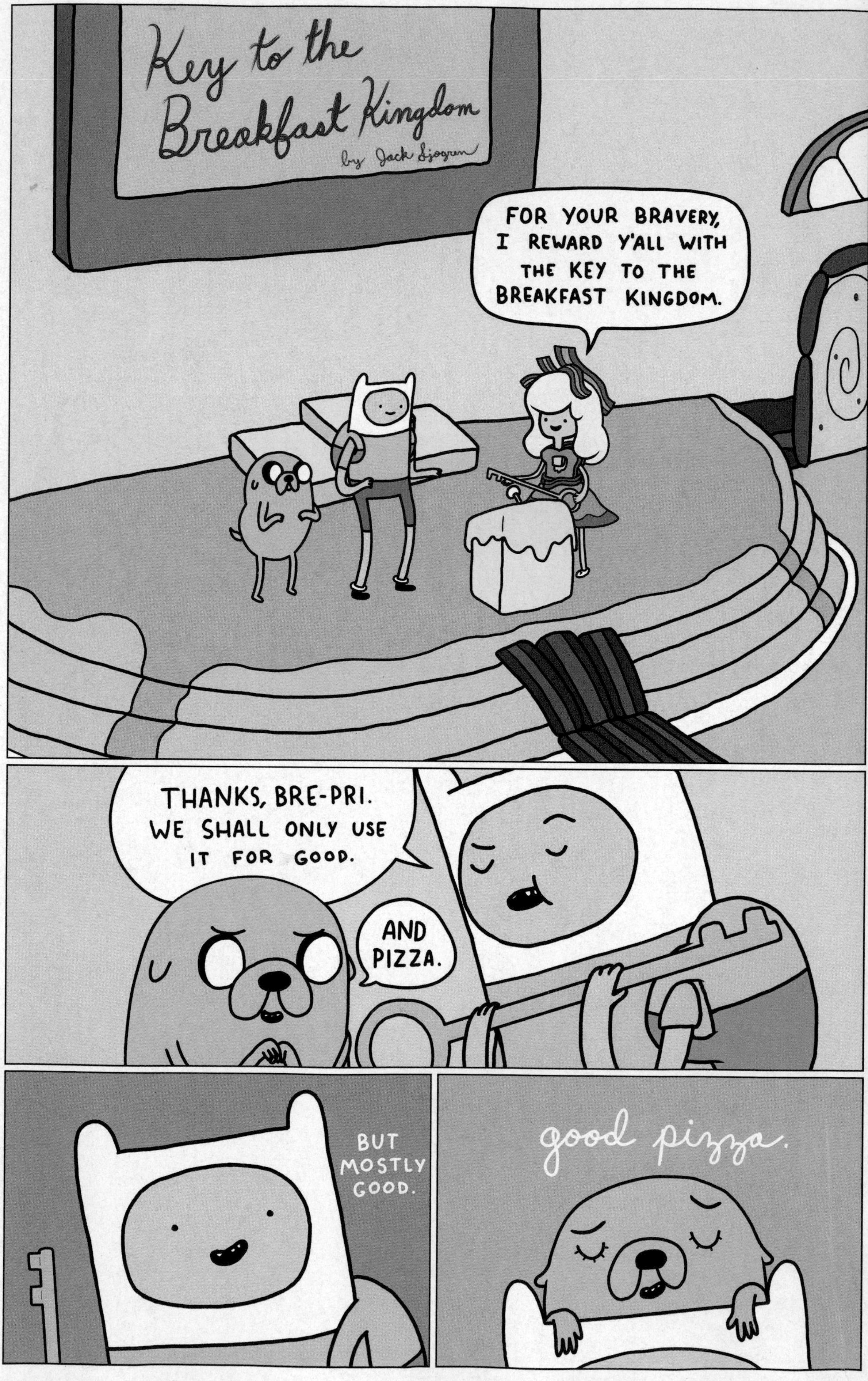
Key to the Breakfast Kingdom
by Jack Sjogren
FOR YOUR BRAVERY, I REWARD Y'ALL WITH THE KEY TO THE BREAKFAST KINGDOM.
THANKS, BRE-PRI. WE SHALL ONLY USE IT FOR GOOD.
AND PIZZA.
BUT MOSTLY GOOD.
good pizza.

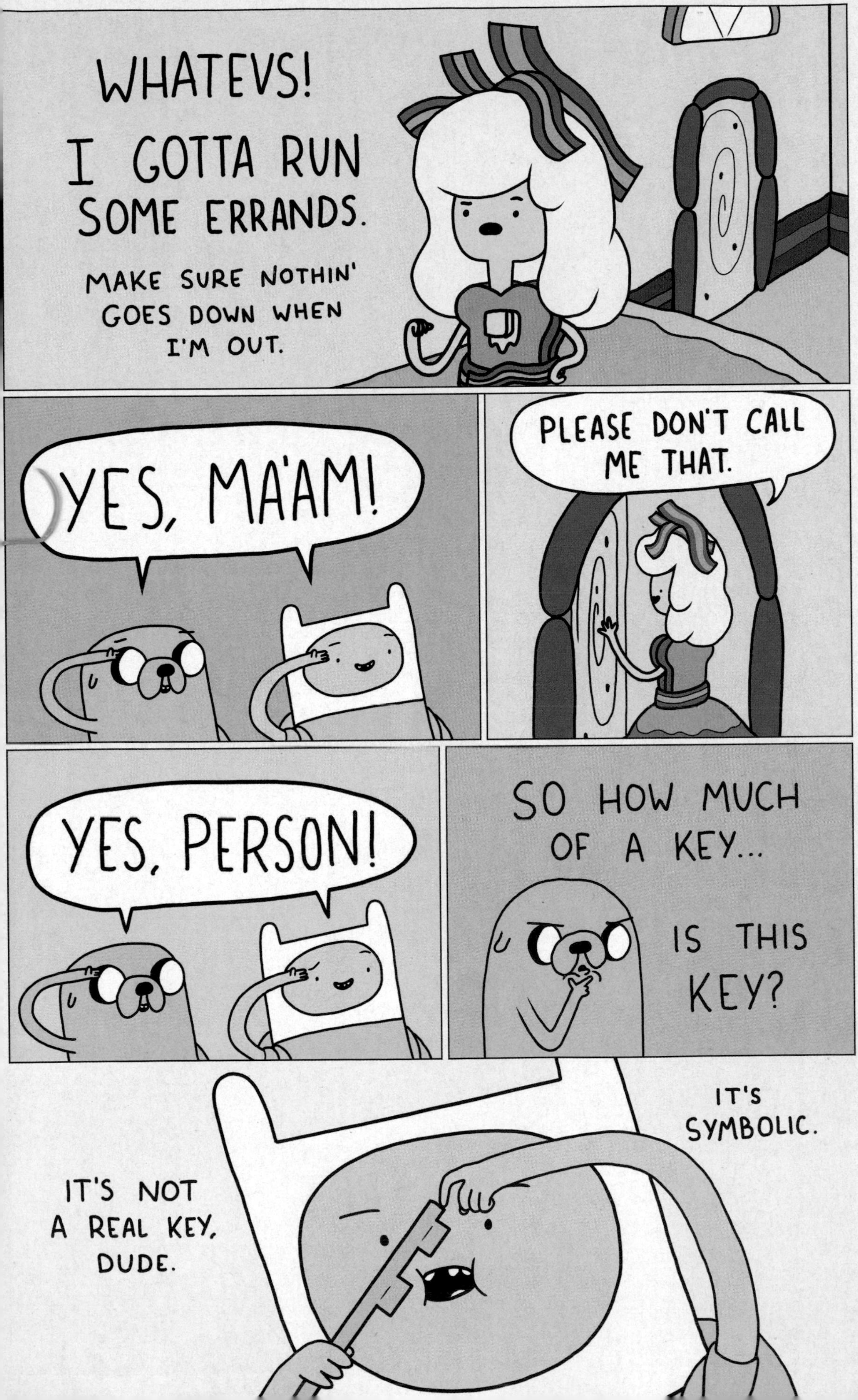

WHATEVS! I GOTTA RUN SOME ERRANDS.
MAKE SURE NOTHIN' GOES DOWN WHEN I'M OUT.
YES, MA'AM!
PLEASE DON'T CALL ME THAT.
YES, PERSON!
SO HOW MUCH OF A KEY...
IS THIS KEY?
IT'S NOT A REAL KEY, DUDE.
IT'S SYMBOLIC.

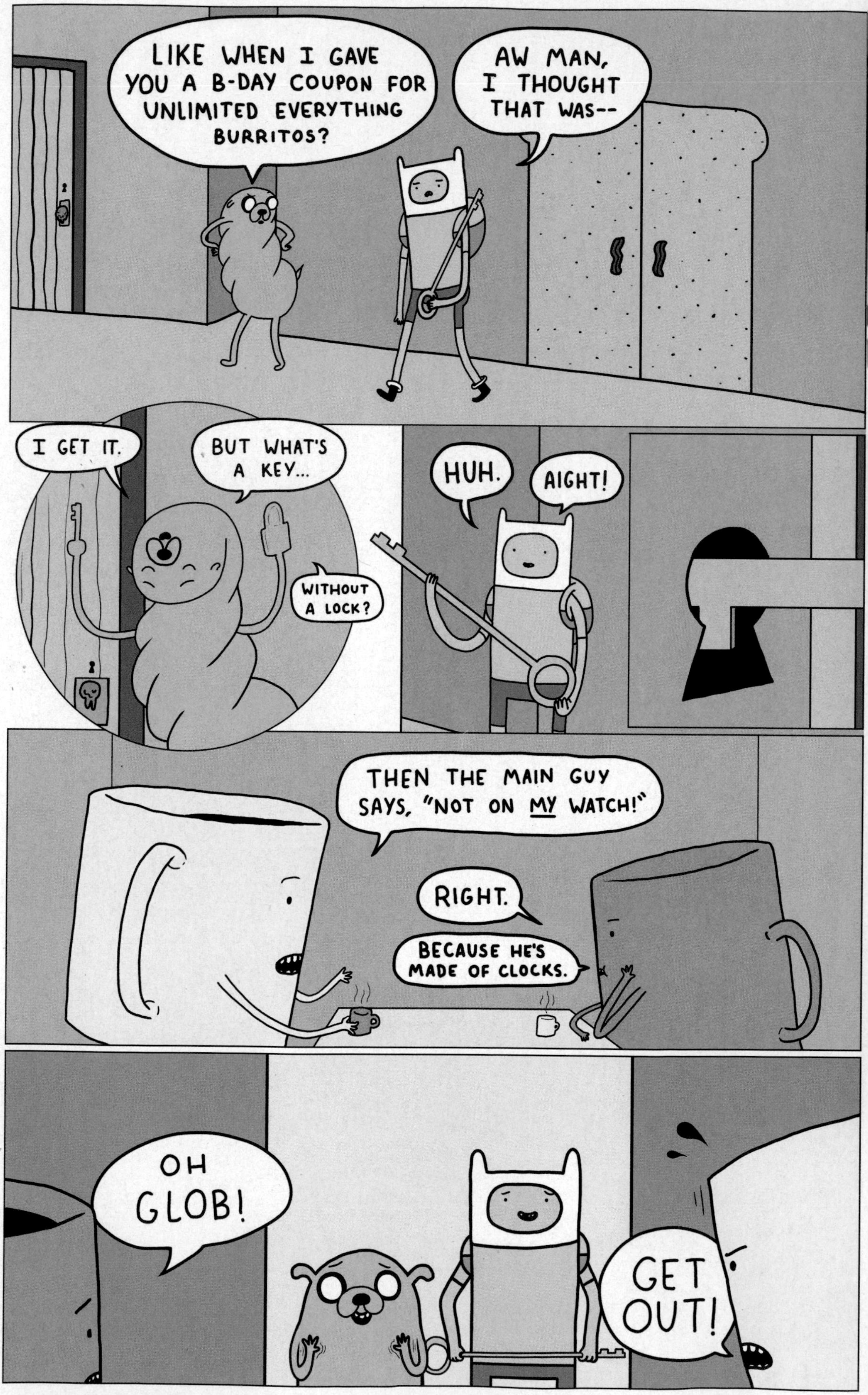
LIKE WHEN I GAVE YOU A B-DAY COUPON FOR UNLIMITED EVERYTHING BURRITOS?
AW MAN, I THOUGHT THAT WAS--
I GET IT.
BUT WHAT'S A KEY...
WITHOUT A LOCK?
HUH.
AIGHT!
THEN THE MAIN GUY SAYS, "NOT ON MY WATCH!"
RIGHT.
BECAUSE HE'S MADE OF CLOCKS.
OH GLOB!
GET OUT!

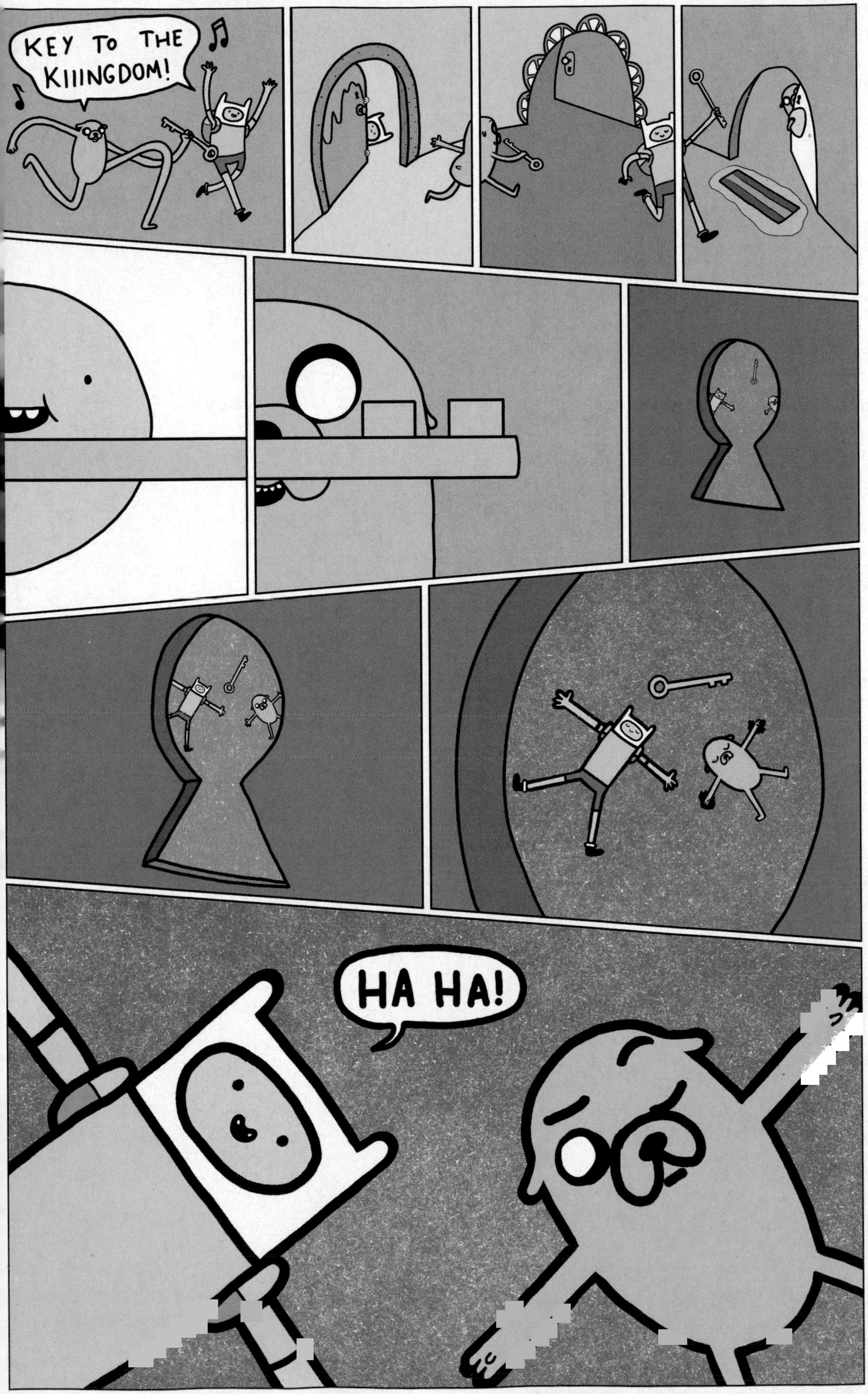
KEY TO THE KIIINGDOM!
HA HA!

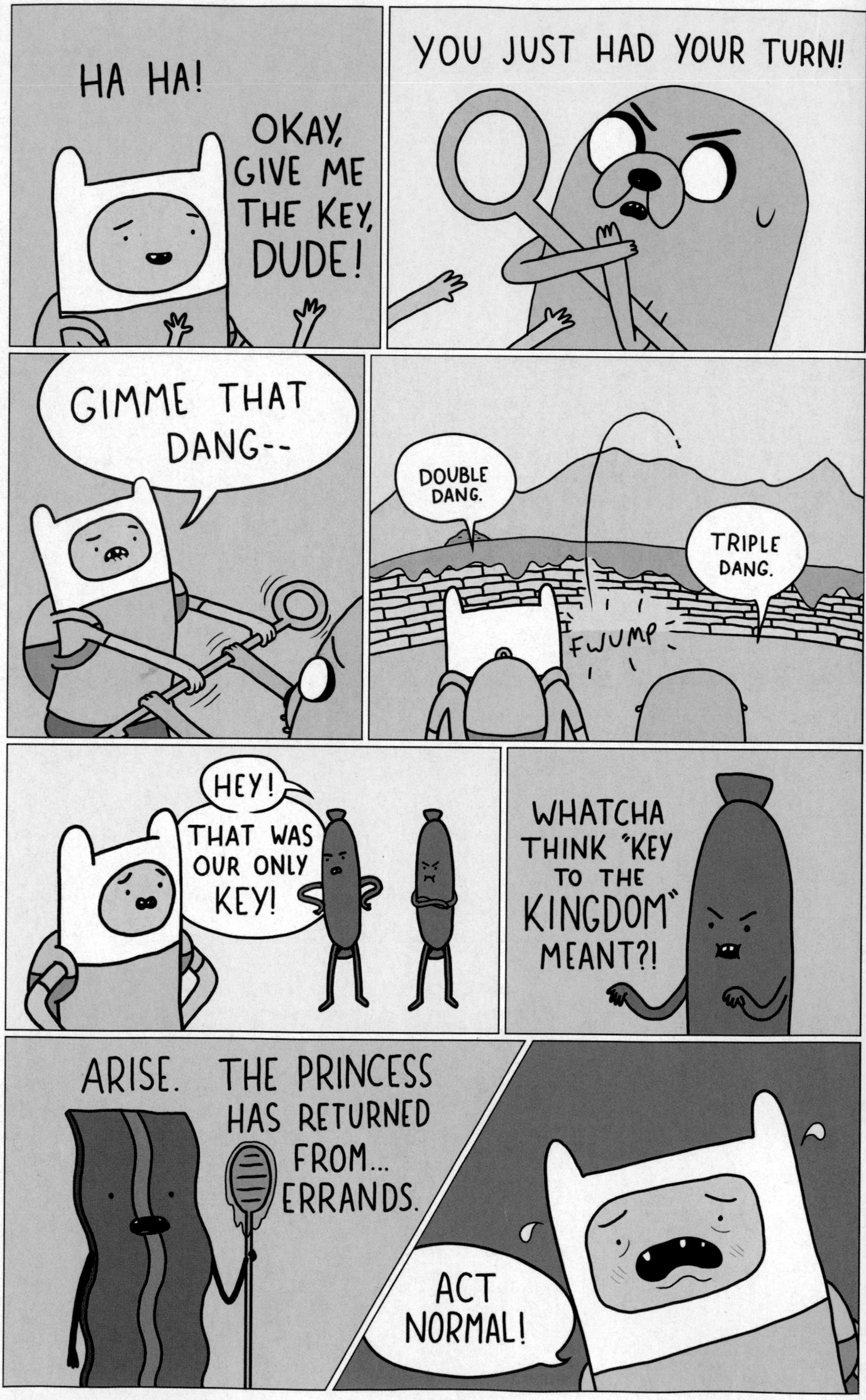
HA HA!
OKAY, GIVE ME THE KEY, DUDE!
YOU JUST HAD YOUR TURN!
GIMME THAT DANG--
DOUBLE DANG.
FWUMP
TRIPLE DANG.
HEY!
THAT WAS OUR ONLY KEY!
WHATCHA THINK "KEY TO THE KINGDOM" MEANT?!
ARISE. THE PRINCESS HAS RETURNED FROM... ERRANDS.
ACT NORMAL!

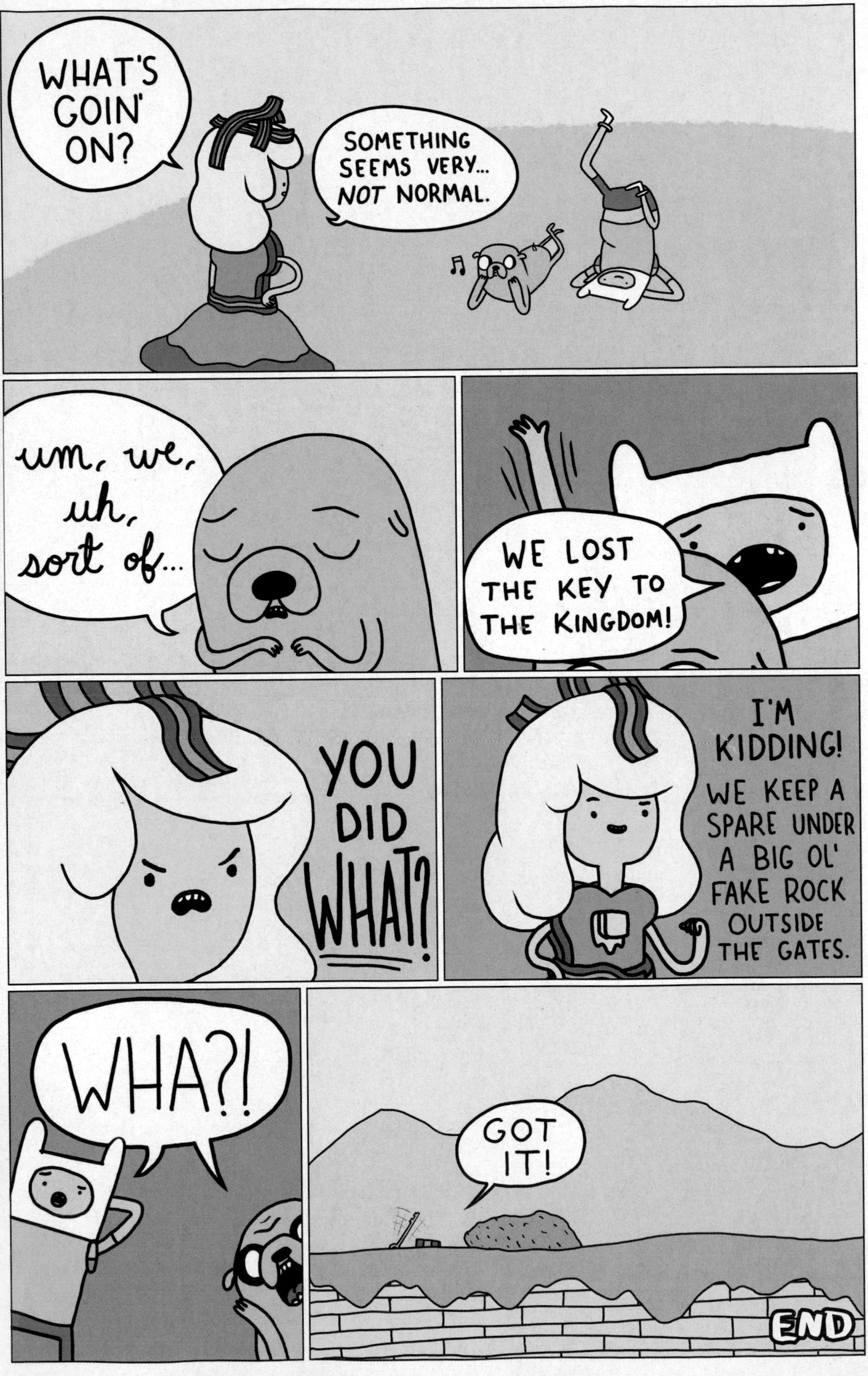
WHAT'S GOIN' ON?
SOMETHING SEEMS VERY... NOT NORMAL.
um, we, uh, sort of...
WE LOST THE KEY TO THE KINGDOM!
YOU DID WHAT?!
I'M KIDDING!
WE KEEP A SPARE UNDER A BIG OL' FAKE ROCK OUTSIDE THE GATES.
WHA?!
GOT IT!
END

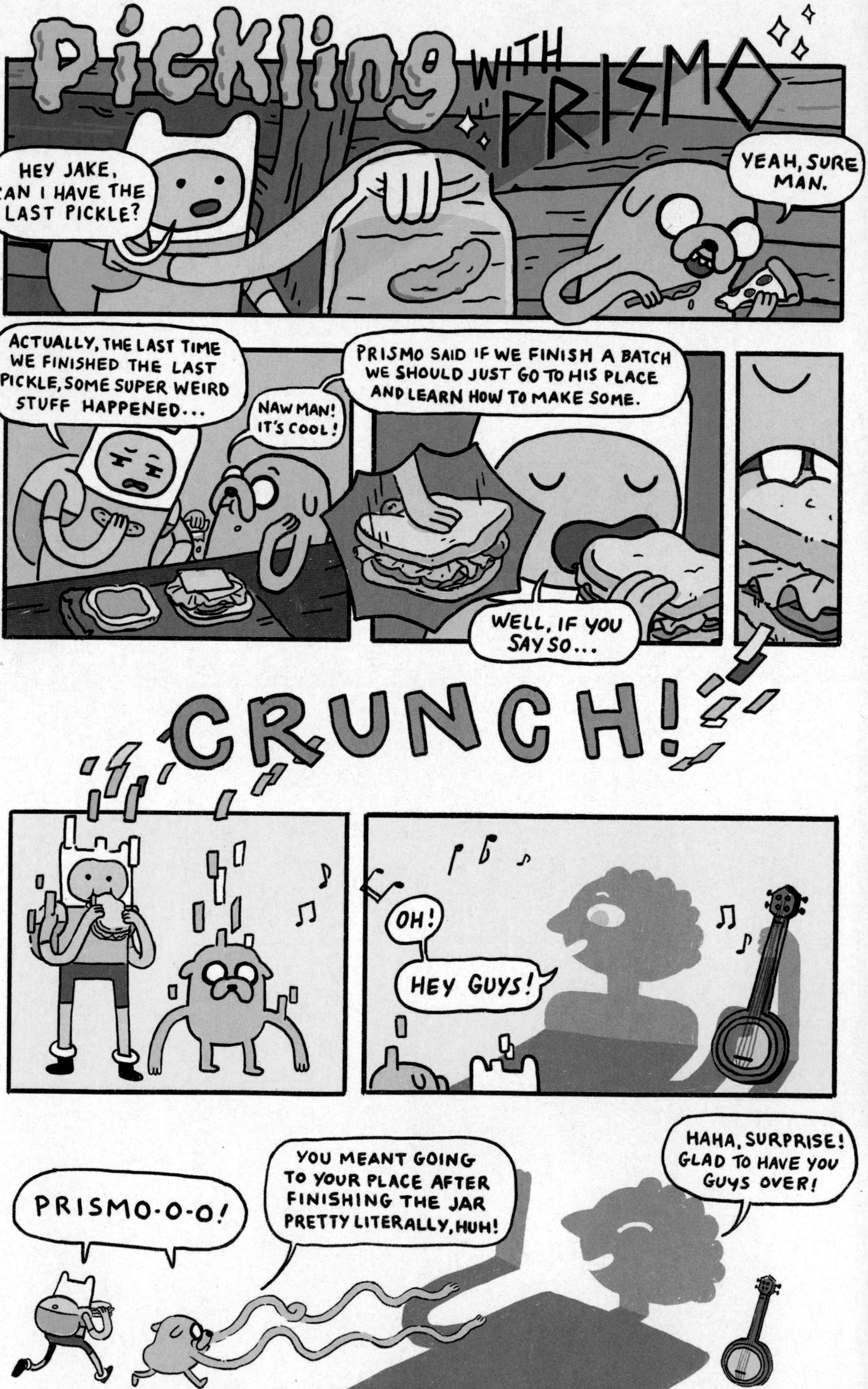
Pickling WITH PRISMO
HEY JAKE, CAN I HAVE THE LAST PICKLE?
YEAH, SURE MAN.
ACTUALLY, THE LAST TIME WE FINISHED THE LAST PICKLE, SOME SUPER WEIRD STUFF HAPPENED...
NAW MAN! IT'S COOL!
PRISMO SAID IF WE FINISH A BATCH WE SHOULD JUST GO TO HIS PLACE AND LEARN HOW TO MAKE SOME.
WELL, IF YOU SAY SO...
CRUNCH!
OH!
HEY GUYS!
PRISMO-O-O!
YOU MEANT GOING TO YOUR PLACE AFTER FINISHING THE JAR PRETTY LITERALLY, HUH!
HAHA, SURPRISE! GLAD TO HAVE YOU GUYS OVER!

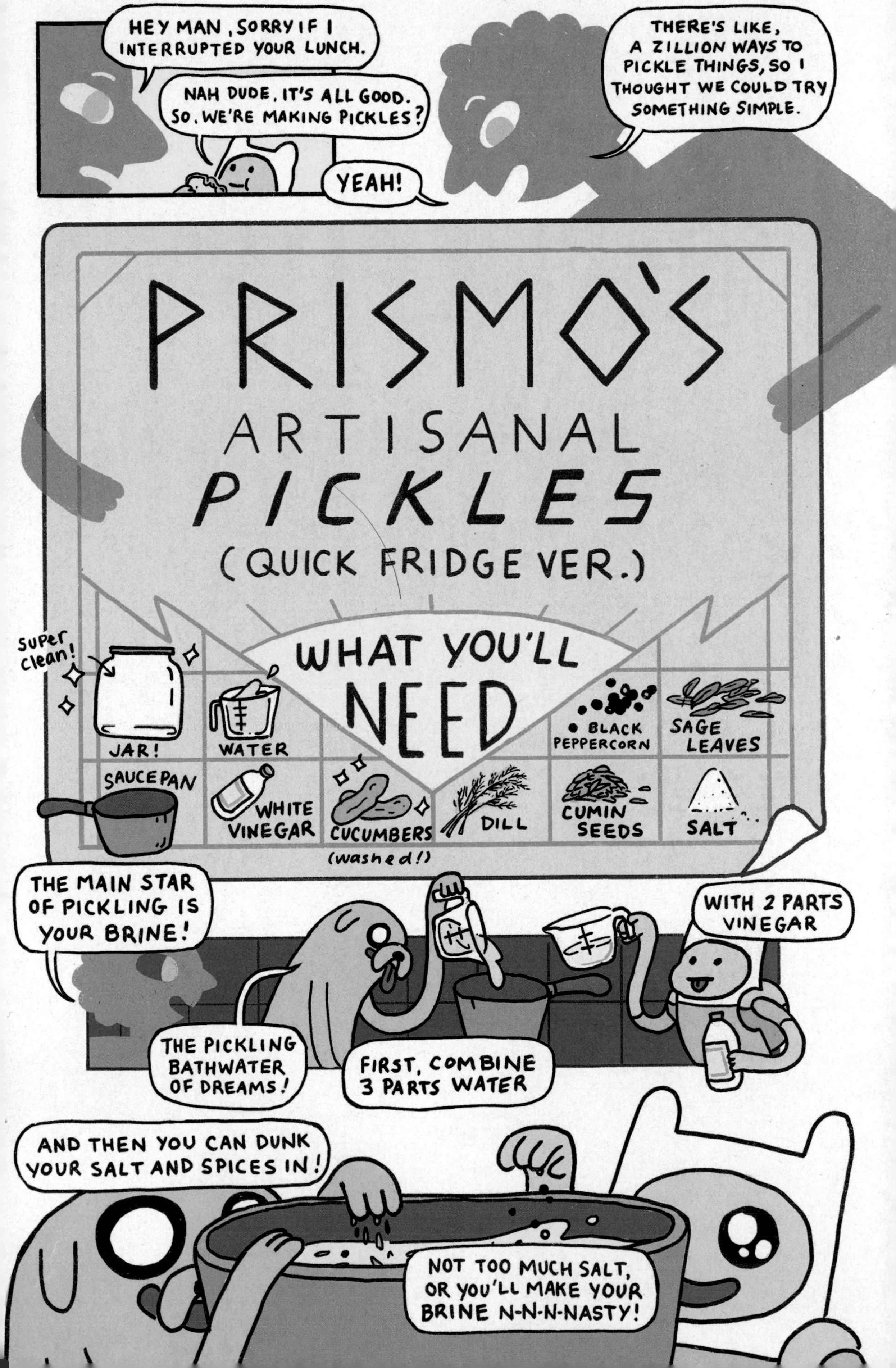
HEY MAN, SORRY IF I INTERRUPTED YOUR LUNCH.
NAH DUDE, IT'S ALL GOOD. SO, WE'RE MAKING PICKLES?
YEAH!
THERE'S LIKE, A ZILLION WAYS TO PICKLE THINGS, SO I THOUGHT WE COULD TRY SOMETHING SIMPLE.
PRISMO'S ARTISANAL PICKLES (QUICK FRIDGE VER.)
WHAT YOU'LL NEED
super clean!
JAR!
WATER
BLACK PEPPERCORN
SAGE LEAVES
SAUCEPAN
WHITE VINEGAR
CUCUMBERS (washed!)
DILL
CUMIN SEEDS
SALT
THE MAIN STAR OF PICKLING IS YOUR BRINE!
THE PICKLING BATHWATER OF DREAMS!
FIRST, COMBINE 3 PARTS WATER
WITH 2 PARTS VINEGAR
AND THEN YOU CAN DUNK YOUR SALT AND SPICES IN!
NOT TOO MUCH SALT, OR YOU'LL MAKE YOUR BRINE N-N-N-NASTY!

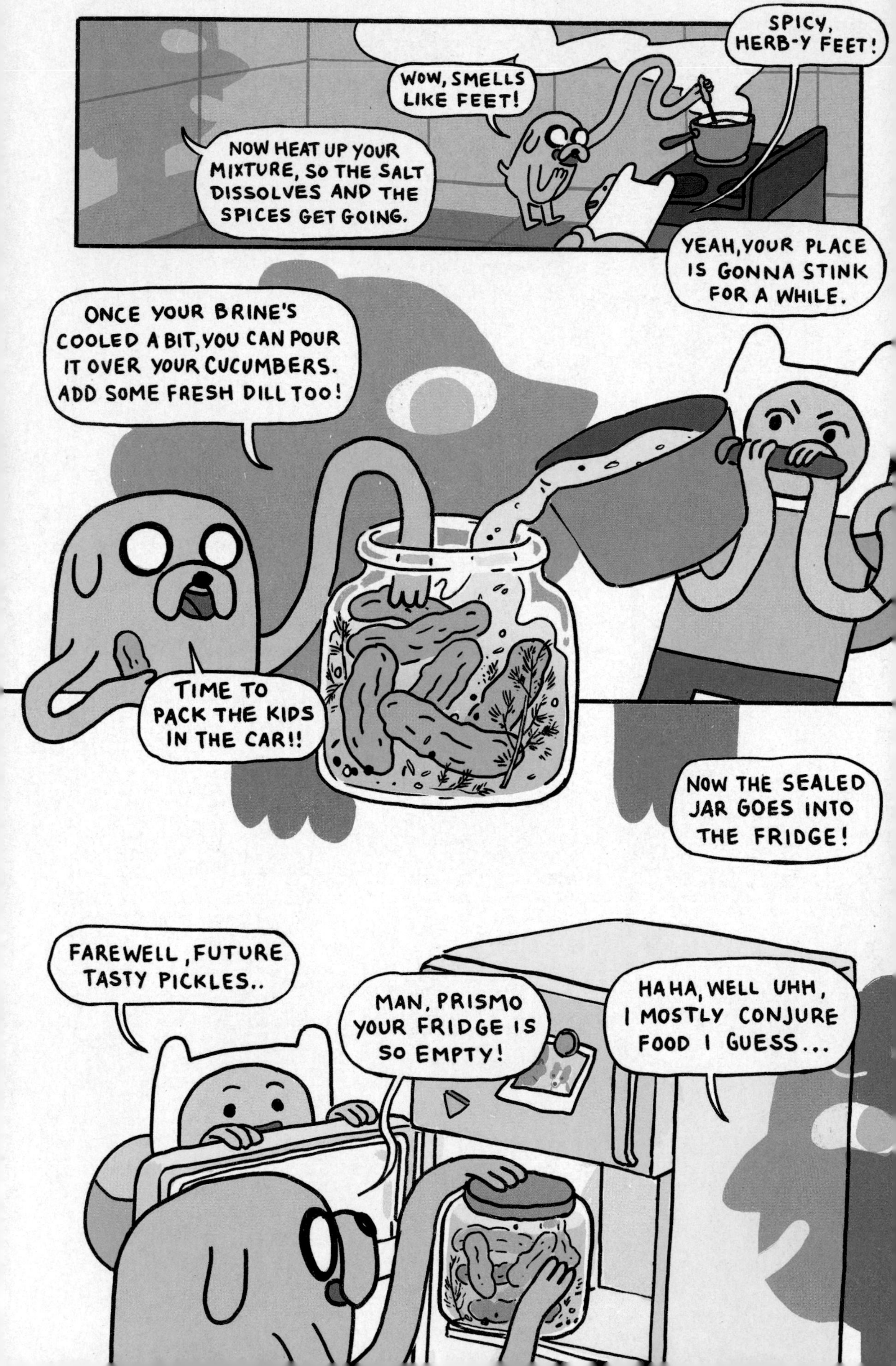
NOW HEAT UP YOUR MIXTURE, SO THE SALT DISSOLVES AND THE SPICES GET GOING.
WOW, SMELLS LIKE FEET!
SPICY, HERB-Y FEET!
YEAH, YOUR PLACE IS GONNA STINK FOR A WHILE.
ONCE YOUR BRINE'S COOLED A BIT, YOU CAN POUR IT OVER YOUR CUCUMBERS. ADD SOME FRESH DILL TOO!
TIME TO PACK THE KIDS IN THE CAR!!
NOW THE SEALED JAR GOES INTO THE FRIDGE!
FAREWELL, FUTURE TASTY PICKLES..
MAN, PRISMO YOUR FRIDGE IS SO EMPTY!
HAHA, WELL UHH, I MOSTLY CONJURE FOOD I GUESS...

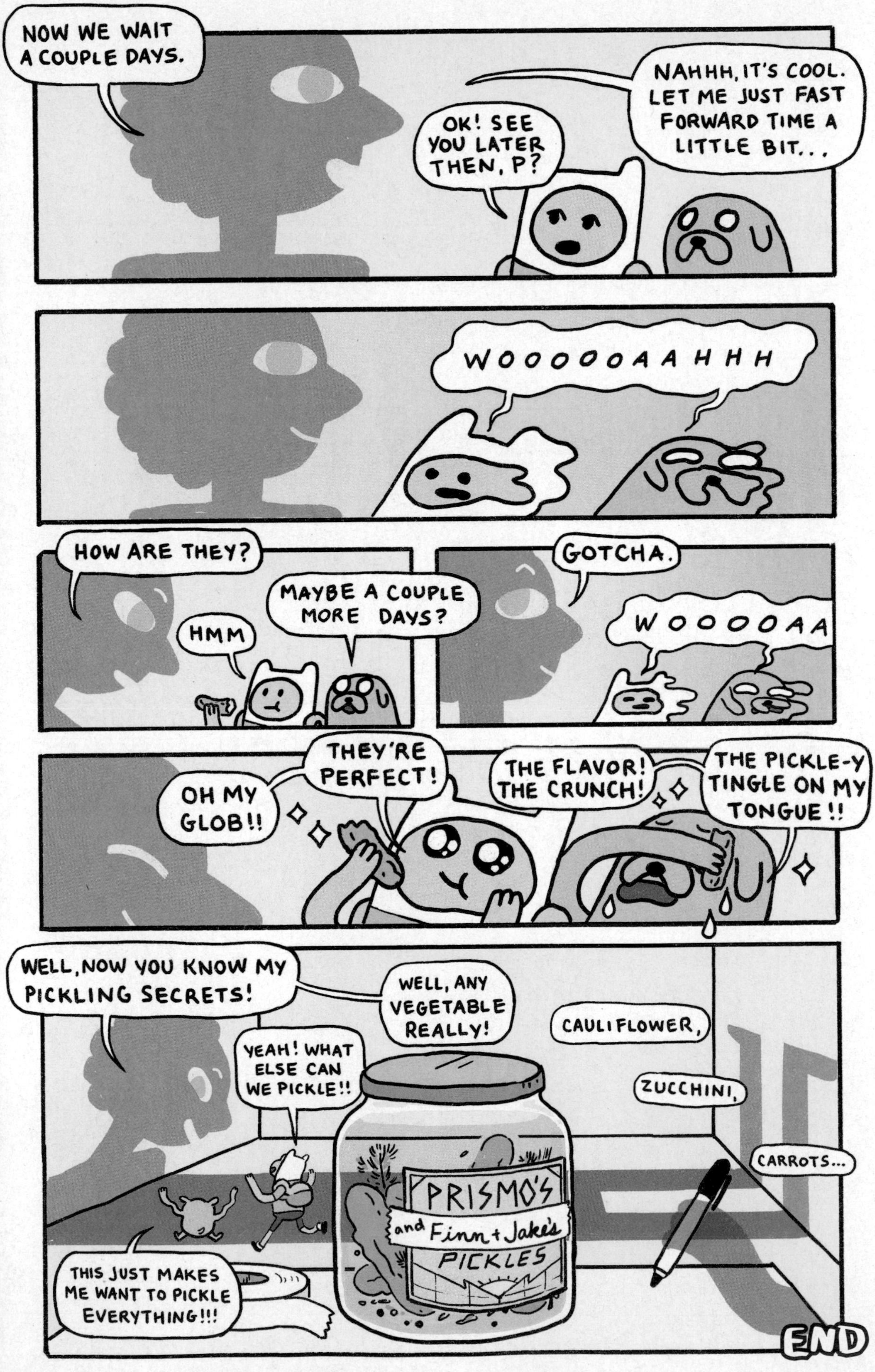
NOW WE WAIT A COUPLE DAYS.
OK! SEE YOU LATER THEN, P?
NAHHH, IT'S COOL. LET ME JUST FAST FORWARD TIME A LITTLE BIT...
WOOOOOOAAHHH
HOW ARE THEY?
HMM
MAYBE A COUPLE MORE DAYS?
GOTCHA.
WOOOOOAA
OH MY GLOB!!
THEY'RE PERFECT!
THE FLAVOR! THE CRUNCH!
THE PICKLE-Y TINGLE ON MY TONGUE!!
WELL, NOW YOU KNOW MY PICKLING SECRETS!
YEAH! WHAT ELSE CAN WE PICKLE!!
WELL, ANY VEGETABLE REALLY!
CAULIFLOWER,
ZUCCHINI,
CARROTS...
THIS JUST MAKES ME WANT TO PICKLE EVERYTHING!!!
PRISMO'S and Finn + Jake's PICKLES
END

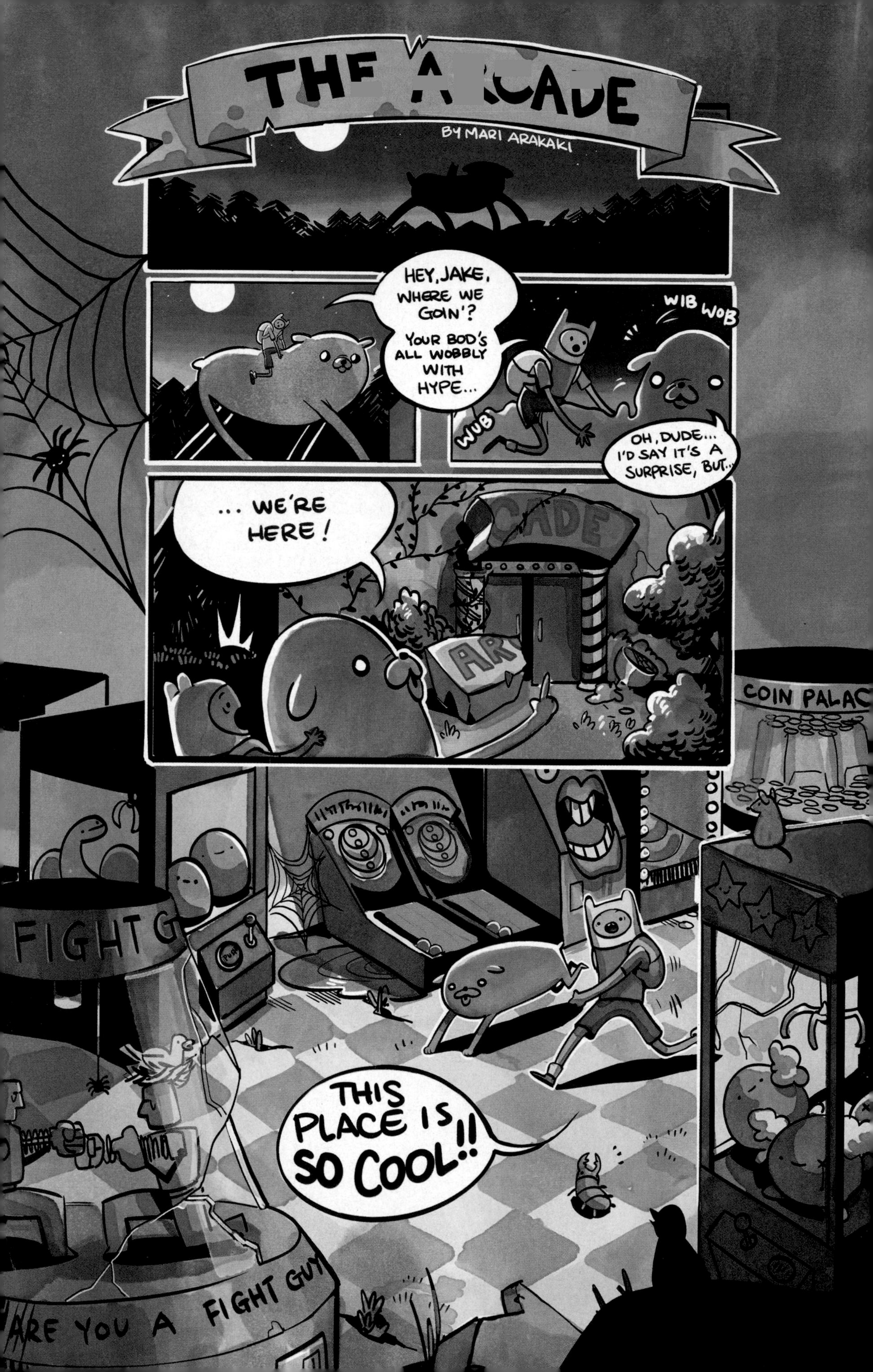
THE ARCADE
BY MARI ARAKAKI
HEY, JAKE, WHERE WE GOIN'? YOUR BOD'S ALL WOBBLY WITH HYPE...
WIB WOB
WUB
OH, DUDE... I'D SAY IT'S A SURPRISE, BUT...
... WE'RE HERE!
CADE
AR
COIN PALAC
FIGHT G
PUSH
THIS PLACE IS SO COOL!!
ARE YOU A FIGHT GUY

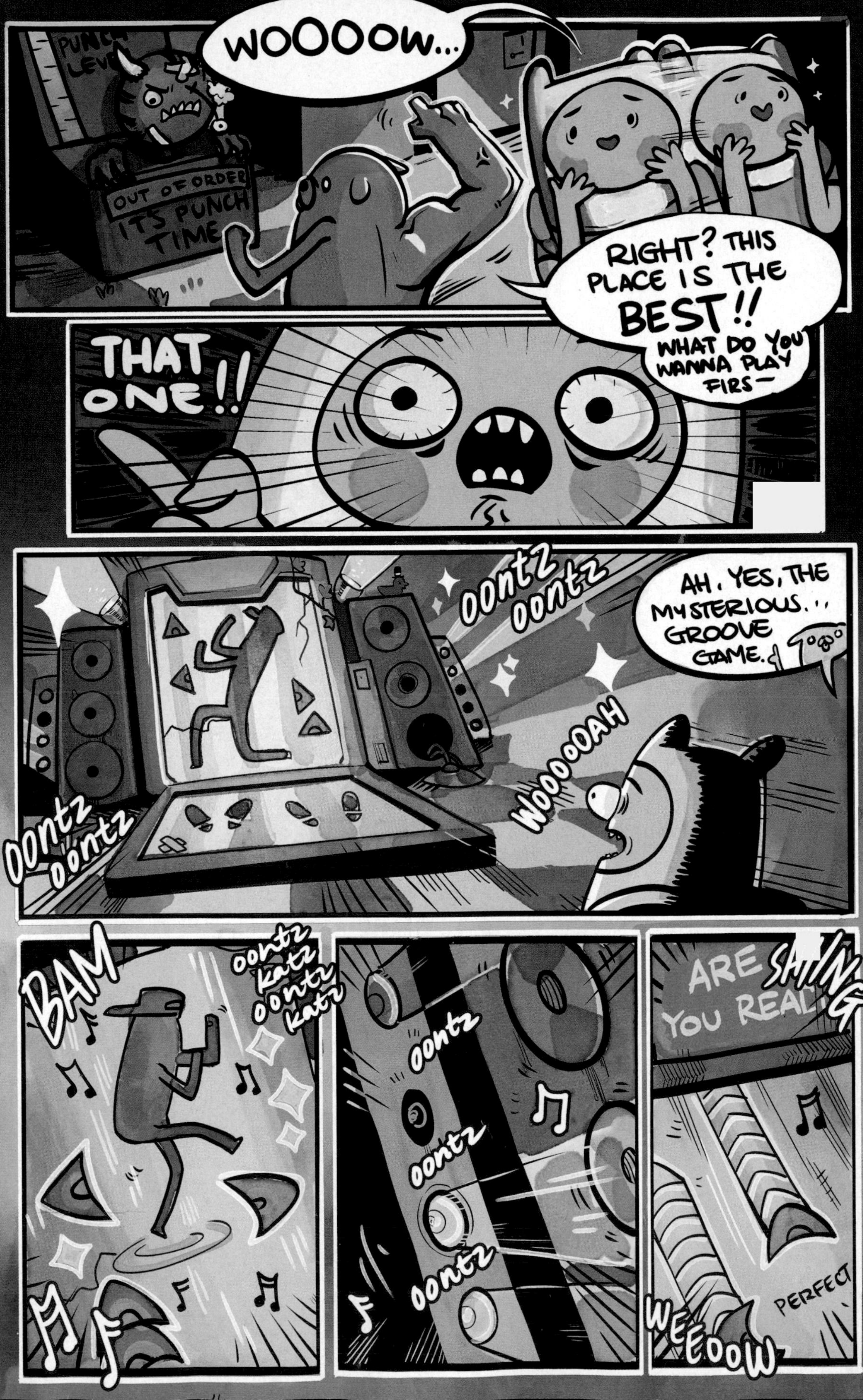

PUNCH LEVEL
OUT OF ORDER
IT'S PUNCH TIME
WOOOOW...
RIGHT? THIS PLACE IS THE BEST!!
WHAT DO YOU WANNA PLAY FIRS—
THAT ONE!!
oontz oontz
AH. YES, THE MYSTERIOUS... GROOVE GAME.
WOOOOOAH
oontz oontz
BAM
oontz katz oontz katz
oontz
oontz
oontz
ARE YOU REAL
SHING
PERFECT
WEEOOOW

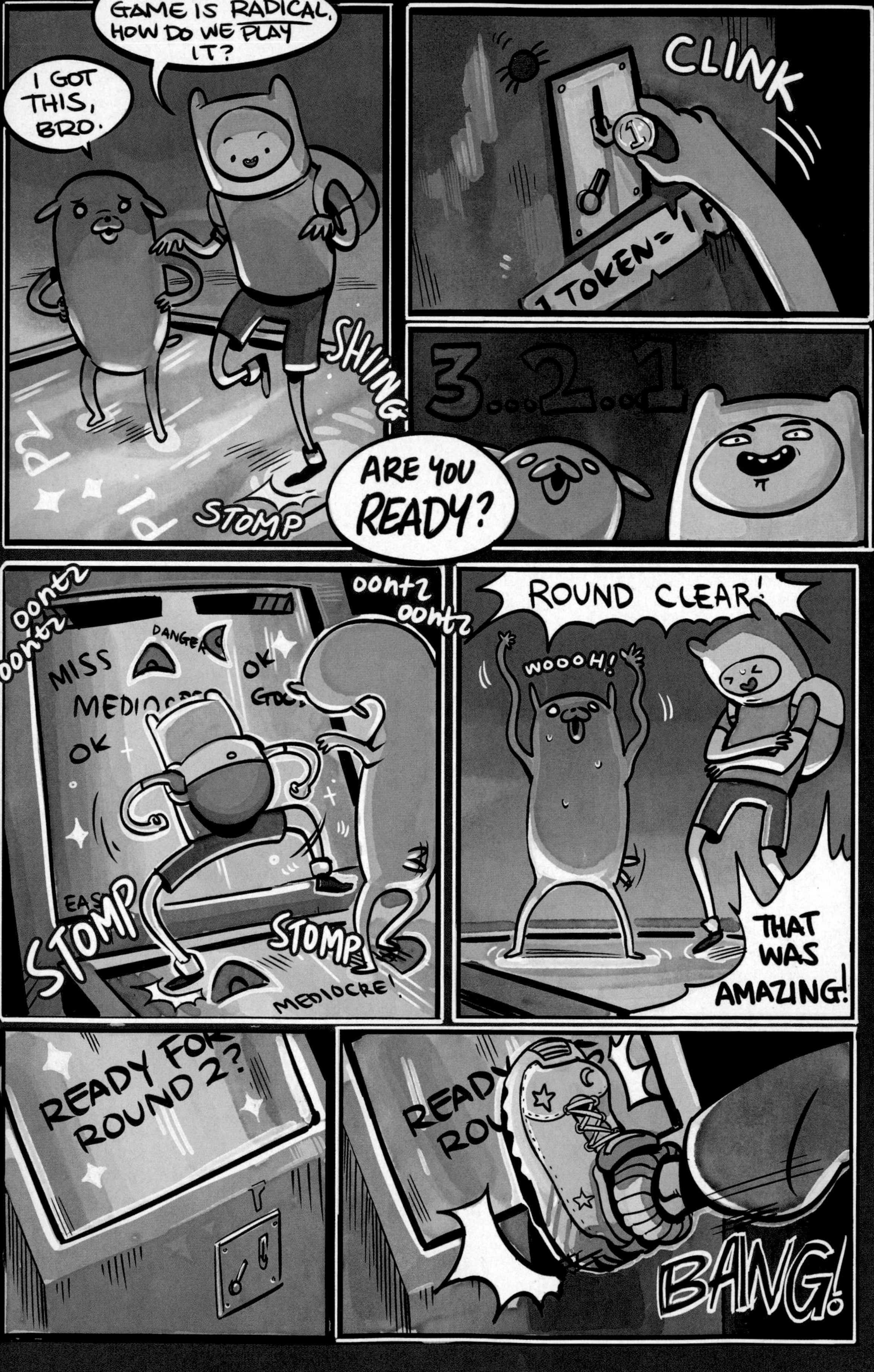
DUDE, THIS GAME IS RADICAL. HOW DO WE PLAY IT?
I GOT THIS, BRO.
SHING
STOMP
CLINK
1 TOKEN=
3...2...1
ARE YOU READY?
oontz oontz
oontz oontz
DANGER
MISS
OK
OK
STOMP
STOMP
MEDIOCRE!
ROUND CLEAR!
WOOOH!
THAT WAS AMAZING!
READY FOR ROUND 2?
BANG!

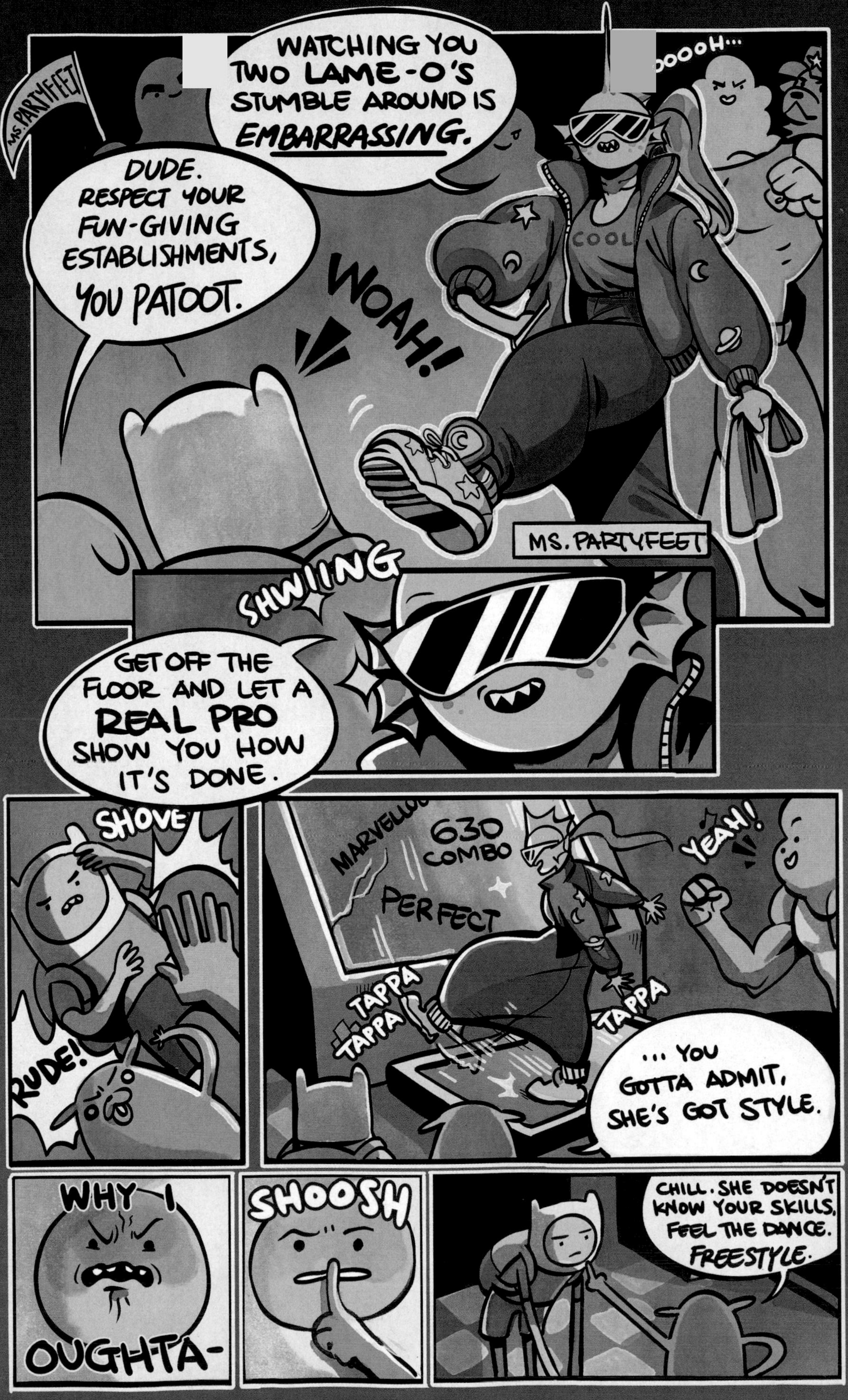

MS. PARTYFEET
WATCHING YOU TWO LAME-O'S STUMBLE AROUND IS EMBARRASSING.
OOOOH...
DUDE. RESPECT YOUR FUN-GIVING ESTABLISHMENTS, YOU PATOOT.
WOAH!
COOL
MS. PARTYFEET
SHWIING
GET OFF THE FLOOR AND LET A REAL PRO SHOW YOU HOW IT'S DONE.
SHOVE
RUDE!
MARVELLO
630 COMBO
PERFECT
YEAH!
TAPPA
TAPPA
TAPPA
... YOU GOTTA ADMIT, SHE'S GOT STYLE.
WHY I
OUGHTA-
SHOOSH
CHILL. SHE DOESN'T KNOW YOUR SKILLS. FEEL THE DANCE. FREESTYLE.

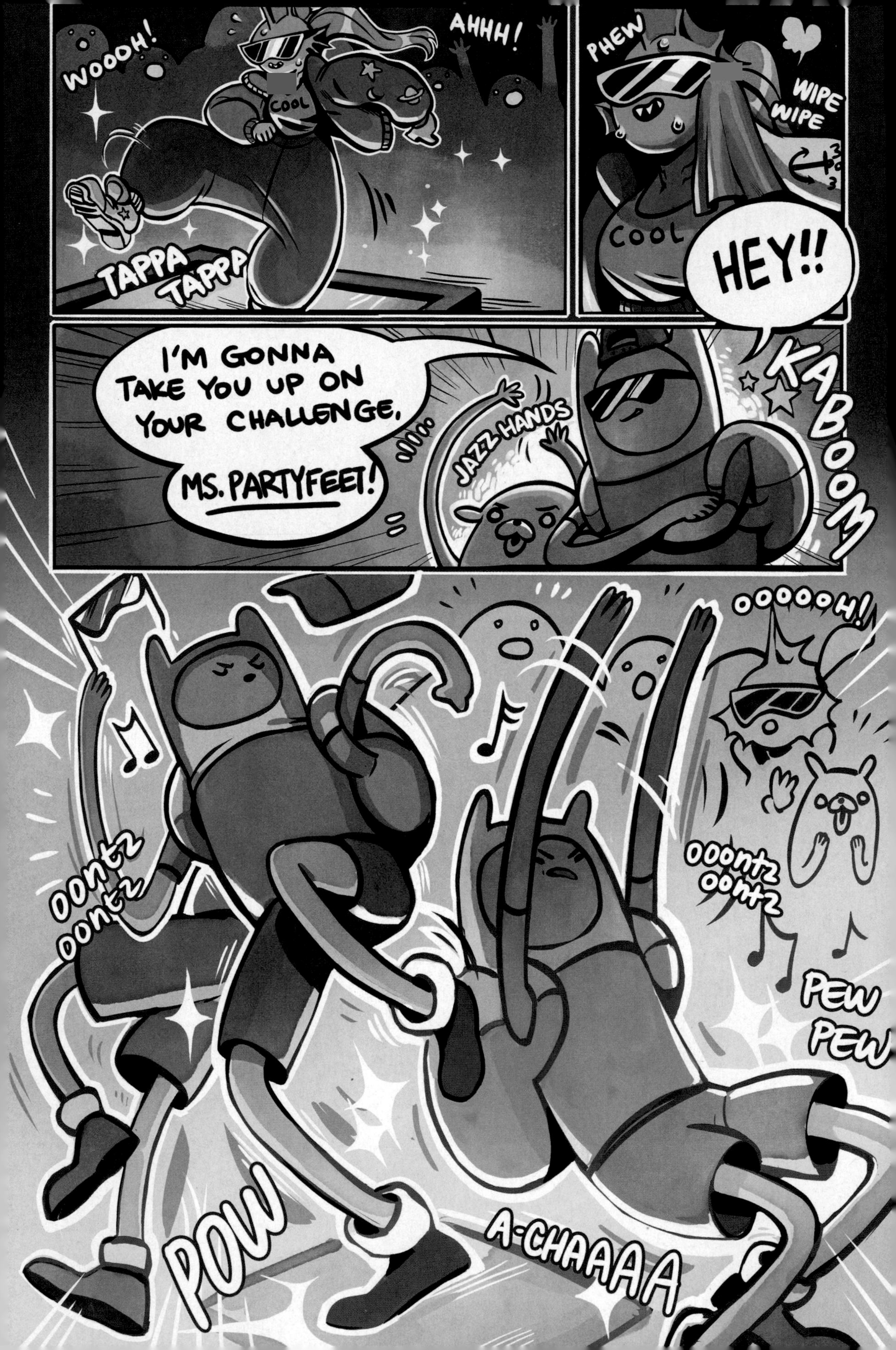
WOOOH!
AHHH!
COOL
TAPPA
TAPPA
PHEW
WIPE
WIPE
COOL
HEY!!
I'M GONNA TAKE YOU UP ON YOUR CHALLENGE, MS. PARTYFEET!
JAZZ HANDS
KABOOM
OOOOOOH!
oontz
oontz
ooontz
oontz
PEW
PEW
POW
A-CHAAAAA

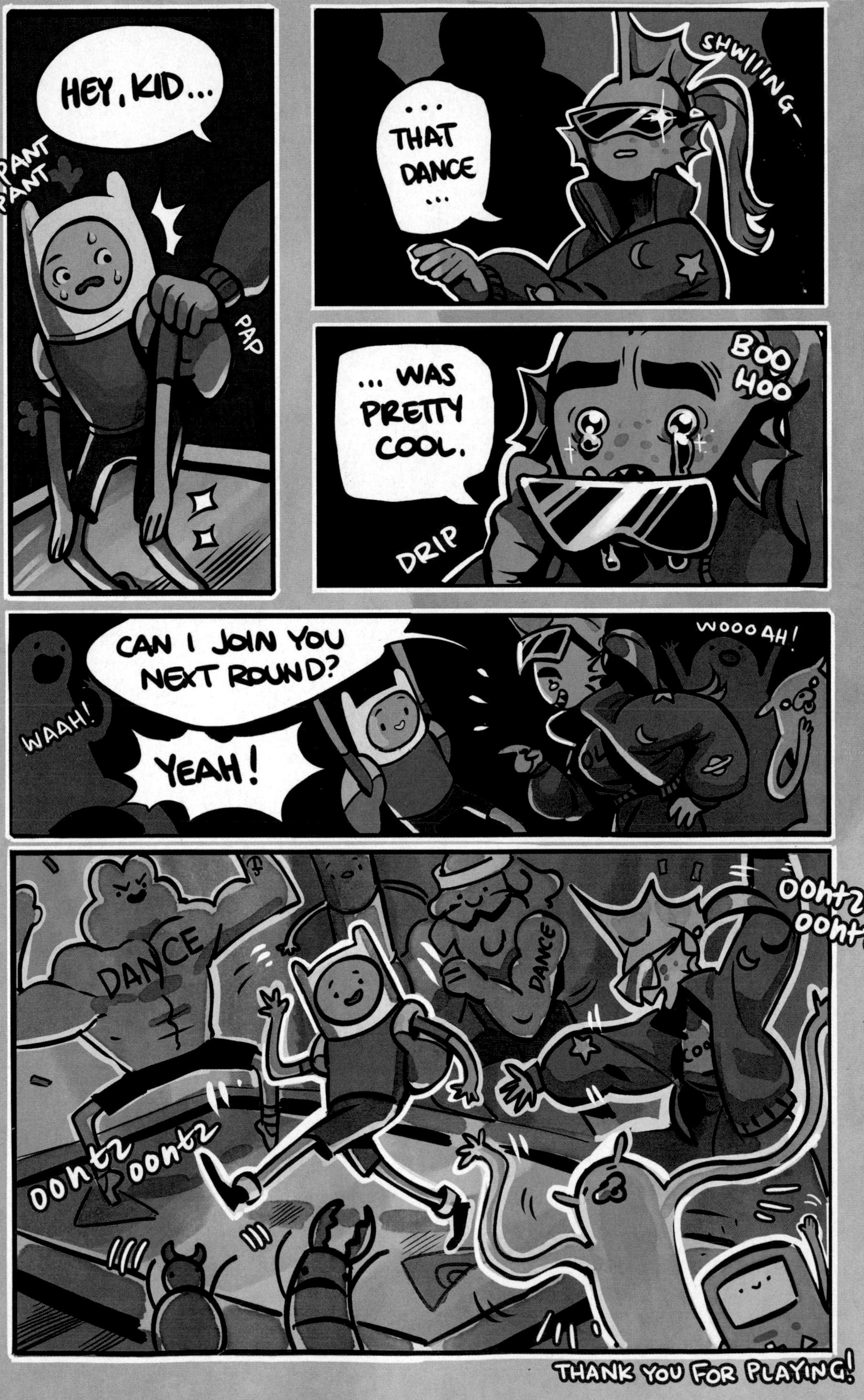
HEY, KID...
PANT PANT
PAP
...THAT DANCE...
SHWIIING
...WAS PRETTY COOL.
BOO HOO
DRIP
CAN I JOIN YOU NEXT ROUND?
YEAH!
WAAH!
WOOOAH!
DANCE
DANCE
DANCE
oontz oontz
oontz oontz
THANK YOU FOR PLAYING!

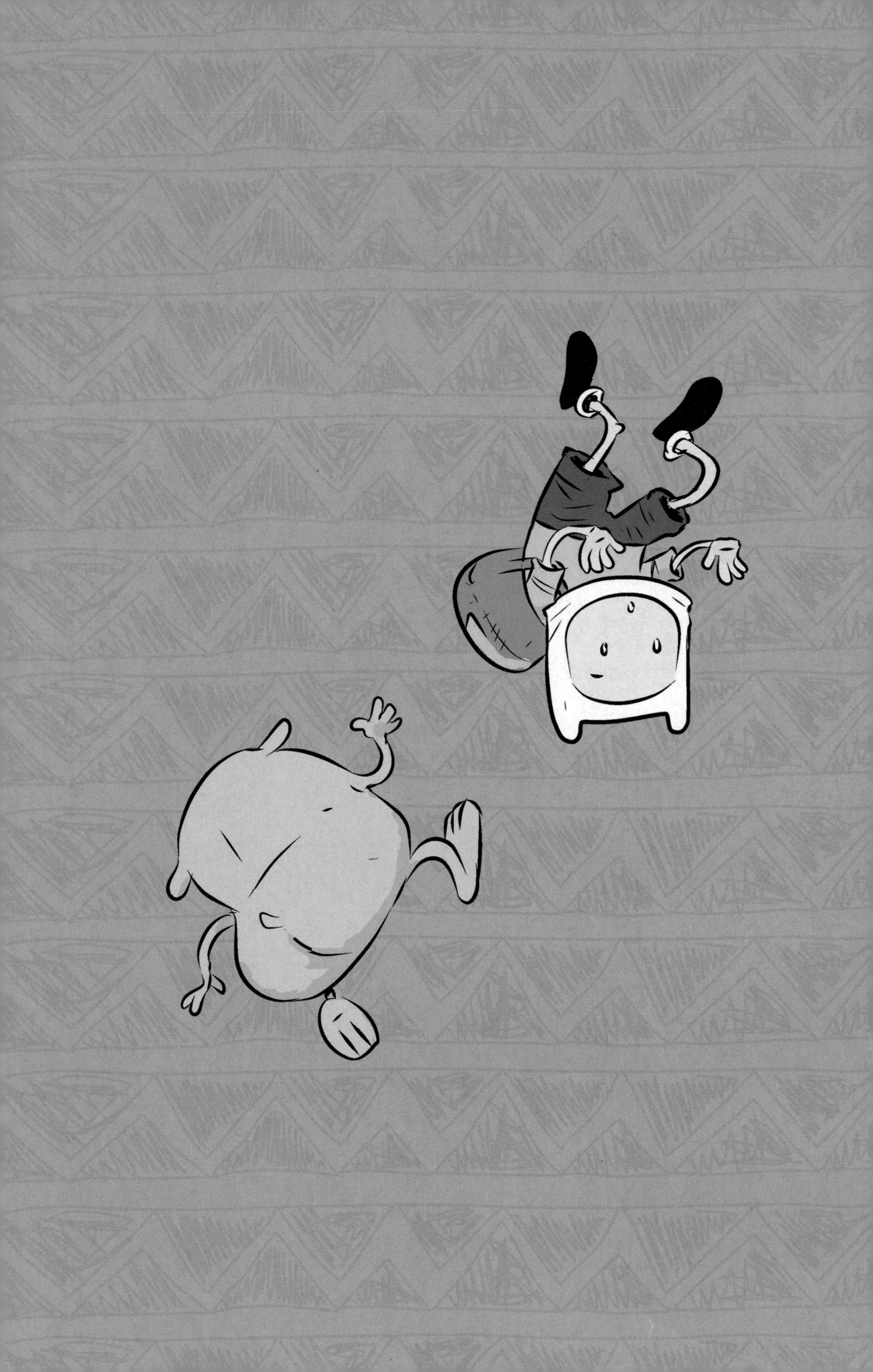

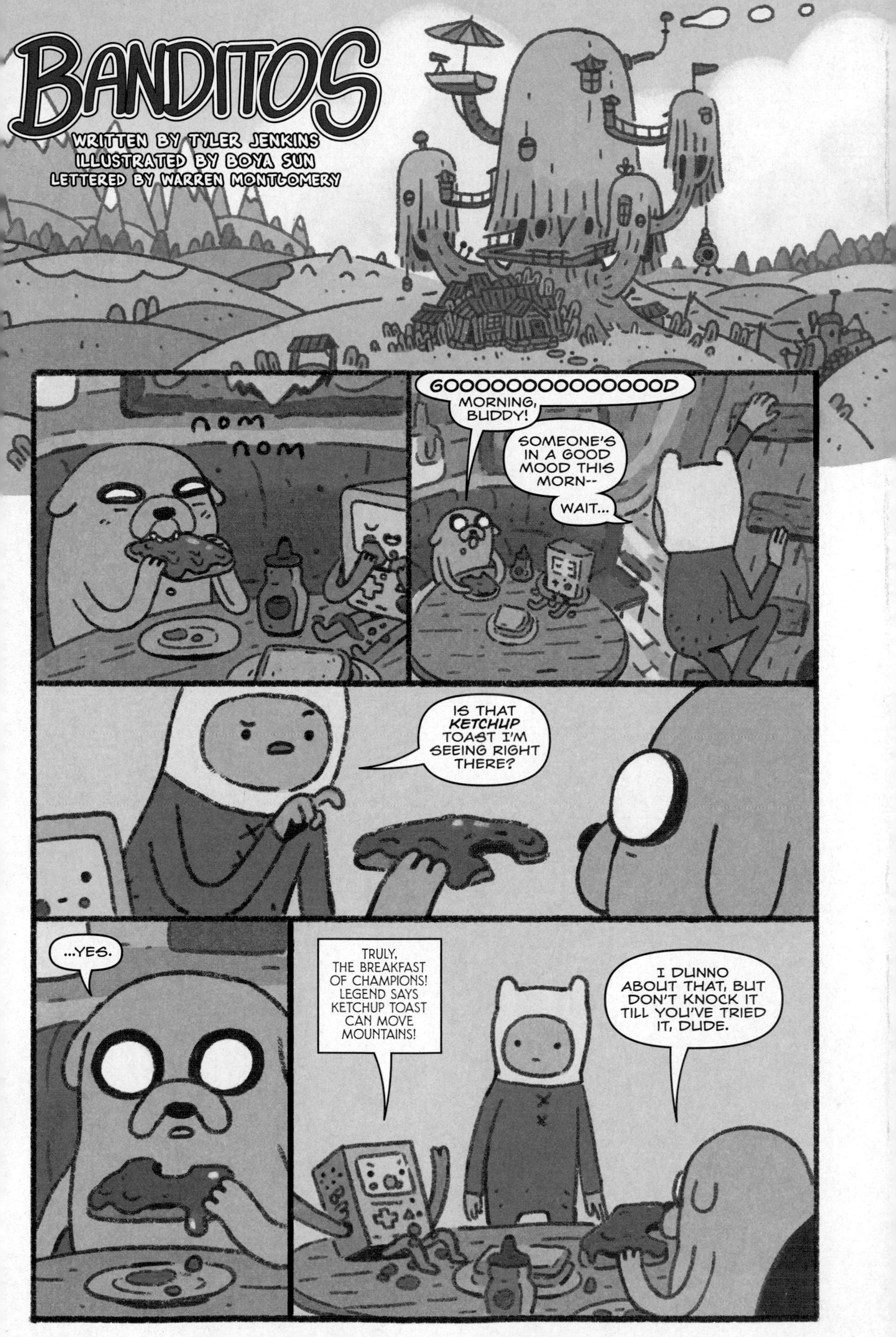
BANDITOS
WRITTEN BY TYLER JENKINS
ILLUSTRATED BY BOYA SUN
LETTERED BY WARREN MONTGOMERY
nom nom
GOOOOOOOOOOOOOOOD MORNING, BUDDY!
SOMEONE'S IN A GOOD MOOD THIS MORN--
WAIT...
IS THAT KETCHUP TOAST I'M SEEING RIGHT THERE?
...YES.
TRULY, THE BREAKFAST OF CHAMPIONS! LEGEND SAYS KETCHUP TOAST CAN MOVE MOUNTAINS!
I DUNNO ABOUT THAT, BUT DON'T KNOCK IT TILL YOU'VE TRIED IT, DUDE.

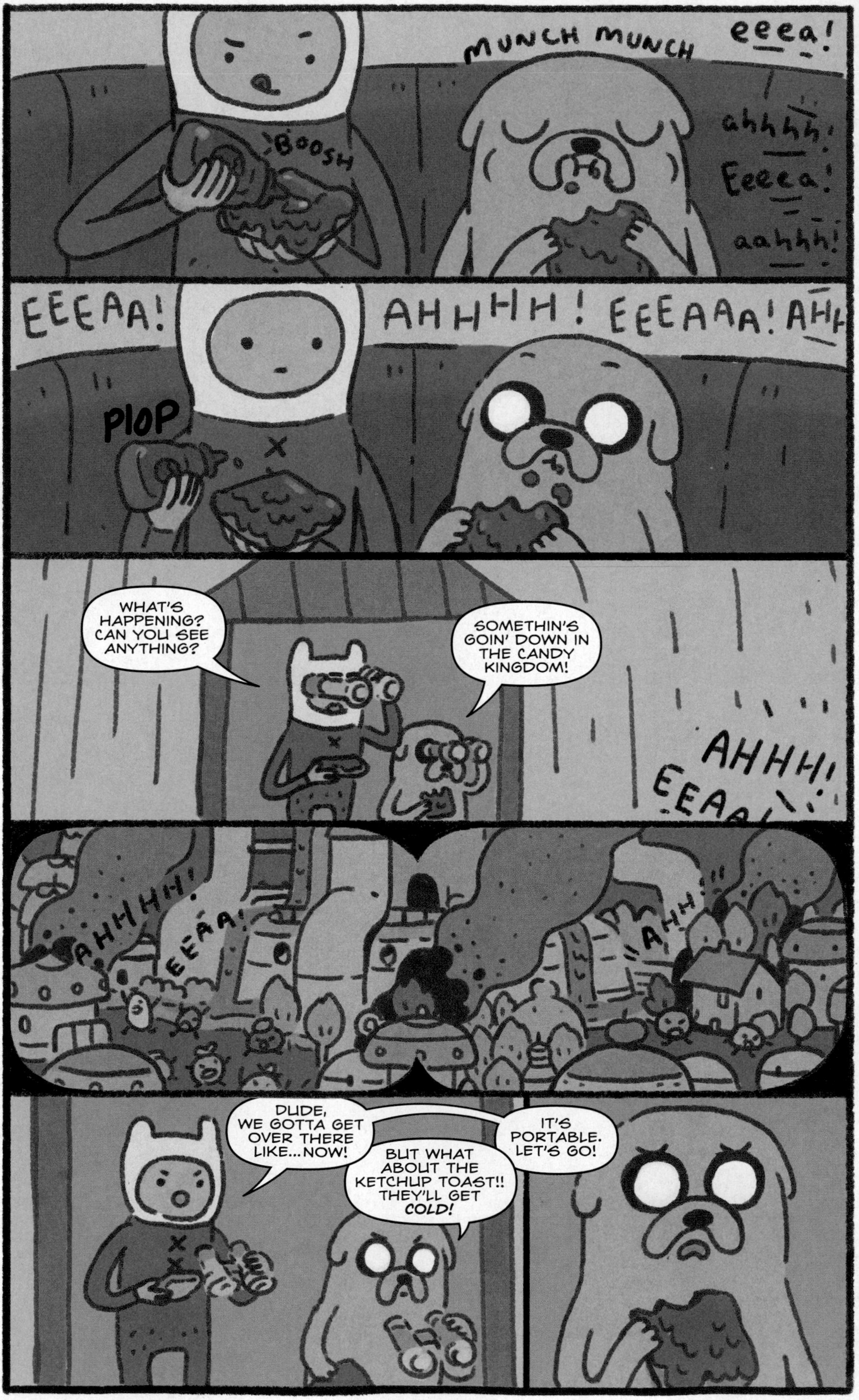

BOOSH
MUNCH MUNCH
eeea!
ahhhh!
Eeeea!
aahhh!
EEEAA!
AHHHH! EEEAAA! AHH
PLOP
WHAT'S HAPPENING? CAN YOU SEE ANYTHING?
SOMETHIN'S GOIN' DOWN IN THE CANDY KINGDOM!
AHHH!
EEAA
AHHHH!
EEEAA!
AHH
DUDE, WE GOTTA GET OVER THERE LIKE...NOW!
BUT WHAT ABOUT THE KETCHUP TOAST!! THEY'LL GET *COLD!*
IT'S PORTABLE. LET'S GO!

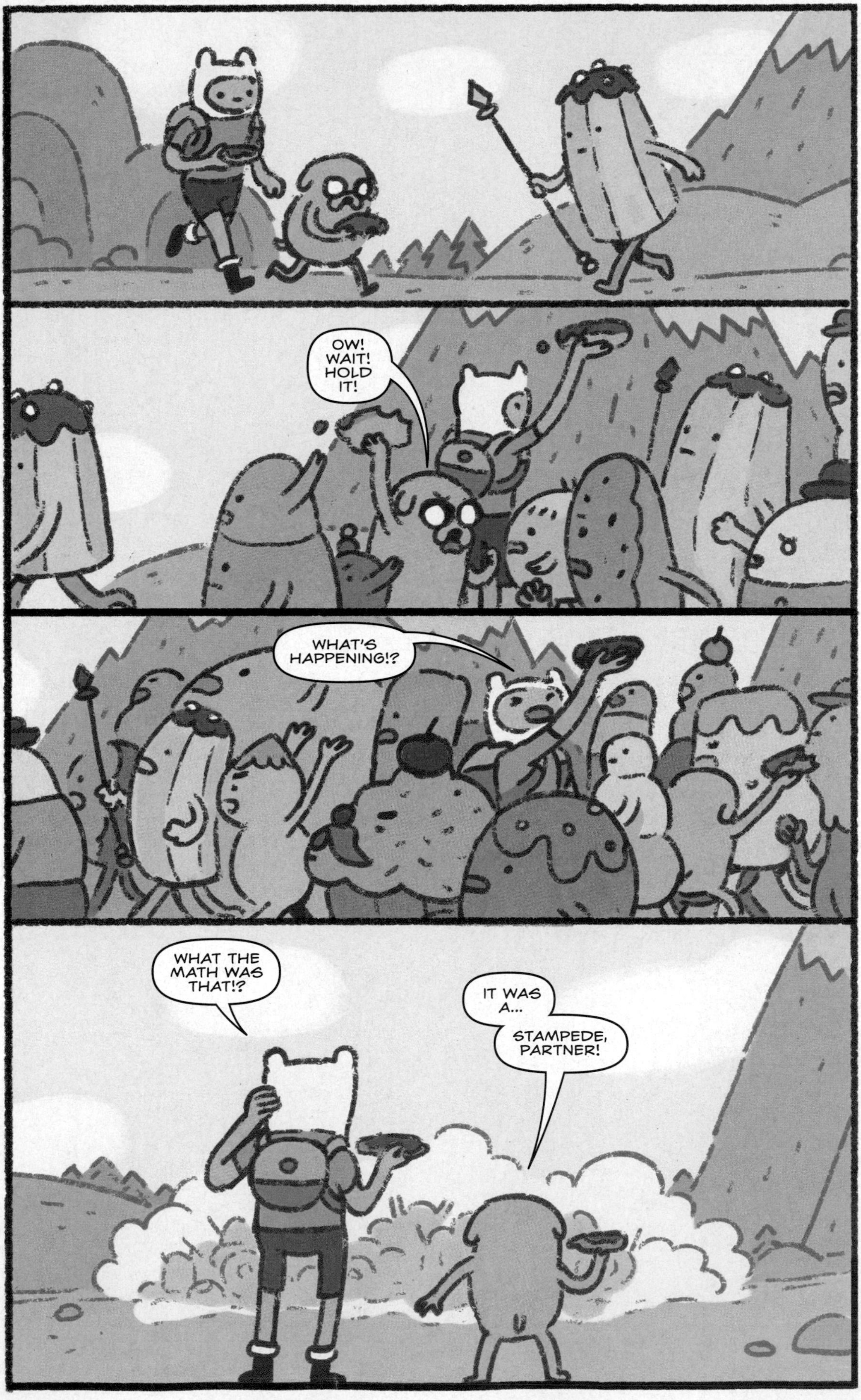
OW! WAIT! HOLD IT!
WHAT'S HAPPENING!?
WHAT THE MATH WAS THAT!?
IT WAS A...
STAMPEDE, PARTNER!

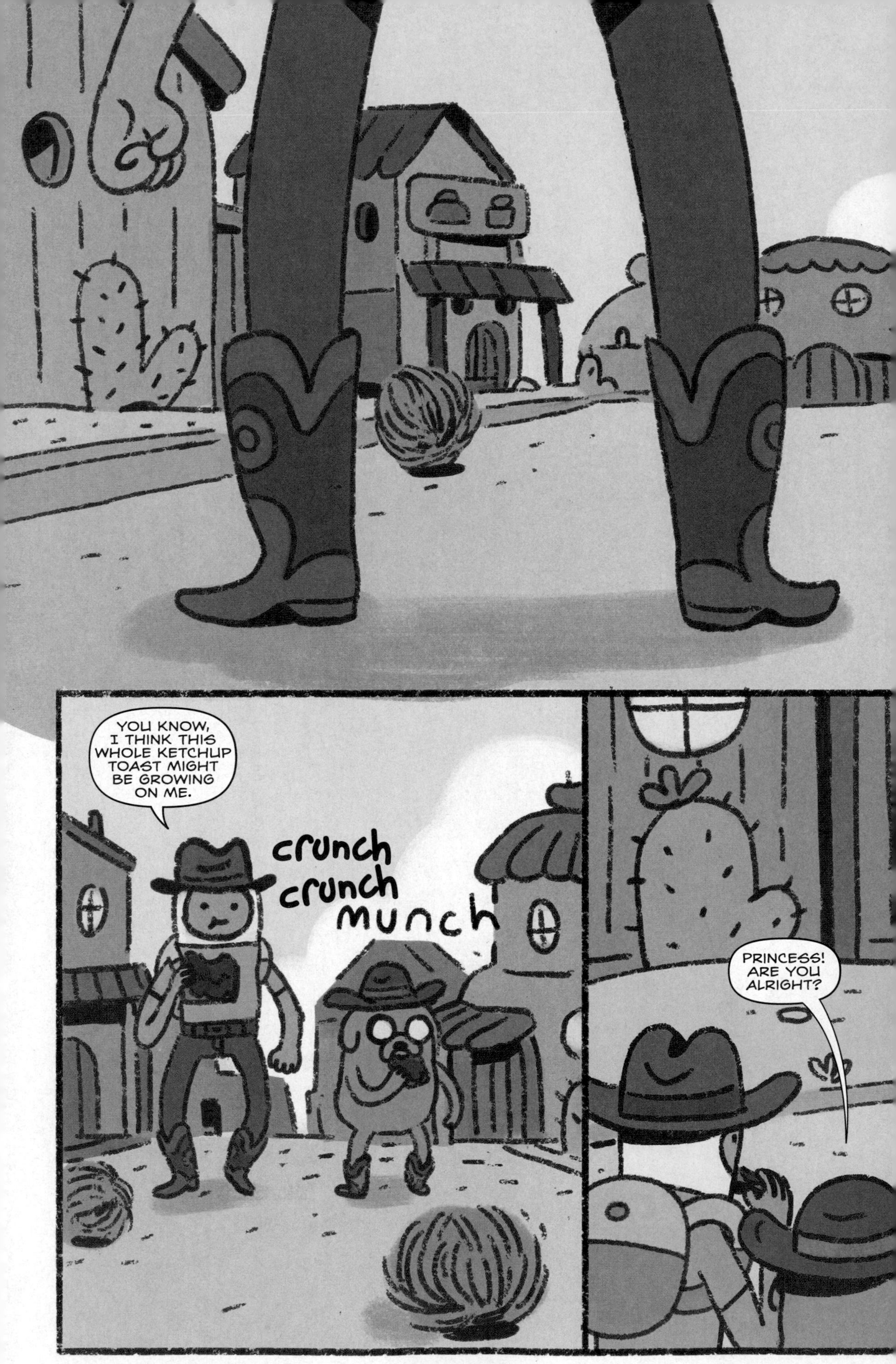
YOU KNOW, I THINK THIS WHOLE KETCHUP TOAST MIGHT BE GROWING ON ME.
crunch
crunch
munch
PRINCESS! ARE YOU ALRIGHT?

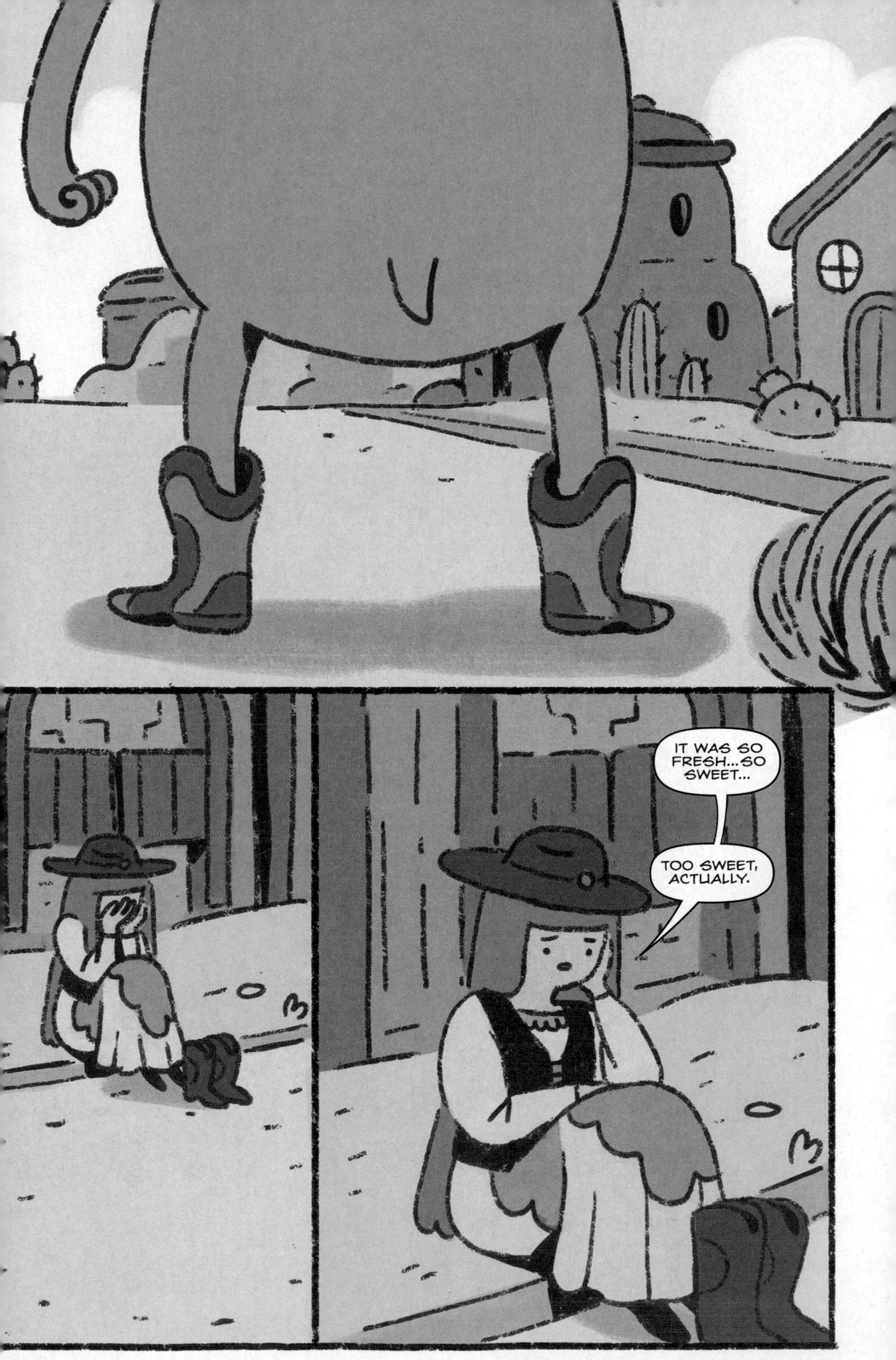
IT WAS SO FRESH...SO SWEET...
TOO SWEET, ACTUALLY.

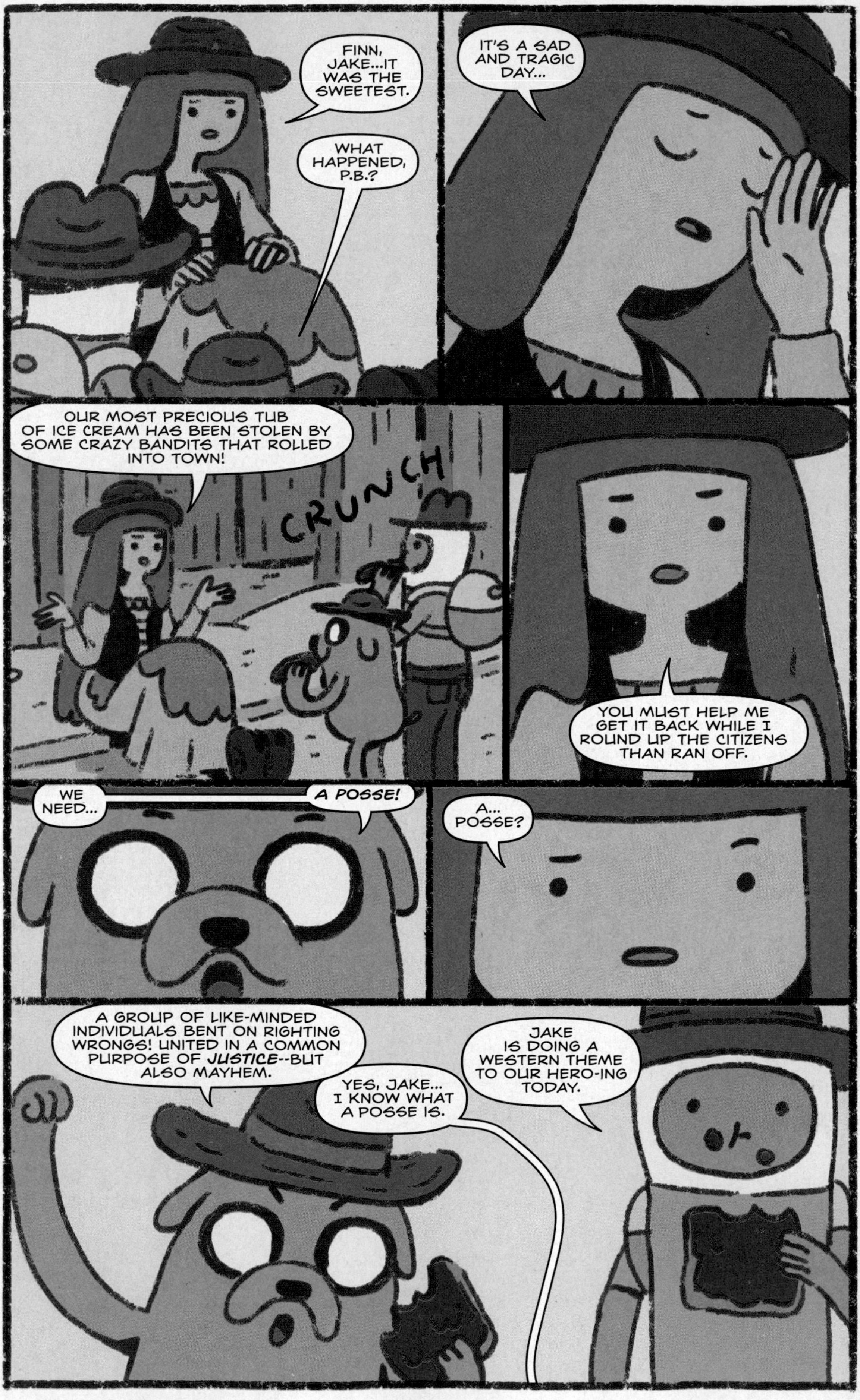

FINN, JAKE...IT WAS THE SWEETEST.
WHAT HAPPENED, P.B.?
IT'S A SAD AND TRAGIC DAY...
OUR MOST PRECIOUS TUB OF ICE CREAM HAS BEEN STOLEN BY SOME CRAZY BANDITS THAT ROLLED INTO TOWN!
CRUNCH
YOU MUST HELP ME GET IT BACK WHILE I ROUND UP THE CITIZENS THAN RAN OFF.
WE NEED...
A POSSE!
A... POSSE?
A GROUP OF LIKE-MINDED INDIVIDUALS BENT ON RIGHTING WRONGS! UNITED IN A COMMON PURPOSE OF JUSTICE--BUT ALSO MAYHEM.
YES, JAKE... I KNOW WHAT A POSSE IS.
JAKE IS DOING A WESTERN THEME TO OUR HERO-ING TODAY.

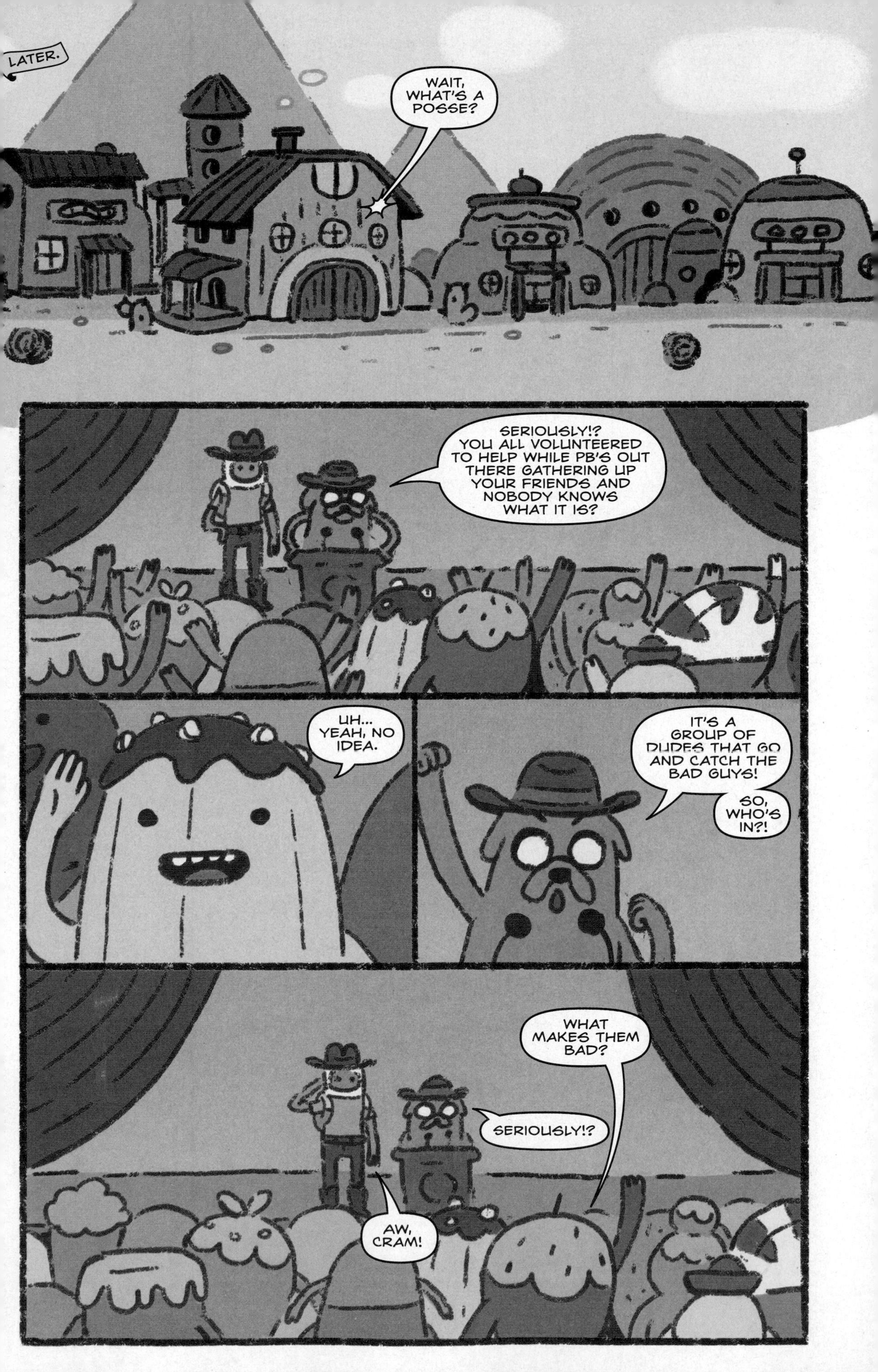
LATER.
WAIT, WHAT'S A POSSE?
SERIOUSLY!? YOU ALL VOLUNTEERED TO HELP WHILE PB'S OUT THERE GATHERING UP YOUR FRIENDS AND NOBODY KNOWS WHAT IT IS?
UH... YEAH, NO IDEA.
IT'S A GROUP OF DUDES THAT GO AND CATCH THE BAD GUYS!
SO, WHO'S IN?!
WHAT MAKES THEM BAD?
SERIOUSLY!?
AW, CRAM!

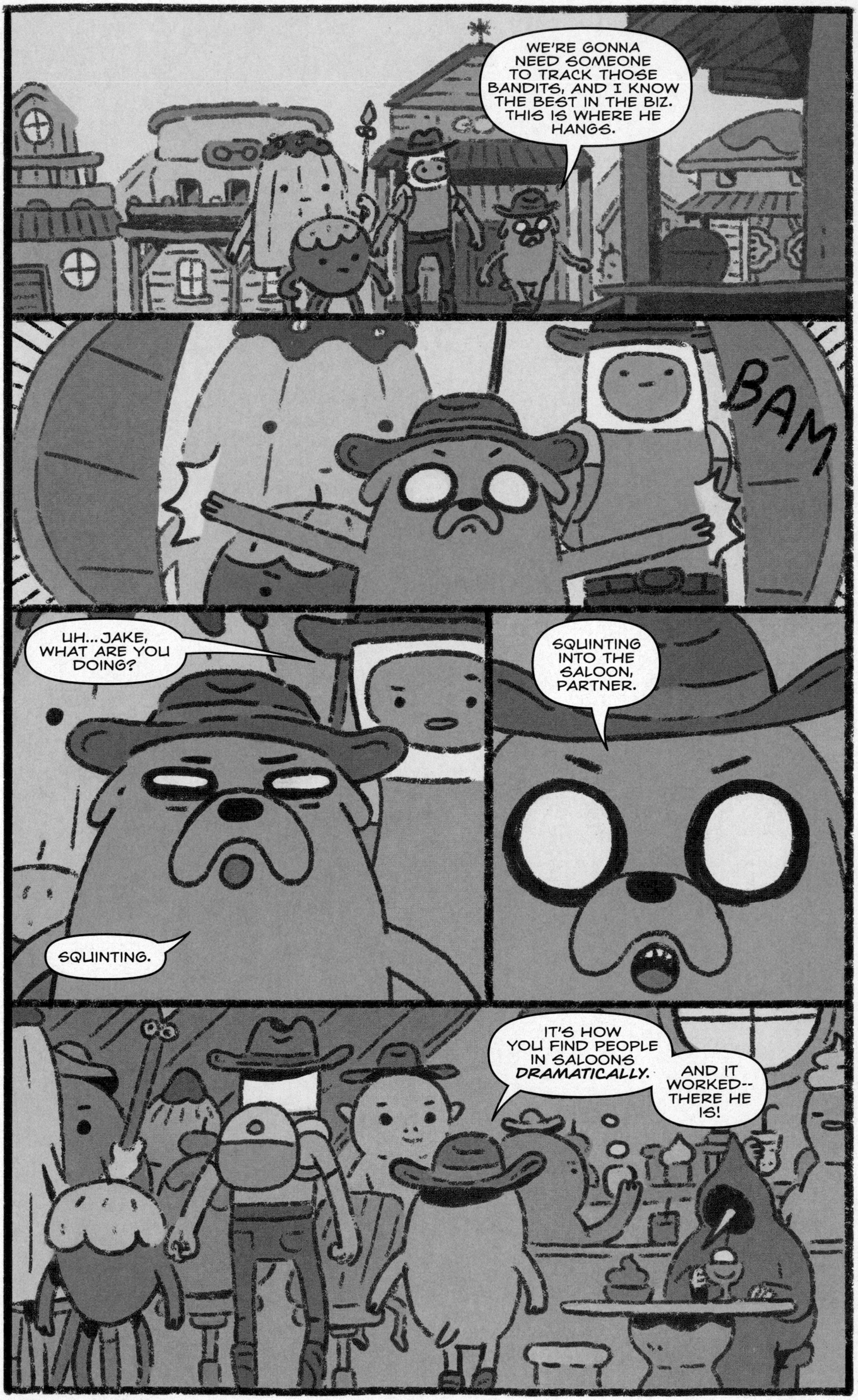
WE'RE GONNA NEED SOMEONE TO TRACK THOSE BANDITS, AND I KNOW THE BEST IN THE BIZ. THIS IS WHERE HE HANGS.
BAM
UH... JAKE, WHAT ARE YOU DOING?
SQUINTING.
SQUINTING INTO THE SALOON, PARTNER.
IT'S HOW YOU FIND PEOPLE IN SALOONS *DRAMATICALLY*.
AND IT WORKED-- THERE HE IS!

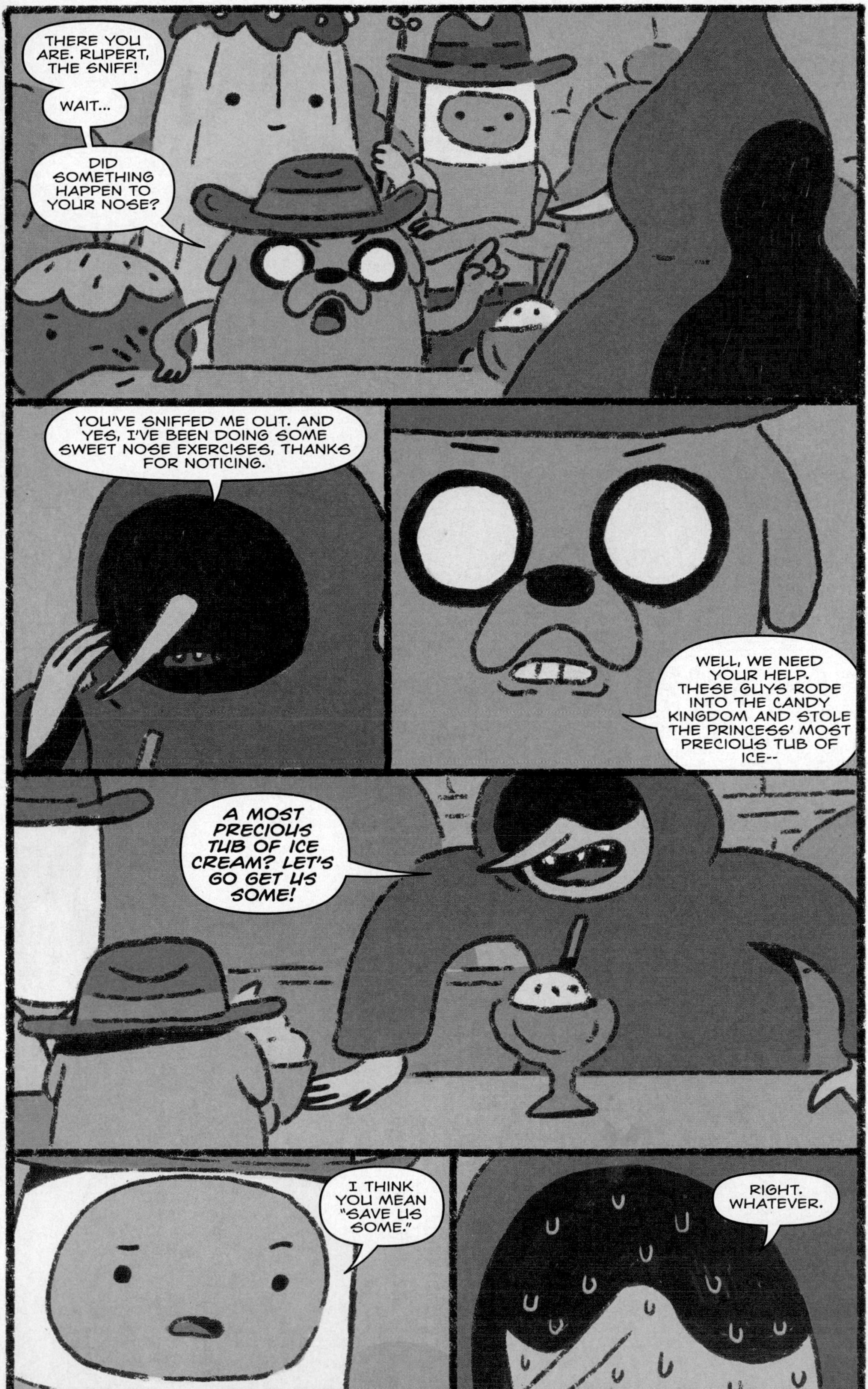
THERE YOU ARE. RUPERT, THE SNIFF!
WAIT...
DID SOMETHING HAPPEN TO YOUR NOSE?
YOU'VE SNIFFED ME OUT. AND YES, I'VE BEEN DOING SOME SWEET NOSE EXERCISES, THANKS FOR NOTICING.
WELL, WE NEED YOUR HELP. THESE GUYS RODE INTO THE CANDY KINGDOM AND STOLE THE PRINCESS' MOST PRECIOUS TUB OF ICE--
A MOST PRECIOUS TUB OF ICE CREAM? LET'S GO GET US SOME!
I THINK YOU MEAN "SAVE US SOME."
RIGHT. WHATEVER.

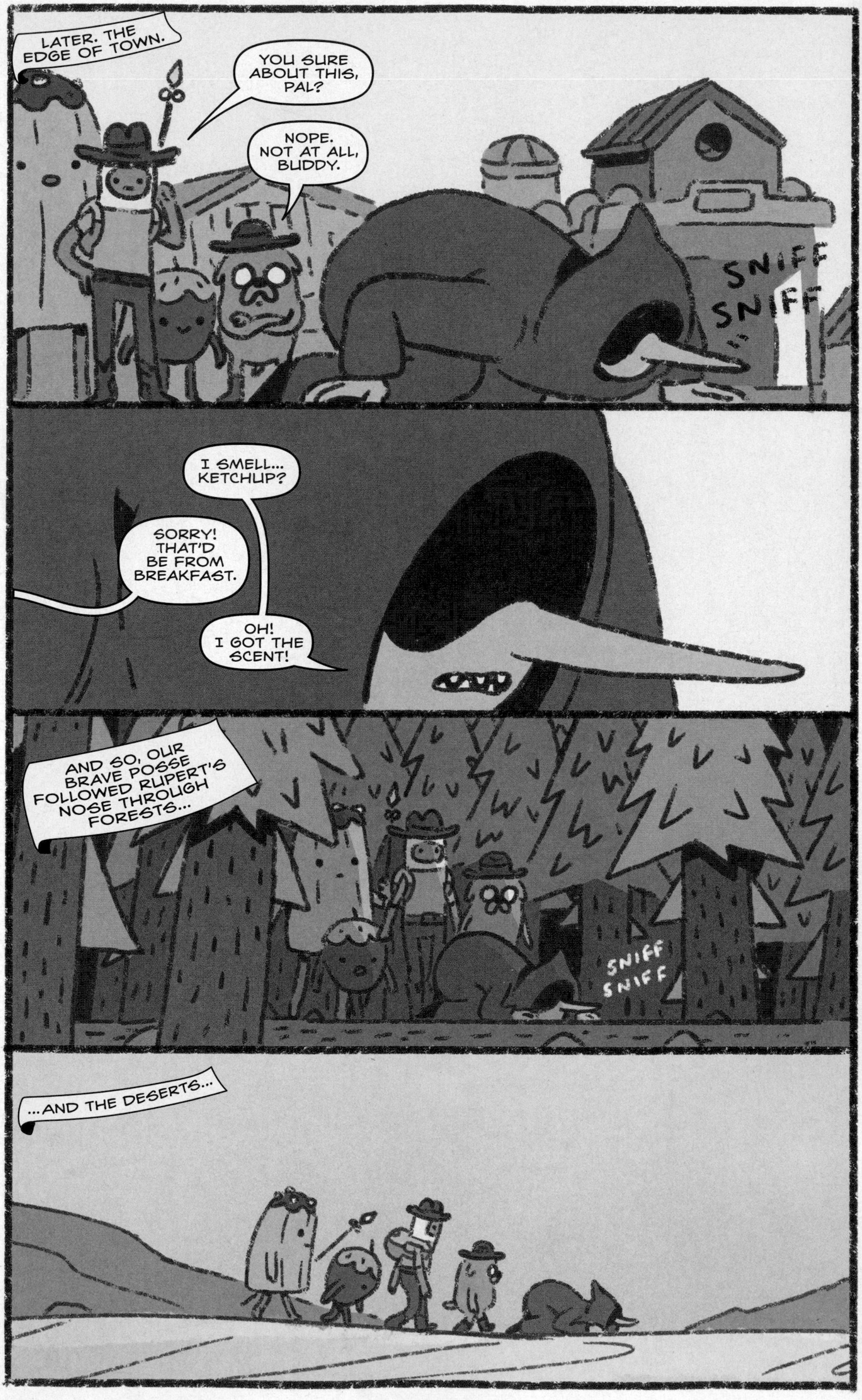
LATER. THE EDGE OF TOWN.
YOU SURE ABOUT THIS, PAL?
NOPE. NOT AT ALL, BUDDY.
SNIFF SNIFF
I SMELL... KETCHUP?
SORRY! THAT'D BE FROM BREAKFAST.
OH! I GOT THE SCENT!
AND SO, OUR BRAVE POSSE FOLLOWED RUPERT'S NOSE THROUGH FORESTS...
SNIFF SNIFF
...AND THE DESERTS...

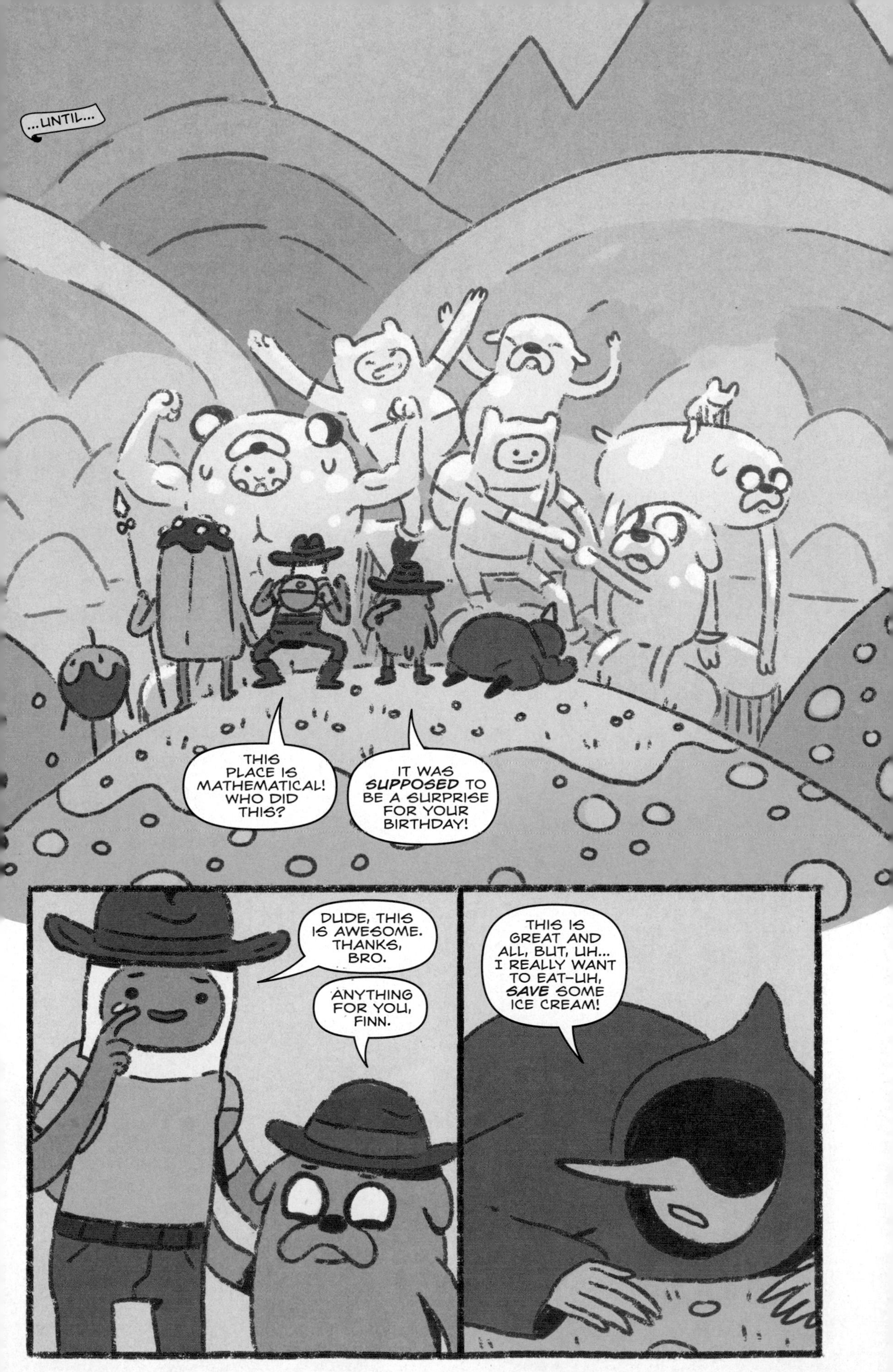

...UNTIL...
THIS PLACE IS MATHEMATICAL! WHO DID THIS?
IT WAS **SUPPOSED** TO BE A SURPRISE FOR YOUR BIRTHDAY!
DUDE, THIS IS AWESOME. THANKS, BRO.
ANYTHING FOR YOU, FINN.
THIS IS GREAT AND ALL, BUT, UH... I REALLY WANT TO EAT-UH, **SAVE** SOME ICE CREAM!

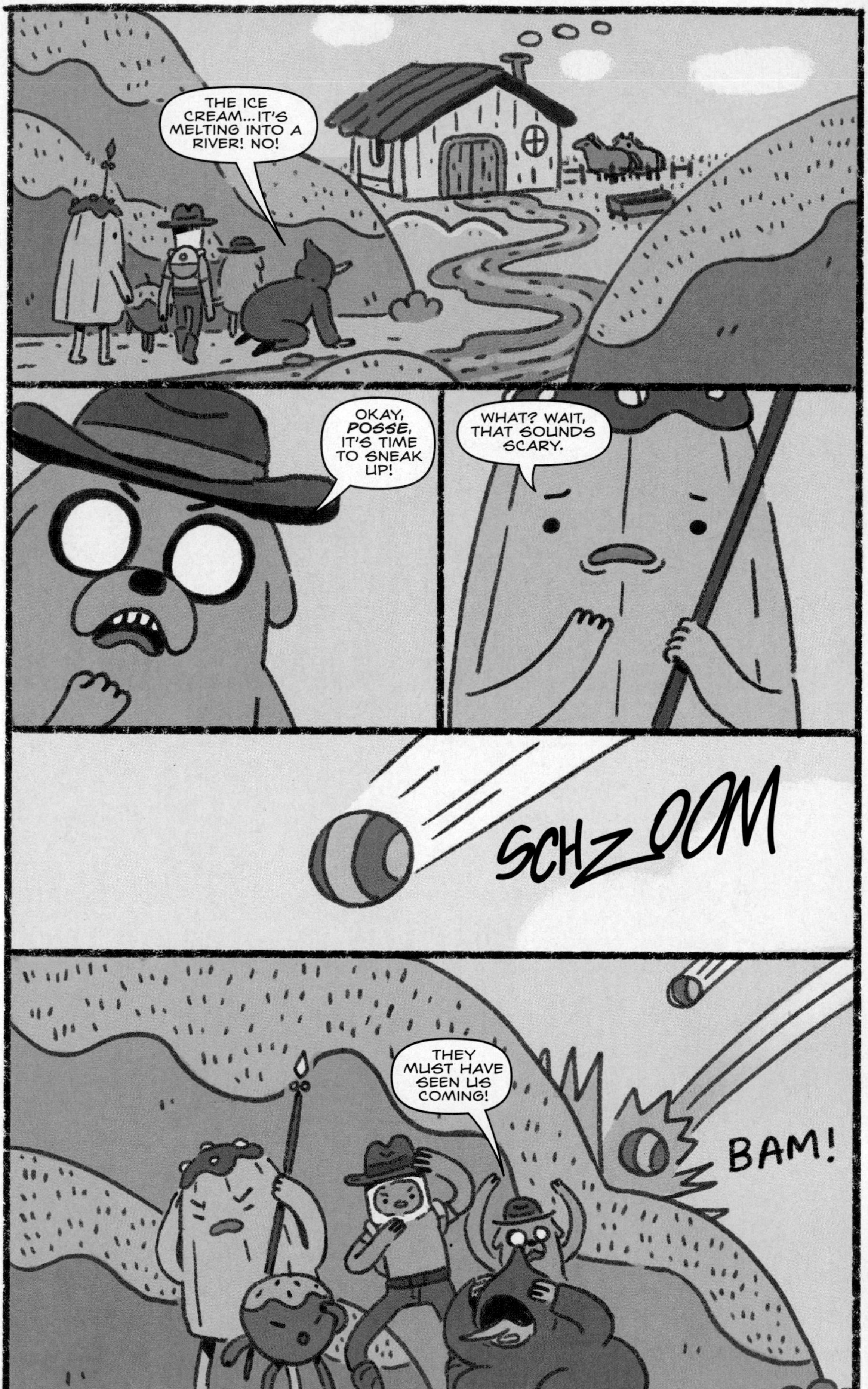
THE ICE CREAM...IT'S MELTING INTO A RIVER! NO!
OKAY, POSSE, IT'S TIME TO SNEAK UP!
WHAT? WAIT, THAT SOUNDS SCARY.
SCHZOOM
THEY MUST HAVE SEEN US COMING!
BAM!

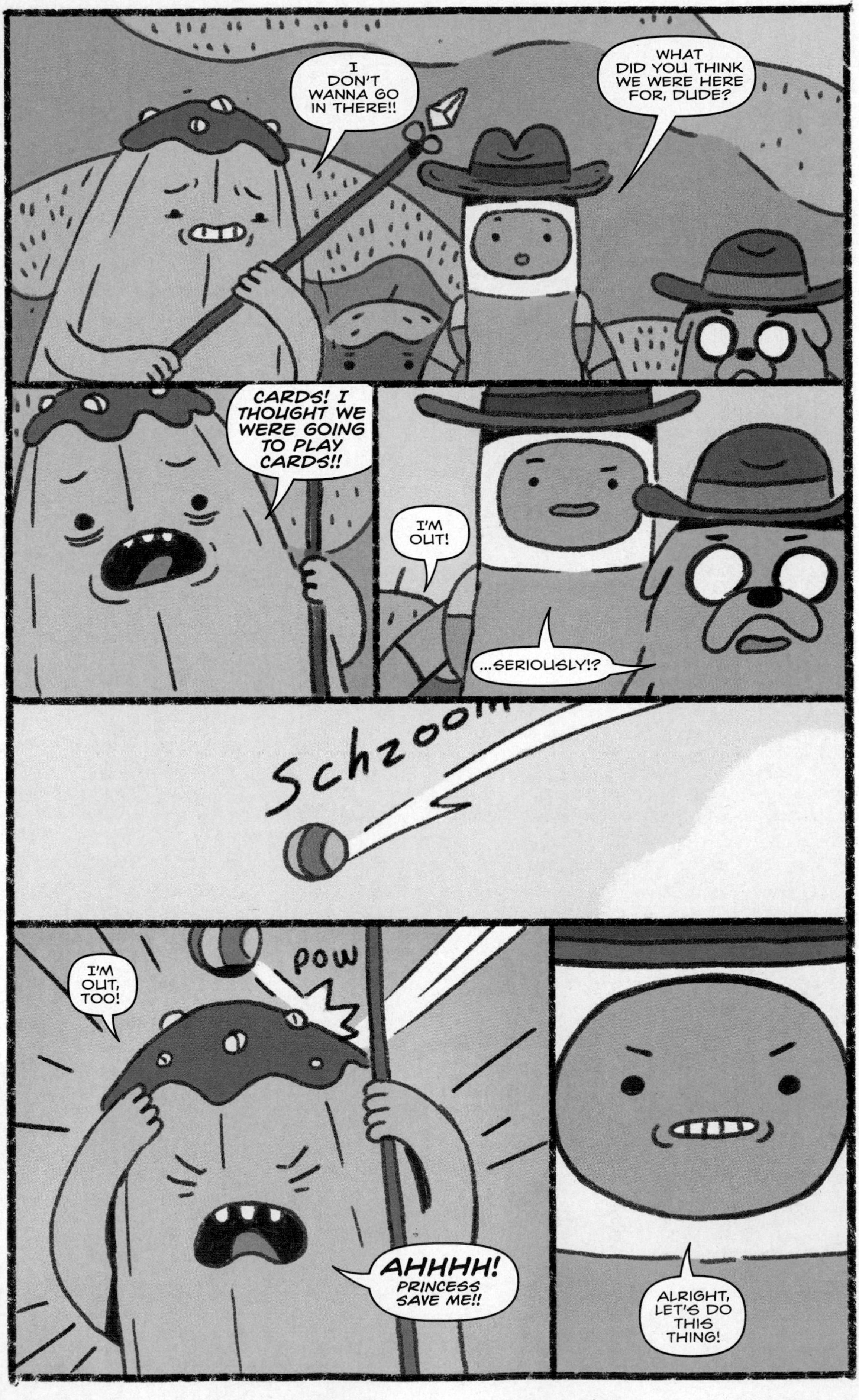
I DON'T WANNA GO IN THERE!!
WHAT DID YOU THINK WE WERE HERE FOR, DUDE?
CARDS! I THOUGHT WE WERE GOING TO PLAY CARDS!!
I'M OUT!
...SERIOUSLY!?
Schzoom
I'M OUT, TOO!
pow
AHHHH! PRINCESS SAVE ME!!
ALRIGHT, LET'S DO THIS THING!

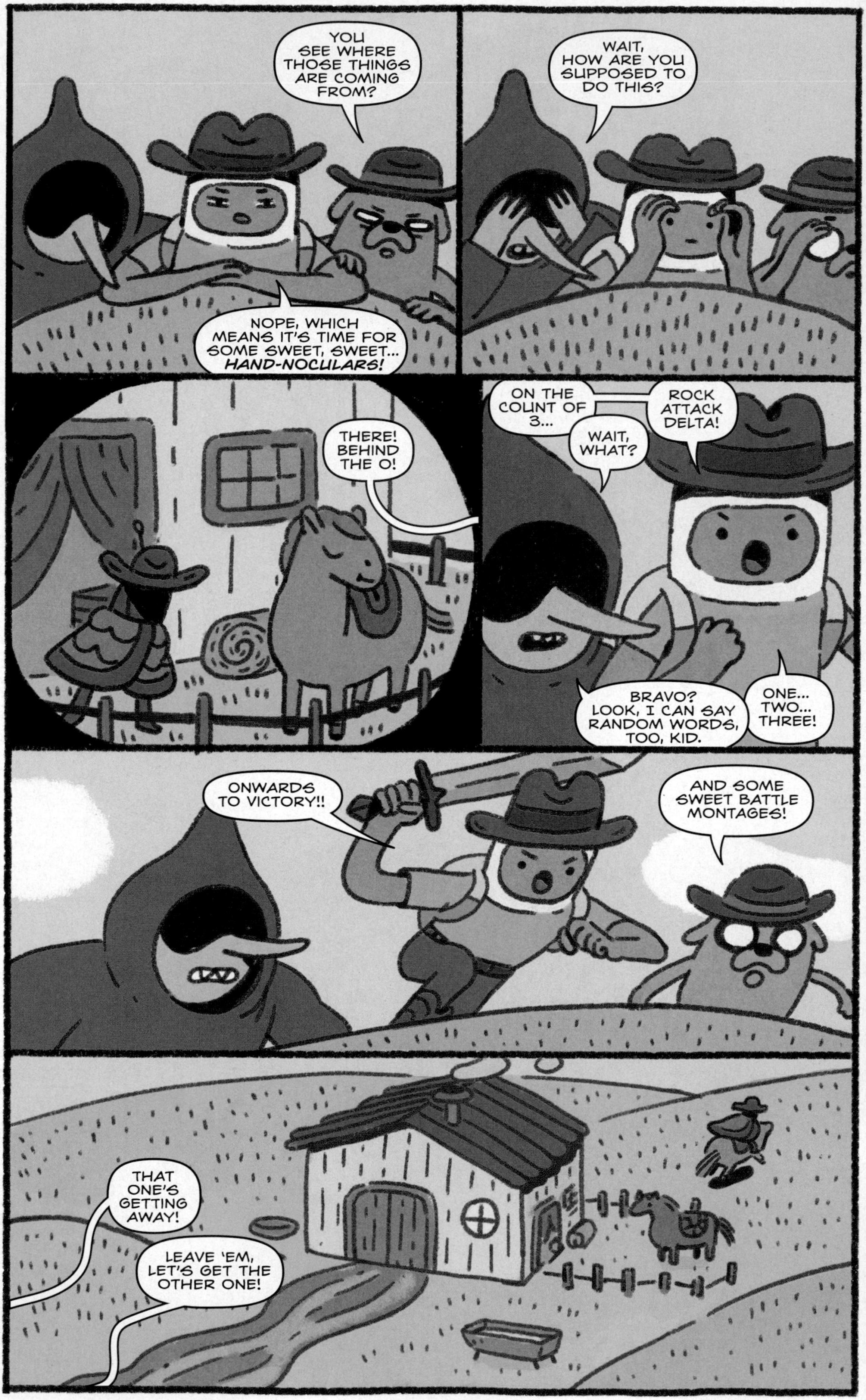
YOU SEE WHERE THOSE THINGS ARE COMING FROM?
NOPE, WHICH MEANS IT'S TIME FOR SOME SWEET, SWEET... *HAND-NOCULARS!*
WAIT, HOW ARE YOU SUPPOSED TO DO THIS?
THERE! BEHIND THE O!
ON THE COUNT OF 3...
ROCK ATTACK DELTA!
WAIT, WHAT?
BRAVO? LOOK, I CAN SAY RANDOM WORDS, TOO, KID.
ONE... TWO... THREE!
ONWARDS TO VICTORY!!
AND SOME SWEET BATTLE MONTAGES!
THAT ONE'S GETTING AWAY!
LEAVE 'EM, LET'S GET THE OTHER ONE!

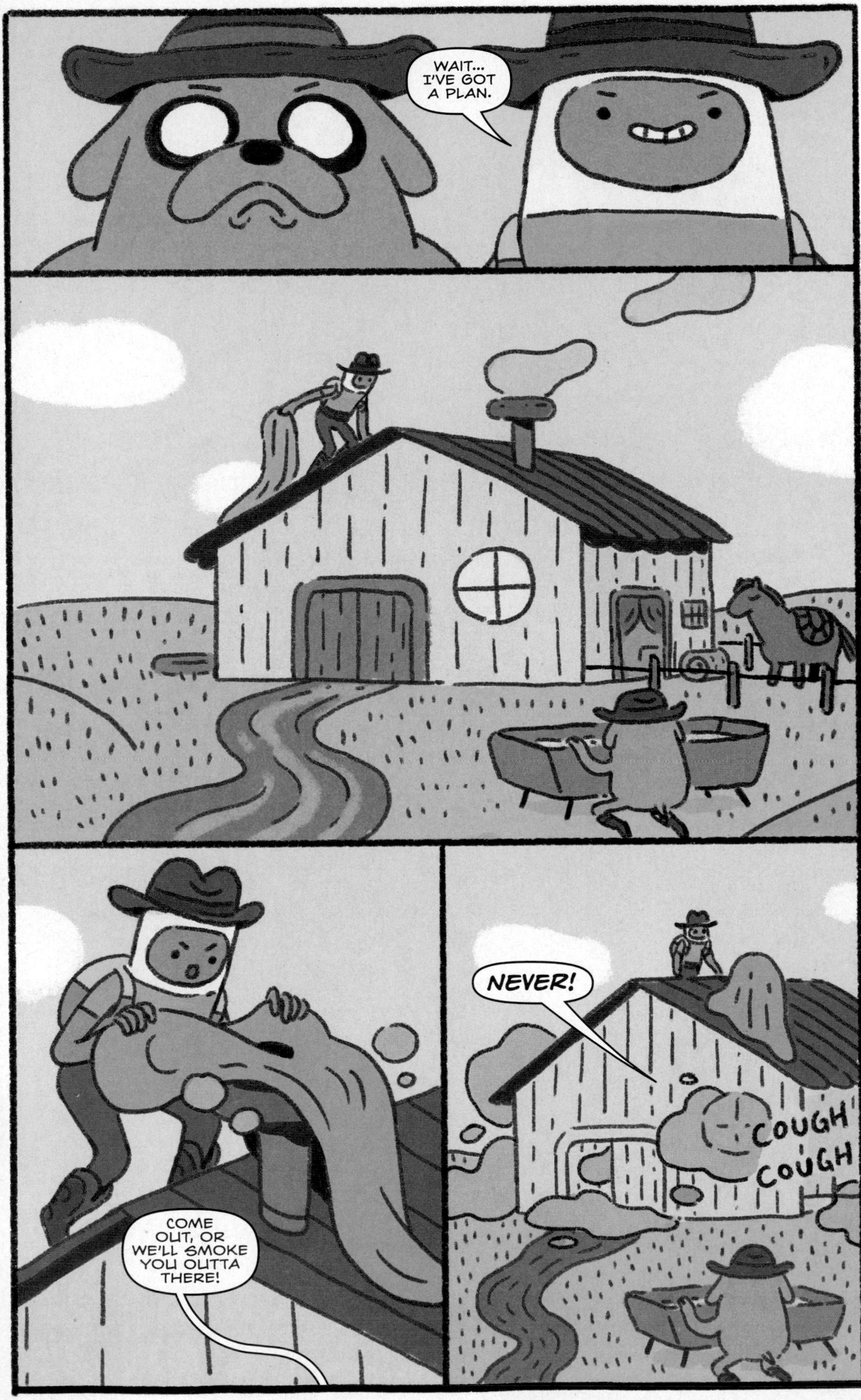
WAIT... I'VE GOT A PLAN.
COME OUT, OR WE'LL SMOKE YOU OUTTA THERE!
NEVER!
COUGH
COUGH

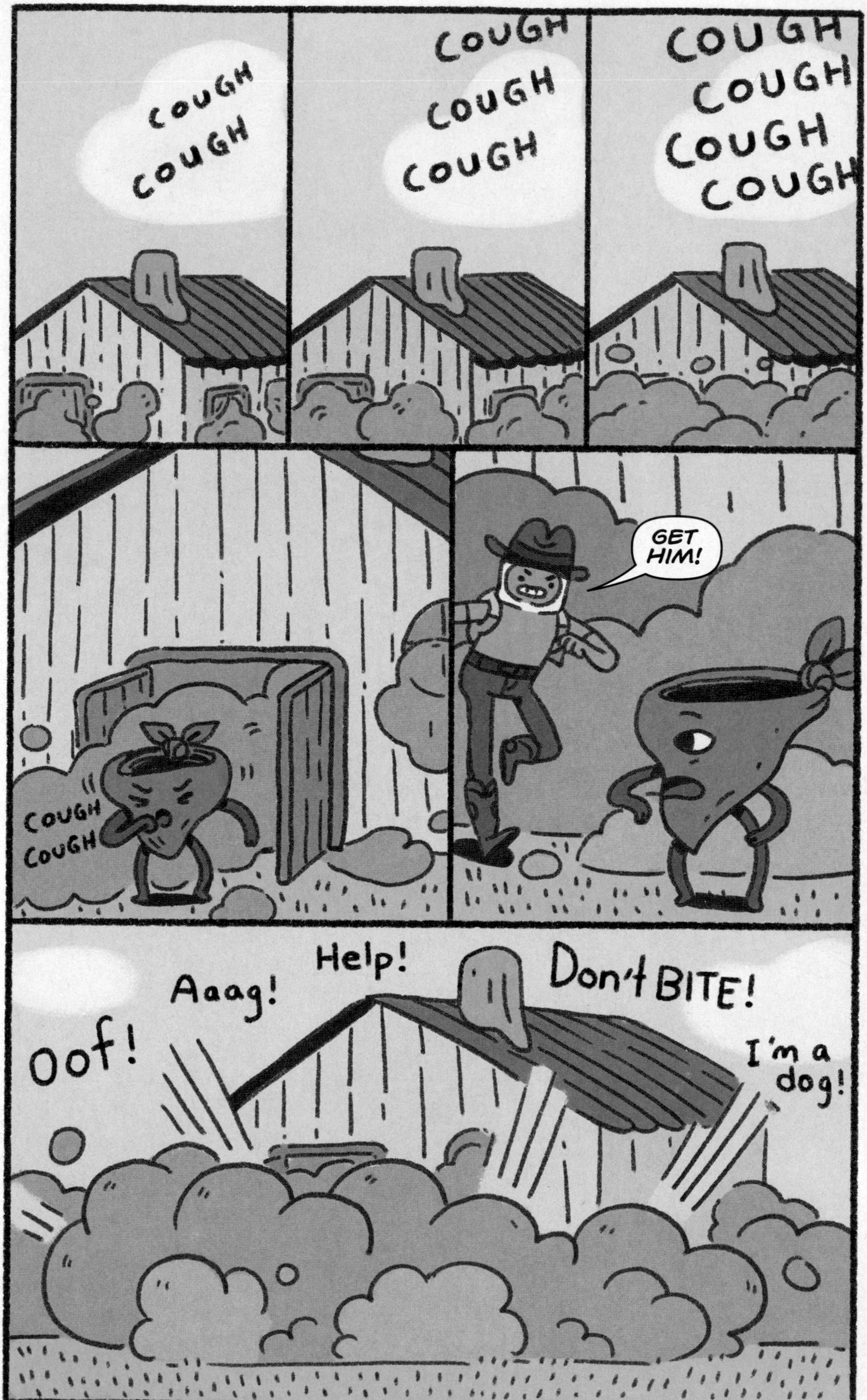
COUGH
COUGH
COUGH
COUGH
COUGH
COUGH
COUGH
COUGH
COUGH
COUGH
COUGH
GET HIM!
Oof!
Aaag!
Help!
Don't BITE!
I'm a dog!

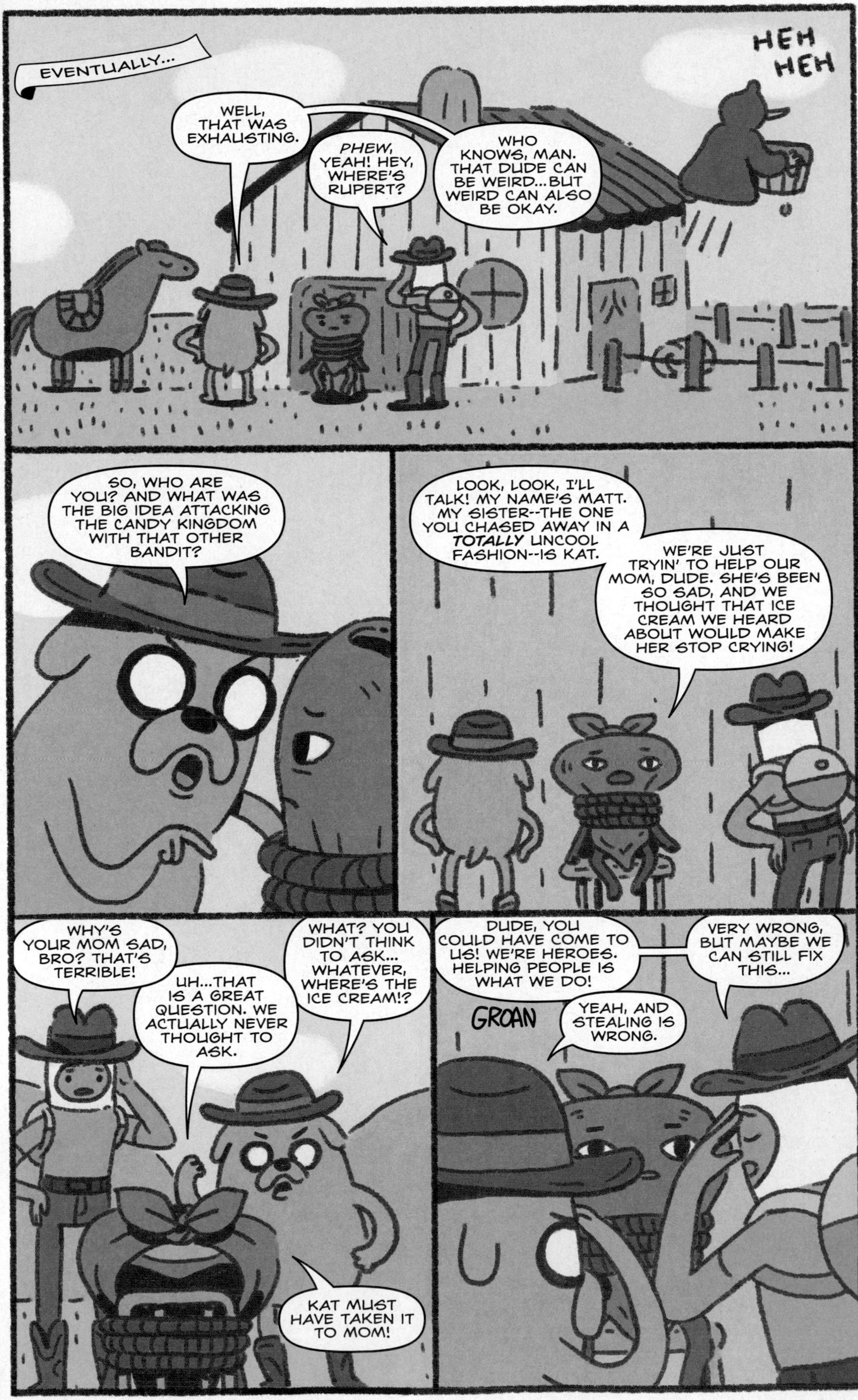
EVENTUALLY...
HEH HEH
WELL, THAT WAS EXHAUSTING.
PHEW, YEAH! HEY, WHERE'S RUPERT?
WHO KNOWS, MAN. THAT DUDE CAN BE WEIRD...BUT WEIRD CAN ALSO BE OKAY.
SO, WHO ARE YOU? AND WHAT WAS THE BIG IDEA ATTACKING THE CANDY KINGDOM WITH THAT OTHER BANDIT?
LOOK, LOOK, I'LL TALK! MY NAME'S MATT. MY SISTER--THE ONE YOU CHASED AWAY IN A TOTALLY UNCOOL FASHION--IS KAT.
WE'RE JUST TRYIN' TO HELP OUR MOM, DUDE. SHE'S BEEN SO SAD, AND WE THOUGHT THAT ICE CREAM WE HEARD ABOUT WOULD MAKE HER STOP CRYING!
WHY'S YOUR MOM SAD, BRO? THAT'S TERRIBLE!
UH...THAT IS A GREAT QUESTION. WE ACTUALLY NEVER THOUGHT TO ASK.
WHAT? YOU DIDN'T THINK TO ASK... WHATEVER, WHERE'S THE ICE CREAM!?
KAT MUST HAVE TAKEN IT TO MOM!
DUDE, YOU COULD HAVE COME TO US! WE'RE HEROES. HELPING PEOPLE IS WHAT WE DO!
VERY WRONG, BUT MAYBE WE CAN STILL FIX THIS...
GROAN
YEAH, AND STEALING IS WRONG.

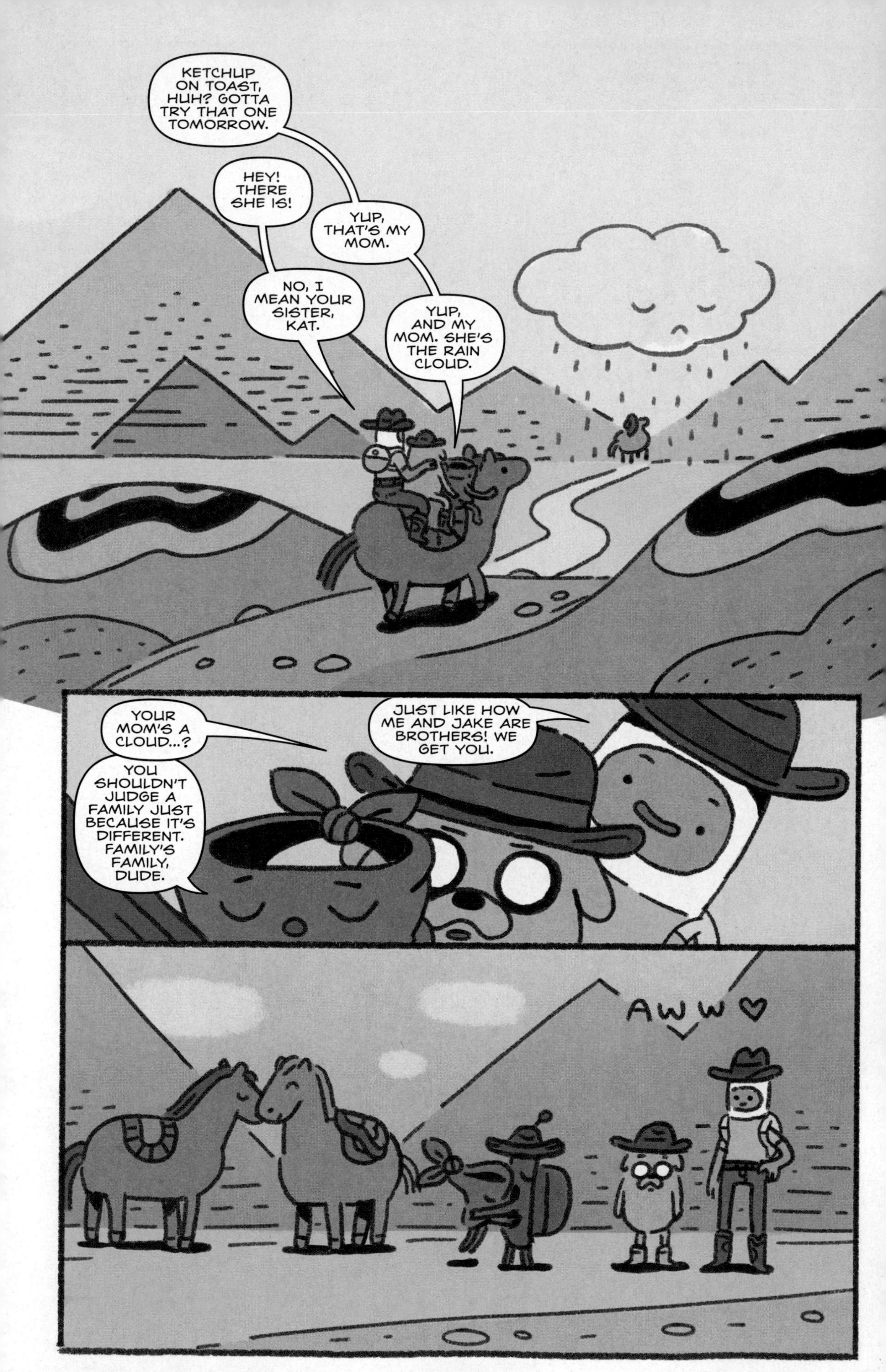
KETCHUP ON TOAST, HUH? GOTTA TRY THAT ONE TOMORROW.
HEY! THERE SHE IS!
YUP, THAT'S MY MOM.
NO, I MEAN YOUR SISTER, KAT.
YUP, AND MY MOM. SHE'S THE RAIN CLOUD.
YOUR MOM'S A CLOUD...?
JUST LIKE HOW ME AND JAKE ARE BROTHERS! WE GET YOU.
YOU SHOULDN'T JUDGE A FAMILY JUST BECAUSE IT'S DIFFERENT. FAMILY'S FAMILY, DUDE.
AWW ♡

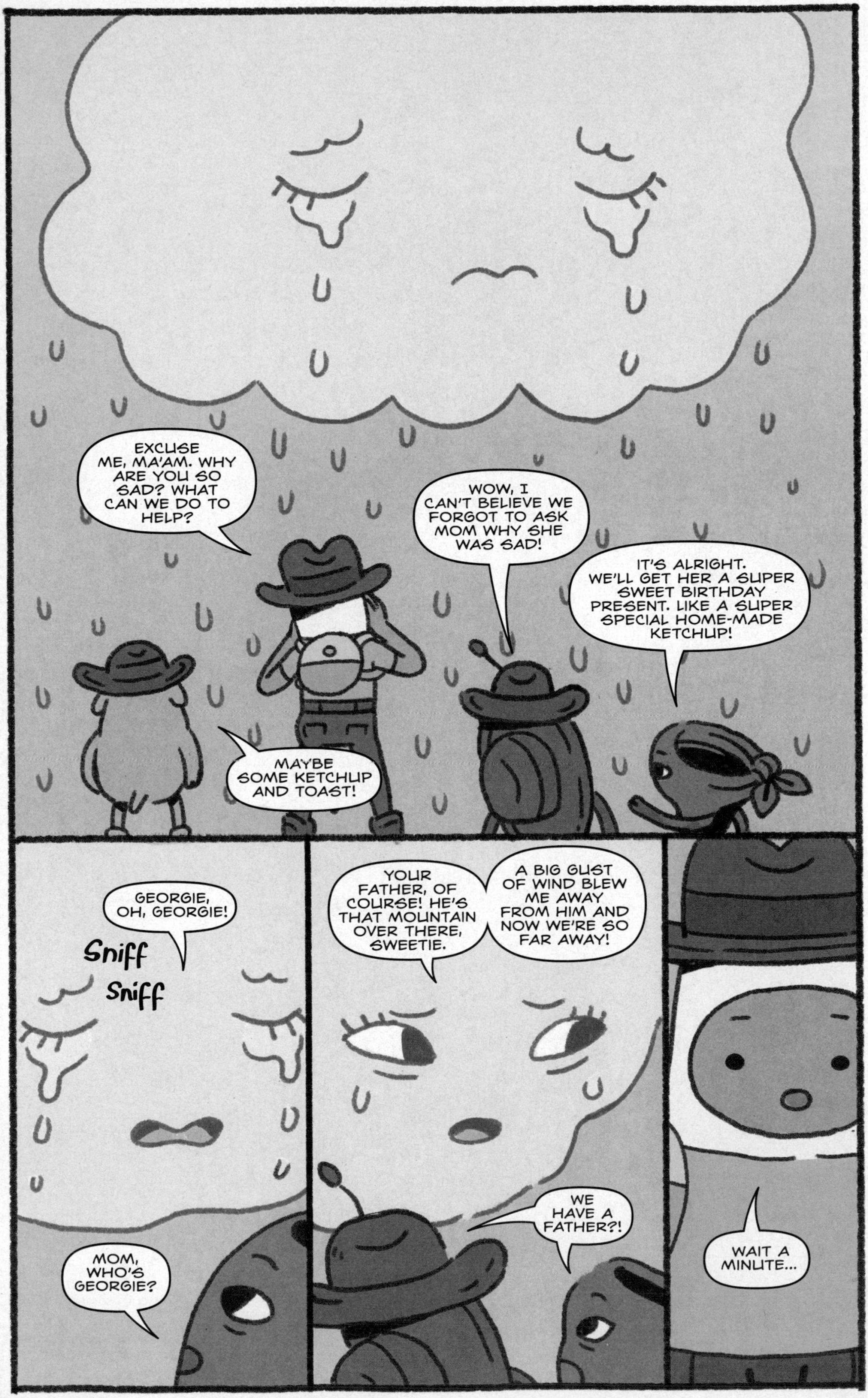
EXCUSE ME, MA'AM. WHY ARE YOU SO SAD? WHAT CAN WE DO TO HELP?
WOW, I CAN'T BELIEVE WE FORGOT TO ASK MOM WHY SHE WAS SAD!
IT'S ALRIGHT. WE'LL GET HER A SUPER SWEET BIRTHDAY PRESENT. LIKE A SUPER SPECIAL HOME-MADE KETCHUP!
MAYBE SOME KETCHUP AND TOAST!
GEORGIE, OH, GEORGIE!
Sniff
Sniff
MOM, WHO'S GEORGIE?
YOUR FATHER, OF COURSE! HE'S THAT MOUNTAIN OVER THERE, SWEETIE.
A BIG GUST OF WIND BLEW ME AWAY FROM HIM AND NOW WE'RE SO FAR AWAY!
WE HAVE A FATHER?!
WAIT A MINUTE...

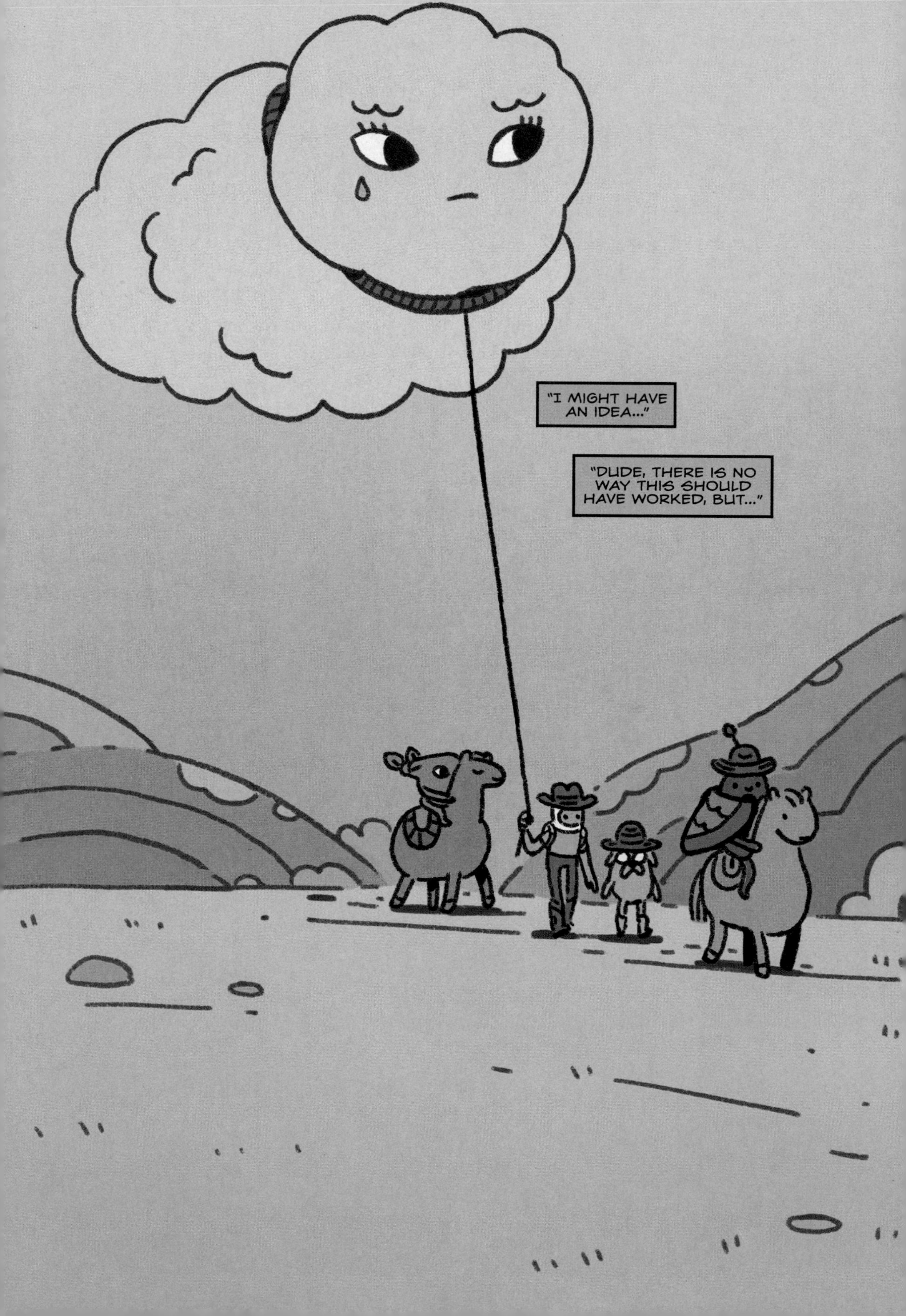
"I MIGHT HAVE AN IDEA..."
"DUDE, THERE IS NO WAY THIS SHOULD HAVE WORKED, BUT..."

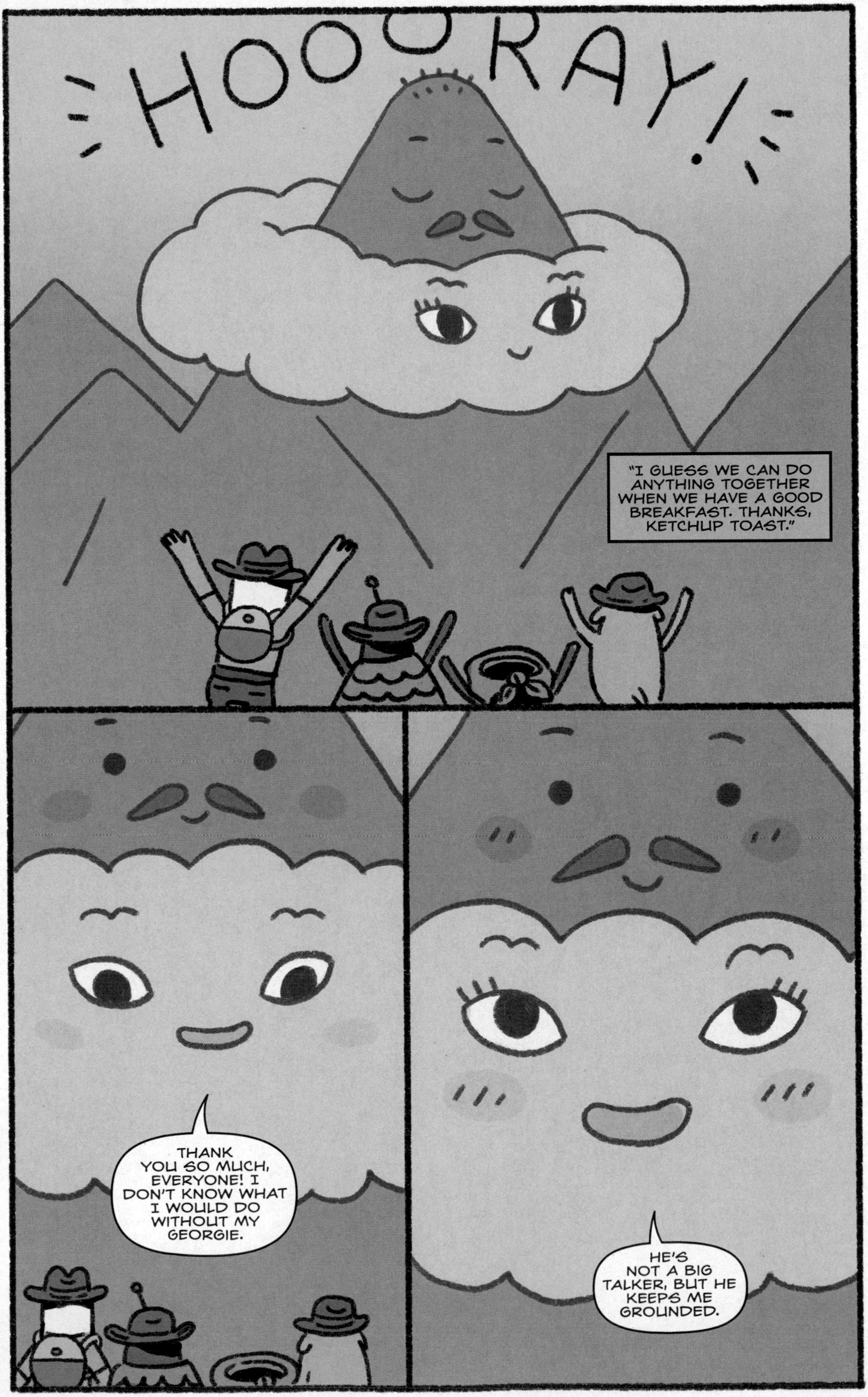
HOOORAY!
"I GUESS WE CAN DO ANYTHING TOGETHER WHEN WE HAVE A GOOD BREAKFAST. THANKS, KETCHUP TOAST."
THANK YOU SO MUCH, EVERYONE! I DON'T KNOW WHAT I WOULD DO WITHOUT MY GEORGIE.
HE'S NOT A BIG TALKER, BUT HE KEEPS ME GROUNDED.

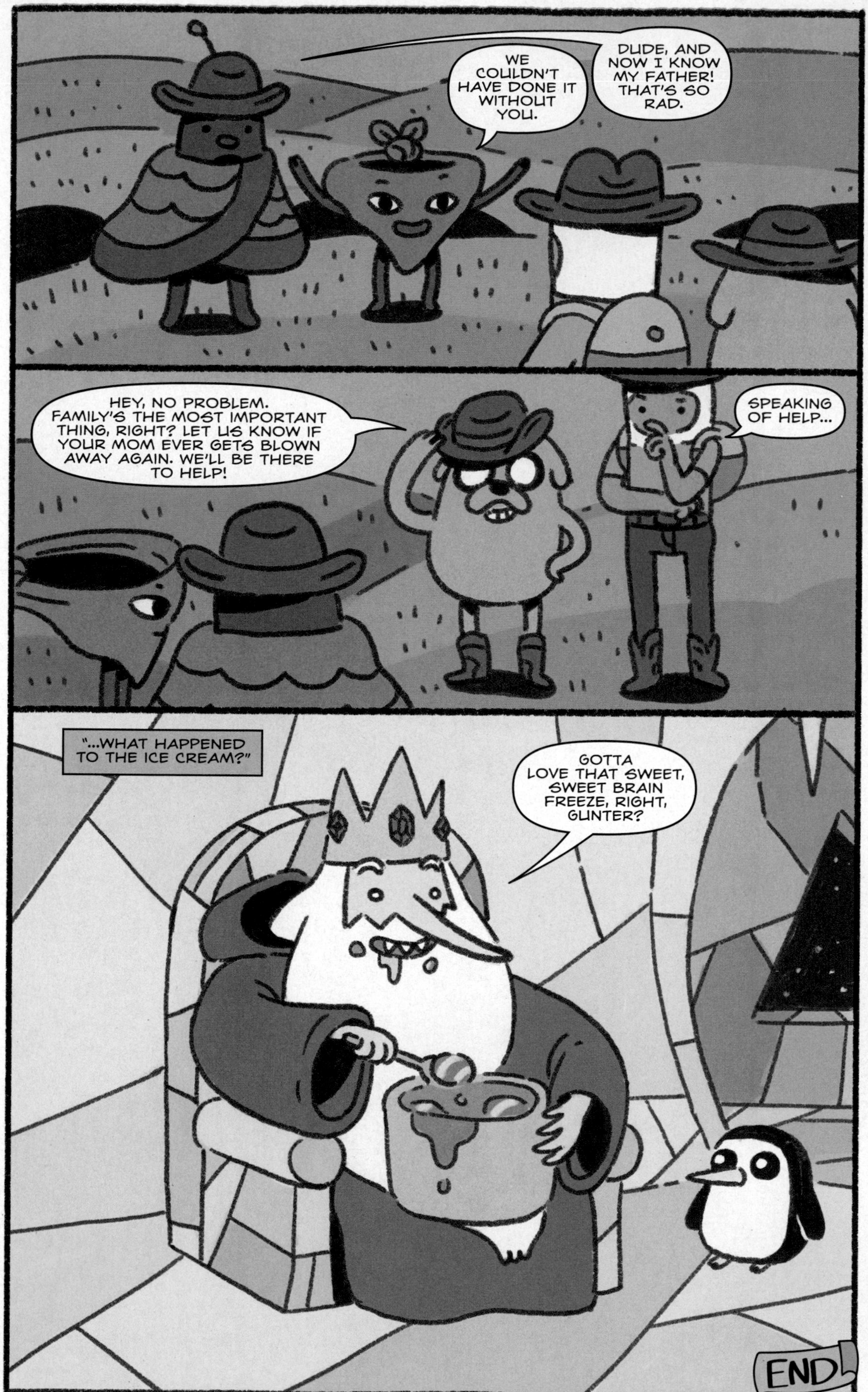
WE COULDN'T HAVE DONE IT WITHOUT YOU.
DUDE, AND NOW I KNOW MY FATHER! THAT'S SO RAD.
HEY, NO PROBLEM. FAMILY'S THE MOST IMPORTANT THING, RIGHT? LET US KNOW IF YOUR MOM EVER GETS BLOWN AWAY AGAIN. WE'LL BE THERE TO HELP!
SPEAKING OF HELP...
"...WHAT HAPPENED TO THE ICE CREAM?"
GOTTA LOVE THAT SWEET, SWEET BRAIN FREEZE, RIGHT, GUNTER?
END

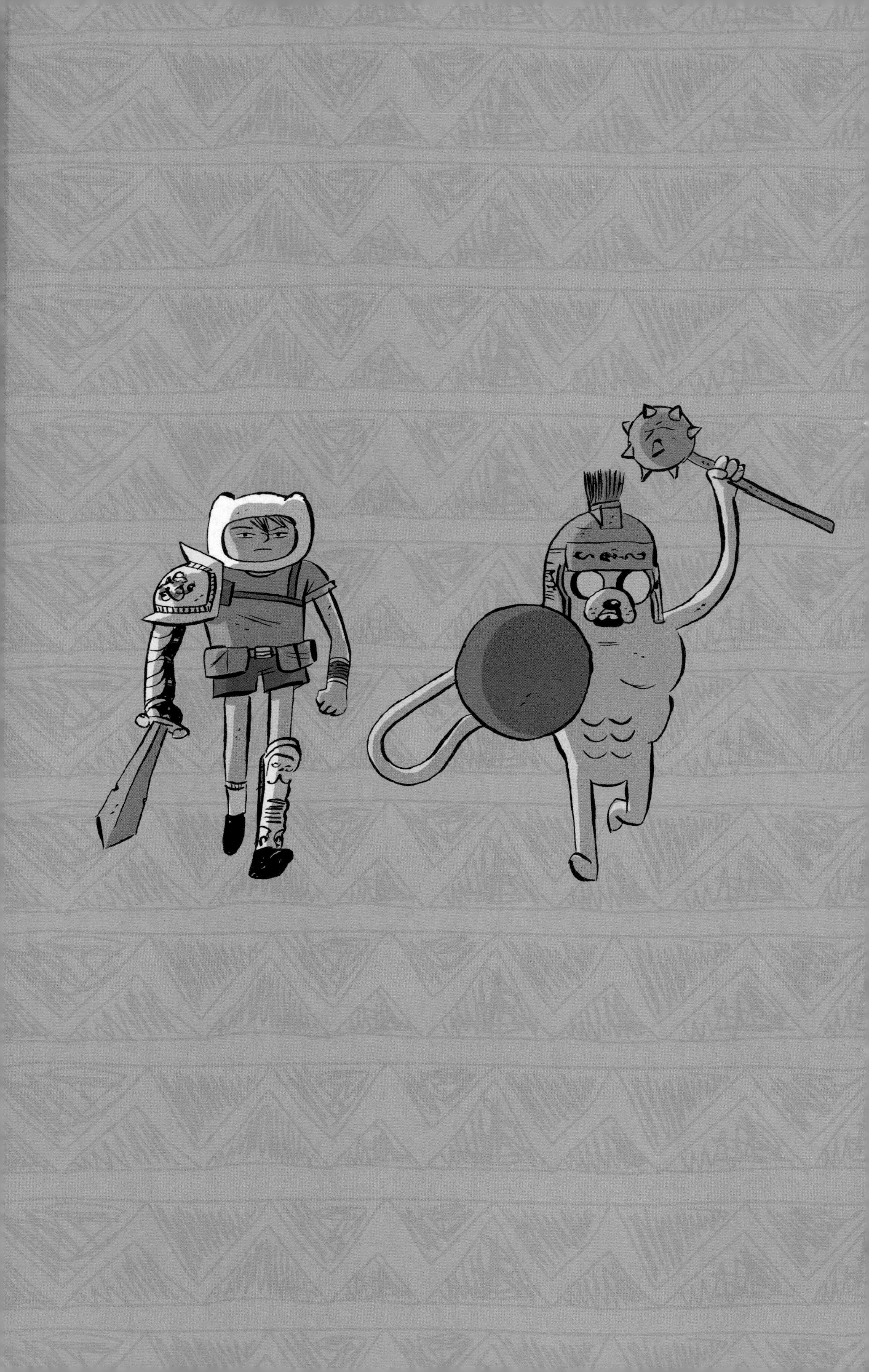

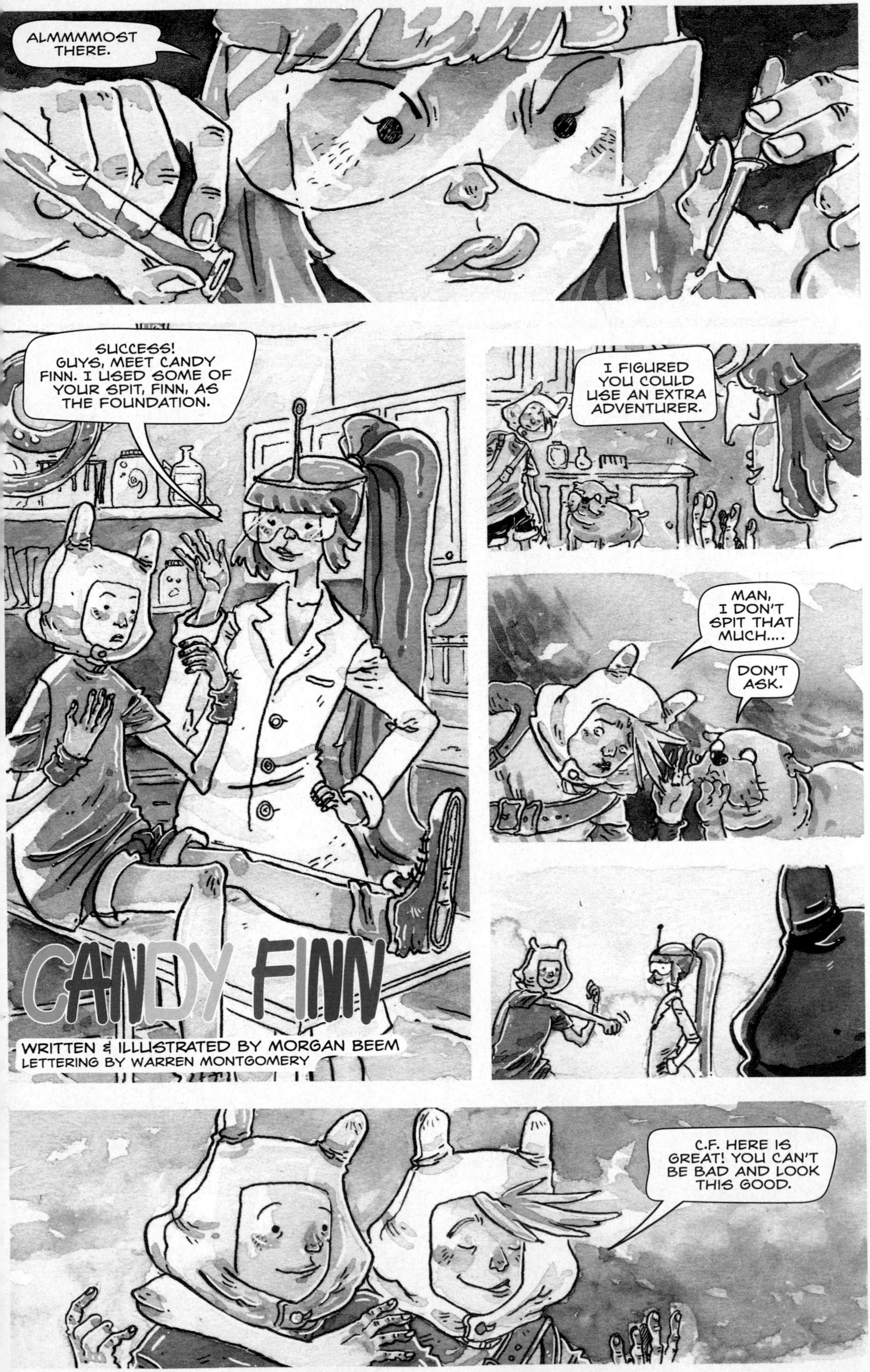
ALMMMMOST THERE.
SUCCESS! GUYS, MEET CANDY FINN. I USED SOME OF YOUR SPIT, FINN, AS THE FOUNDATION.
CANDY FINN
WRITTEN & ILLUSTRATED BY MORGAN BEEM
LETTERING BY WARREN MONTGOMERY
I FIGURED YOU COULD USE AN EXTRA ADVENTURER.
MAN, I DON'T SPIT THAT MUCH....
DON'T ASK.
C.F. HERE IS GREAT! YOU CAN'T BE BAD AND LOOK THIS GOOD.

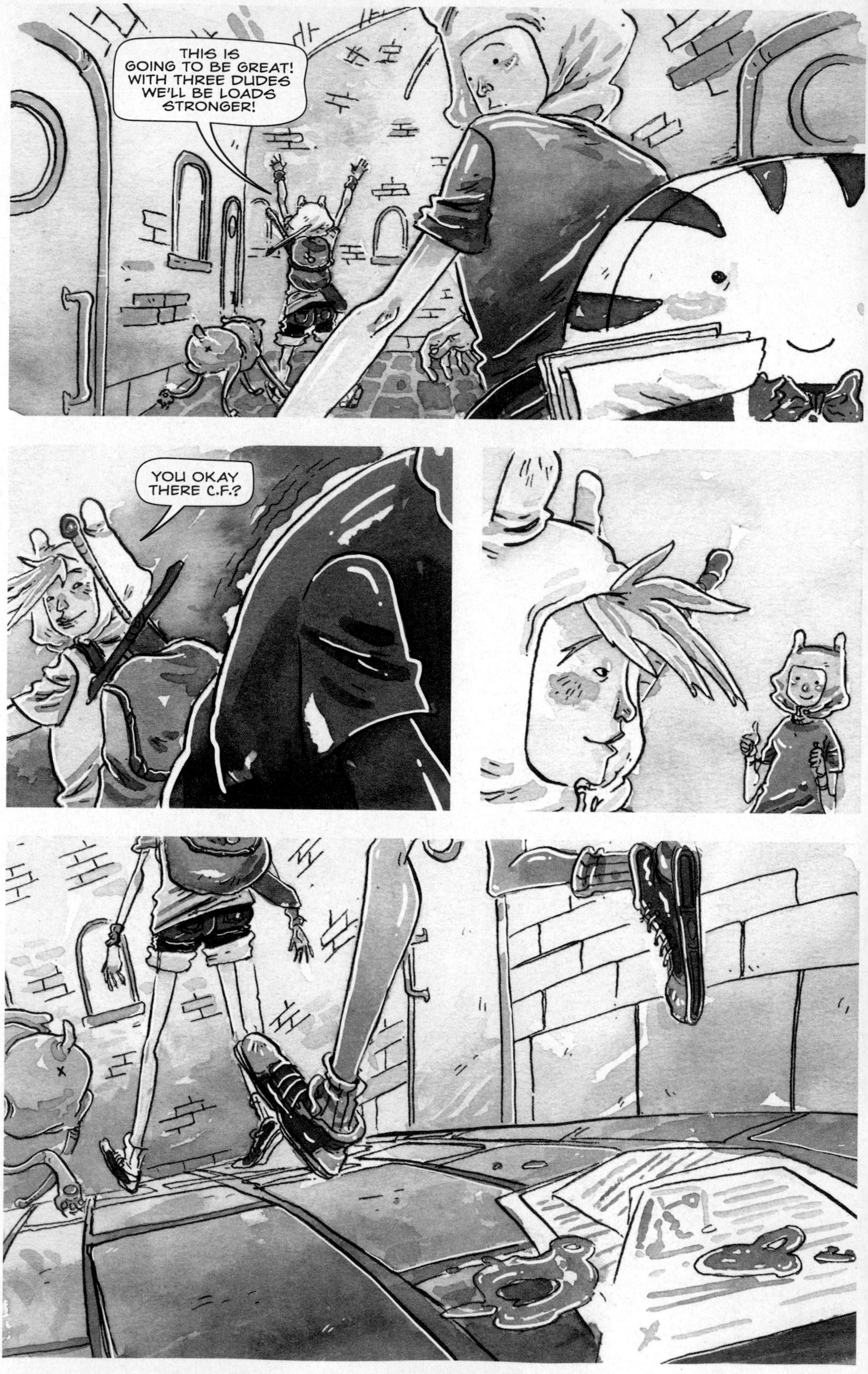
THIS IS GOING TO BE GREAT! WITH THREE DUDES WE'LL BE LOADS STRONGER!
YOU OKAY THERE C.F.?

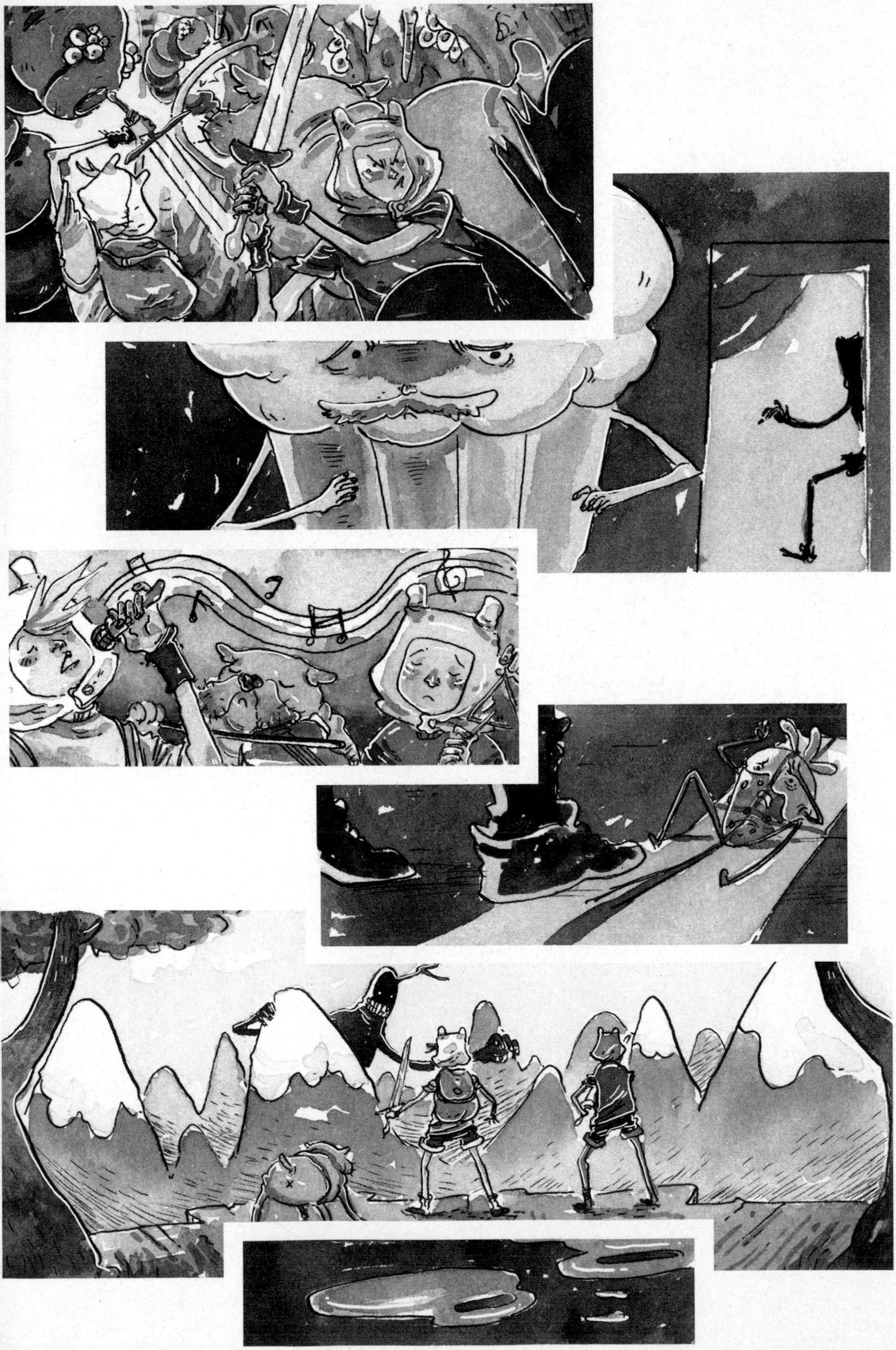

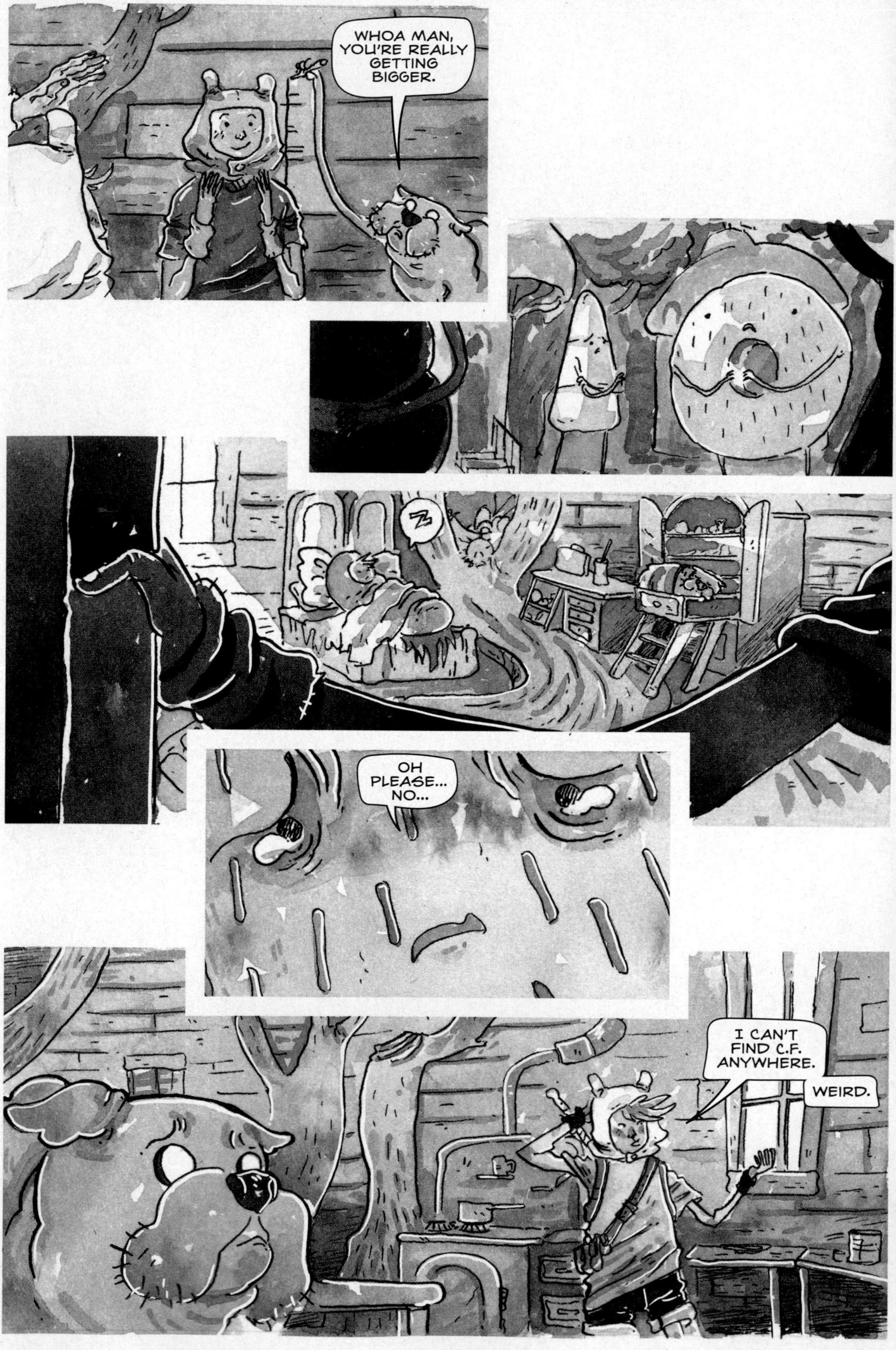
WHOA MAN, YOU'RE REALLY GETTING BIGGER.
Z
OH PLEASE... NO...
I CAN'T FIND C.F. ANYWHERE.
WEIRD.

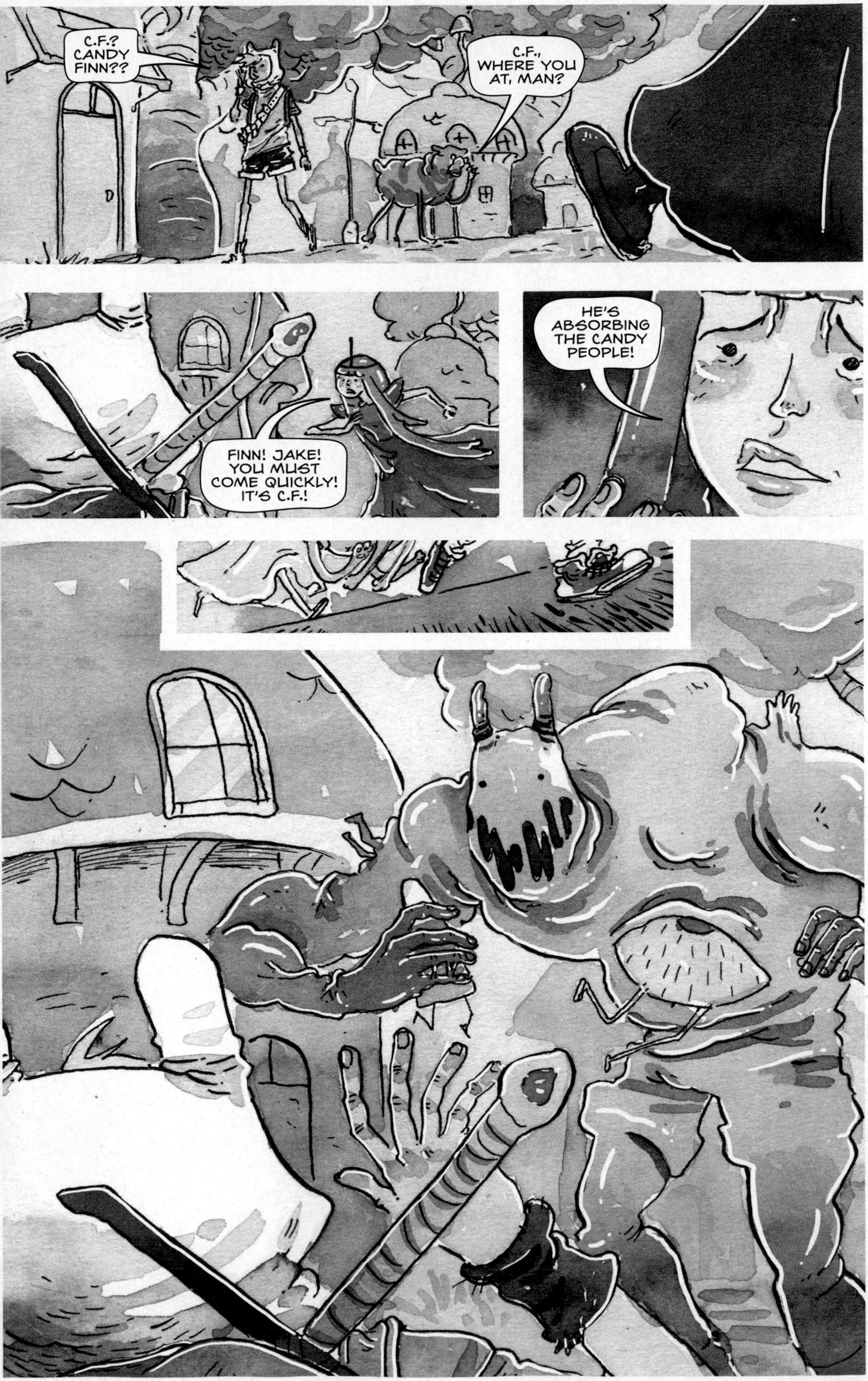
C.F.? CANDY FINN??
C.F., WHERE YOU AT, MAN?
FINN! JAKE! YOU MUST COME QUICKLY! IT'S C.F.!
HE'S ABSORBING THE CANDY PEOPLE!

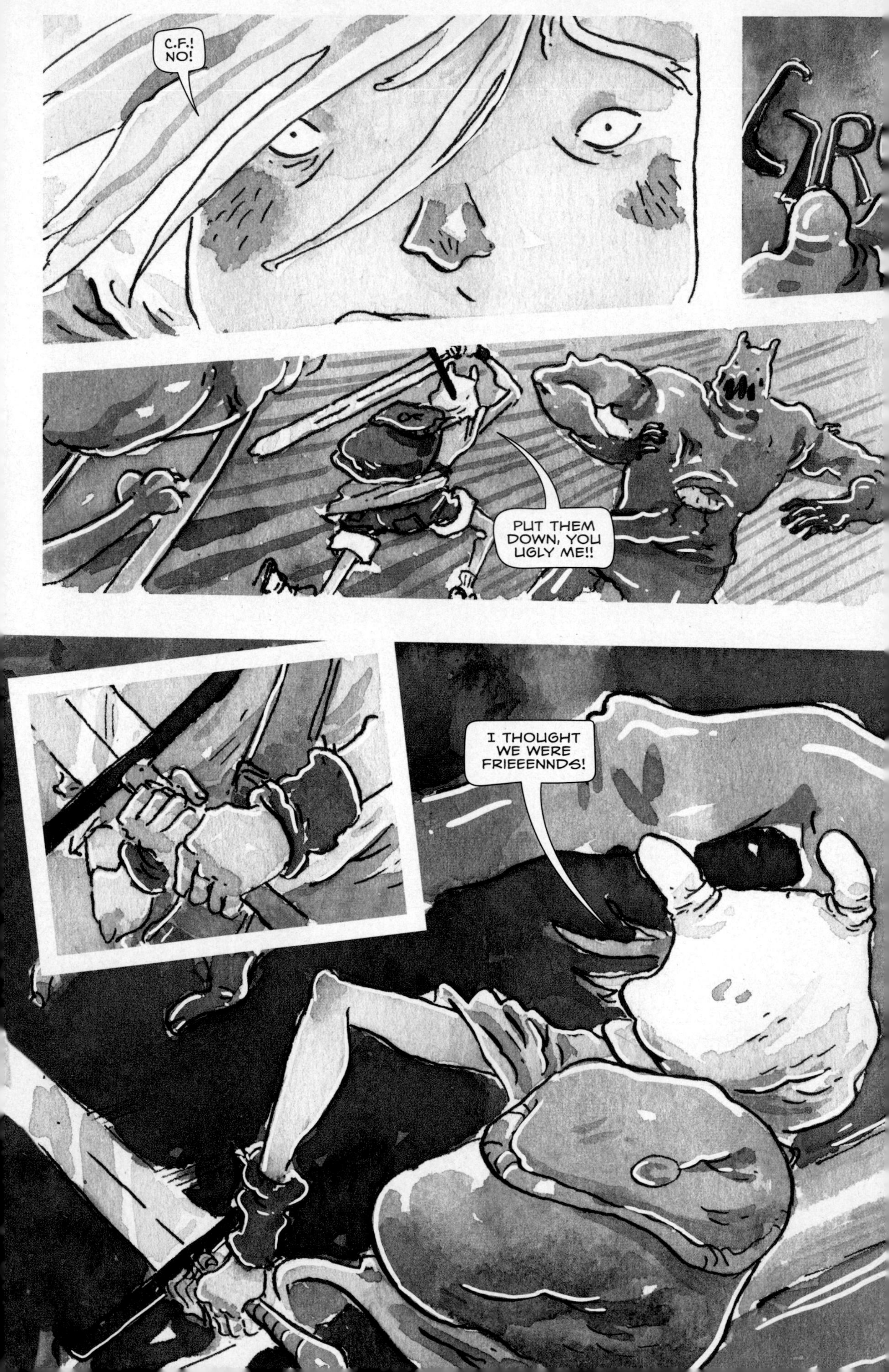
C.F.! NO!
PUT THEM DOWN, YOU UGLY ME!!
I THOUGHT WE WERE FRIEEENNDS!

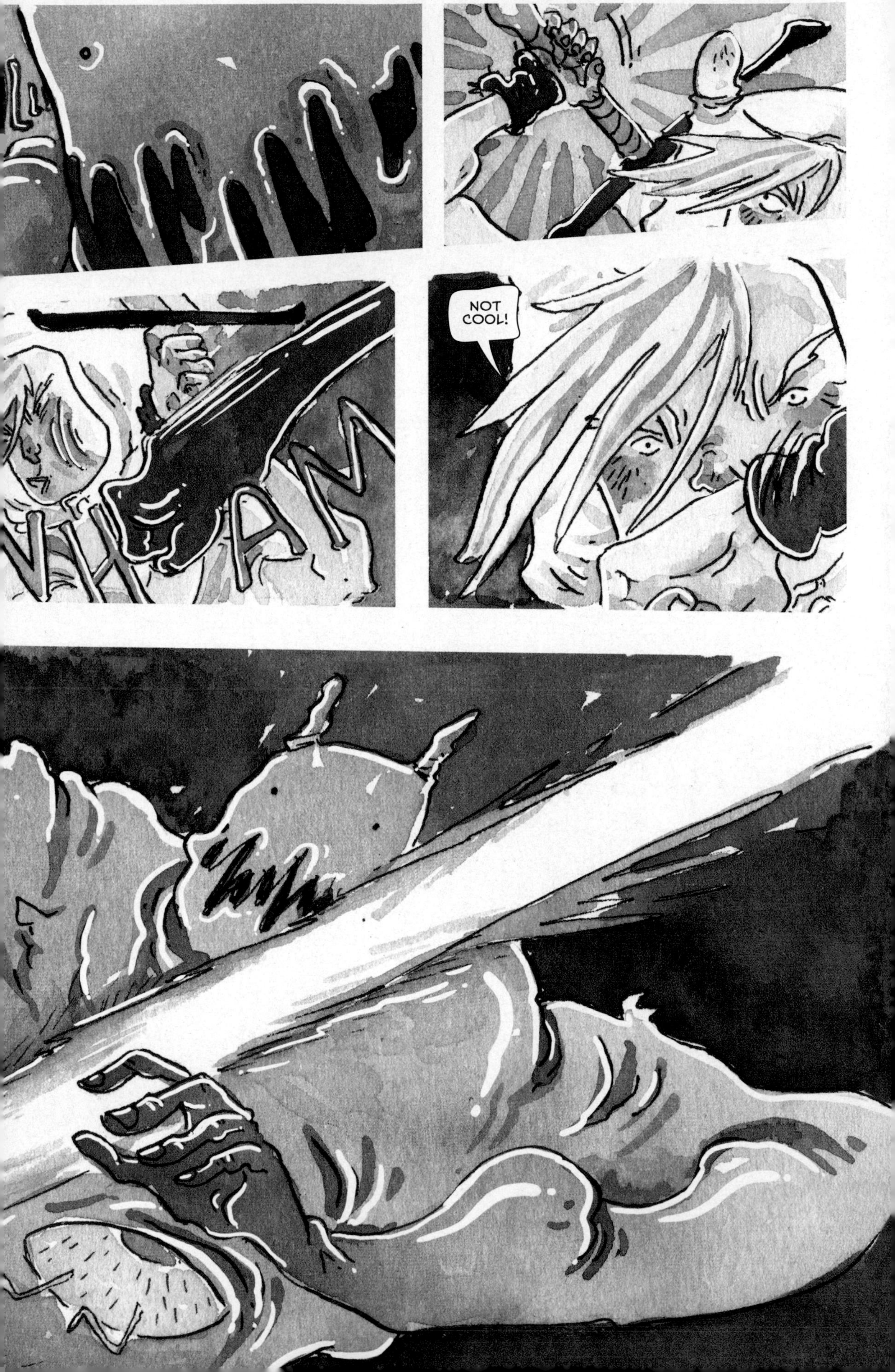
NOT COOL!

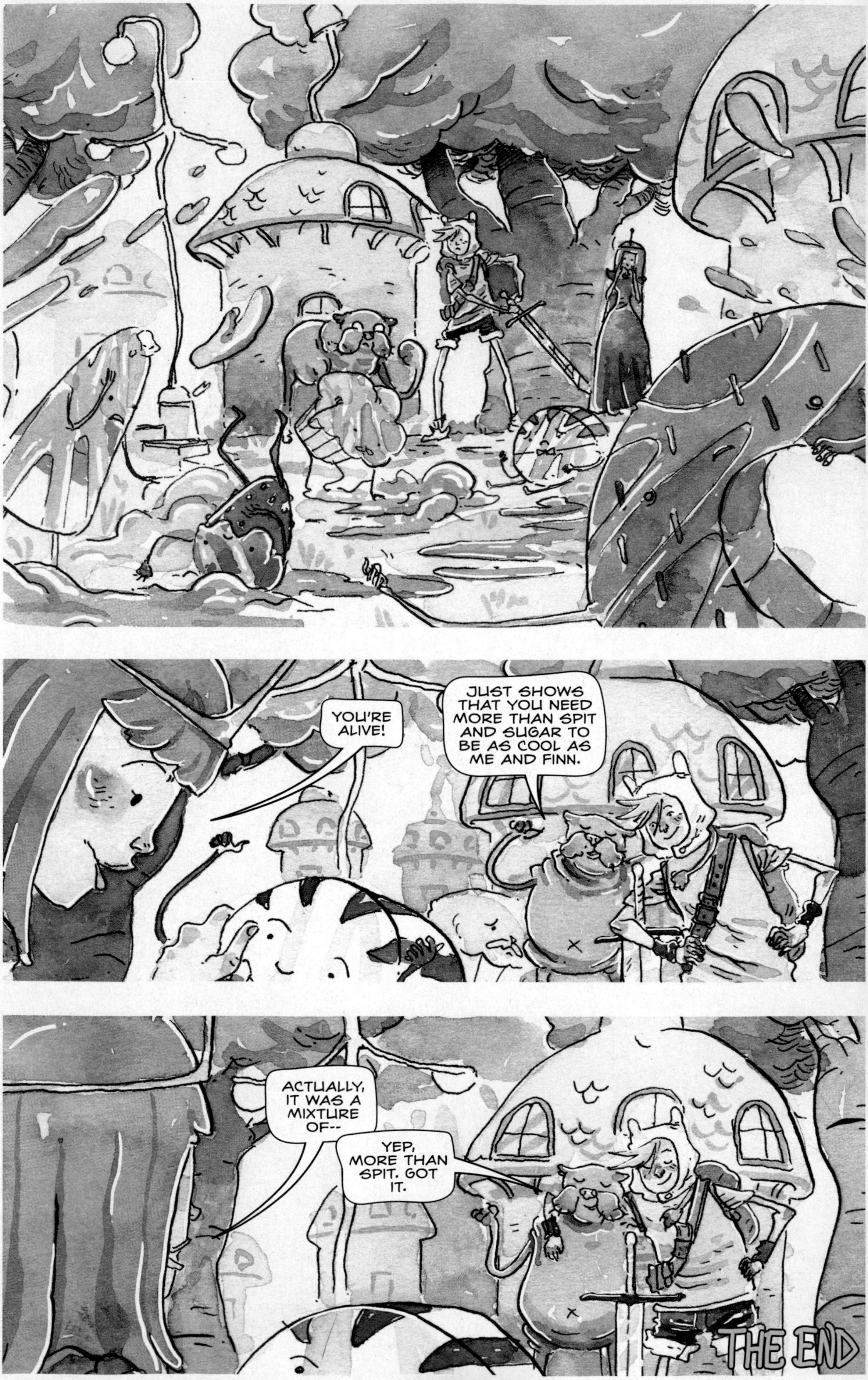
YOU'RE ALIVE!
JUST SHOWS THAT YOU NEED MORE THAN SPIT AND SUGAR TO BE AS COOL AS ME AND FINN.
ACTUALLY, IT WAS A MIXTURE OF--
YEP, MORE THAN SPIT. GOT IT.
THE END

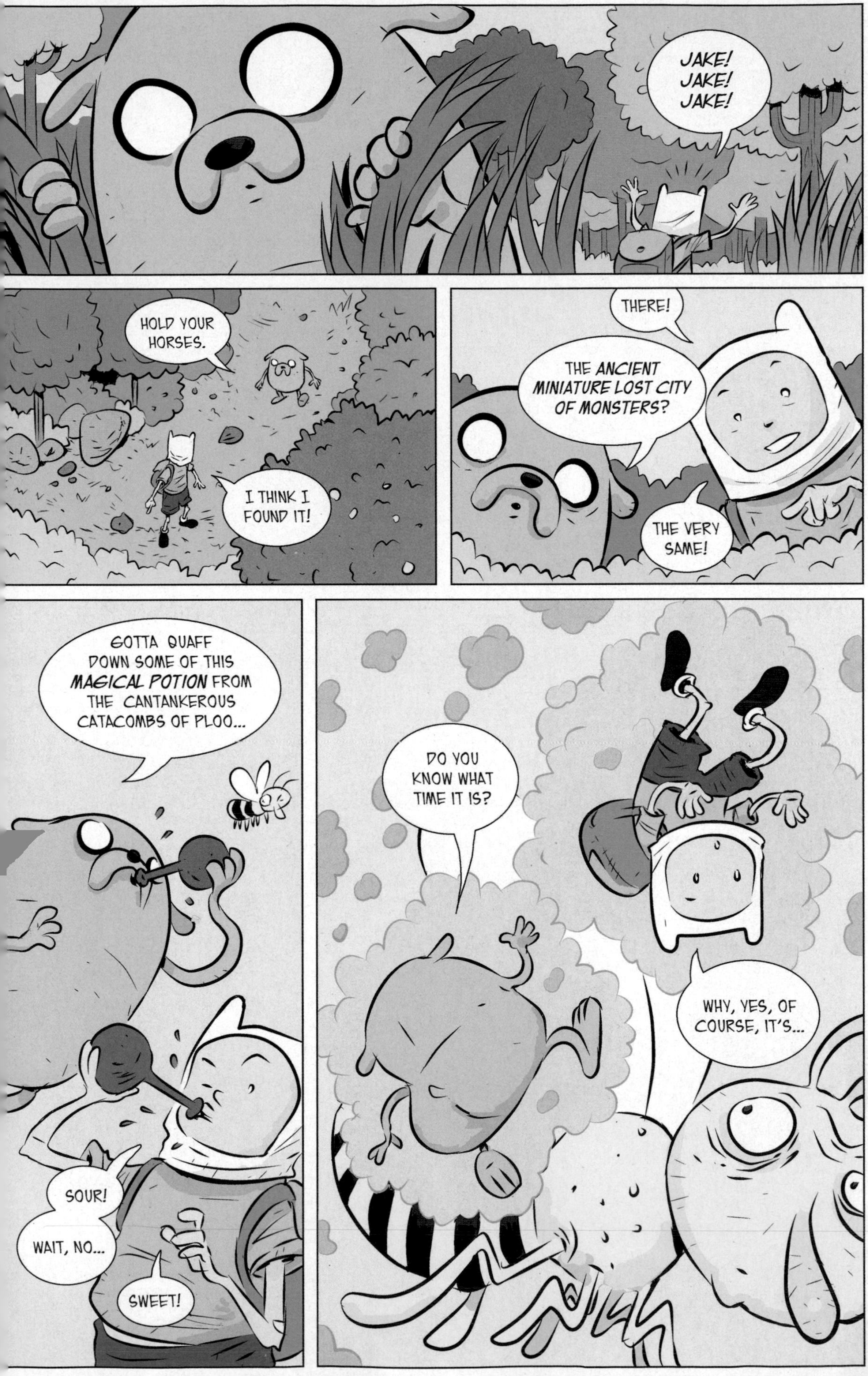

JAKE! JAKE! JAKE!
HOLD YOUR HORSES.
I THINK I FOUND IT!
THERE!
THE ANCIENT MINIATURE LOST CITY OF MONSTERS?
THE VERY SAME!
GOTTA QUAFF DOWN SOME OF THIS MAGICAL POTION FROM THE CANTANKEROUS CATACOMBS OF PLOO...
SOUR!
WAIT, NO...
SWEET!
DO YOU KNOW WHAT TIME IT IS?
WHY, YES, OF COURSE, IT'S...

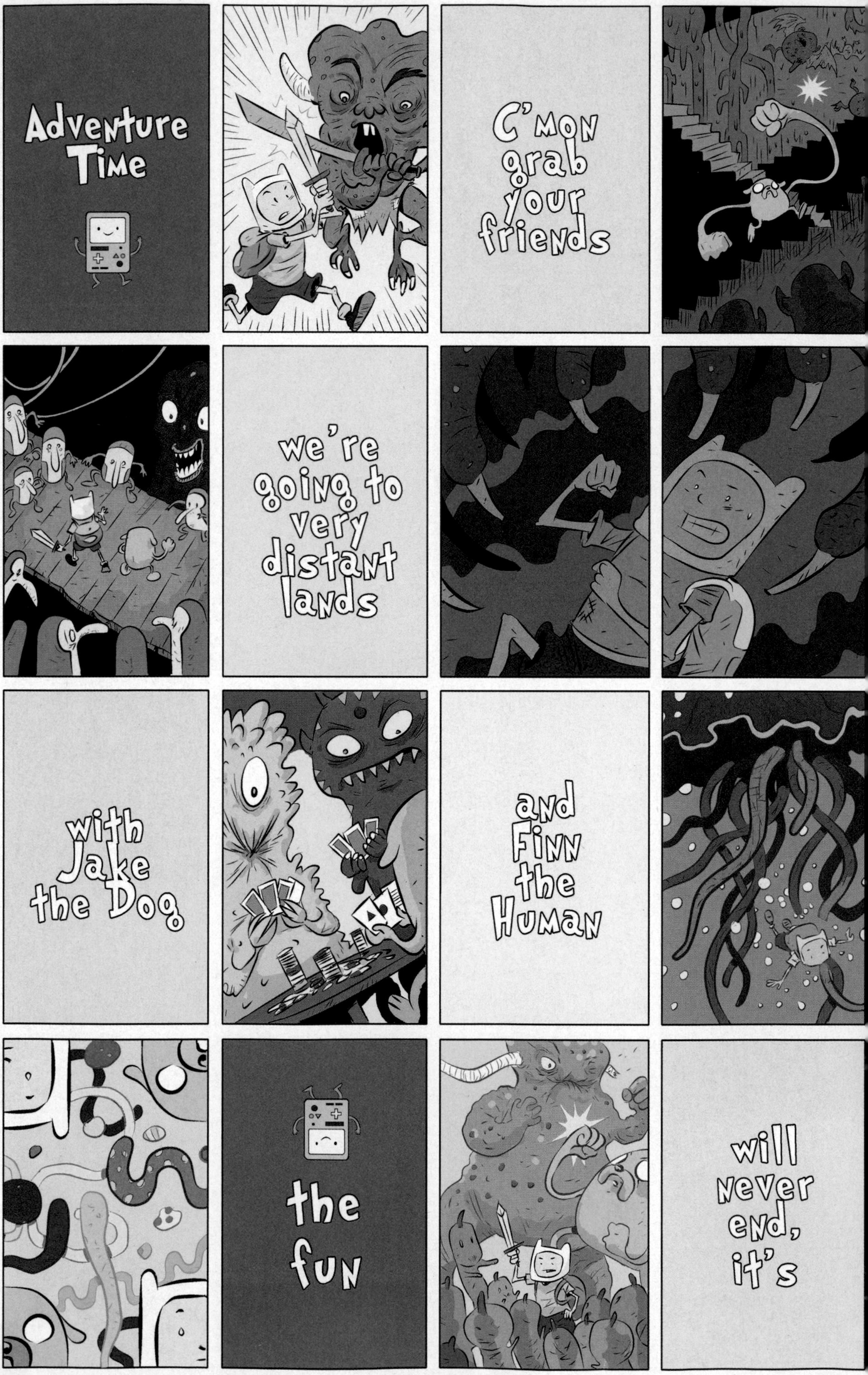
Adventure Time
C'mon grab your friends
we're going to very distant lands
with Jake the Dog
and Finn the Human
the fun
will never end, it's

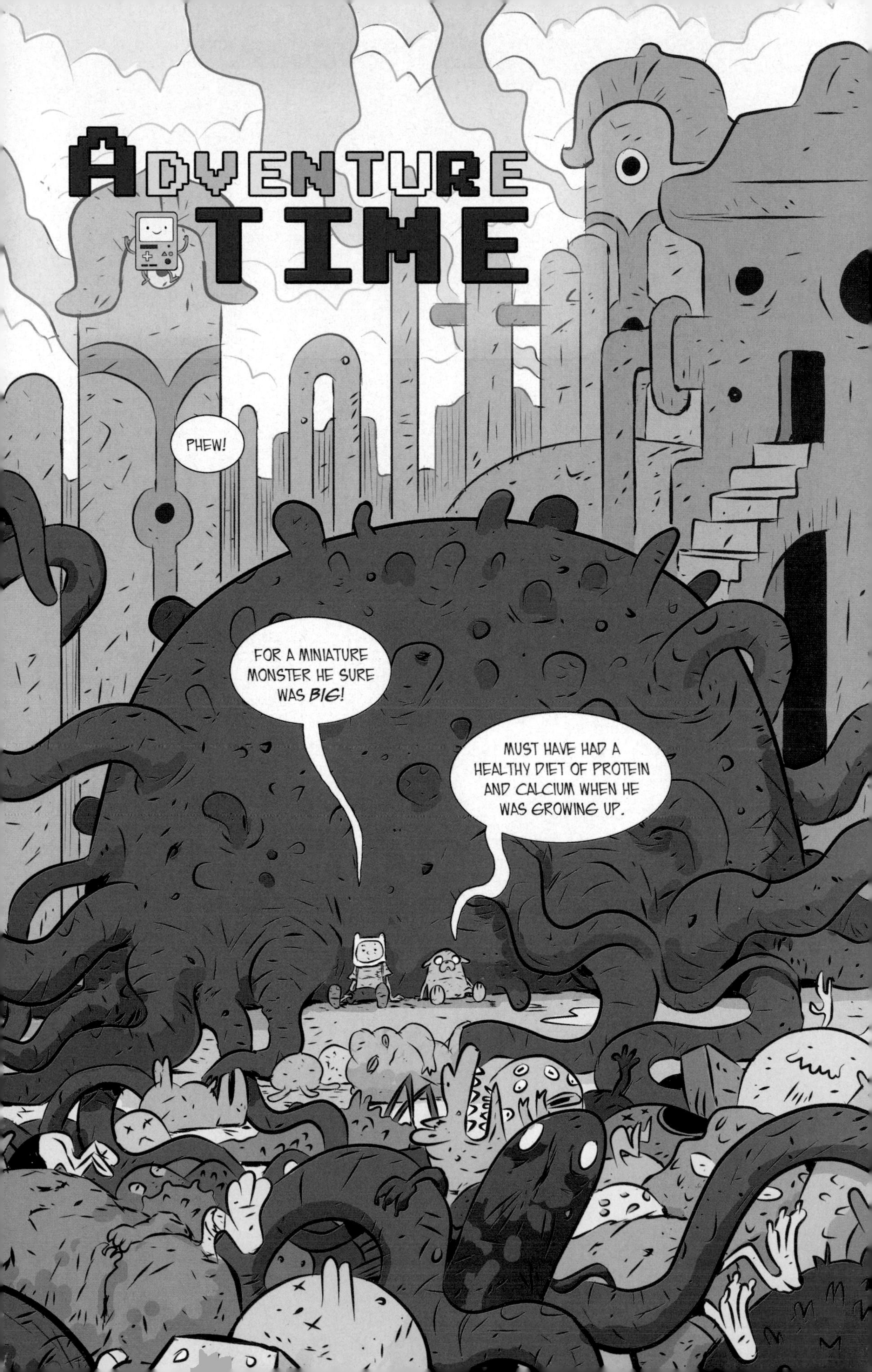
ADVENTURE TIME
PHEW!
FOR A MINIATURE MONSTER HE SURE WAS *BIG*!
MUST HAVE HAD A HEALTHY DIET OF PROTEIN AND CALCIUM WHEN HE WAS GROWING UP.

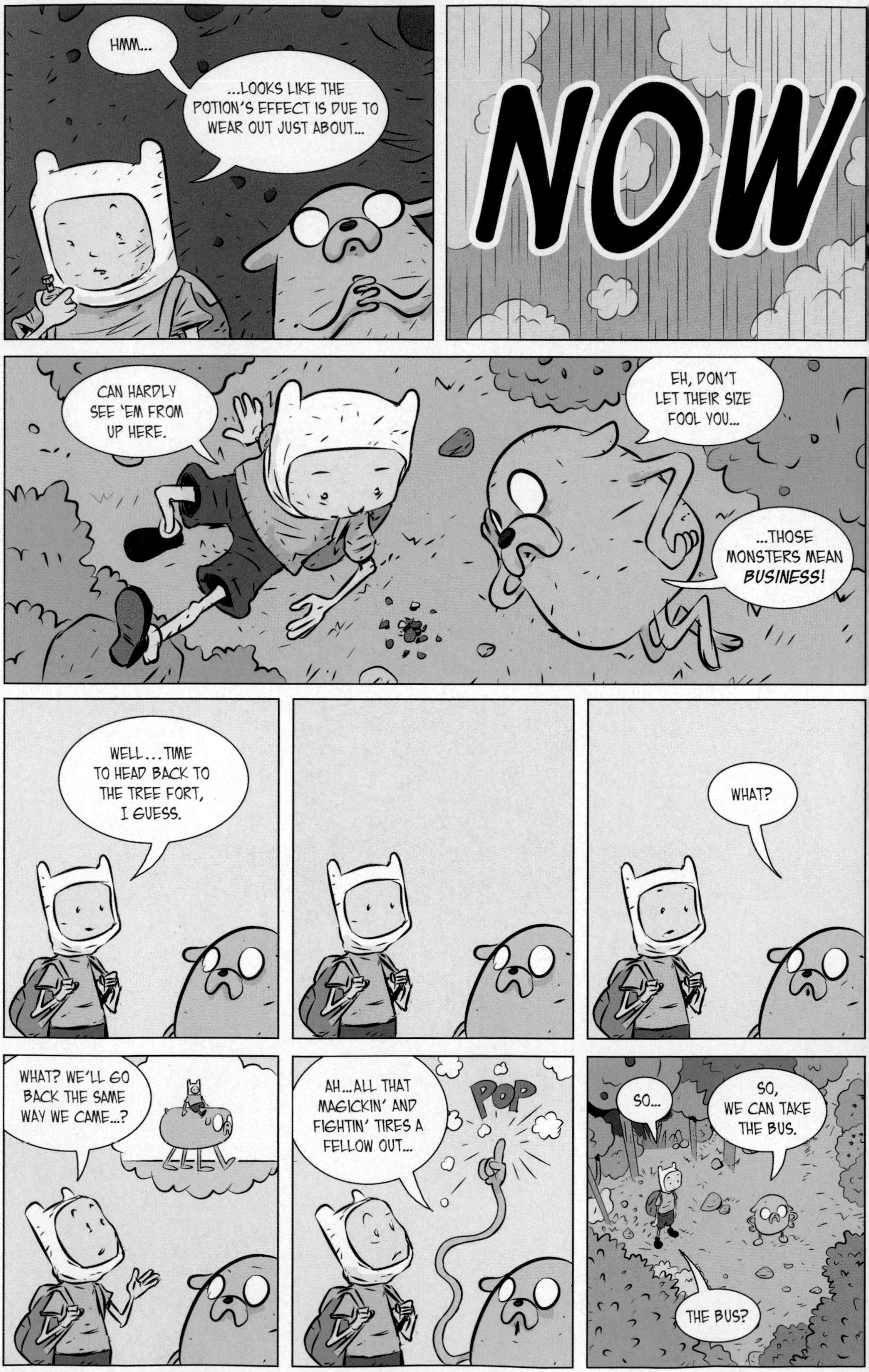
HMM...
...LOOKS LIKE THE POTION'S EFFECT IS DUE TO WEAR OUT JUST ABOUT...
NOW
CAN HARDLY SEE 'EM FROM UP HERE.
EH, DON'T LET THEIR SIZE FOOL YOU...
...THOSE MONSTERS MEAN *BUSINESS!*
WELL... TIME TO HEAD BACK TO THE TREE FORT, I GUESS.
WHAT?
WHAT? WE'LL GO BACK THE SAME WAY WE CAME...?
AH...ALL THAT MAGICKIN' AND FIGHTIN' TIRES A FELLOW OUT...
POP
SO...
SO, WE CAN TAKE THE BUS.
THE BUS?

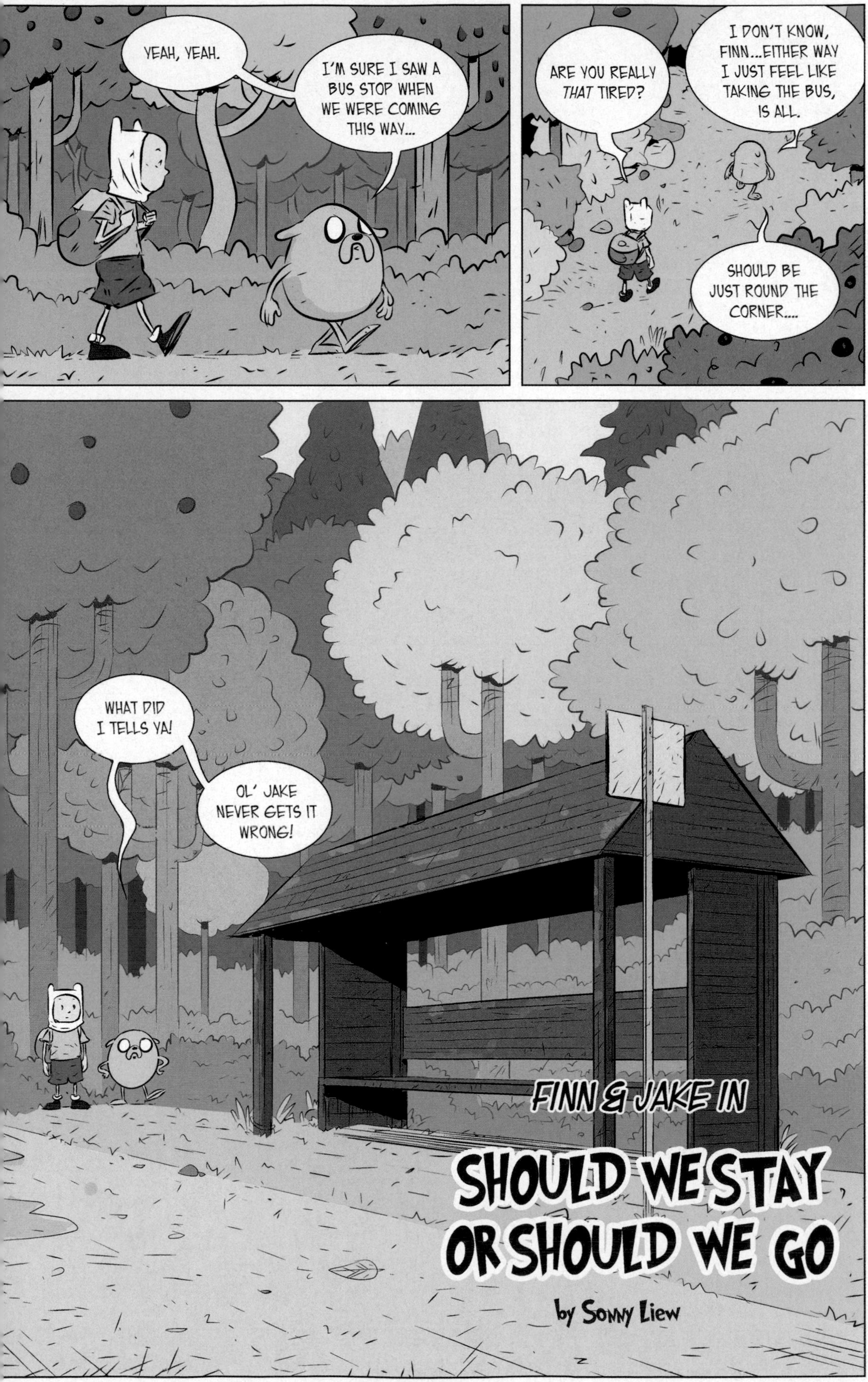
YEAH, YEAH.
I'M SURE I SAW A BUS STOP WHEN WE WERE COMING THIS WAY...
ARE YOU REALLY *THAT* TIRED?
I DON'T KNOW, FINN...EITHER WAY I JUST FEEL LIKE TAKING THE BUS, IS ALL.
SHOULD BE JUST ROUND THE CORNER....
WHAT DID I TELLS YA!
OL' JAKE NEVER GETS IT WRONG!
FINN & JAKE IN
SHOULD WE STAY OR SHOULD WE GO
by Sonny Liew

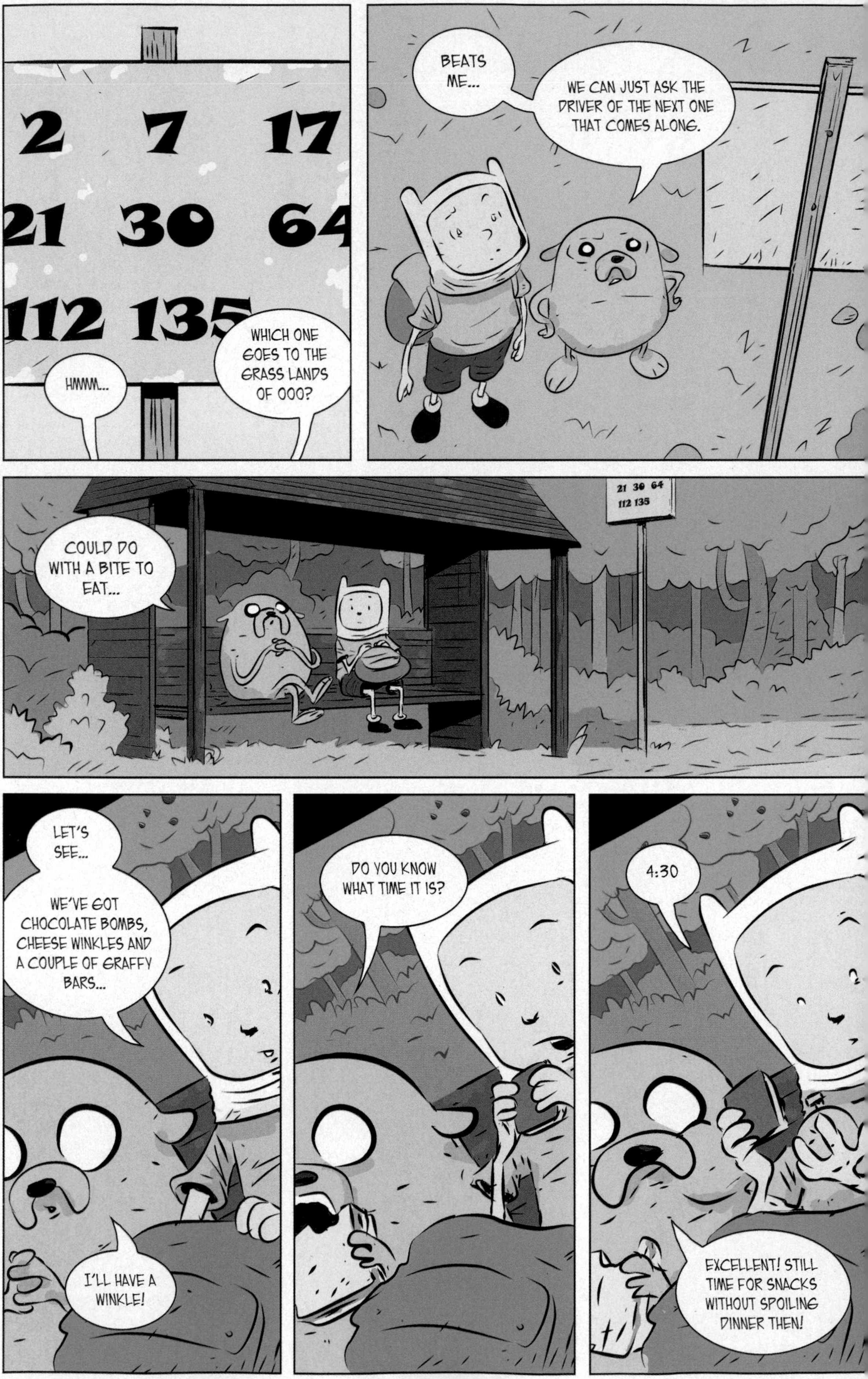
2 7 17
21 30 64
112 135
WHICH ONE GOES TO THE GRASS LANDS OF OOO?
HMMM...
BEATS ME...
WE CAN JUST ASK THE DRIVER OF THE NEXT ONE THAT COMES ALONG.
21 30 64
112 135
COULD DO WITH A BITE TO EAT...
LET'S SEE...
WE'VE GOT CHOCOLATE BOMBS, CHEESE WINKLES AND A COUPLE OF GRAFFY BARS...
I'LL HAVE A WINKLE!
DO YOU KNOW WHAT TIME IT IS?
4:30
EXCELLENT! STILL TIME FOR SNACKS WITHOUT SPOILING DINNER THEN!

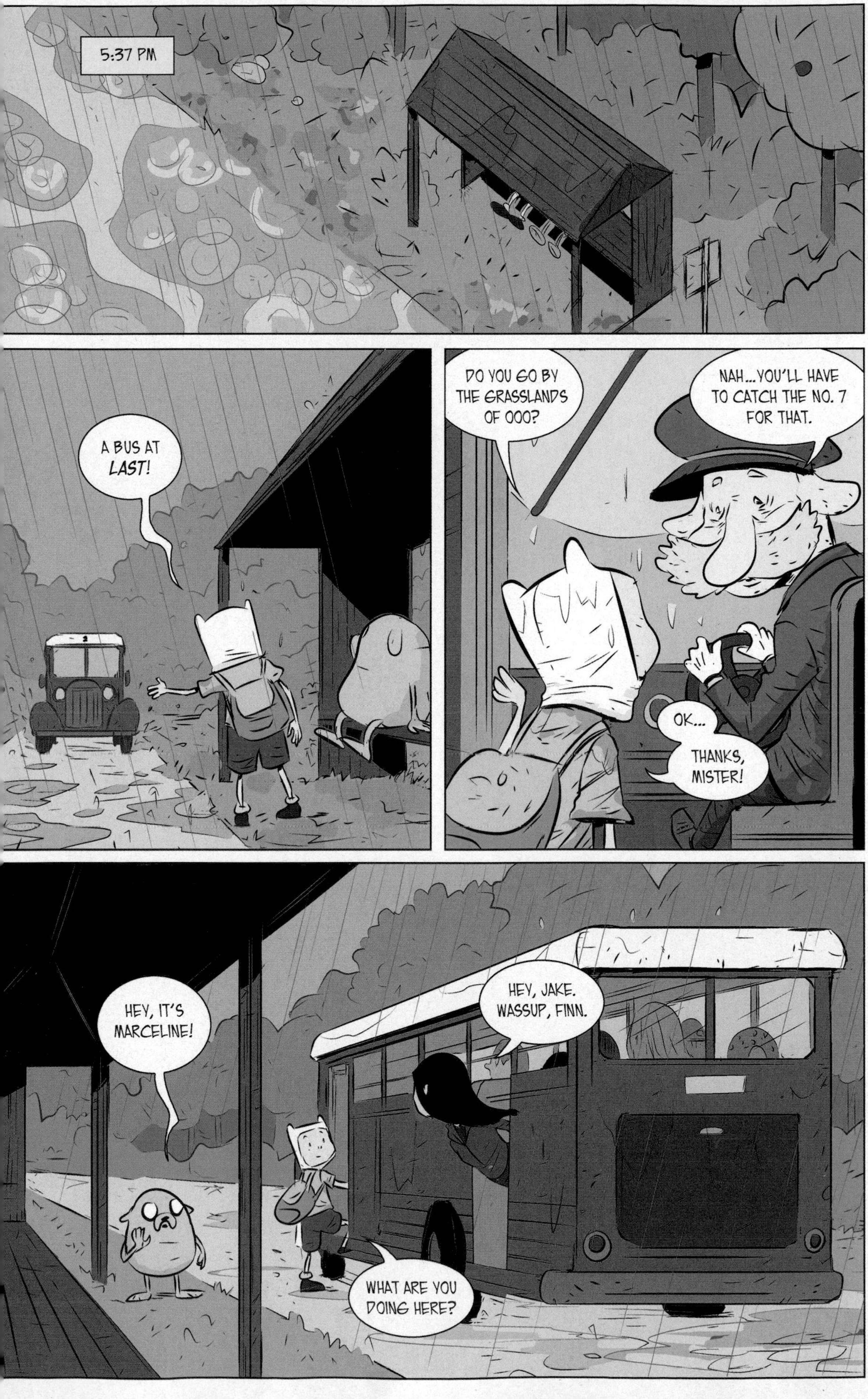
5:37 PM
A BUS AT LAST!
DO YOU GO BY THE GRASSLANDS OF OOO?
NAH...YOU'LL HAVE TO CATCH THE NO. 7 FOR THAT.
OK...
THANKS, MISTER!
HEY, IT'S MARCELINE!
HEY, JAKE. WASSUP, FINN.
WHAT ARE YOU DOING HERE?

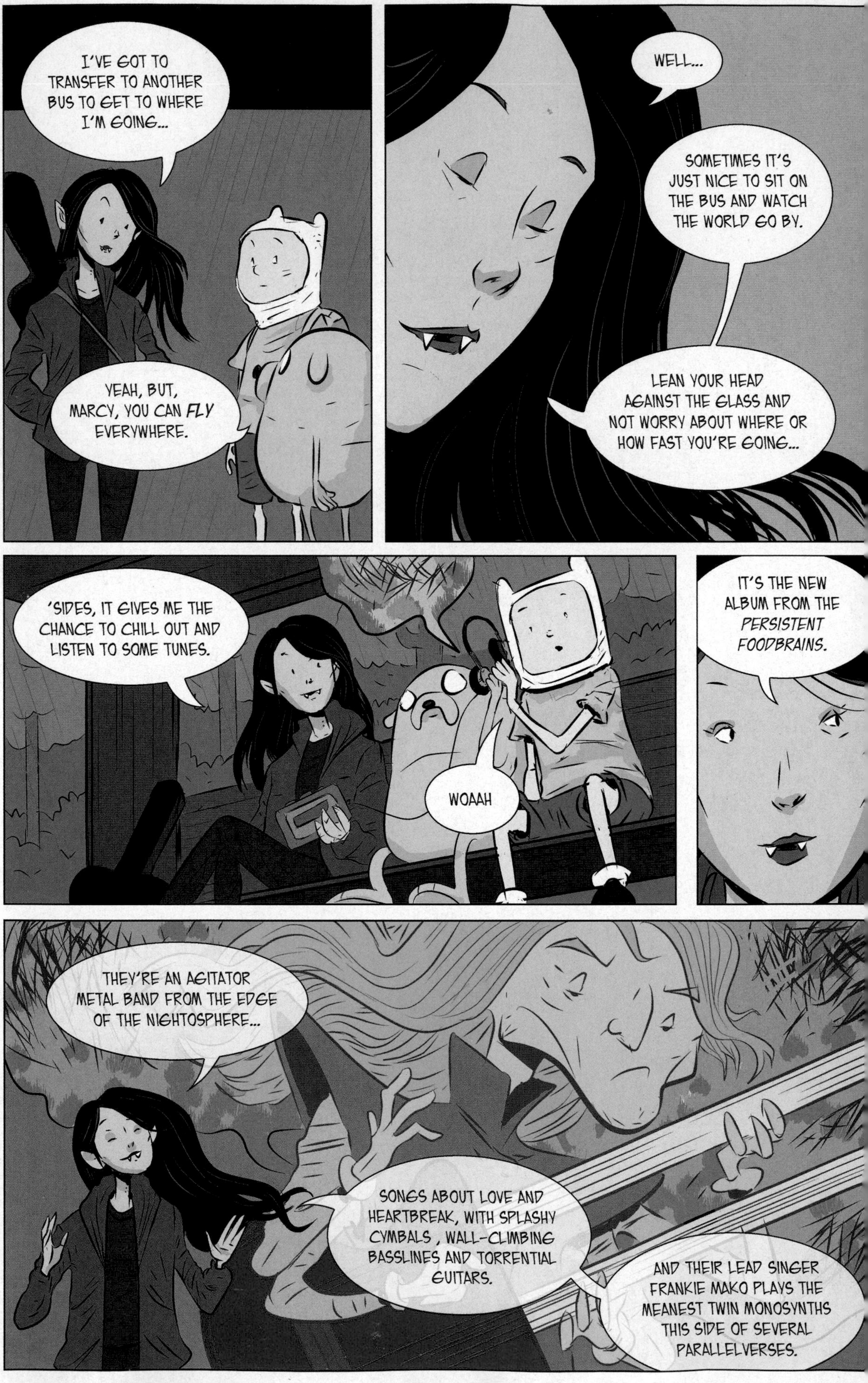
I'VE GOT TO TRANSFER TO ANOTHER BUS TO GET TO WHERE I'M GOING...
YEAH, BUT, MARCY, YOU CAN *FLY* EVERYWHERE.
WELL...
SOMETIMES IT'S JUST NICE TO SIT ON THE BUS AND WATCH THE WORLD GO BY.
LEAN YOUR HEAD AGAINST THE GLASS AND NOT WORRY ABOUT WHERE OR HOW FAST YOU'RE GOING...
'SIDES, IT GIVES ME THE CHANCE TO CHILL OUT AND LISTEN TO SOME TUNES.
WOAAH
IT'S THE NEW ALBUM FROM THE *PERSISTENT FOODBRAINS.*
THEY'RE AN AGITATOR METAL BAND FROM THE EDGE OF THE NIGHTOSPHERE...
SONGS ABOUT LOVE AND HEARTBREAK, WITH SPLASHY CYMBALS , WALL-CLIMBING BASSLINES AND TORRENTIAL GUITARS.
AND THEIR LEAD SINGER FRANKIE MAKO PLAYS THE MEANEST TWIN MONOSYNTHS THIS SIDE OF SEVERAL PARALLELVERSES.

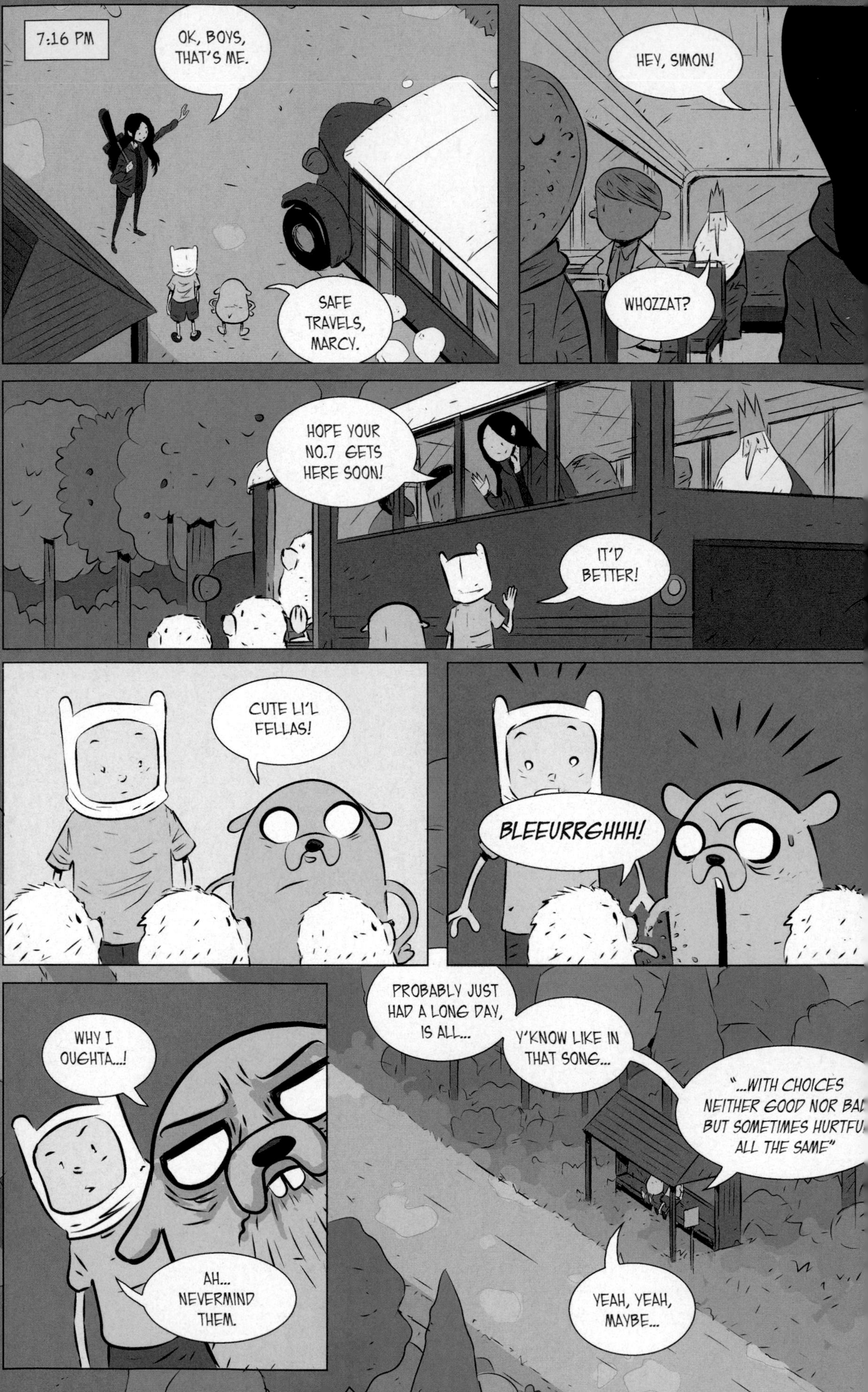
7:16 PM
OK, BOYS, THAT'S ME.
SAFE TRAVELS, MARCY.
HEY, SIMON!
WHOZZAT?
HOPE YOUR NO.7 GETS HERE SOON!
IT'D BETTER!
CUTE LI'L FELLAS!
BLEEURRGHHH!
WHY I OUGHTA...!
AH... NEVERMIND THEM.
PROBABLY JUST HAD A LONG DAY, IS ALL...
Y'KNOW LIKE IN THAT SONG...
"...WITH CHOICES NEITHER GOOD NOR BA
BUT SOMETIMES HURTFU
ALL THE SAME"
YEAH, YEAH, MAYBE...

Should We Stay or Should We Go

by The Mathematicals

Should we stay or should we go

Neither seems to be particularly bad

Except that sometimes it's

Hurtful just the same

If we stayed it could be alright

A collision of planets in the inky dark

Some things lost

Other things found

Should we stay or should we go

I guess there are choices

Neither good nor bad

But sometimes

Hurtful all the same

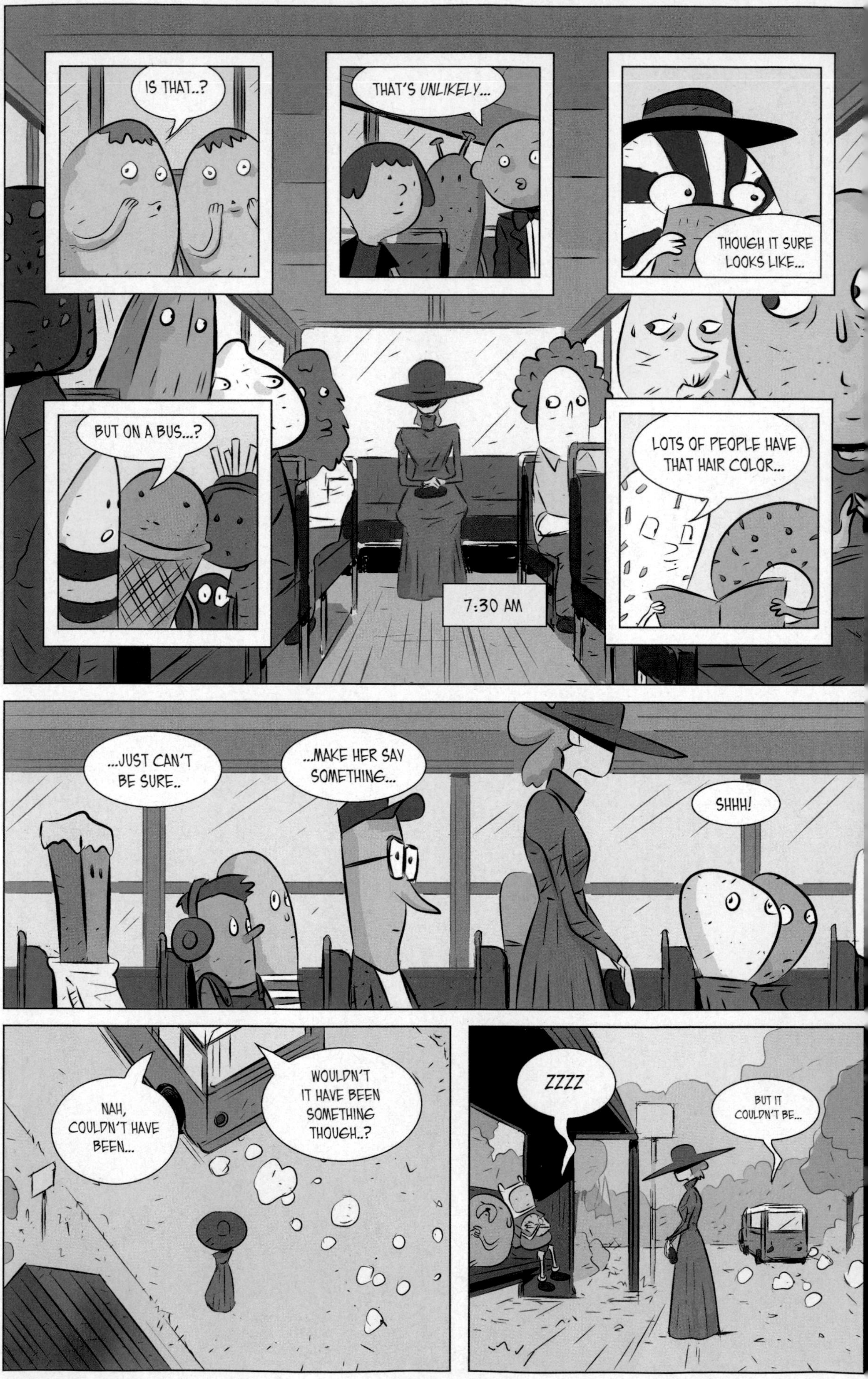
IS THAT..?
THAT'S UNLIKELY...
THOUGH IT SURE LOOKS LIKE...
BUT ON A BUS...?
LOTS OF PEOPLE HAVE THAT HAIR COLOR...
7:30 AM
...JUST CAN'T BE SURE..
...MAKE HER SAY SOMETHING...
SHHH!
NAH, COULDN'T HAVE BEEN...
WOULDN'T IT HAVE BEEN SOMETHING THOUGH..?
ZZZZ
BUT IT COULDN'T BE...

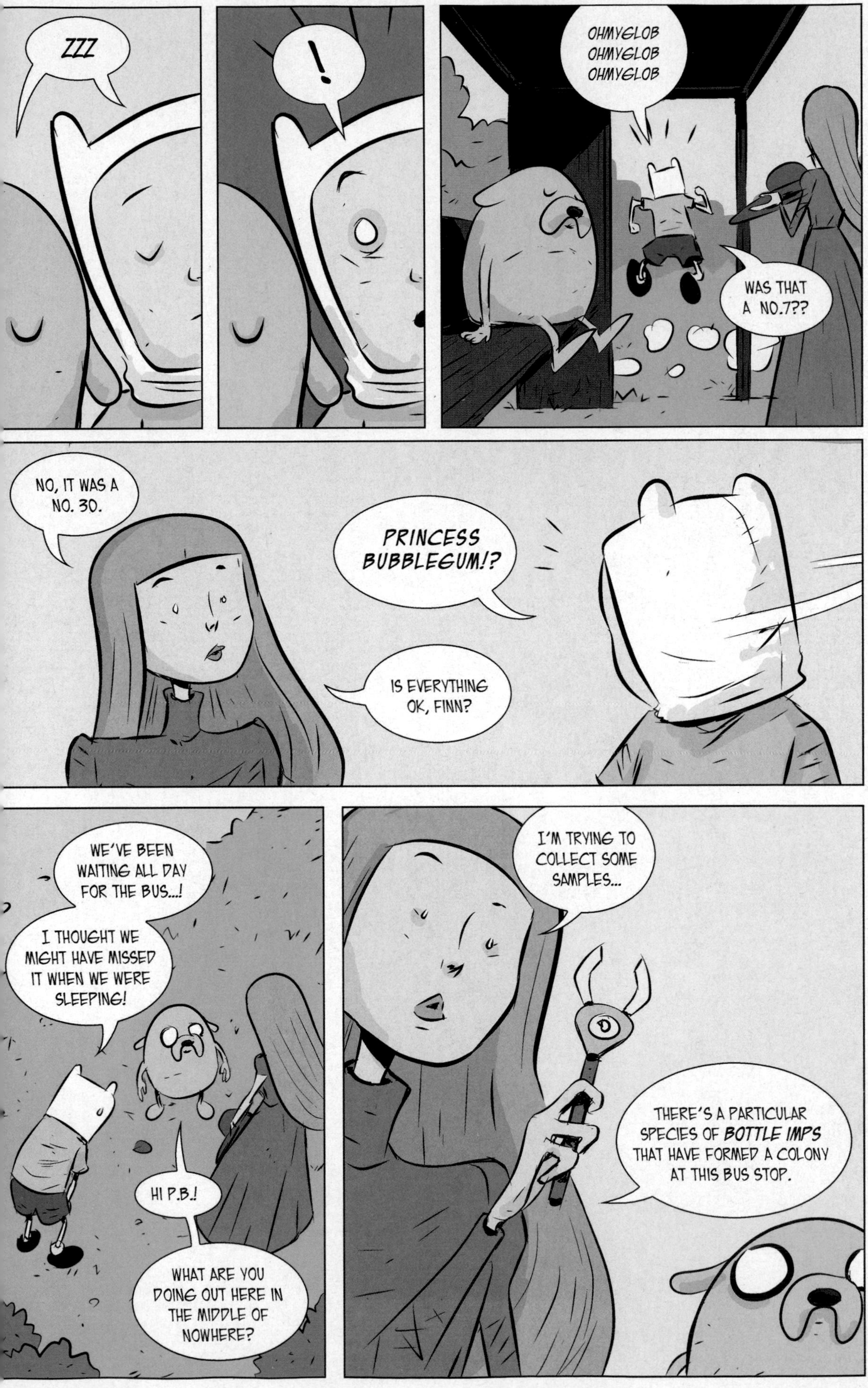
ZZZ
!
OHMYGLOB
OHMYGLOB
OHMYGLOB
WAS THAT A NO.7??
NO, IT WAS A NO. 30.
PRINCESS BUBBLEGUM!?
IS EVERYTHING OK, FINN?
WE'VE BEEN WAITING ALL DAY FOR THE BUS...!
I THOUGHT WE MIGHT HAVE MISSED IT WHEN WE WERE SLEEPING!
HI P.B.!
WHAT ARE YOU DOING OUT HERE IN THE MIDDLE OF NOWHERE?
I'M TRYING TO COLLECT SOME SAMPLES...
THERE'S A PARTICULAR SPECIES OF BOTTLE IMPS THAT HAVE FORMED A COLONY AT THIS BUS STOP.

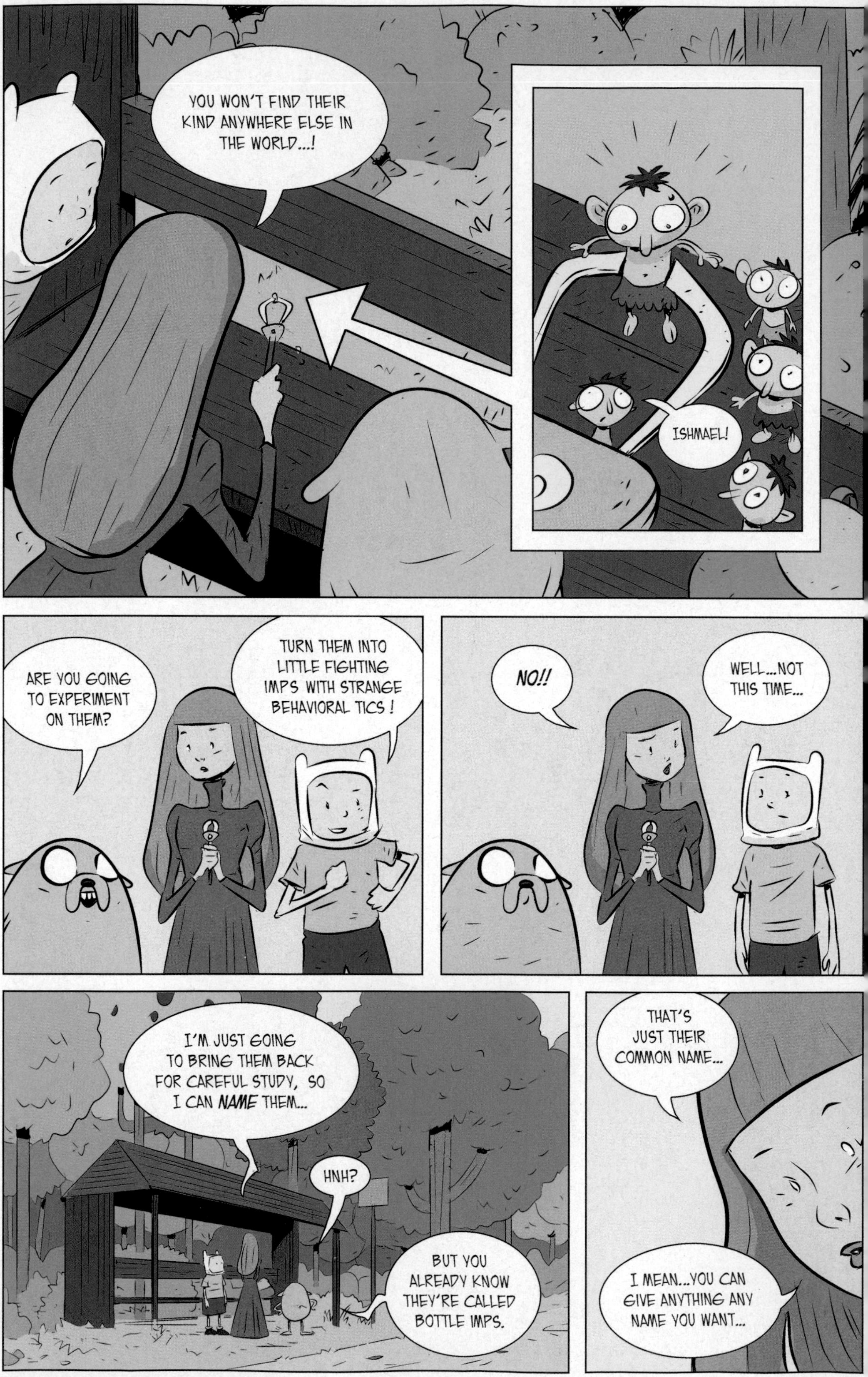
YOU WON'T FIND THEIR KIND ANYWHERE ELSE IN THE WORLD...!
ISHMAEL!
ARE YOU GOING TO EXPERIMENT ON THEM?
TURN THEM INTO LITTLE FIGHTING IMPS WITH STRANGE BEHAVIORAL TICS !
NO!!
WELL...NOT THIS TIME...
I'M JUST GOING TO BRING THEM BACK FOR CAREFUL STUDY, SO I CAN *NAME* THEM...
HNH?
BUT YOU ALREADY KNOW THEY'RE CALLED BOTTLE IMPS.
THAT'S JUST THEIR COMMON NAME...
I MEAN...YOU CAN GIVE ANYTHING ANY NAME YOU WANT...

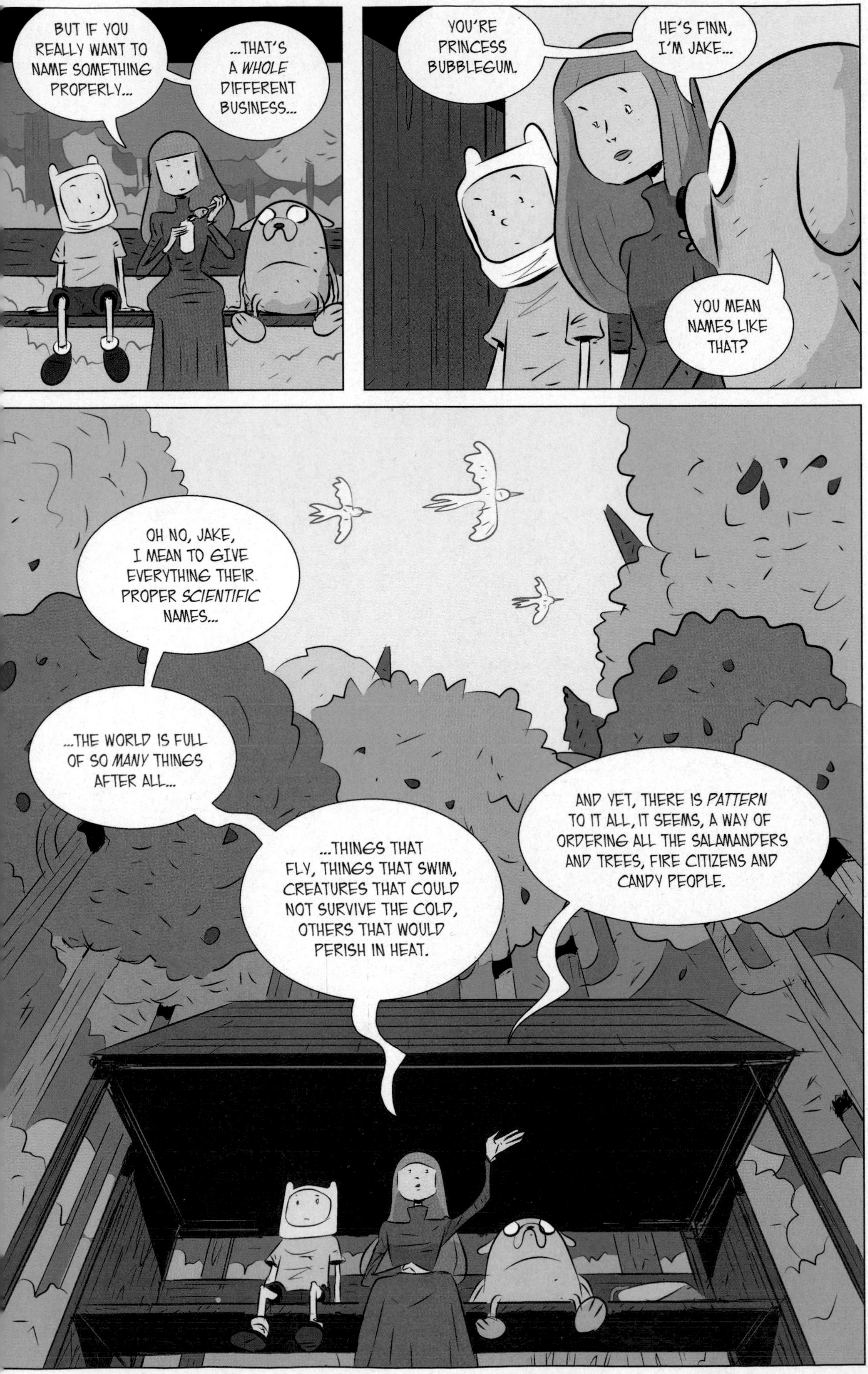
BUT IF YOU REALLY WANT TO NAME SOMETHING PROPERLY...
...THAT'S A *WHOLE* DIFFERENT BUSINESS...
YOU'RE PRINCESS BUBBLEGUM.
HE'S FINN, I'M JAKE...
YOU MEAN NAMES LIKE THAT?
OH NO, JAKE, I MEAN TO GIVE EVERYTHING THEIR PROPER *SCIENTIFIC* NAMES...
...THE WORLD IS FULL OF SO *MANY* THINGS AFTER ALL...
...THINGS THAT FLY, THINGS THAT SWIM, CREATURES THAT COULD NOT SURVIVE THE COLD, OTHERS THAT WOULD PERISH IN HEAT.
AND YET, THERE IS *PATTERN* TO IT ALL, IT SEEMS, A WAY OF ORDERING ALL THE SALAMANDERS AND TREES, FIRE CITIZENS AND CANDY PEOPLE.

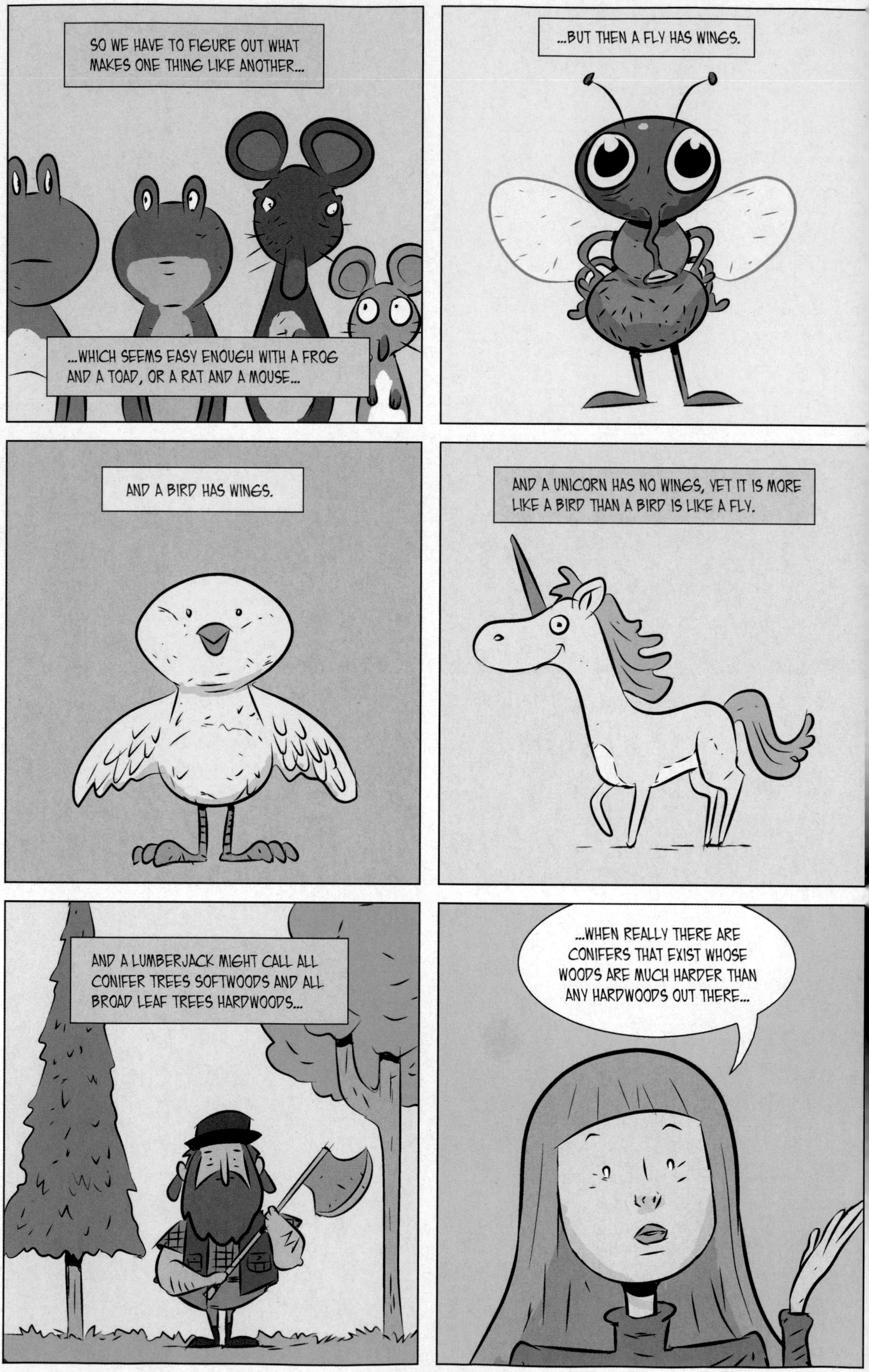
SO WE HAVE TO FIGURE OUT WHAT MAKES ONE THING LIKE ANOTHER...
...WHICH SEEMS EASY ENOUGH WITH A FROG AND A TOAD, OR A RAT AND A MOUSE...
...BUT THEN A FLY HAS WINGS.
AND A BIRD HAS WINGS.
AND A UNICORN HAS NO WINGS, YET IT IS MORE LIKE A BIRD THAN A BIRD IS LIKE A FLY.
AND A LUMBERJACK MIGHT CALL ALL CONIFER TREES SOFTWOODS AND ALL BROAD LEAF TREES HARDWOODS...
...WHEN REALLY THERE ARE CONIFERS THAT EXIST WHOSE WOODS ARE MUCH HARDER THAN ANY HARDWOODS OUT THERE...

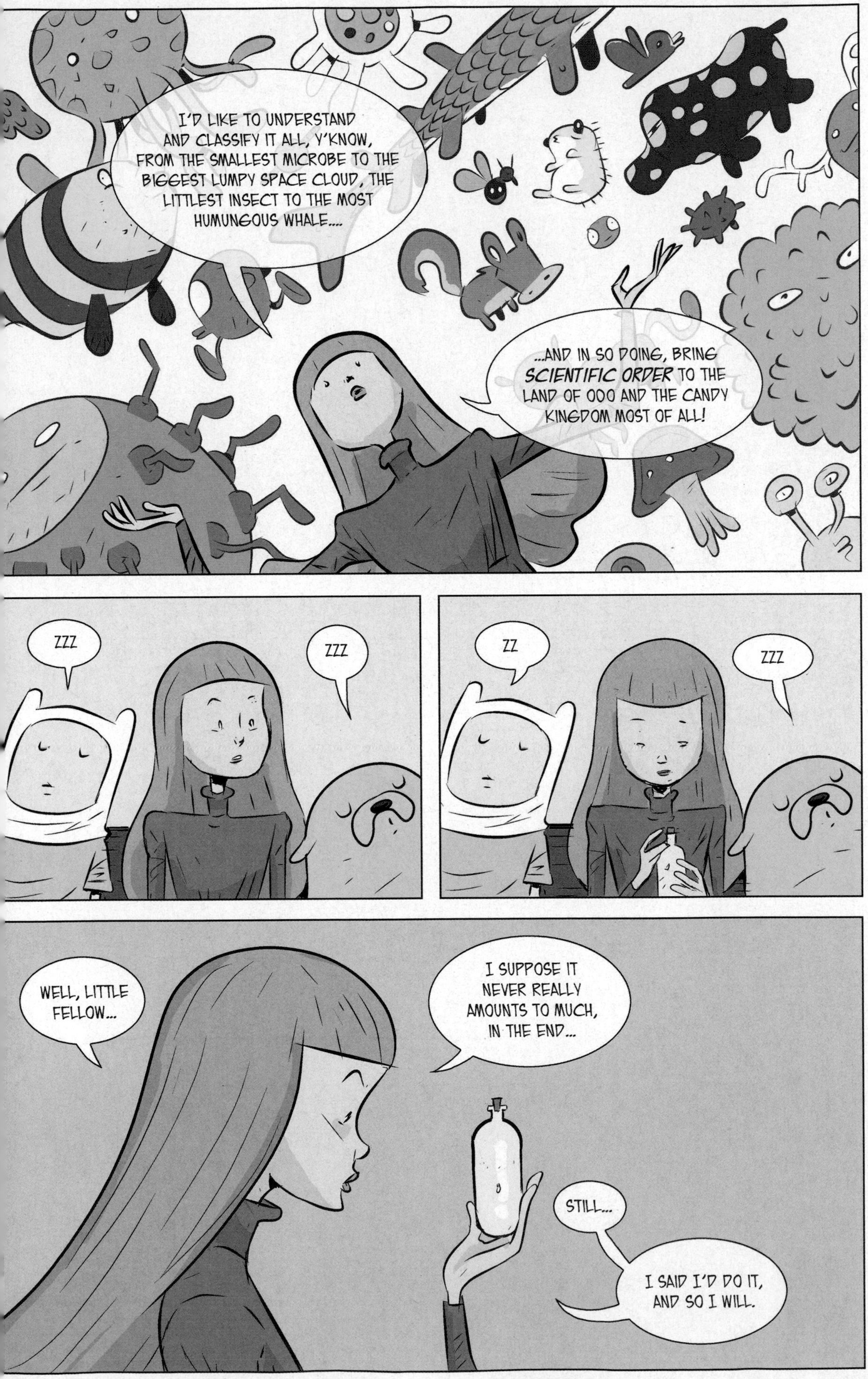
I'D LIKE TO UNDERSTAND AND CLASSIFY IT ALL, Y'KNOW, FROM THE SMALLEST MICROBE TO THE BIGGEST LUMPY SPACE CLOUD, THE LITTLEST INSECT TO THE MOST HUMUNGOUS WHALE....
...AND IN SO DOING, BRING SCIENTIFIC ORDER TO THE LAND OF OOO AND THE CANDY KINGDOM MOST OF ALL!
ZZZ
ZZZ
ZZ
ZZZ
WELL, LITTLE FELLOW...
I SUPPOSE IT NEVER REALLY AMOUNTS TO MUCH, IN THE END...
STILL...
I SAID I'D DO IT, AND SO I WILL.

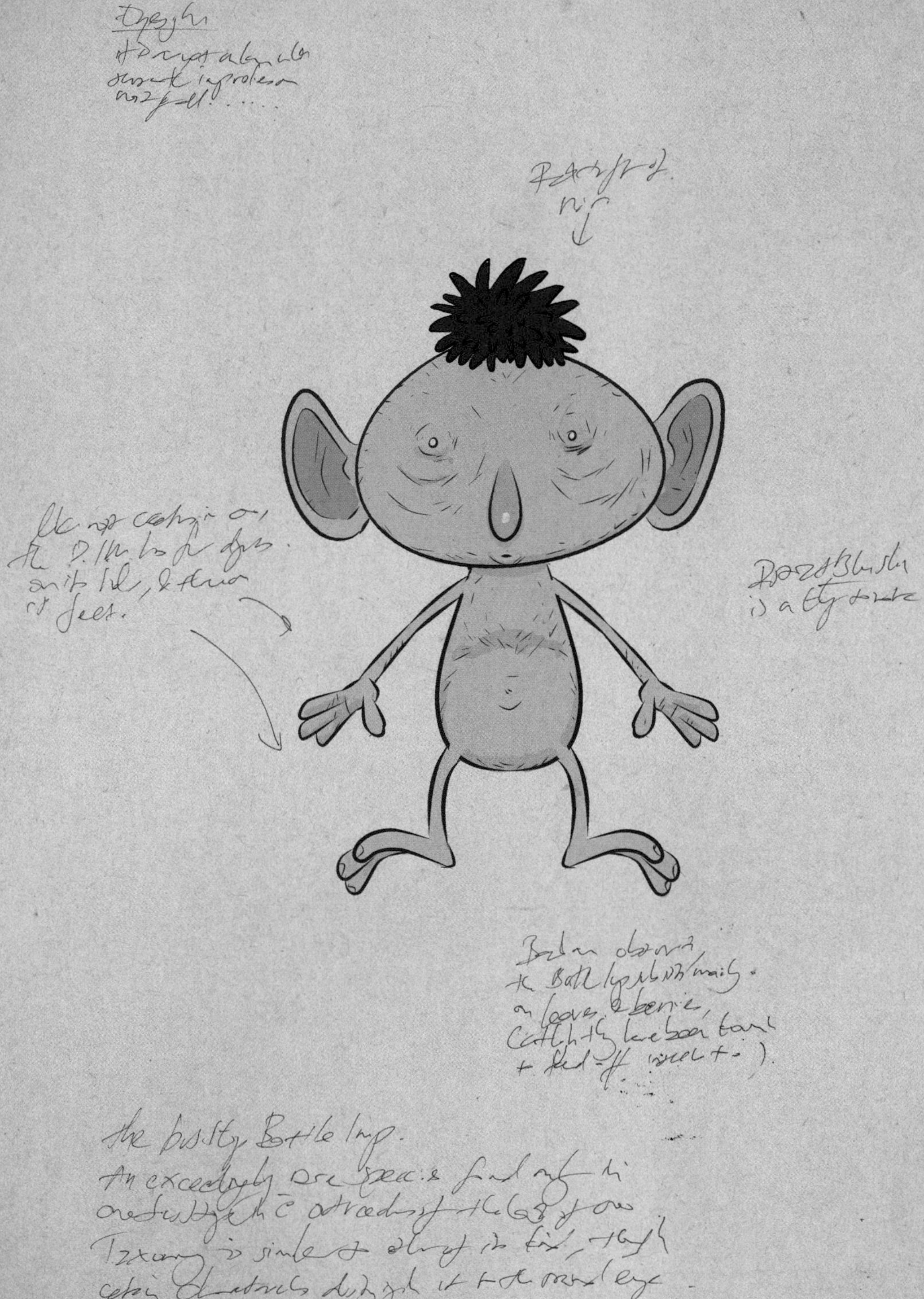
on leaves & berries,
the Bristly Bottle Imp.
An exceedingly rare species
certain characteristics

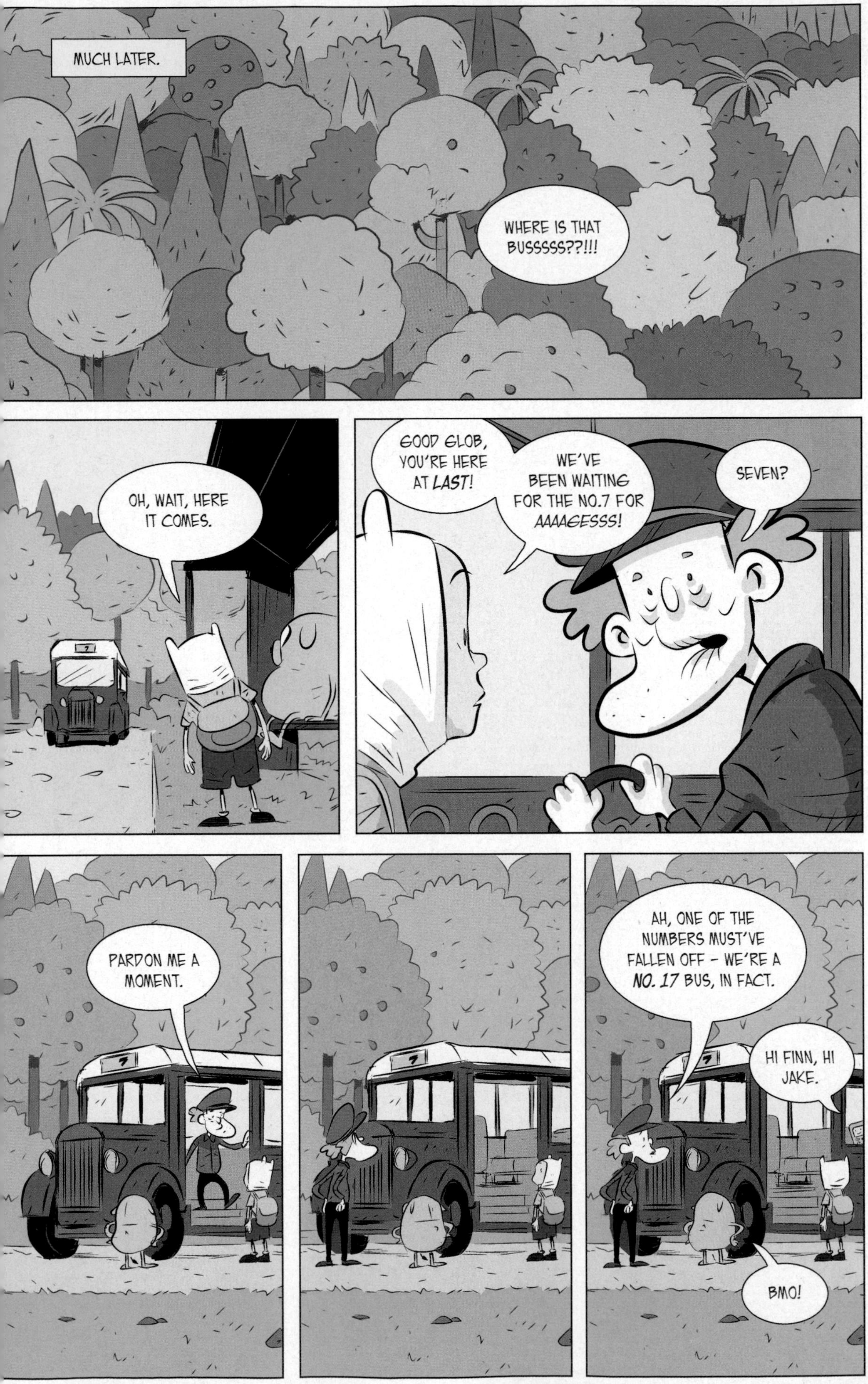
MUCH LATER.
WHERE IS THAT BUSSSSS??!!!
OH, WAIT, HERE IT COMES.
GOOD GLOB, YOU'RE HERE AT LAST!
WE'VE BEEN WAITING FOR THE NO.7 FOR AAAAGESSS!
SEVEN?
PARDON ME A MOMENT.
AH, ONE OF THE NUMBERS MUST'VE FALLEN OFF - WE'RE A NO. 17 BUS, IN FACT.
HI FINN, HI JAKE.
BMO!

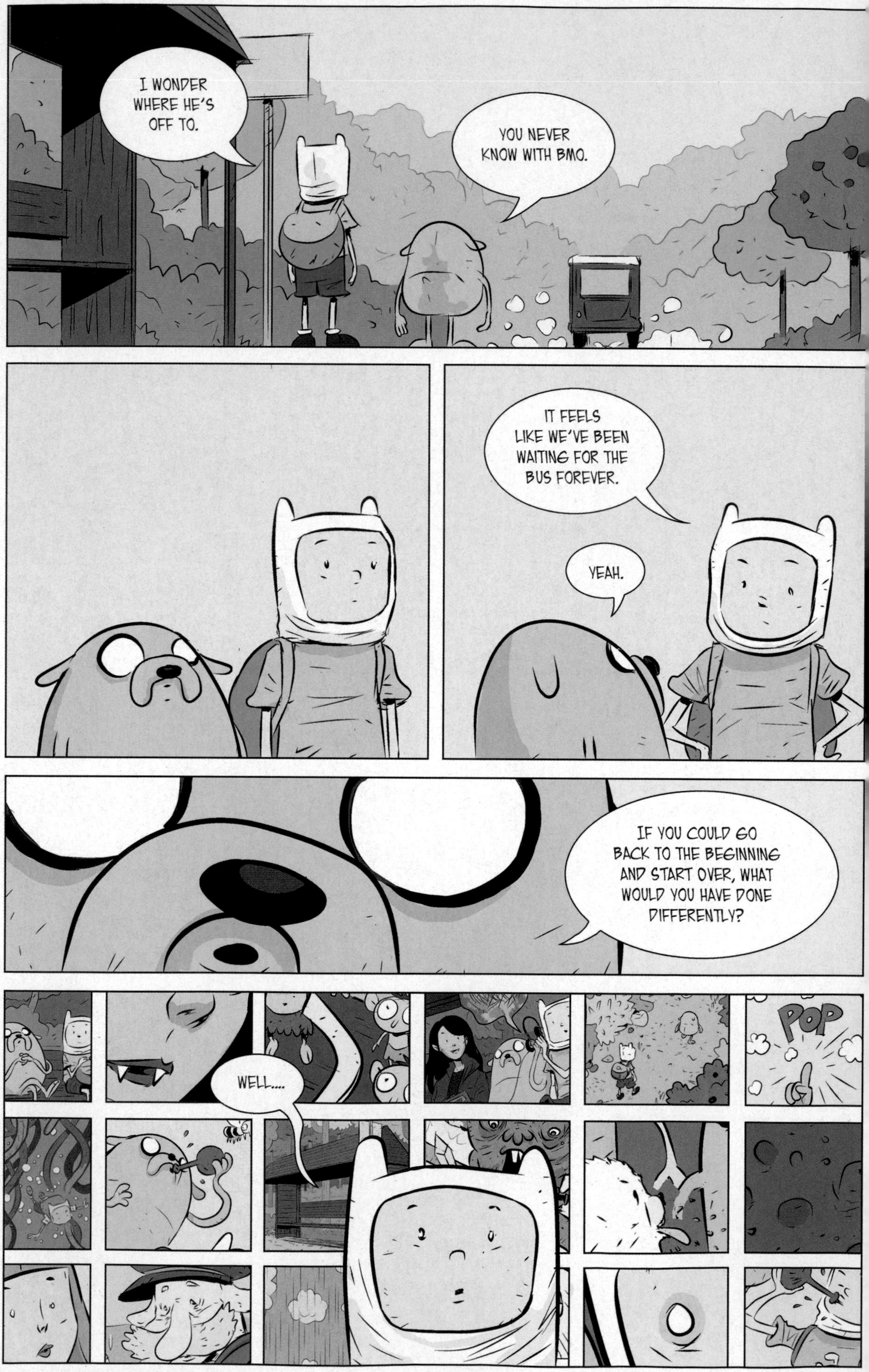

I WONDER WHERE HE'S OFF TO.
YOU NEVER KNOW WITH BMO.
IT FEELS LIKE WE'VE BEEN WAITING FOR THE BUS FOREVER.
YEAH.
IF YOU COULD GO BACK TO THE BEGINNING AND START OVER, WHAT WOULD YOU HAVE DONE DIFFERENTLY?
POP
WELL....

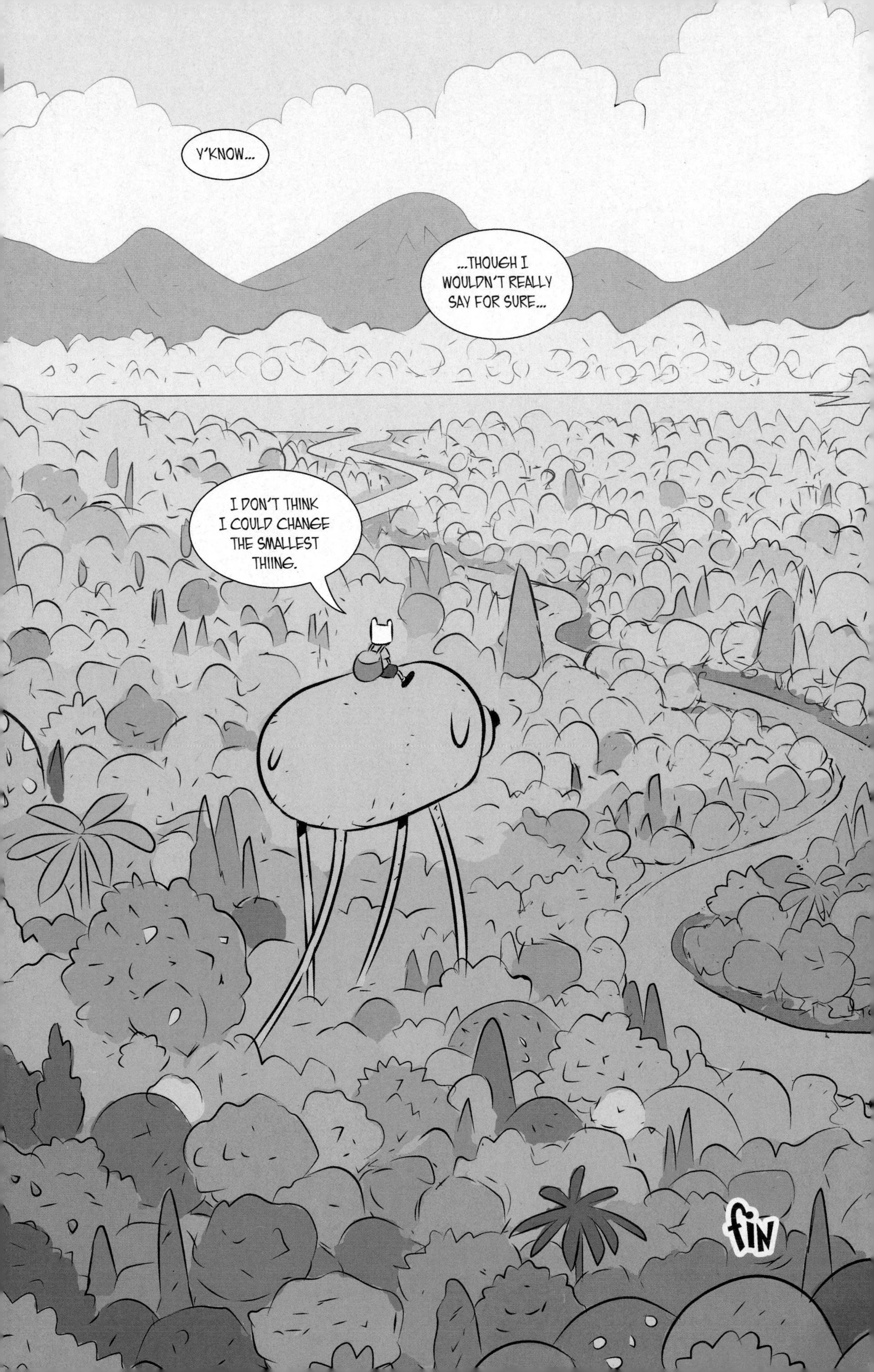
Y'KNOW...
...THOUGH I WOULDN'T REALLY SAY FOR SURE...
I DON'T THINK I COULD CHANGE THE SMALLEST THIING.
fin

COVER
GALLERY

Issue #21 Main Cover

BETHANY SELLERS

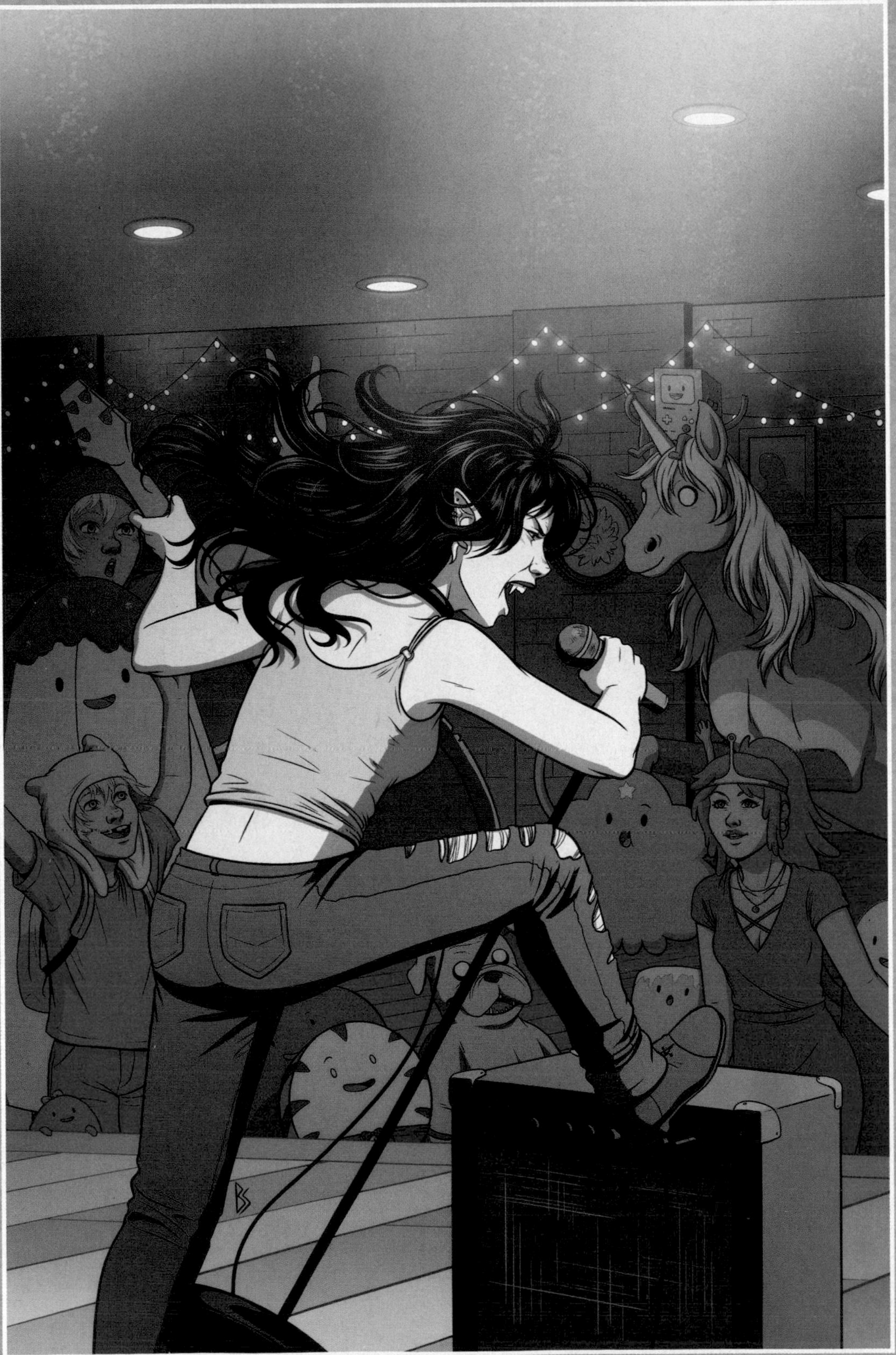

Issue #21 Subscription Cover

NUNO PLATI

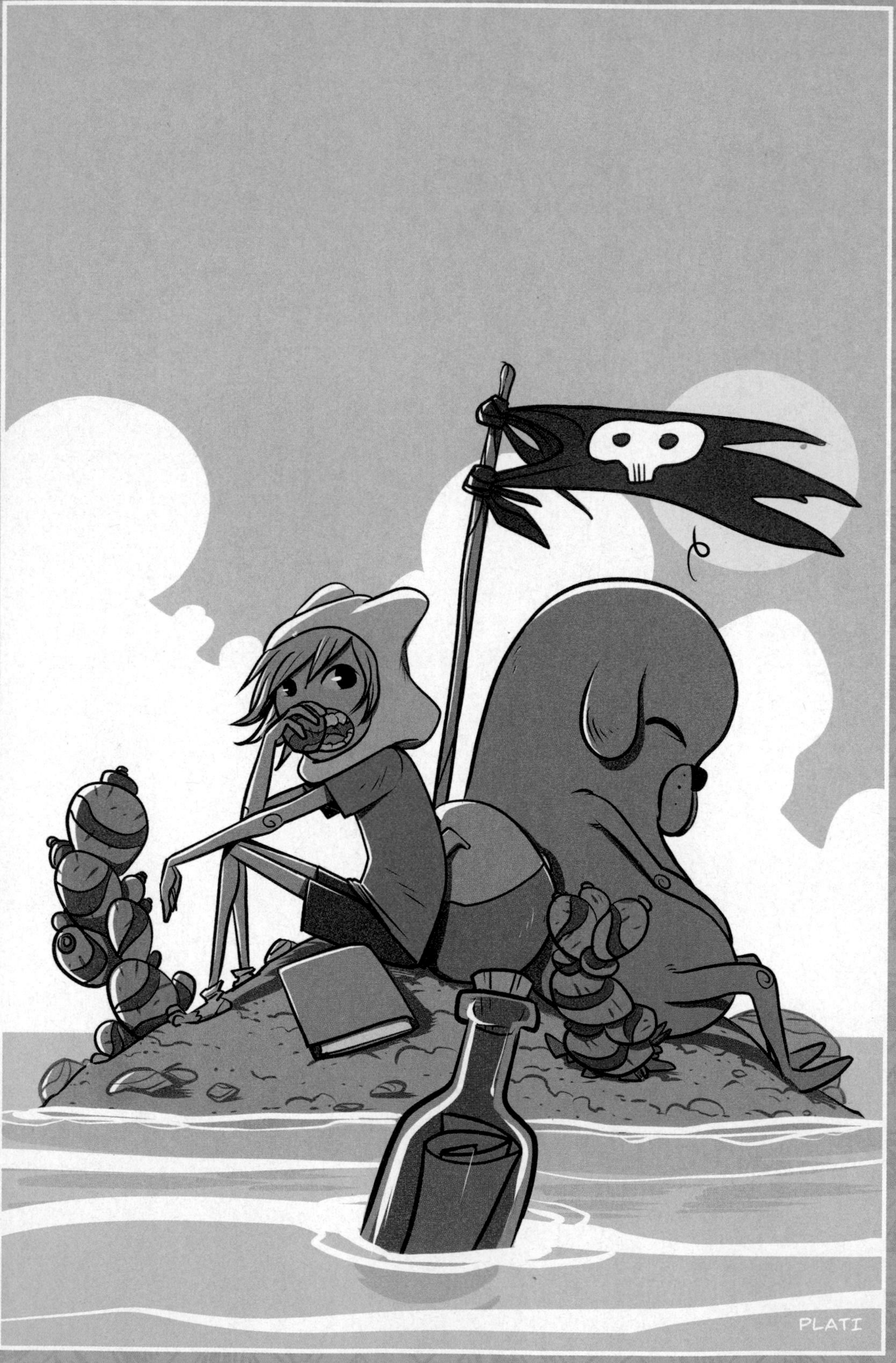
PLATI

Issue #21 Variant Cover

SAPO LENDARIO

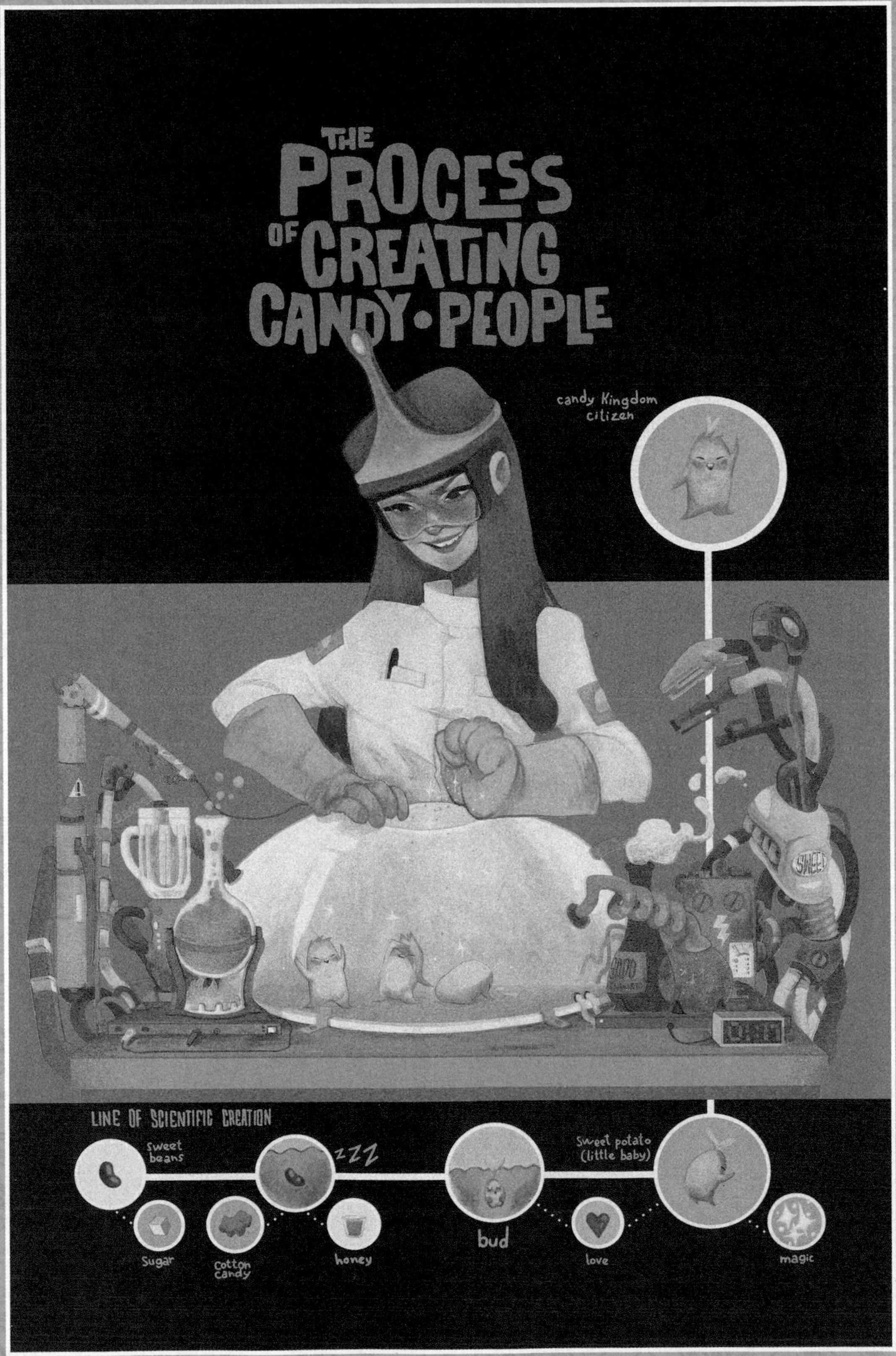
THE PROCESS OF CREATING CANDY•PEOPLE
candy Kingdom citizen
LINE OF SCIENTIFIC CREATION
sweet beans
ZZZ
sweet potato (little baby)
sugar
cotton candy
honey
bud
love
magic

Issue #22 Main Cover

KYLE SMART

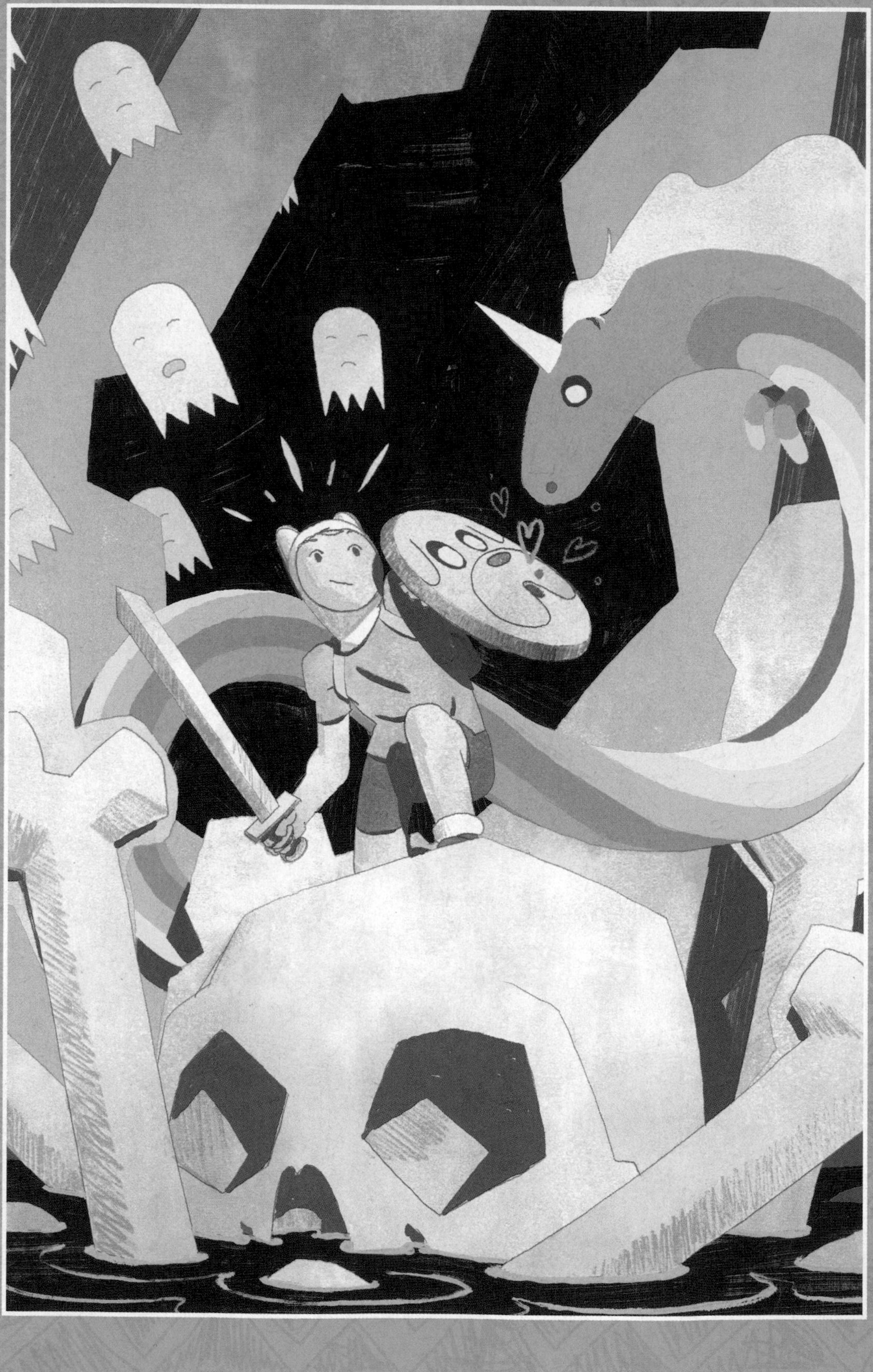

Issue #22 Subscription Cover

BENJAMIN DEWEY

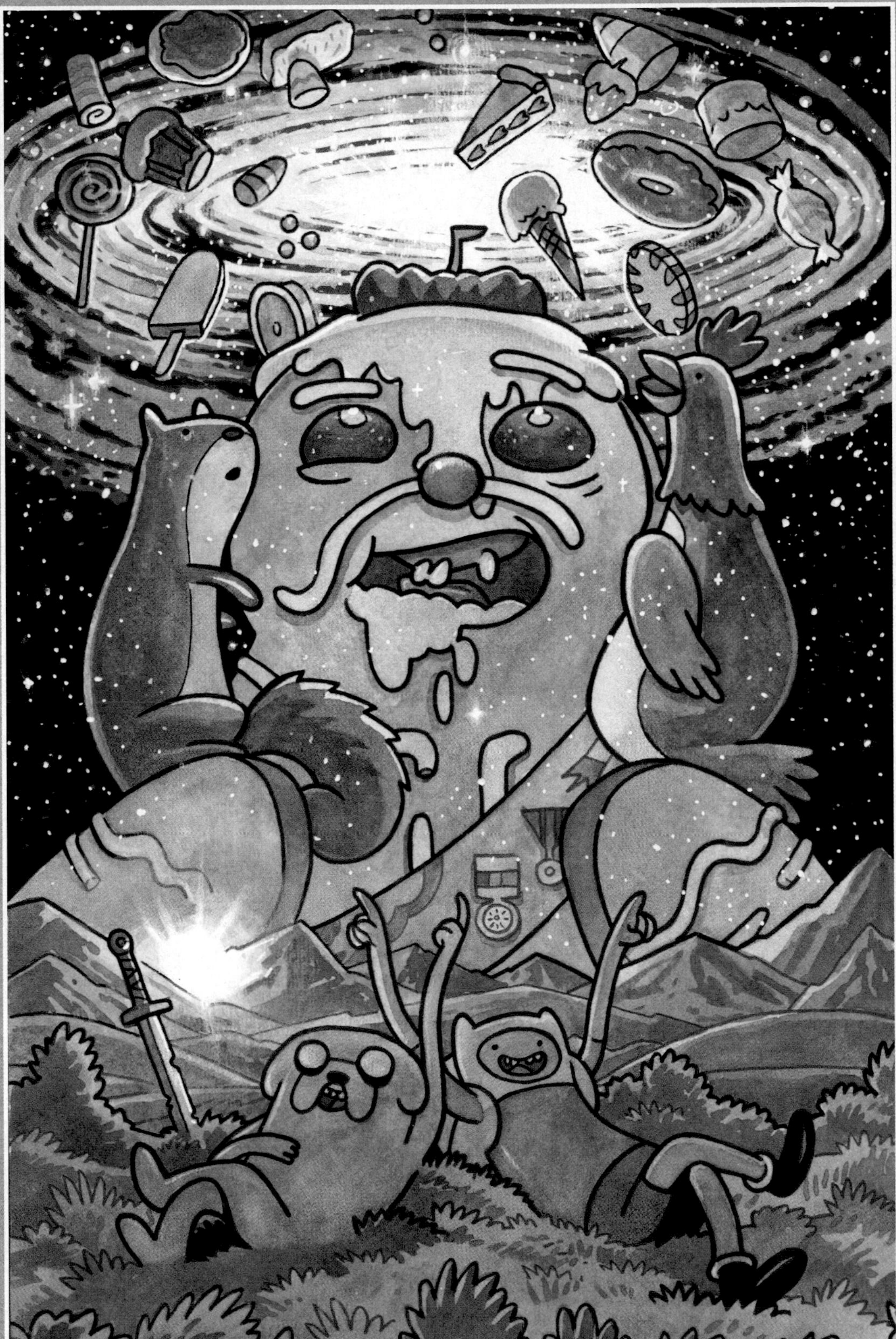

Issue #22 Variant Cover

MIKE HENDERSON

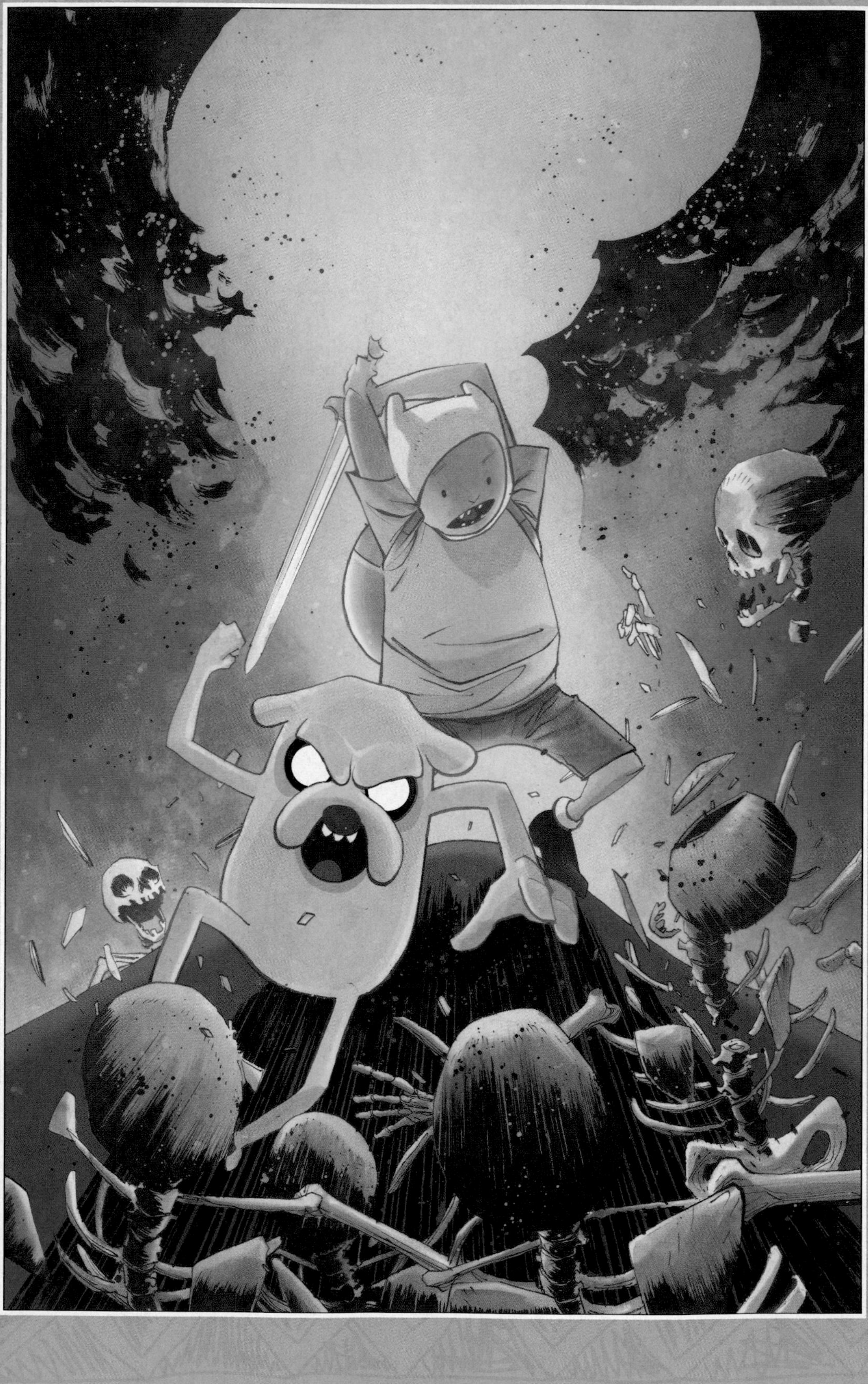

Issue #23 Main Cover

JONATAN CANTERO

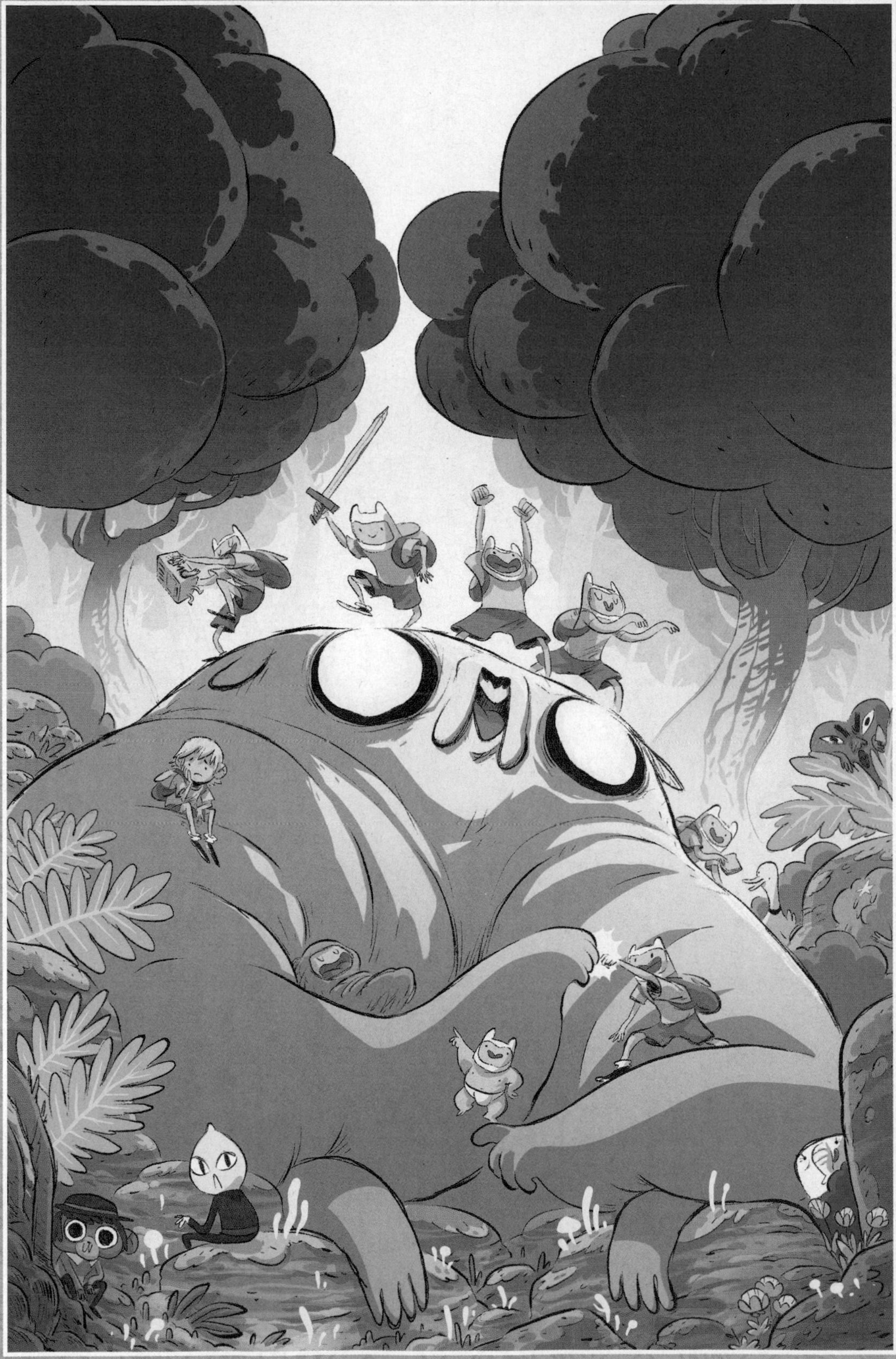

Issue #23 Subscription Cover

GUSTAVO DUARTE

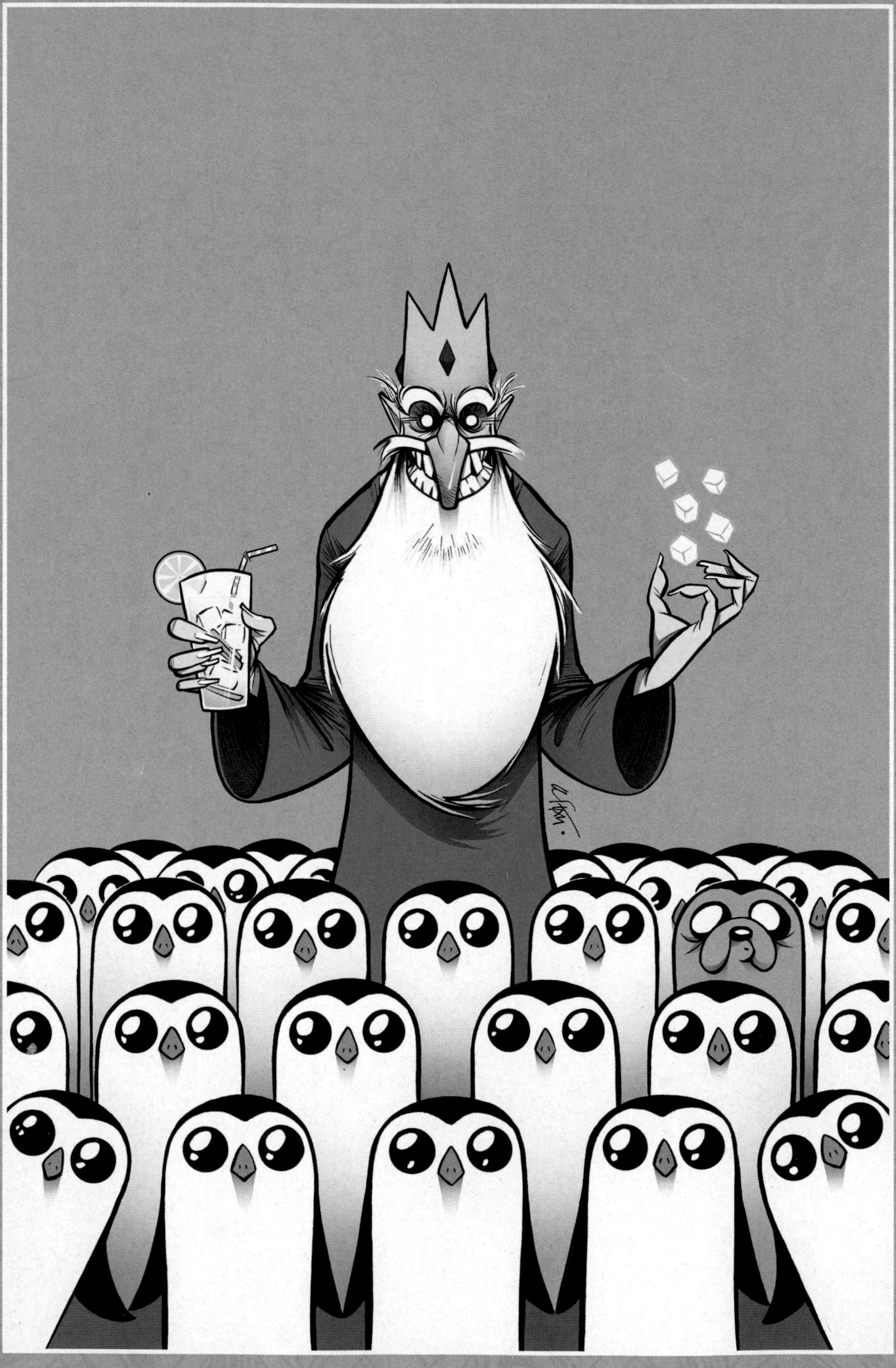

Issue #23 Variant Cover

IGOR WOLSKI

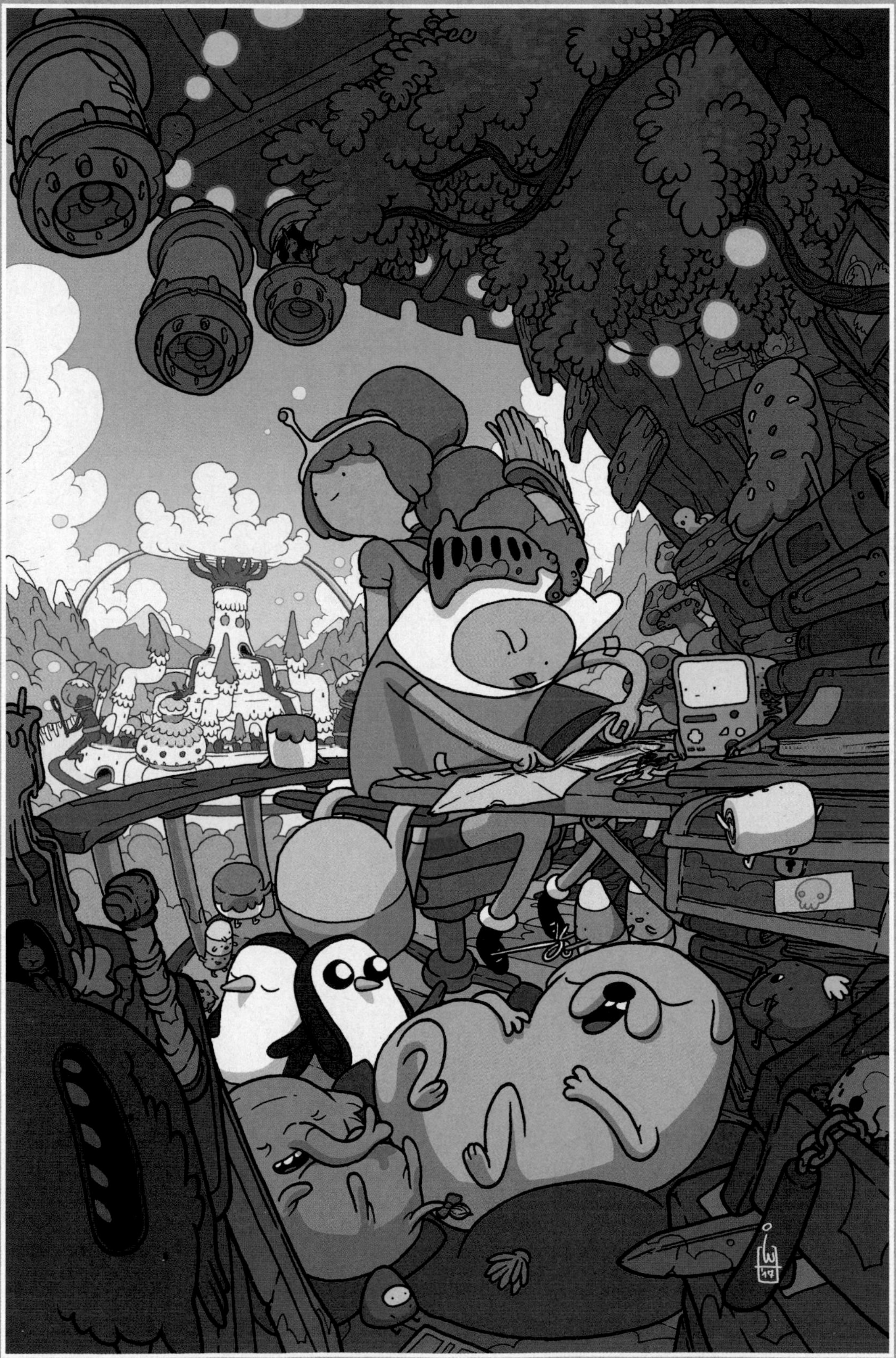

Issue #24 Variant Cover

MIKE LOWERY

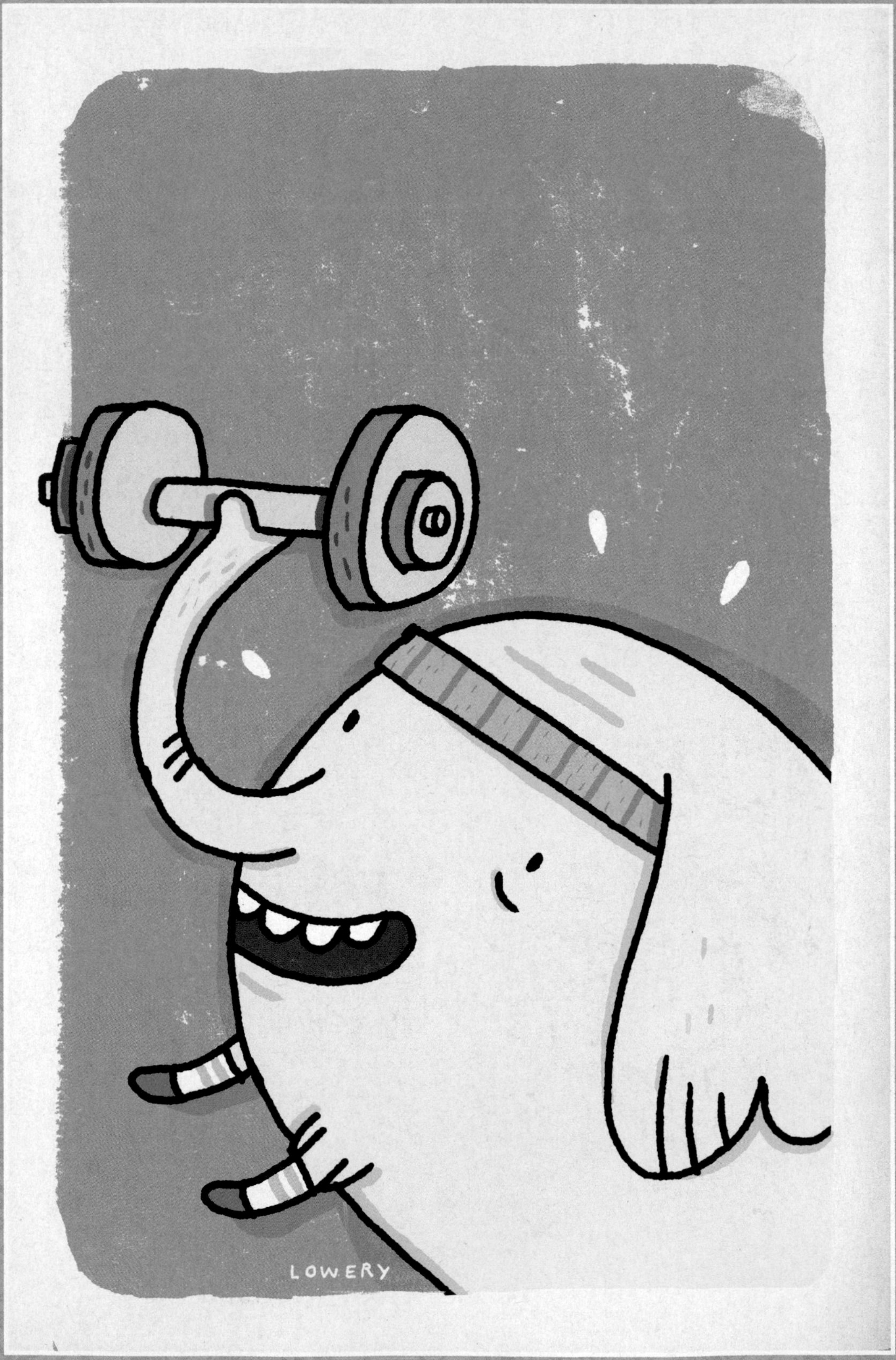
LOWERY

Issue #24 Subscription Cover

ROBERT HACK

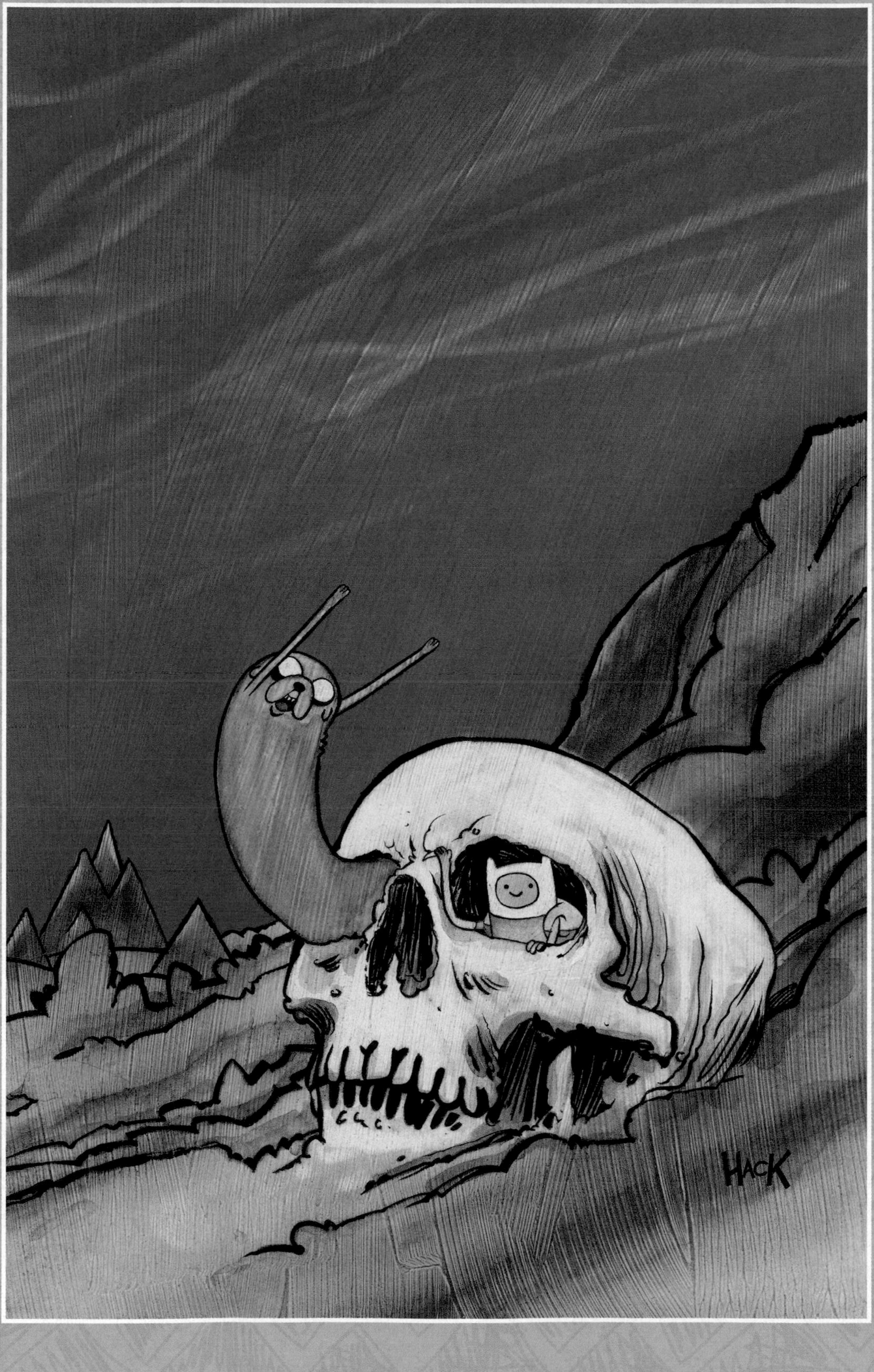
HACK

Issue #24 Main Cover

LESLEY VAMOS

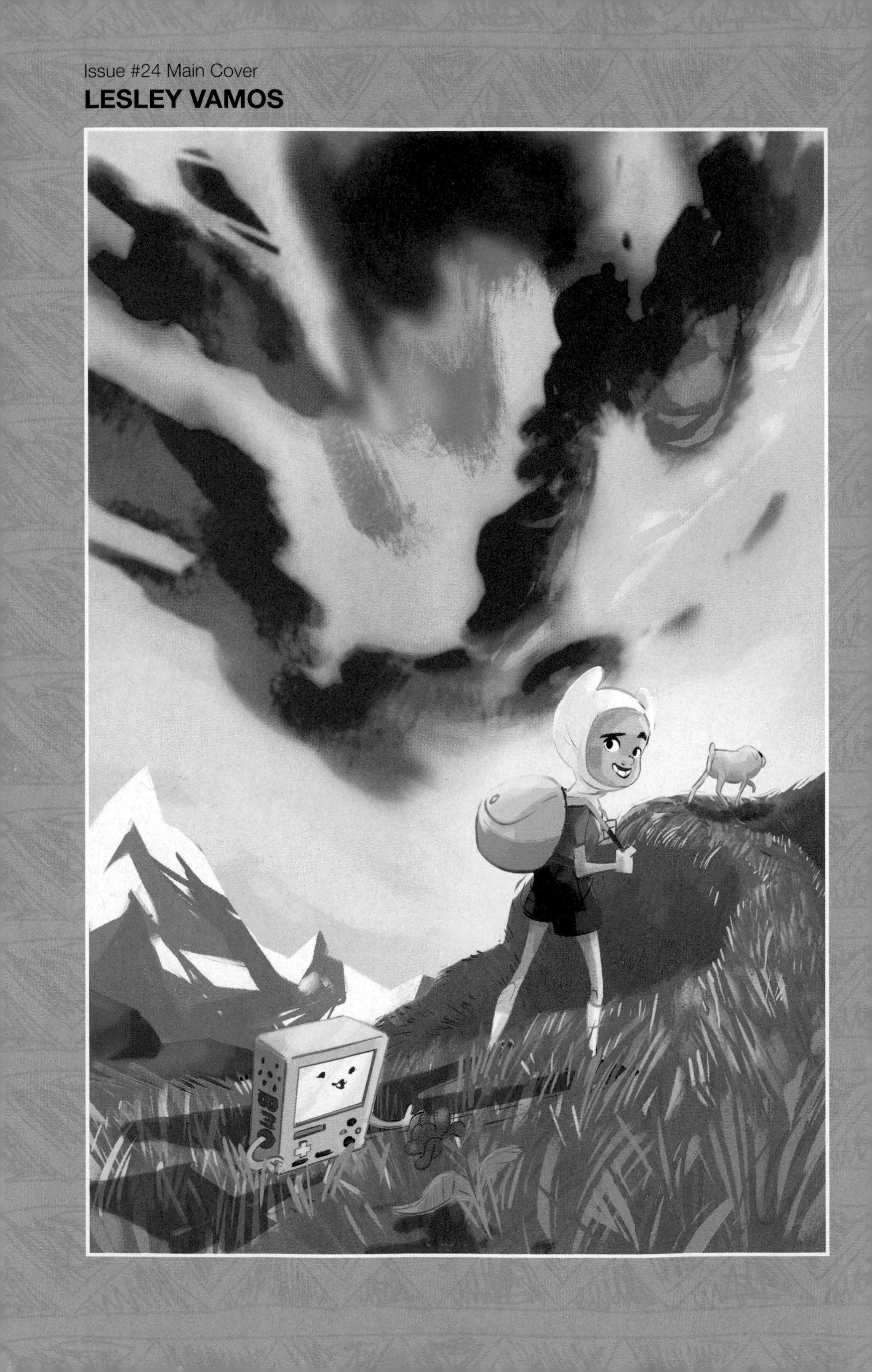

BMO

Issue #25 Main Cover

LIZ PULIDIO

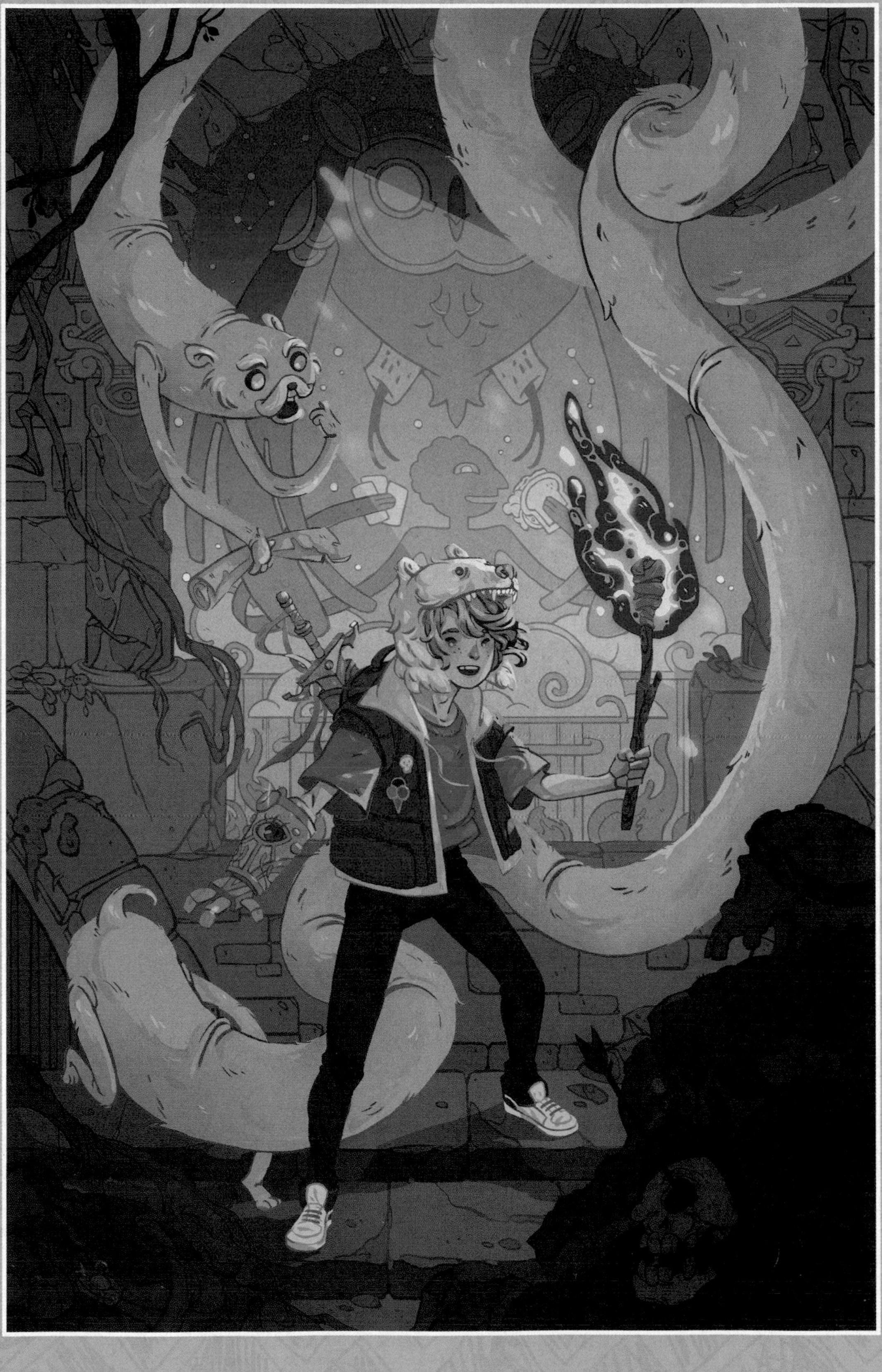

Issue #25 Subscription Cover

PIUS BAK

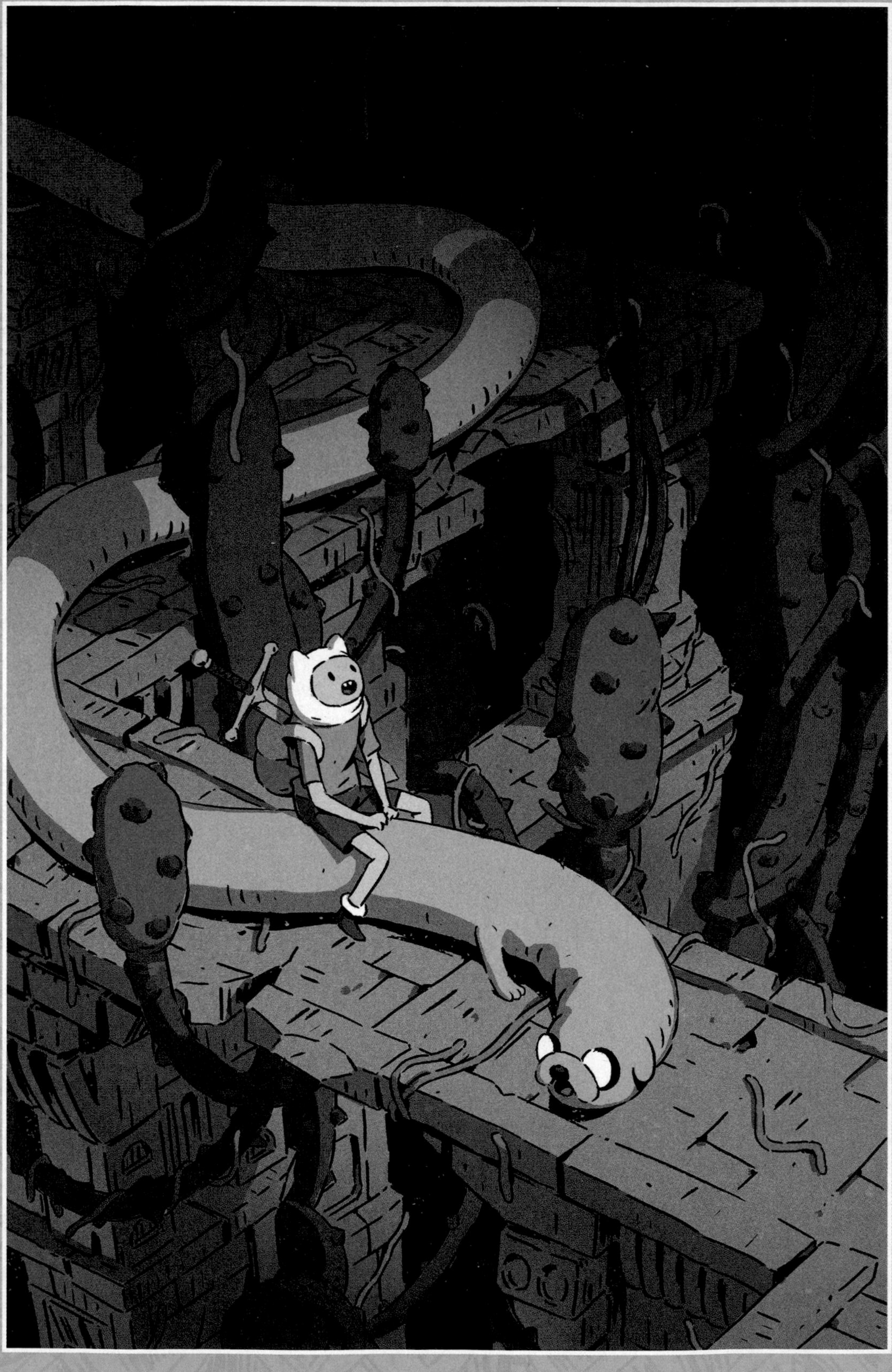

Issue #25 Variant Cover

NATALIE ANDREWSON

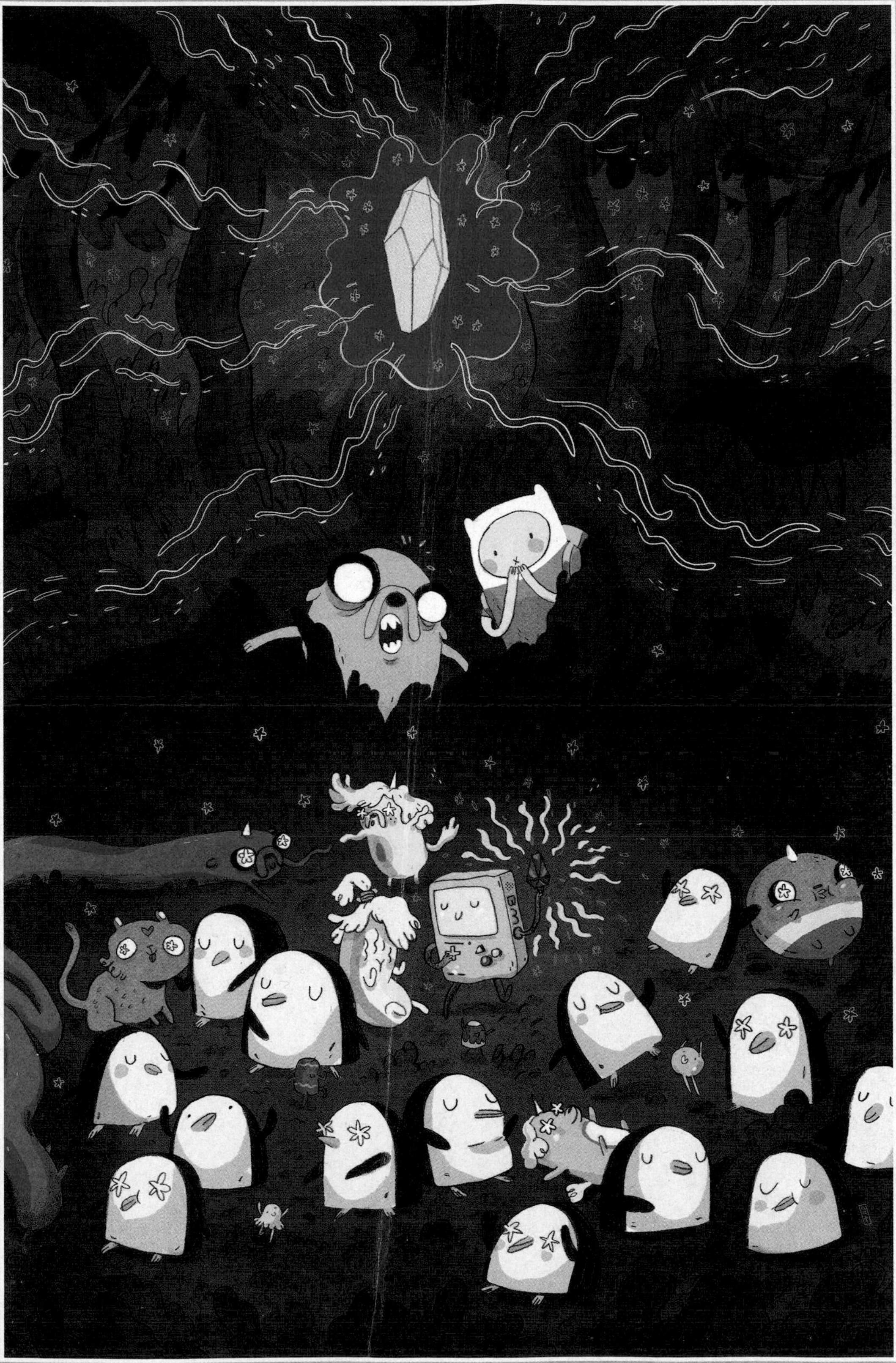
BMO

Adventure Time

Volume 1
ISBN: 978-1-60886-280-1 | $14.99 US

Volume 2
ISBN: 978-1-60886-323-5 | $14.99 US

Volume 3
ISBN: 978-1-60886-317-4 | $14.99

Volume 4
ISBN: 978-1-60886-351-8 | $14.99

Volume 5
ISBN: 978-1-60886-401-0 | $14.99

Volume 6
ISBN: 978-1-60886-482-9 | $14.99

Volume 7
ISBN: 978-1-60886-746-2 | $14.99

Volume 8
ISBN: 978-1-60886-795-0 | $14.99

Volume 9
ISBN: 978-1-60886-843-8 | $14.99

Volume 10
ISBN: 978-1-60886-909-1 | $14.99

Volume 11
ISBN: 978-1-60886-946-6 | $14.99

Volume 12
ISBN: 978-1-68415-005-2 | $14.99

Volume 13
ISBN: 978-1-68415-051-9 | $14.99

Volume 14
ISBN: 978-1-68415-144-8 | $14.99

Volume 15
ISBN: 978-1-68415-203-2 | $14.99

Volume 16
ISBN: 978-1-68415-272-8 | $14.99

Adventure Time Comics

Volume 1
ISBN: 978-1-60886-934-3 | $14.99

Volume 2
ISBN: 978-1-60886-984-8 | $14.99

Volume 3
ISBN: 978-1-68415-041-0 | $14.99

Volume 4
ISBN: 978-1-68415-133-2 | $14.99

Volume 5
ISBN: 978-1-68415-190-5 | $14.99

Volume 6
ISBN: 978-1-68415-258-2 | $14.99

Adventure Time Original Graphic Novels

Volume 1 Playing With Fire
ISBN: 978-1-60886-832-2 | $14.99

Volume 2 Pixel Princesses
ISBN: 978-1-60886-329-7 | $11.99

Volume 3 Seeing Red
ISBN: 978-1-60886-356-3 | $11.99

Volume 4 Bitter Sweets
ISBN: 978-1-60886-430-0 | $12.99

Volume 5 Graybles Schmaybles
ISBN: 978-1-60886-484-3 | $12.99

Volume 6 Masked Mayhem
ISBN: 978-160886-764-6 | $14.99

Volume 7 The Four Castles
ISBN: 978-160886-797-4 | $14.99

Volume 8 President Bubblegum
ISBN: 978-1-60886-846-9 | $14.99

Volume 9 The Brain Robbers
ISBN: 978-1-60886-875-9 | $14.99

Volume 10 The Orient Express
ISBN: 978-1-60886-995-4 | $14.99

Volume 11 Princess & Princess
ISBN: 978-1-68415-025-0 | $14.99

Volume 12 Thunder Road
ISBN: 978-1-68415-179-0 | $14.99